Also available from Kasey Michaels and HQN Books

KASEY MICHAELS

A Scandalous Proposal

&

How to Woo a Spinster

HQN™

HQN™

ISBN-13: 978-0-373-78916-0

Recycling programs for this product may not exist in your area.

A Scandalous Proposal

Copyright © 2016 by Kathryn Seidick

The publisher acknowledges the copyright holder of the additional work:

How to Woo a Spinster
Copyright © 2009 by Kathryn Seidick

CONTENTS

Dear Reader,

A journalist once asked then president John F. Kennedy, who had captained a PT boat during World War II, just how he had come to be a war hero. His answer was given with a wink and a grin: "It was involuntary. They sank my boat."

That quote has always stayed with me: *It was involuntary.*

Nobody gets up in the morning and says, "Today I shall become a hero." Heroism, rather, is thrust upon them.

That's pretty much what happened to Cooper McGinley Townsend at the battle of Quatre Bras. Coop had gotten up that morning wanting only to be able to return to his tent in one piece that night. But between the hours of dawn and dusk, without warning, and although he was far from the sea, the fates figuratively sank his boat.

Honors commenced to rain down on our hero, including the presentation of a rather lovely estate, a fat purse and the title of baron to go along with it. Coop, a modest man by nature, was grateful, said thank you very much, and figured that was the end of that.

Except it wasn't. Some "close friend and confidant of the hero" published *Volume One* of a chapbook so stuffed with nonsense and purported feats of Coop's derring-do (most especially with the ladies), that only a fool would give countenance to a word of it. Except that London did believe it, swallowed the nonsense whole and turned Coop's life into a chapbook of its own.

Fame was one thing. Notoriety was a complete other kettle of fish. Coop found himself besieged by giggling young misses and their ambitious parents, all while the words *Volume One* warned of further ridiculousness to come.

What to do, what to do?

Let's find out, shall we?

Happy reading,

Kasey Michaels

A SCANDALOUS PROPOSAL

To Sally Hawkes, a true friend.

PROLOGUE

COOPER TOWNSEND STOOD facing the tall dressing table, looking at his expression in the attached mirror, watching as he saw his usually clear green eyes going dark. He had to control himself, get past his anger, or else he wouldn't be able to think clearly.

He'd also run out of neck clothes, as this was the third he'd managed to mangle since his friend Darby showed up in his dressing room waving a copy of Volume Two of what was becoming known as *The Chronicles of a Hero.*

As if the first one hadn't been enough: *The Daring and Amorous Exploits of His Lordship Cooper McGinley Townsend, Compleat with Firsthand Accounts of His Extraordinary Missions Against the Frogs in England's Glorious Victory Over the Devil Bonaparte: Volume One.*

Indeed, Volume One had been sufficient to send him off within a fortnight to the supposed safety of his newly acquired estate, where he'd hoped sanity might rule the day (even considering that his mother was in residence).

He'd returned to London only at the behest of his friend Gabriel Sinclair, and that was for only a week, at which point the delivery of a copy of the soon-to-be published Volume Two had sent him to his estate once more. But this time it was only to pack up the majority of his new wardrobe, fail to talk his mother out of returning with him and head back to the Little Season, where he would find himself a wife. He didn't want a wife—who did? Except Gabriel, and contrary to all that was rational, his friend seemed deliriously happy contemplating the loss of his freedom.

A hasty betrothal might not solve all his problems, but it would be a start. The matchmaking mamas were getting much too clever, and at least this way his wife would be of his own choosing, and not the result of waking up one morning with a giggling debutante tucked up beside him in his bed, her mother ready to burst in— with witnesses—to cry, "You cad! We post the banns yet today!"

Which would seem silly and self-serving to consider… except for the fact that one ambitious damsel had already made it all the way into the bedchamber in his hotel suite before Ames could scoop her up and deposit her back in the lobby, where her infuriated mama grabbed her by the ear and harangued her incompetence, presumably all the way back to her coach.

Yes, he would take himself off the market. Only then would he be able to concentrate on the rest of it.

"Did you read this? I only saw it this morning, so maybe you haven't yet had the pleasure," Darby Travers, also Viscount Nailbourne when he chose to impress, asked, tearing himself away from the printed page in order to wave the chapbook at him.

"Yes, I've read it. The perpetrator—I won't call him *author*—was kind enough to send me an early copy when I was in town last week. For God's sake, Darby, put it down."

"Not quite yet. It's obvious you're going to wrest the fair maiden from a fate worse than death, hero that you are. Just let me read the ending."

"All right, since it's unfortunately important. Go on. Damn, Darby—I didn't say for you to read it aloud."

But the viscount continued in his pleasant baritone, now heavily laden with amused emphasis.

"The most Beauteous and Grateful young lady, her name always to be a mystery, her Cornflower Blue Eyes awash in Diamond-Bright tears, turned to our Modest and Abashed Hero and, quite to his Astonished Surprise, flung her soft round body straight at his chest, so that he was Without Recourse save to Hold Her Close as He could feel the Frantic Beating of her Virgin Heart, the rapid rise and fall of her Perfect Bosoms, as she extolled his Virtues, his immense Bravery and indeed, Overcome by her Emotions, she cried out in Near Ecstasy as she grasped his strong shoulders, claiming the world could safely rest on their Broad Expanse, just as her fate had so lately done, and Never Fear for her honor, that which she then so Earnestly Offered Him."

"It's even worse than I remember," Cooper grumbled. "And did the man never hear about the glories of a *period*? You almost ran out of breath there, Darby, unless you were being 'overcome by your emotions.'"

"A little of both, I believe. You lucky dog, you." Darby struggled to turn the last page of the cheaply made chapbook, and frowned.

"Coming soon, *Volume Three: The Further Adventures and Exploits of Baron Cooper McGinley Townsend, Hero, Wherein All Is Revealed as to His Character and Private Nature, Whether Be He Devil or Saint.*"

He looked up at his friend. "That's it? There's nothing more? My God, Coop, and with all the ripping retorts that have come rushing into my head reluctantly pushed to one side, this isn't good. Anyone with a drop of imagination would think you took advantage of her virtue, and Lord knows what the ton lacks in intelligence it more than makes up for in lurid imagination."

"I'm aware of that, yes, thank you." Coop stripped off the abused neck cloth and tossed it to Sergeant Major Ames, who had been his aide-de-camp during the final defeat of Bonaparte at Waterloo, and who could now lay claim to being the most burly, most foulmouthed and most sartorially bankrupt valet in all of England.

"Man needs his digits hacked off, that's what he needs," Ames said, tossing a new neck cloth Coop's way. "And then stuffed up his arse."

"Oh, I wouldn't go that far, Ames," Darby drawled as he stepped forward and snatched the fresh linen out of midair. "He's usually bearably adequate, but clearly he's overset at the moment. Here, Coop, let me do it for you, or else we'll be spending the remainder of our lives here in your dressing room."

Two tall, handsome but very different men were now reflected in the mirror. Coop could have been the angel, with his blond good looks, and Darby the dark-haired devil, somehow made even more attractive with the black satin eye patch covering his left eye.

"Ames meant my anonymous good friend," Coop pointed out, grinning as he raised his chin and allowed Darby to position the neck cloth around his raised shirt points. "And he was being kind, if not civil. It's quite another part of the scribbler's anatomy Ames truly has designs on, don't you, Ames?"

"First have to find them, my lord, and I doubt the rascal has the least trouble fitting into his breeches, if you take my meaning."

"Give me that before you choke me," Coop said, grabbing one end of the linen strip as Darby's bark of laughter blasted in his ear. "I returned to the city for assistance from my friends, and not only is Gabe gone to his estate, but he left you behind, which is less than helpful in any circumstance. I've got enough going upside down in my life as it is, and you have all the makings of a menace."

"I'd be bereft, did I not choose to take that as a compliment. But please, a menace that can tie the Waterfall with his eyes—pardon me, *eye*—closed. Very well, make your own mess. We'll even name it. The Hero's Knot. Good choice, Sergeant Major, wouldn't you say, because I think he's fashioned a noose."

"You're quite the wit, Darby," Cooper said as Ames helped him into his jacket. "I don't know how you ever stop laughing. You really think this whole thing is hilariously funny, don't you?" he asked as Darby replaced his handkerchief after lifting the black patch over his left eye and dabbing at a nonexistent tear of amusement.

"In most cases, no, I suppose not, but to see the calm, never-ruffled Cooper so flummoxed? Yes, I admit to enjoying myself. Really, is it so very terrible, Sobersides, being cast in the role of a hero? Damsels must be sighing and swooning over their hot chocolate all over Mayfair right now, their tiny pink toes curling in delight. I repeat, you lucky dog."

Coop and Ames exchanged glances, and the valet retrieved a folded sheet of paper from the desk in the bedchamber Coop occupied at the Pulteney Hotel. "This arrived earlier, shoved under the door just as messages are in all inferior novels. Take it down to the lobby with you, read it and decide for yourself. I'll just say a quick good-morning to my mother and join you there shortly."

"Am I going to be amused?" Darby asked, sliding the paper inside his jacket. "Never mind, I can see I'm not. And does it explain the neck cloth, and your jolly good humor? I suppose so. Very well, ten minutes, or else I'll be back."

With Darby out of the room, Coop picked up his silver-backed brushes and concentrated on taming his thick thatch of annoyingly unruly dark blond hair, or

…his Glorious Crown of sun-Kissed locks reminiscent of a Veritable Halo of Goodness even while he ran his long, straight fingers through the Mass as he stepped over the Broken Body of the Wretched Attacker and shyly smiled at the Unknown Damsel he'd Rescued from a Fate Worse Than Death.

Fate worse than death. Just what Darby had said in jest. It only went to prove anyone could write a chapbook—as long as one didn't bother stretching his imagination beyond the trite and prurient. "Oh, God, now I'm poking sticks at one of my best friends." Cooper sighed as he put down the brushes and spoke to the air. "'Is it so terrible being cast in the role of a hero?' Darby, my friend, you have no idea."

Admittedly, at first it hadn't been *that* awful. He'd served his country not once, but twice, donning the colors again after being invalided back to England in 1814 with his friends Darby, Gabriel and Jeremiah Rigby, baronet. He'd gone on to become quite the celebrity after a small yet fierce battle just outside Quatre Bras, just before Wellington's final victory at Waterloo.

The world would never know the full truth of what had transpired that day, which was pointed out to Cooper quite forcefully by His Royal Highness, the Prince Regent himself, before he presented the hero with a small estate, a comfortably heavy purse and the title of baron. It was a magnificent reward...although some might call it a bribe, or even the hint of a threat. In any event, Cooper quickly realized he would be wise, and perhaps safer, to accept it.

But the world didn't know any of that.

Of most interest to the average John Bull and the newspapers had been Cooper's daring rescue of several towheaded tots (the number varied from three to a full dozen, depending on who told the story), who had wandered into the midst of what was soon to be a battlefield. Some versions included a beauteous older cousin who had been *most* grateful for their rescue...but then, there were romantics everywhere, weren't there?

Three or twelve, lovely and anonymous, profoundly grateful blonde beauty or not, on his return to London Cooper found himself more popular than Christmas pudding. In the months since Waterloo he had not been able to take more than a few steps in any direction without someone calling out, "It's him—Townsend! There he is!"

Everyone clapped him on the back. Everyone stood him up for a bottle or two. Everyone treated this son of a genteel but never more than comfortably well-off family as if he was the best of good fellows, and he'd been invited to so many house parties and boxing matches and the like that it would have taken a squadron of heroes to accept all of the invitations.

Still, the whole thing was fairly enjoyable.

But then Volume One was handed out free on the street corners, and everything changed.

Coop remembered waking one morning to have Ames present him with *it*. There he was on the cover of the cheap chapbook, or at least Ames told him the garish print was supposed to represent him. He was pictured as tall and lean, which he was, but with a highly exaggerated shock of unruly blond hair and vividly green eyes that had him peeking into a pier glass to check on the intensity of his own. They were green—he'd give the artist that—but certainly not *that* green.

The streets were flooded with the damned book that was complete with a notice on its back cover that the next in the series would reveal

The Further Adventures of Our Glorious Baron Returned from the War, Secretly Performing Heroic Acts in England, Champion of the People and Rescuer of Delicate Females in Dire Straits and Needful of His Valiant Assistance.

Now mamas wanted him for their daughters. Fathers wanted him because he was a hero, and wouldn't

"M'son-in-law the hero, yes, indeed" sound all the crack in the clubs? Married women wanted him because— good Lord, who knew why married women wanted anything…and sweet young damsels considered Coop the catch of the year.

"And now *this*. So much for my plan of throwing myself into the Little Season and finding a wife in order to put an end to the nonsense."

"My lord? I didn't quite catch all of that?"

"Never mind, Ames. I was thinking about that damn note again."

He had already committed that to memory, as well.

Ten thousand pounds or the next volume will be *Our Hero Falls from Grace as the True Identity of the Supposed Innocents Rescued at Quatre Bras is Revealed, Much to the Shame That Rises to the Highest Reaches of the Crown Itself.* Yes, my hero, this is blackmail, and I'm quite good at it. Remain in London, Baron Townsend, no more dashing to hide yourself at your estate. I will be in touch.

"Ah, Ames. So much for brilliant ideas, not to mention the size of the cow Prinny will birth if the truth were to become known. We can only hope to God Darby has had his fill of poking fun and is about to offer his help," he said now, accepting his gloves and curly brimmed beaver from Ames before heading for the stairs leading to the lobby.

"You didn't want to get bracketed, anyway," his man reminded him.

"True enough, but if I can't find our underendowed bastard of a biographer, we can probably wave goodbye to the estate and you can stop addressing me as 'my lord.' I don't even want to think what my mother would say."

Ames screwed his face into a grimace. "That could be the worst, my lord, I agree. She says more than enough as it is, don't she?"

Coop laughed. "Thank you, Ames, for that reminder. Please tell her I was called away and will see her at dinner tonight. I go forth now with doubled determination, and twice the haste."

The sergeant major sharply saluted. "Just as a hero should, sir."

"I'm quite fond of you, Ames, but I could still sack you," Coop warned him as the other man quickly hid his grin beneath his prodigiously large mustache.

Darby was waiting, pacing, in the lobby. "You get yourself into the damnedest predicaments, don't you?" he said, handing back the folded paper.

"You mistake the matter. That's you, along with Gabe and Rigby. I'm the sensible one, remember, always there to pull you three free of the briars at every turn."

"Point taken. And what does your sensible self plan to do now that the thorns are sticking into your own backside? I hope it includes finding this bastard and wringing his scrawny neck."

Darby's outrage soothed Coop somewhat. "Yes, that was the plan, as a matter of fact. How did you know?"

"I didn't know, not with you. You're too damn civilized. You're not going to tell me the lady's name, are you? The fair damsel who could or, perhaps, could not have been there the day of your daring rescue."

"Why, Darby, I do believe I've forgotten it. Imagine that." Then he flinched, knowing his friend had tricked him. How could he have forgotten, even for a moment, that his friend could pry a secret from a clam.

"Aha! Then there was a woman. At least I've gotten that out of you. You are a hero, you know, pure of heart and straight as the best-carved arrow. That, and a damn fool, now that I know our own fat Florizel is somehow involved. Baron? Seems to me you could have held out for earl. Shall we get started?"

CHAPTER ONE

THE WALK FROM the Pulteney to the nearest club was too short for any but an old man or an utter twit with pretensions of grandeur to bother bringing around his curricle from the stables or hailing a hackney, or so Darby protested when Coop suggested they do the latter.

"I could be recognized," Coop pointed out quietly.

Darby was busy pulling on his gloves. "By whom? Not that I'm lobbing stones at your usual modesty, but that remark could be thought by some to verge on the cocky. I suppose vanity comes along with this heroing business."

"You're enjoying yourself again, aren't you? You know *who—whom*. By everybody. Sometimes I want to turn myself around to see if there's some sort of sign pinned to my back."

"Really? Draw a crowd wherever you go, do you? Well, good on you. And good on me, for I am the favored one, aren't I, out on the strut on this lovely, sunshiny day with the hero of all these brave, not to mention *amorous*, exploits. Gabe and Rigby don't know what they're missing. Come on, I want to see this. Maybe you'll find another fair damsel to rescue along the way."

Barely a block from the hotel, Coop was fighting an impulse to turn to his friend and utter the classic words of any bygone childhood: "I *told* you so."

"G'day ta yer, guv'nor," the first to recognize him had called out, the man bowing and tugging at a non-existent forelock as Coop and Darby approached the corner.

"Yes, good day," Coop responded, slightly tipping his head to the hawker balancing a ten-foot pole stacked high with curly brimmed beavers that had seen better days, even better decades.

"It's the *tip* I think he's wanting, not a tip of your head. That is, unless you wish to purchase one, which I wouldn't recommend. Lice, you understand, nasty things," Darby informed him, not bothering to lower his voice. "But since you're a hero, and *heroing* comes with certain expectations from the hoi polloi—yes, you fine fellow, that indeed was a compliment, and your smile is quite in order—I'll handle this. Here, my good man," he said, reaching into his pocket, and flipped a copper into the air for the fellow to snag with the skill of long prac-tice. "Compliments of the baron. On your way now."

Cooper looked around to see that the two of them were rapidly becoming the cynosure of all eyes. "Now you've done it, you fool."

"Done what? I can't let our hero's brass be tarnished because you're a skinflint. Have a bit of pride, man."

"Pride, is it? How fast can you run in those shiny new boots?"

After a suspicious bite at the copper, the grinning man raised his hand, showing his prize, and called out, "Make way! Make way! The hero passes! Make way for the brave Baron Townsend!"

"Oh, for the love of… See what you've started?"

"I'm beginning to, yes. I thought you might be ex-aggerating, but I should have known better. I'm the one who does that." Darby turned in a graceful circle. "Shall we be off? Standing still doesn't seem a prudent option."

On all sides, people were beginning to cross the intersection, heading directly for Coop while, in front of them, a pair of eager lads carrying homemade brooms raced to be the first to clear the street so that the hero could cross without, well, stepping in anything. In their zeal, they fell to battling each other with their broomsticks, and the smaller one could have come to grief had not Coop stepped in to separate them.

Holding his handkerchief to his bruised cheek—the one that had been more than delicately kissed by one of the broom handles—he and Darby continued on their way, not quite at a run, but certainly they stepped sharply to avoid the gathering crowd.

Just before they turned the corner into an alley, Darby wisely tossed several coins over his shoulder and the pursuers slid to a collective halt so quickly they tumbled over one another like ninepins as they dived for the coins, fists already flying.

"Ah, a smile, and bloody well time. I'd wondered if you'd completely lost your sense of delight thanks to your biographer. Shall we be off?"

"More at a canter than a trot? Yes, I do believe so."

At a renewed shout from the mob, they upped their pace to a near-gallop, dodging suspicious puddles, ducking under sagging lengths of gray laundry, tipping their hats to a toothless hag who offered to show her "wares" for a penny.

Twist here, turn there, retreat at the sight of a dead-ended alley. They didn't stop until they'd lost the last of their pursuers, but by that time Cooper was hard-pressed to do so much as figure out the direction of north, trapped as they were beneath ramshackle structures whose upper stories leaned out of the alley, nearly touching each other, blocking out the sun.

"Where are we?" he asked, not quite liking the look of a rather burly man who was watching them from his seat on the threshold of a building lacking a door.

"Sorry," Darby whispered, stopping to put his hands on his knees and catch his breath. "But were you asking me, or that faintly terrifying creature over there currently eyeing us as if we'd look good circling on a spit for dinner?"

"You, of course, and don't stop. I thought you knew where we're headed?"

"I did," Darby said, "about three turns ago. But I was much younger last time I pulled a stunt like this, and considerably less sober. Ah, damn, Coop. I think you might owe me a new pair of boots."

Coop didn't bother inspecting his friend's new boots—friendship had its limits—but did give Darby a mighty shove to safety as he heard a female voice from above warning that she was about to empty a slop bucket. Which she did a half second later, cackling merrily as her targets barely escaped her fine joke.

"You can't say everyone in London has read about your exploits, unless that was the woman's way of expressing her joy at seeing you," Darby said as they finally halted once more just before somehow reaching Bond Street, both of them brushing at their sleeves, checking for dirt that may have been left behind by grubby hands, for everyone had wanted to touch the great hero. "You know, all in all—my poor boots to one side—that was fairly exhilarating. Pity Rigby wasn't with us. Our plump friend could do with a bit of exercise."

Coop was still trying to catch his breath. "That's it? That's all you can say? You didn't hear the demands to know the name of the latest fair beauty I've supposedly saved? You didn't hear the suggestions called out as to what I should *do* with her? A few were quite specific."

"Yes, I heard, but chose to pretend I didn't. Your blushes were more than enough. At least one of them should probably be chained up in Bedlam, or else gelded. Why didn't I notice this when you were in town last week?"

"The second volume of my supposed exploits only surfaced once I was gone back to the country. When Prinny first honored me I was treated rather well, pointed to, yes, spoken to—more than a few wishing to shake my hand, clap me on the back, introduce their daughters to me. The added attention brought to me by the appearance of Volume One came as a jolt, especially when it somehow fostered a nearly unnatural interest from the ladies. It's Volume Two, though—all this business about my supposed heroics since returning to England—which has seemed to raise quite another emotion besides simple gratitude. It was bad enough when I first returned. Crowds did tend to gather. But this is the first time I've actually had to run from them. Things can't continue this way, Darby, they just can't."

"True. Only imagine what it would be like if your blackmailer makes good on his threat—the one I don't quite understand and apparently am not allowed to know, even as I am applied to for assistance. You'd have to emigrate. The admiration of the mob has always been known to turn into hatred at the drop of a pin."

"The thought has crossed my mind, yes. But in the meantime, let's go find us both a bootblack."

"And after that, a bird and a bottle," Darby agreed. "But I'm not a demanding sort. I'm willing to make do without the bird."

CHAPTER TWO

DANIELLA FOSTER, VARIOUSLY known to her family as Dany, the Baby or, not all that infrequently, the Bane of Mama's Existence, eyed the purple silk turban perched on a wooden stand in the corner of the fitting room. It felt as if she'd been there for a small eternity, and she'd already inspected most every inch of the crowded room at the back of the dress shop.

She wasn't bored, because Dany was never bored. She was interested in everything around her, curious about the world in general, which had led her, in her youth, to getting down on the muddy ground to be nose to nose with an earthworm, all the way up to the present, which just happened to include wondering how it would feel to wear a turban. Would it itch? Probably, but how could she know for certain if she didn't try?

"I still say it's pretty," she announced, "and would fit me perfectly."

Her sister, Marietta, Countess of Cockermouth, just now being pinned into the last new gown she'd commissioned, did not agree. "I've told you, Dany, purple is reserved for dowagers, as are turbans. No, don't touch it."

"Why not?" Dany plucked the turban from its stand. "That doesn't seem fair, you know," she said, demonstrating her version of *fairness* as she lowered the thing onto her newly cropped tumble of red-gold hair. "Do you see that? The color very nearly matches my eyes."

"Your eyes are blue."

"Not in this turban, they're not. Look."

Dany stepped directly in front of her sister, who was a good eight inches taller than her at the moment, as she was standing on a round platform for the fittings.

Marietta frowned. "Some would say you're a witch, you know. That thing should clash with your hair, what you left of it when you had that mad fit and took a scissors to it. Your skin is too pale, your eyes are ridiculously large and your hair is… I'm surprised Mama didn't have an apoplexy. Yet you…yes, Dany, you look wonderful. Petite, and fragile, and innocent as any cherub. You always look wonderful. You don't know how to appear as anything less than winsome and adorable. It's one of the things I like least about you."

Dany went up on tiptoe and kissed her sister's cheek. "Thank you, Mari. But you know I don't hold a candle to your serene beauty. Why, it took only a single look at you across the floor at Almacks for Oliver to fall madly and hopelessly and eternally in love with— Oh, Mari, don't cry."

Turning to the seamstress, who was looking at both of them curiously, and Marietta's maid, who was already hunting a handkerchief in her mistress's reticule, Dany quickly asked the women to please leave them alone for a bit.

"Increasing, is the countess, and good for her," the seamstress said, nodding her gray head toward the maid. "They gets like that, you know, all weepy and such for no reason at all. I'll be certain to leave plenty of fabric for lettin' out the seams."

"I'm not—"

"Crying," Dany interjected quickly, squeezing Marietta's hands so tightly her sister winced. "No, darling, of course you're not crying. We neither of us think any such thing." Then she winked at the seamstress, who reluctantly let the drape fall shut over the doorway, she and the maid on the other side of it. Let the woman think Mari was increasing. Anything was better than the real reason her sister had turned into a watering pot. "You were going to blurt out the truth, weren't you?" she asked—perhaps accused—as she helped her sister down from the hemming platform.

"I most certainly was not. I'm still wondering what on earth prompted me to say anything to you. I must have suffered a temporary aberration of the mind."

"No," Dany said flatly as she watched her sister gingerly lower herself onto a chair, making sure she didn't encounter any pins on the way down. "You did that when you wrote those silly letters to your *secret admirer*. And Mama says you're the sensible one, and I'm to imitate you in all you do. But you know what, Mari? *I* would have at least asked my admirer's *name*. Oh, here, take this, and blow your nose," she ended, fishing an embroidered hankie from her own reticule and all but shoving it in her sister's face.

"Lower your voice, Dany." Marietta looked left to right and back again, as if making certain no one was hiding in the cluttered room, possibly taking notes, and then whispered, "And it wasn't my fault. All the married ladies of the ton have secret admirers. It's just silly fun. Especially when our husbands desert us to go off to hunting lodges and gambling parties and whatever it is gentlemen who wish to avoid their wives call amusement."

Dany replaced the turban on its stand. It had been interesting to see how she looked in the thing, but it definitely was beginning to itch. When she became a dowager she would make sure all her turbans were lined with soft cotton.

"Is that so? And is it all still silly fun for you now that your admirer is demanding five hundred pounds for his silence, his promise to return your notes to you? Is that just another part of the game?"

Marietta blew her nose none too delicately. "You know it isn't. I don't have five hundred pounds, Dany, and Oliver will be home in a fortnight. Oh, this is all his fault. If he'd only paid me more *attention*. It used to be I couldn't budge him out of my bed, but—no, don't listen to me, Dany. You're an unmarried woman."

"True, but I'm not still in the nursery. Oliver is sadly lacking in romance, isn't that it?"

Her sister's shoulders slumped. "He…he forgot my birthday. He went traipsing off to Scotland with his ramshackle friends, and totally forgot my birthday. Our first year together he bought me diamond eardrops, the second a ruby bracelet and the third a three-strand pearl necklace. Now? Now nothing." She looked up at Dany, her blue eyes awash in tears. "I don't want to be a wife, Dany. He's clearly bored, having a wife. I want to be his *love*."

Dany motioned for her sister to stand up, and began helping her out of the gown. "I remember when you nearly called off the wedding."

"That was all Dexter's fault," Marietta pointed out as she bent her knees, her arms straight up over her head, and allowed Dany to remove the gown. "And we don't talk about that."

Dany, carefully holding the gown at the neck, stuck it past the slight gap in the curtain, feeling confident the seamstress would be standing there to receive it (and anything she might overhear). No, they didn't talk about it, what Dex had said, not after their father had threatened to disown him if he did anything to cost his sister a wealthy, eligible earl.

Oliver Oswald, Earl of Cockermouth. Marietta had written those words in an old copybook at least two hundred times, along with Marietta Foster Oswald, Her Ladyship Countess Cockermouth. She'd been so proud, right up until the moment Dex had whispered a less than civilized definition of the word as seen by youths who found such things giggle-worthy.

"Oliver explained it all," Marietta said now, diving into the sprigged muslin gown she'd chosen for her shopping trip to Bond Street. "The name is derived from the proud and ancient town's position…"

"…at the mouth of the Cocker River, just as it joins with the River Derwent. Yes, I know. Papa made me commit that to memory. He also gave me a pretty pearl ring when I promised to stop calling you…"

"You promised!"

Dany held up her hands in submission. "I was only fourteen, still sadly innocent in the way of things, and didn't know what I was saying. Which, as I've pointed out many times, you can blame on Mama, not me. Now strap on your armor, and let's go home. We'll put our heads together and find some way to get you out of the bramble bush you so blithely flung yourself into in the name of revenge."

Marietta carefully smoothed on her gloves, finger by finger. "Never should have told her," she scolded herself. "What in God's name possessed me to think she'd be of the least assistance?" Still, now armed once again with her bonnet and gloves, outwardly she looked the epitome of calm, her fine features carefully composed in what Dany thought of as her sister's "smug face." Her "I am a countess, you know" face. If Marietta wasn't so heart-stoppingly beautiful, and Dany didn't love her so much, she would laugh.

"It's going to be fine, Mari. It's all going to be fine. I promise."

"Humph, humph." More than a polite throat-clearing, the sound was full of suggestion, or innuendo, or perhaps even hope. Or at least Dany chose to think so.

Both young women turned about to see the elderly seamstress had reentered the fitting room.

Lady Cockermouth raised her chin. "I believe we were not to be disturbed. However, as we're finished here, you may simply send along the gowns when they are done, and we'll be on our way."

Marietta, embarrassed and caught off guard, was making an attempt at haughtiness, intending to put the seamstress firmly in her place by playing at the grande dame. So typical of her, and so wrong, at least in her sister's opinion. Dany believed herself not to be so cork-brained. It would be much better, even safer, to play on the woman's sympathy.

And then there was the "humph, humph" to consider. The woman was clearly dying to know *something*.

"Mrs. Yothers, I think it is? Was there perhaps something you'd like to say to Lady Cockermouth?"

"What could she possibly have to—"

"Mari, there's a wrinkle in your right glove," Dany interrupted, knowing it was one thing that would silence her. She abhorred wrinkles in her gloves, which was why they were so tight they nearly cut off her circulation. "Mrs. Yothers?"

"Yes, miss, my lady. I apologize, I truly do, but so as to be sure no one else disturbed you two fine ladies, I took it upon myself to send your maid outside and station myself right on the other side of the curtain. I couldn't do much besides clap my hands over my ears not to hear that her ladyship is in a bit of a pickle."

"I am not in a—"

"Oh, I was wrong, it isn't a wrinkle. Why, Mari, I do believe you've picked up a smudge. Go on, please, Mrs. Yothers."

"Yes, miss. And seeing as how we're all women here, even you, young miss, and with the poor dear increasing and all…"

"I am *not*—"

"Here, Mari, you don't want to forget your reticule," Dany said, shoving the thing in her sister's gut, leaving the latter rather breathless. And mercifully silent. "Mrs. Yothers? You were saying?"

The seamstress shot a compassionate glance at Marietta. "I remember how I was with my first. It does get better, my lady, as the months go on. Before it gets worse again, that is, but that's over quickly enough and you're back to doing what got you in the delicate way in the first place. But that's not what I'm here to say.

I think, Your Ladyship, what you need right now is a hero."

Dany rolled her eyes. *That's* what the "humph, humph" was about? How depressing. "A hero, Mrs. Yothers? What a splendid idea. Would you perhaps know where to locate one?"

The woman smiled as she reached into the pocket of her apron, pulling out a wrinkled, dog-eared chapbook. "I do indeed, yes. Here you go, miss. You can keep it, seeing as how I know it all by heart, anyway, and there's a whole new one waiting for me upstairs when I go up for my tea. I hear it's even better than the first."

Dany was already reading the title on the front cover: *The Chronicles of a Hero.*

"A hero? But, Mrs. Yothers, surely this is just a made-up story? This man, this—" she looked at the cover again "—His Lordship Cooper McGinley Townsend? He's no more real than Miss Austen's Mr. Darcy."

"He looked passably real to me about an hour ago, when he and his companion sauntered past, out on the strut. Spied one of my girls staring bug-eyed at him through the window, and gave her a tip of his hat, he did. Such a gentleman. Everyone knows him, miss. Purest, bravest man alive, and bent on helping other people out of their troubles, especially pretty young ladies. Prinny himself handed over a title and an estate to him. I do nothing but hear about him in here, miss. He's a hero to all the ladies, who chase him something terrible, poor man."

Dany looked down at the cover once more. What a ridiculous print. Nobody looked like that, at least nobody real. But if he did…

"Dany? Daniella, for pity's sake, what are you staring at?"

"I wasn't staring," Dany answered quickly, folding the chapbook and stuffing it into her pocket. "I was thinking. Mrs. Yothers, you just might be right. Mari, shall we go? Thank you so much, and I'm certain Lady Cockermouth will return in the next week or less to order at least another half dozen gowns, four of them for me, as a matter of fact."

"I'm what?" But even Marietta wasn't *that* thick. "Oh, yes. Yes, indeed. And bonnets. And…and scarves. I do favor scarves. You know, the sheer flowy ones. And…and…"

A young boy hastened to open the door to the street for them, and Dany took her sister by the elbow, ready to pull her out of the shop if necessary before she bankrupted the earl. "Mrs. Yothers understands, don't you, Mrs. Yothers, and is terribly appreciative of your custom?"

The seamstress blushed, and bobbed several quick curtsies. "I do indeed, miss. As my son says, mum's the word."

"Thank you. Mari, we should be going now."

"We should have gone long since," her sister pointed out as her lady's maid rose from a bench outside the shop and fell into place three paces behind them. "We shouldn't have come at all, not in the delicate state I'm in, and certainly I shouldn't have dragged your flapping mouth along with me. Now look where I am—beholden to Mrs. Yothers."

"She'll be worth every penny if she's right, and she doesn't really know anything. She was being nice mostly because you're pregnant."

"I am *not*—oh, the devil with it. Tell me what's going on in your mind, Dany, even though I'm not going to like it, nor will I approve. Mama placed you in my hands, remember."

"The answer's obvious, Mari. You can't fix what's wrong, and heaven knows I have no idea how to fix what's wrong. But a hero? Morally upright, generous of heart and spirit, wonderfully hand—*handy*. I think we should apply to him for his assistance."

"Don't even think such a thing," Marietta said, her voice trembling. "The poor man is absolutely *besieged* with all matter of ladies of the ton. Young, old, eligible misses and their mamas, married women—they're after him day and night. Oliver told me the man had to flee London, in fact, to get away from their flirtatious entreaties and embarrassing importunities. Now he's back, according to Mrs. Yothers, and I'm certain the ladies are making utter fools of themselves yet again. I couldn't possibly be so bold."

And there was the smile that had launched a thousand nervous tremors within her family. "That's all right, Mari, because I could. In fact, I'm quite looking forward to it."

"Dany, you wouldn't dare! Oh, what am I saying? Of course you'd dare. But you cannot, Daniella. You simply cannot!"

"Why? At least I'd know his name, which is more than you took the time to find out when you were punishing Oliver with your unknown lothario, offering up your reputation to be shredded—and even signing your name to those dangerous notes. You couldn't have scratched 'Your Beloved Snookums' or some such equally cloying and anonymous?"

"That would have been silly. He already knew my name."

"Exactly. You didn't have to sign your notes at all. Oh, don't start crying again. I'm merely pointing out the obvious. Now let me think more about how I'm going to approach your hero."

"The baron is not my hero, and you are definitely not going to attempt to run him to ground like some fox. I can't let you do it. I'll say it again. Mama sent you here to practice for the spring Season. I'm to tutor you, train you, set a good example for you."

"And you're doing a whacking great job of that so far," Dany said, grinning. "Rule number one. I now know, as if I didn't before, never to exchange silly letters with unknown men."

Marietta probably hadn't pouted so forcefully since she was twelve. "One mistake. I made one mostly innocent mistake."

"And Oliver deserves half the blame for that. Possibly more, as there was jewelry involved. I remember. See? Lesson two, learned. If jewelry is involved, there may be exceptions to rule number one."

"You're being facetious."

"And enjoying myself mightily. And more than slightly excited, I'll admit that as well, considering I'd come to town believing I would be bored spitless. How do you propose we go at this, Mari? If we knew the baron's direction, I could simply pen him a *formal* note, asking him to meet with me on an urgent personal matter involving an innocent woman's virtue. Or do you think my chances would be better if I approach him in public, perhaps at the theater or one of the parties we're committed to this week?"

She reached into her pocket and withdrew the chap-book. Truly, she could stare at the print for hours, just to look into those green eyes. "I believe I'd recognize him if I could somehow manage to casually bump into— *Oh!*"

CHAPTER THREE

"Oh, for the love of…" Baron Cooper Townsend instinctively grabbed the young woman by the shoulders. He'd been watching her, the way she was clinging to her companion's arm as they proceeded along the flagway, the two of them chattering like magpies, definitely not looking where they were headed.

He believed the taller one to be the Countess of Cockermouth, although he couldn't be certain. Besides, it was the other young lady who somehow seemed to demand his attention, simply because she existed.

And then she'd apparently tripped and all but propelled herself into his arms.

"My, my, Coop, look what you found," his friend Darby teased, never one to fail to see the amusement in most any situation. "Or is that look what found you? I've lost count—is that four? Two on the way down, and now two coming back? Alas, our English misses seem sadly lacking in imagination, as well as balance."

Cooper ignored the man, concentrating on the small, upturned face and the pair of huge indigo eyes looking up into his. They had to be the most unusual and intriguing eyes he'd ever seen; they all but swallowed him up, leaving him shocked and nearly breathless.

This did not please Baron Townsend. Levelheaded Baron Townsend. Wasn't his world topsy-turvy enough, without adding unexpected attraction to his budget of woes?

Still, he watched, fascinated, as those eyes, like a mirror into her soul, told him her every thought, each rapidly transitioning emotion. Wide-eyed shock. Embarrassed innocence. Questioning. Recognition. Amusement, almost as if she was laughing at their situation, perhaps even at him. No, that couldn't be possible.

"I didn't mean that quite so literally, but how very convenient," she said as if to herself, and her smile almost physically set him back on his heels. Damn, it had been amusement he'd seen, and it definitely was at his expense.

Wonderful. It wasn't enough that they chased him. Did this one have to find the pursuit so amusing?

"Are you all right, miss?" he asked tightly, still lightly holding her upper arms, because that seemed to be his required opening line in these tiring encounters. "Perhaps you've twisted your ankle and require my assistance?"

"I seem to have tripped over an uneven brick. How careless of me, not to watch where I'm stepping. No, I don't think I'm injured," she said, and her voice, rather low and husky for such a small thing, surprised and further intrigued him, much against his will. "Not precisely at any rate. But if you'd be so kind as to support me over to that bench?"

Those eyes, that voice, the unique color of the little bit of her hair he could see, the alabaster skin set against those eyes and a fetchingly curved pink mouth. So much danger in such a small package.

You said hello, Coop, he reminded himself. *Now say goodbye.*

"I don't think so. Why don't you hop?" he heard himself say, and let her go.

And damn if she didn't immediately being listing to one side, so that he was forced to swoop her up into his arms before she could collapse on the flagway.

"Why didn't you tell me you hurt your ankle?" he demanded as he carried her over to the bench outside a milliner's shop, her companion right behind him asking, "Dany, are you all right?"

"I told you I wasn't injured, not *precisely.* I asked for your assistance, remember? I seem to have lost the heel to my shoe, see?" The beauty incongruously named Dany raised her right leg to display the damaged shoe (and give him a brief but delightful sight of her shapely ankle). She looked up at him, understanding rising in her eyes even as the sun rises at dawn. "You didn't believe me. Are you often accosted in the street by admiring and hopeful females, my lord Townsend?"

Coop straightened. "So you do know who I am?"

"And you said it wasn't a good likeness," Darby said, holding out a copy of the damned Volume One. "This fell out of the young lady's hand as you performed your less than impressive imitation of Sir Galahad to the rescue."

"Give that back," Dany demanded, holding out her hand. "I've yet to read it."

"And that's how it will remain, unread," Coop said. "Put that in your pocket, if you please."

"Excuse me," the older of the two women said imperiously, inserting her body between that of Coop and Dany. "I don't know who you gentlemen are, but you would both please me very much by taking yourselves off now so that I may attend to my sister."

"You hear that?" Darby clapped Coop on his back. "The hero of Quatre Bras and all points west has just been dismissed. How lowering."

Coop took a step back and bowed. "A thousand pardons, ladies. We'll be on our way. But first, if I may be so bold as to ask we exchange introductions? I believe you might be Oliver's countess. My friend here is the viscount Nailbourne, and I am…"

"He's Baron Cooper McGinley Townsend, Mari, *hero*, as if you didn't know, or would if you'd lower your chin enough to be able to look at him. Just the man we were talking about before I so providentially tripped and landed in his arms. Twice."

"Dany!"

The countess sat down beside her sister all at once, rather as if someone had pushed her onto the bench.

Dany looked up at Coop, those huge eyes of hers filled with amusement and obvious mischief. "While my sister plots ways to gag me and have me sent back to the country, please allow me to introduce myself. I am Daniella Foster, here in London, according to my fond papa, to obtain a little town polish before I'm officially sicced on Society in the spring. And sadly failing to acquire any, if my sister's forlorn sighs mean anything. I've been looking for you, Your Lordship. It would appear my sister needs a hero."

"I'm not looking for…" the countess began, but then subsided.

Dany got to her feet, Darby stepping forward to assist her, moving faster than Coop, who was still repeating her outlandish words in his head. This left him to hold out his arm to the countess, who ignored the gesture, instead grabbing on to her maid in a near-death grip.

When he did open his mouth, it was to hear himself solemnly pronounce as he bowed to the countess, "My lady, I am of course your servant," as if he was penning his own silly chapter in Volume Three. Apparently he'd lost half his mind in the past few minutes. And here he'd always thought it was only other men who made cakes out of themselves at the bat of an eyelash.

Just then a town coach bearing the Cockermouth crest on its door pulled to the curb. A liveried groom hopped down from the bench to open said door and let down the stairs.

And none too soon, Coop realized as the maid assisted the countess to the equipage, *before I shove my other foot in my mouth and volunteer Darby's assistance, as well*.

But it was already too late.

"Miss Foster, although there have been no written reports of my derring-do, I should be honored to likewise offer my assistance," Darby said, smiling at his friend. "Isn't that right, Baron? Two heads always being better than one when it comes to this heroing business."

"Why, thank you, my lord," she responded even as she half hopped toward the coach with his support. "Number Eleven Portman Square in an hour? Although I doubt the countess will join us. She's found herself in a rather delicate situation."

The countess's voice rang out from the coach. "I am not in a delicate…! Daniella, get in this coach. At once!"

The two gentlemen watched as the coachman drove off.

"Our Miss Foster is going to get an earful all the way back to Portman Square," Darby said once they turned to continue their walk. "And it won't be her first,

I'd imagine. What an odd little creature. Not a drop of guile anywhere—honest, forthright and apparently amused even as she clearly wants to help the countess. Society will have her for lunch, you know, even here, in the Little Season."

"Or she'll have all of Society at her feet," Coop countered, realizing he was none too happy with his conclusion. "The ton has often embraced the eccentric, and she certainly at least qualifies as an Original."

"Oh, she's more than that, old friend. I've just realized she managed to remove the chapbook from my pocket."

"She what?" Coop turned to look at the flagway, hoping the chapbook had simply fallen to the ground once more. It wasn't there, just the broken heel of Dany's right shoe, which he quickly retrieved. "My God. Forward, cheeky *and* a pickpocket. What do you think we've gotten ourselves into, Darby? I won't help with an elopement, and neither will you, if that's what this is about. Oliver's a friend."

"And as our friend, we have offered our services to his wife, or at least to find out what's going on so that we might warn him. It's probably all a tempest in a teapot, anyway, knowing women, and easily put to rights, whatever her problem. If nothing else, it should serve to take your mind off your blackmailer for a few hours."

Coop frowned. "Nothing will take my mind off the bastard," he said, but as they wisely hailed a hackney to take them back to the Pulteney for what Darby had called "a wash and a brush-up," it was thoughts of Daniella Foster that most occupied his mind.

He had originally come back to London to find himself a wife, there was that.

CHAPTER FOUR

IT WAS QUIET in the Portman Square drawing room now that the countess had retired to her bedchamber, led there by the promise of tea and freshly baked lemon cakes. She'd run out of complaints and threats, anyway, emptied her budget of Things Ladies of Good Breeding Do Not Say or Do and thrown up her hands in defeat when her sister grinned and asked, "So, *are* you breeding, Mari? You've been rather overset lately. Perhaps you haven't been counting?"

Having successfully routed her sister at last, Dany looked across the room, to where her maid, Emmaline, had been told to take up residence on a chair positioned close by a front-facing window. There were two reasons for that. One, Emmaline would be able to watch out the window to alert her mistress when one of the carriages stopped in front of Number Eleven, and two, the carriage traffic would help muffle voices while Dany and the gentlemen spoke.

Oh, and a third: young unmarried ladies needs must be chaperoned at all times or else the entire world just might disintegrate into cinders, or some such calamity. Of course, were that true, Dany would have destroyed the world at least six times over by now. And that was just this year.

In any event, Emmaline was discreet. She'd kept

many a secret for Dany over the years, either out of affection or because she'd be sacked on the spot for having allowed any of her mistress's daring exploits, many of which had necessarily included her cooperation. Dany preferred to believe it was affection.

She glanced at the mantel clock, mentally calculating the time between their departure from Bond Street and now, and pulled the chapbook from her pocket. The thing was thin of pages, no more than thirty at the most, quite shopworn, and with luck she could finish it before the hero and his viscount friend arrived.

But first she'd look at the cover again. The baron truly owned one of the most pleasing collections of features she'd ever seen gathered together all in one place. Hair so thick and blond that it would have to be the envy of all the many women who both dyed their locks and supplemented them with itchy bunches of wool to help conceal the thin patches.

Not that Dany had that problem. When it came to her own hair, the true bane of her existence was its color. Not red, not chestnut, not even orange, thank God and all the little fishies. Her mother (believing herself to be out of her younger daughter's hearing), had once described the curious mix of red and gold as *trashy*, the sort of hair that couldn't possibly come from nature, and was favored by loose women who flaunt their bosoms and kick up their skirts to expose their ankles in the chorus in order to delight the randy young gentlemen in the pit at Covent Garden.

Although sometimes Dany thought that might not exactly be considered a *bane* on her existence, as at least the kicking up of her heels sounded rather fun. To date, the only thing *growing up* had proved to Dany was that the mere passing of years could turn a female's life into one long, boring existence, with nothing to look forward to but purple turbans.

She'd marry somewhere in between some sort of hopeful kicking up of her heels and the turbans, she supposed, although she was in no hurry to please her parents by accepting the first gentleman willing to take her off their hands. She hoped for at least two Seasons before anyone was that brave, anyway.

But on to the baron's eyes. The engraver had been a tad too generous with the green, but by and large, they were the most compelling eyes Dany had seen outside of her childhood pet beagle, which somehow had managed one blue and one brown eye. And they were sweet, and sympathetic, just like her puppy's eyes when he wanted to convince her he deserved a treat. Winsome, yet wise, and not a stranger to humor.

Yes, she really did admire the baron's eyes. They were nearly as fascinating as her own, she thought immodestly—she would have said *truthfully*—which seemed to change color with her mood or what she wore. Not that she was in any great hurry to be limited to dowager purple.

His nose definitely surpassed hers. She liked the small bump in it just below the bridge, which kept him from being too pretty. Hers was straight, perhaps a bit pert. In short, it was simply a nose. It served its purpose but would never garner any accolades.

And then there was his mouth. Oh, my, yes, his mouth. Her father had no upper lip, none at all, as if he'd been hiding behind a door when they were handed out. The baron's upper lip was generously formed, and nicely peaked into the bargain, and his bottom lip full, just pronounced enough that there was a hint of shadow beneath it.

He didn't favor side-whiskers, for which she was grateful, seeing that her brother, Dexter, he of the madly curling black hair, had taken to wearing his long enough to clump around the bottom of his ears, making him look rather like a poodle.

And he was tall—the baron, that is—so that the top of her head didn't quite reach his shoulders. Ordinarily that would annoy her. She'd always thought she would be attracted to shorter men, so that she didn't feel over-powered. But she didn't feel small or powerless beside the baron. She felt...protected. Most especially when he had caught her as she fell and lifted her high in his arms. It had been quite the extraordinary experience.

"I suppose I can't trip again, because that would be too obvious. Pity," she said to herself, opening the chapbook. It was time to stop thinking and start reading. Time to see just what sort of hero the baron was, if he was a hero at all. She hoped at least part of the story would turn out to be real.

She had only two pages to go when the mantel clock struck the hour of one, but she pressed on, determined to finish.

The April day was made for Pic-a-nicks beneath the Budding trees, a day for Good Food, Fine Wine and Lovers. Instead, it was a Day for Kill-ing and Dying, and by evening the green field would Run Red with blood and gore. The En-glish soldiers looked out across the field, wonder-ing if they would by lying there within the next few hours, Broken in body and Food only for the

worms. This was not their Choice—it was their
Duty—and they would Fight to the Death for both
King and Country, for the Little Corporal had
broken free of his prison and had marched nearly
into Brussels, threatening the Entire World once
again with his Insane Ambition.

The troops had hoped to reach the High Ground
above them, and from there Defend their Position
if an attack should come. But they'd been Too
Late, and when a scout reported seeing French
troops Advancing Toward Them, there'd been no
choice but to take refuge in the trees at the Bottom
of the hill, hoping the French would not Detect
them until they'd come too far down the hill to
Retreat without Tripping over one another.

But something was wrong. The Fates had
placed a low Stone Wall and the Ruins of an old
Kiln halfway up to the top of the hill. Several
Small Figures huddled there inside the Kiln, at
least a half dozen Children and a heavily veiled
Lady who could be their nurse or their mother.
Whether they hid from the English or the French
could not be known. Either way, they were about
to be Caught smack in the middle of a Battle.

It was the Worst of all possible Nightmares.
How could the English fire, knowing the Children and a Frail Female were between them and
the French? No man of merit would Dare such
a thing. Even the officers had sent Whispered
Commands down the line. *Keep your positions!
Hold your fire!*

But one Brave Man broke ranks, tossing away
his rifle and uniform cap, crouching nearly in half

as he ran Up the Hill without regard to his own safety. Every last man held his breath as Captain Cooper McGinley Townsend seemed to be Arguing with the woman, convincing her to Leave her ill-chosen safe harbor.

And still the Enemy advanced. It was now possible to see the distinctive Brass Eagle topping a tall staff, and the French Colors flapping in the breeze. Their Full Force would crest the hill in Mere Seconds, hopefully stop to assay the land below. Could they See beyond the wall? Would the sunlit blaze of the captain's Distinctive Blond Mane catch the sunlight and give away his Position?

With one breath, one silent collective thought, the troops prayed: *Run! Run now, before it's Disaster for all of us!*

And run he did. Gathering the youngest against his chest even as he Threw the protesting woman over his shoulder, he motioned for the other children to Run on Ahead as he Raced across the field, out from behind the Fragile Safety of the Broken stone wall, and toward the trees, Throwing Himself and His Precious Burdens into concealment mere seconds before the first horse and rider could be seen Cresting the Hilltop.

The English General dismounted and began walking the Line. "Now that's how to disobey orders, hmm? Bloody well done, Townsend. Today, gentlemen, we have witnessed the birth of a Hero. Now, what say we rid the World of a few of these hopping frogs, hmm? They'll send Infantry first. Ah, and here they come a-marching, all smug and unsuspecting. Steady, men. Hold…hold…hold. First rank, Forward if you please. Kneel. Raise your weapons. Hold. Hold. *Fire!*"

Just as it was Coming on to Dusk, our Hero strode into the camp, bloodied but not bowed, the rescued Innocents, orphans all, skipping merrily behind him, a sweet, towheaded cherub no more than three perched on his Strong Shoulders, waving his small cap in Victory, but with the heavily veiled Lady Curiously Absent.

Huzzah! the assembled soldiers cried out, raising their rifles in Salute after Salute, for they had lost many Brave Men that day and the sight of the Children once again firmed their resolve to Fight On. *Huzzah! Huzzah! Huzzah!*

The women of the camp Raced forward, gathering the Children against their skirts and hustling them off to the cook tents to be fed, and our brave Captain was swiftly surrounded by his soldiers in arms, All of Them wishing to pat his back, shake his hand.

Huzzah! Huzzah! May the whole world Rejoice in such Modest Bravery!

…and thus, Dear Readers, is how the Baron Cooper McGinley Townsend, Hero, came to be.

There is just a bit More before we term this story Told, although it will not, alas, Satisfy the Curious among Us.

A bold Question from one of his acquaintance about the Scratches on his cheek, followed by the Assumption as to how they'd gotten there, elicited a Warning Green Flash from Townsend's narrowed eyes before he smiled and Explained that a Holy Nun had been taking the Children to her convent for Safekeeping, but had gladly turned them over since food at the convent was limited.

A search of the area days after Bonaparte's final defeat elicited No Nunnery in the area. There was, however, Dear Readers, a lovely Country Cottage, clearly quite hastily Abandoned, and a single remaining caretaker who Confirmed that a young woman, always Heavily Veiled, had been in Residence for some Weeks before rushing off, leaving behind nothing more than a Curious Signet Ring as payment, a ring now in the Possession of one whose Discretion can always be Trusted.

But not to fret, Loyal Readers, for our hero's Daring Adventures do not end with this Single tale of bravery. Upon his return to our faire isle, now Baron Cooper McGinley Townsend, at the Behest of the Crown, has continued his Deeds of Bravery and Rescue, personally preserving the Honor of several damsels in Mortal Danger of their Virtue even while the Mystery persists— who is the Veiled Lady?

Dany let out a breath, not realizing she'd been holding it, and closed the chapbook. "A veiled lady? What a hum," she said, for her interest lay more in the feat of derring-do than in anything so obviously fictitious as a veiled lady. And a signet ring, no less, also thrown into the mix, a perfect clue for someone with the interest to pursue its origin. But she supposed every story must have a lady in it somewhere, preferably veiled or beautiful or both, or else the gentlemen wouldn't bother racking their brains and running their fingers beneath line after line to keep their place in order to not miss a word. Men were such children. And women, sadly, were possibly even worse, seeing themselves in the role of the rescued.

"Curricle, Miss Dany."

With one last quick look at the cover of the chapbook—had she considered his wonderfully high, strong cheekbones in her initial inventory?—Dany quickly slipped it down behind the cushions of the over-stuffed couch and ran her hands over her hair, bodice and skirts, just to be sure everything was still where it had been when she'd first arranged herself so carefully in anticipation of her guests.

She pressed a hand to her bosom once more, clearing her throat as daintily as possible, hoping the action might help regulate the rather rapid beating of her heart, and then lifted her chin, directing her gaze toward the doorway.

But no! She couldn't look as if she'd been just sitting here, waiting on the man. Certainly a hero was already full enough of himself without thinking she'd been counting the minutes until his arrival. She shot to her feet as she heard Timmerly greet the visitors and direct them toward the stairs, looking about frantically for something she could be doing when the butler announced him.

Propping herself against the mantel was ludicrous, and reserved for gentlemen at any rate, not to mention the fact that she'd practically have to raise her bent arm above her head in order to rest her elbow on the thing. She spied her sister's knitting basket and dismissed it in the same heartbeat. She'd rather be boiled in oil than found knitting, for goodness' sake.

What to do, what to—wait, the flowers! There must be five huge bouquets scattered about the room, each more lovely the other. How impressed the gentleman would be when he saw her handiwork. She raced to a round table holding a perfectly arranged bouquet and yanked four of the blooms from the porcelain vase. In an instant, three of them were on the tabletop, dripping water onto her skirt, and one was in her hand as she posed in the motion of sliding it in with its fellow blooms.

"Ah, gentlemen," she cooed, turning her head ever so slightly as Timmerly announced them, inwardly cursing the viscount for keeping good his promise to lend his help. She'd really rather he'd taken himself off somewhere, to amuse himself at somebody else's expense. "How good of you to come. Timmerly, refreshments if you please."

"Yes, Miss Dany," the butler scolded, bowing. "But if you were to leave off playing with the posies, the countess would be that pleased. It took her ladyship and Mrs. Timmerly a good hour to arrange them this morning."

The viscount's bark of laughter accompanied the high-nosed butler's exit from the drawing room, leaving Dany with nothing to do but pick up the other blooms and jam them back into the vase. Butlers could be such *prunes*.

"I suppose I'm caught out," she recovered swiftly, wiping her damp hands against each other as she returned to the couch. "I was hoping to look accomplished, but the truth is, I have very few skills welcomed in polite company. Please, gentlemen, be seated."

And the maddening viscount was at it again: "Such as picking pockets?"

She turned to the baron, who was looking, or so she hoped, at least slightly amused. Therefore, she would be amused. "Yes, my lords, although I'd rather call it retrieving what's mine. I've now read it cover to cover, of course. How much is truth, sir, and how much could be termed a bag of moonshine? As for the signet ring, the tantalizing clue that just happened to be left behind to be found by your anonymous biographer? I would think both it and the veiled lady were only mentioned to encourage purchase of Volume Two. Do you by chance have a copy in your possession, or know where I might purchase one?"

The handsome, famous Cooper McGinley Townsend, who had been silent until now, his elbow propped on one arm of the chair, his chin in his hand, ignored the question to ask, "Where is the countess? I would have thought she'd had you bound and gagged and locked up in the nursery by now."

"Oh, ouch," the viscount said, wincing rather comically. "Did that hurt, Miss Foster? I rather think it didn't, not from the width of that smile. We can safely ignore him, you know. He's been *locked* in an unpleasant mood all day. Not that he's ever particularly jolly, being by nature a calm, sensible, nearly boring man. My friends and I tolerate him because of his good heart, you understand. Plus, he's managed to rescue us from most of our scrapes since our boyhoods with his good common sense. Haven't you, Coop?"

Dany held her smile, but her heart had never been in it, so that her cheeks were beginning to ache. "The trials and tribulations of being a hero must weigh heavily." She looked almost boldly into those suddenly dark green eyes. She felt he could look straight through her, and it was unnerving, if also faintly delicious. "I feel absolutely terrible, an encroaching beast and any other vile thing you can think of, but I fear I must hold you to your word. My sister truly does need a hero. She's in a terrible pickle."

Cooper got to his feet. "Yes, of course. I'm afraid the viscount is correct. My behavior, both now and on Bond Street, has been beyond reprehensible and far from anyone's fault save my own ill humor." He then proceeded to bow from the waist, rather elegantly, and add, "How may I make it up to you, Miss Foster?"

Dany knew herself to be many things, but a lack of backbone (or a mouth) had never been a problem. "A drive in Hyde Park today at five wouldn't come amiss. Appearing with the hero would probably do my reputation no end of good, which should help placate my sister, who believes I'm nearly past saving even now. My lord Nailbourne? Laughing again? You are easily amused, aren't you? Have you ever considered trotting into Society with a monkey on a chain? You could wear matching hats."

Now, for the first time, Dany heard the baron's laughter, clear and full and wonderfully charming. Even better, he laughed with his entire body—his smile wide, the tanned skin around his eyes crinkling, his shoulders shaking as he showed his pleasure.

"Miss Foster," he said as he seated himself once more, this time with his legs slightly spread, and resting his elbows on his knees as he leaned toward her, "I would be delighted. But on the contrary, being seen with you will do my reputation no end of good, as I do believe you are going to take the Little Season by storm."

Now Dany leaned forward, feeling more comfortable

with each passing moment. "Now you see, that's just what I said," she told him earnestly. "Mari isn't quite so sure, and I know my mother is sitting in her private parlor at home even now, making rash promises to our Lord if He will only keep me mute until some poor fool decides he can't live without red-haired children."

"Miss Foster, you are too candid by half. I think I adore you," Lord Nailbourne interjected.

"Stifle yourself, Darby," the baron warned quietly. "Ignore him, Miss Foster. He's much more used to being the one whose every word should be considered a masterpiece of dry humor."

"Wry humor," the viscount corrected. "I am an observer, Miss Foster, and do occasionally delight in sharing those observations."

"I see. And what are your observations of the situation as it stands at this time, my lord? With the three of us here, that is."

Darby looked at his friend for a long moment, and then shook his head. "No, not today. I think I'll wait. It might be safer." He then got to his feet just as Timmerly entered the room with the teapot and some cakes. "I believe I now should recall that I have an appointment with my tailor. Or perhaps with my vintner. In any case, Miss Foster, I'm going to toddle off and leave the two of you to discuss her ladyship's dilemma without me in the way. Coop, you can fill me in later if it turns out my earlier offer of assistance remains necessary."

"Coward," Coop murmured as the viscount preceded Timmerly out of the room. Then he turned back to Dany, who was hopefully striking her most innocent pose. One, sadly, she had never quite mastered.

"I know you're young, and at least marginally innocent in the ways of the world, but I feel compelled to ask—did you set out deliberately to roust my good friend from the premises?"

Dany sat back against the cushions, one hand to her bosom. "Me? Do something as horridly underhanded as to all but point out that he wasn't necessary at the moment?" She laid her hands in her lap. "Yes, of course. My sister made me promise not to share her humiliation with the viscount."

"You could have asked him to leave."

She rolled her eyes. "Now *that*, my lord, would have been impolite. Shall I pour?"

"Not for me, thank you, as I won't be lingering much longer. You know what you are, Miss Foster? You're the sister I'm so delighted my mother never birthed."

Dany had been reaching for the silver teapot, but withdrew her hand, as she'd never played hostess before and she was more than a tad worried her hand might shake, giving away her true feelings now that she was all but alone with the baron (Emmaline's snores were soft, but audible). She would have felt insulted, if not for the smile on the baron's face. "My sister's feelings, at least very nearly so. She has said she'd often wished I were the sister my parents didn't have, or words to that effect. Of course, she says much the same about Dexter, our brother. But she doesn't mean it."

"Then I suppose I don't, either. In fact, I'm going to convince myself you're no more than a younger sister brimming over with good intentions. Can I safely do that, Miss Foster?"

"Oh, yes, yes. That's exactly what I am. Not that I'm not madder than a hatter that she managed to get herself into such a predicament. Really. It sounds much more like something *I* would have done—at least our mother would say so. Except that I know I'm possibly outrageous at times, even a sad trial, but I'm not a complete looby."

"My friend Oliver married a looby? You must understand that, as much as I wish to be of assistance to his wife, I refuse to do anything that would harm him."

"Your friend Oliver married a smile as sweet as sugar, a pair of soulful blue eyes and a slim soft body he was attracted to as bees are to honey, and then found himself bracketed to a romantic ninny who believes she should continue to be courted day in and day out for the rest of their lives. I've told her, that sort of thing… wears off after a few years, and you become *comfortable* with each other, as our parents have done. But she doesn't believe that. Mari…well, Mari needs *attention*. And…and *drama*."

"Which the earl is no longer supplying? You're putting me to the blush, Miss Foster."

Dany shrugged her slim shoulders. This *explaining* business was more difficult than she had imagined. "As I'm not privy to their private lives, I cannot answer that, and you, my lord, should never have asked the question. I can only tell you that he forgot her birthday before heading north with his chums to hook salmon or shoot winged things, which apparently can only be considered a declaration of his disenchantment with his wife."

Coop scratched at a spot just behind his left ear. "I should probably add this to the list I've been keeping on the perils of matrimony."

"You keep a list? Do you have another on the benefits of the wedded state?"

"No, but if I ever think of anything I'll be sure to

write it down. Miss Foster, can we please get to the point? Your sister revenged herself on Oliver, didn't she? What did she do? And please don't tell me she took a lover, because I don't have the faintest idea how to rescue her from anything like that, unless you expect me to kill somebody for her. Which I won't."

"Ah, such a sad disappointment you are, my lord. So it would be asking too much to have you insult the man's ancestors or some such thing, then demand pistols at dawn? As a hero, I'll assume you're a fairly good shot, so it wouldn't present too much of a problem for you."

"And then I'd escape to the continent for the remainder of my days because duels are outlawed and I'd be hanged if I stayed?"

"Yes, I suppose that is too much to ask. What *are* you prepared to do?"

"Since I don't know the precise nature of the problem, nothing. Again, I remind you, Oliver is a friend."

"I was avoiding the details," Dany told him, feeling fairly certain telling him the truth—that she was thoroughly enjoying their nonsense exchanges—would only encourage more, and she was having enough difficulty not melting each time she looked in his amused green eyes.

"Avoid them no longer, Miss Foster. Has the countess taken a lover she now wishes would disappear, preferably without a trace?"

Dany shook her head. "Nearly as bad, but not so dire as to contemplate a *permanent* solution meted out on the man. She began a correspondence with—and I say this with as much disgust as the words engender—a *secret admirer*."

Now it seemed to be the baron's turn to shrug his

shoulders. "Is that all? I agree with you. If we were to line up the married ladies of the ton who have exchanged silly correspondence with supposed secret admirers, they'd probably stretch from Land's End to John O'Groats. Twice. Simply tell the countess to stop fretting. I'm certain Oliver will understand, although why she'd tell him I have no idea."

"If only it were that easy, my lord, we would not be having this conversation. My sister penned her innermost thoughts to the man, her complaints and misgivings about the beastly, horridly unromantic, probably philandering Oliver, who of course broke her heart into tiny pieces before going off with his male friends to do Lord only knows what. She bared her heart, my lord, her overwrought, melodramatic soul. And everything you can think of she should never have written."

The baron slightly adjusted his posture. His lean cheeks colored slightly, which was so adorable, especially in a hero. "Hmm. Would this confession expand to include, um, matters of…of marital intimacy? Please say no," he added quickly.

Even Dany knew she also should be blushing at this point. But perhaps because this all was rather old news to her, or in the light of her never experiencing "marital intimacy" and therefore not approaching the subject with the amount of gravitas she otherwise might, she answered in her usual amused way. "Or the sad lack thereof, my lord?"

"Not good, not good," he said nearly under his breath.

"Why?"

"Why?" He looked at her directly now. "Because no

man would ever wish his manhood questioned, that's *why*. Who's this secret admirer?"

Dany busied herself with a lemon square, shoving a bite in her mouth and mumbling around it, hoping not to be heard, but knowing she had to tell him the truth. "And therein, my lord, lies the rub. She's never so much as met the man, or if she did, she didn't know he and her admirer are one and the same. It's beyond silly, actually, although she's convinced Oliver won't see the humor I see in the thing. To put it briefly, my lord— we don't know."

"She—*she doesn't know?* For the love of heaven, Miss Foster, how could she not know the name of her secret admir— No, don't answer that. Because then he wouldn't be *secret*, would he? Women, you're all to let in the attic, aren't you?"

Dany felt it necessary to defend her gender, and perhaps even her sister in particular. "Now I may call *you* out. Women, by and large, are ten times more sensible than men. We wouldn't have stupid wars, for one thing. Even my sister isn't usually so empty-headed, if that's what 'to let in the attic' means. She's simply *emotional* at the moment. My God! I wonder if Mrs. Yothers was right, and she is— No, she'd know that, wouldn't she? She'd have to know that, for pity's sake."

The baron got to his feet, beginning to pace. "When you're done debating yourself, Miss Foster, perhaps we can return to this matter of the unknown secret admirer?"

Dany put down the remainder of the lemon square, her very favorite, her appetite having disappeared, perhaps forever. "The dress shop owner believes the countess is...is increasing." She looked up at Cooper, who was now standing stock-still. "A seamstress can't know more than the person in question, could she?"

"You're asking me?"

"No, probably not. You're not as calm and collected as I would have imagined a hero would be, you know."

"I'm not a hero, damn it!" He held up his hands. "I beg your pardon, Miss Foster. But I'm not a hero. Anything you read in that god-awful chapbook was made up out of whole cloth."

Well, wasn't that disappointing. "None of it? You didn't rescue any children?"

He tipped his head to one side for a moment. "Well, that's true. But I didn't plan it. It…it just happened. One minute I was standing there with everyone else, and the next I was tossing down my rifle and running. It seemed like the thing to do. And what does any of that matter?"

"I imagine it matters to the children you saved from being trampled or shot, the Englishmen who were then free to defend themselves from a French slaughter. Oh, and to the veiled lady. Was there a veiled lady?"

"A holy nun. A veiled nun, yes."

"Now you're lying," she said, not knowing why she felt so certain, but certain nonetheless. "You're protecting her, whoever she is. That's why she *disappeared*. You took her somewhere safe, and only then returned to the camp, hours after the battle. Even now, you protect her. She must be very important to someone."

His green eyes flashed, his eyelids narrowed—just the way his unknown biographer had written. "I don't like you, Miss Foster."

"That's understandable. I've rather bullied my way into your life, haven't I? I have no shame in that, however, as my sister desperately needs a hero, unwilling hero or not," she told him brightly. "Inconveniently for you, you're a man of your word, because you're still here, when a lesser man would have broken down the earl's front door in his haste to be gone. He knows who she is, naturally."

"What?"

"Oh, I'm sorry. We're back to my sister and her secret admirer. He knows her because the notes he wrote were delivered here. That's only sensible. But he also knows her because she foolishly signed her name to her notes. Probably with a flourish, and including her title. Mari can be a bit of a twit."

"All right, I think I finally understand. Your sister wants me to discover the identity of her anonymous admirer in order to have her notes returned to her. And how am I supposed to go about that, Miss Foster? Does your sister by chance keep a list of her admirers, as a sort of starting point for me, you understand?"

"No, and it's not that simple. I can show you the letters he wrote to her, I suppose. There may be a hint or two there I've overlooked. But it's his final missive— or should I say *almost* final missive—that is causing all of this trouble."

So saying, she reached into her pocket and drew out a folded note, handing it over to him.

He looked at it, almost as if he didn't want to touch it, and then suddenly all but grabbed it from her. Opening it, he read aloud.

"Five hundred pounds or the next person to read your love notes will be your husband, just before the collection is published in a pamphlet entitled *Confessions of a Society Matron Forced to Seek*

Solace in the Arms of Another, Rejected by Her Husband, Who Apparently Is Immune to Feminine Charms, Preferring the Company of Others of His Own Persuasion.

"Yes, this is blackmail, and I'm quite good at it. Your husband returns soon, my lady, and you have no time to dawdle. I will be in touch."

"You can see he is fairly specific while remaining disturbingly vague. Mari has no idea how to produce five pounds without applying to her husband, let alone five hundred, but she's fairly certain whatever this man is threatening will greatly upset Oliver."

"Upset him? Miss Foster, you have no idea, thankfully. Son of a— When did this arrive?"

"A few days ago. Why? Oh, no, he has not contacted my sister again. Should we be looking for a discreet jeweler to buy some of Mari's necklaces, or are you thinking this is an empty threat?"

"I don't think the countess can assume it's an empty threat, no. May I keep this? And do you have his other notes?"

Did he seem more interested now? Yes, he did. Perhaps it was the hero in him stepping to the fore. Or concerns for Oliver. It certainly couldn't be anything else, could it?

Dany retrieved those from behind the cushions, cloyingly tied up with a pink ribbon, because Mari didn't learn quickly, if she learned at all. She still probably harbored at least a slight hope that the blackmailer was only trying to attempt to get her to write to him again. Which she would only do over Dany's dead body, and so she had informed the countess. Folding up notes and placing them in...

"Oh, you might want to know how they corresponded," she said as the baron pocketed the notes. "The first was delivered by a maid who was handed the note and a copper piece on the street, with instructions for its delivery. I've questioned her, naturally. The man didn't hand off the note himself, but used a young lad who then disappeared. The rest were exchanged by tucking the notes in a knothole in the third tree from the right behind the mansion. My bedchamber windows overlook the mews, and I've done my best for the past several nights to remain awake and watching, but am ashamed to admit I make a poor sentry. I've never lasted much beyond midnight before falling asleep at my post."

He was looking at her oddly now, very nearly *measuring* her. What on earth was he thinking?

"No, I can't do that. Even Darby isn't that foolhardy."

"Pardon me?"

"Nothing, Miss Foster. Is there anything else you wish to tell me?"

"Only my thoughts on how to catch out the rotter so you can teach him a firm lesson. You will do that, correct, or what is the use of finally knowing who he is? So here's the thing, my lord. He has to communicate with my sister again, correct? Threaten her with *dire consequences* and upset her again, then tell her where to place the money and all of that nonsense so that he can swoop down, masked and caped, and disappear with his ill-gotten lucre."

"Read your share of penny dreadfuls, have you?"

"The blame isn't on my head if Mama often forgets to lock them up in her desk. But I'm right, aren't I? He wrote that he would be in touch. I doubt he'll wait too long, don't you? Why, he might even return tonight, to place another message in the tree. Which means you have to be in my bedchamber before midnight. It's the best vantage point. I know that, because I've tried them all. There aren't enough shrubs to constitute a concealed hidey-hole, the windows in the kitchens are barely aboveground and I could only look from my sister's windows if I involved her, which I won't. She would send me straight home if she knew I was making myself personally involved in her misadventure. I'd raise too much attention if I availed myself of the view from the servants' quarters in the attics. Oh, and before you ask, the windows in Oliver's study are stained glass, and impossible to see through."

"You've put a good measure of thought into this, haven't you?"

"I have. Which leaves your only good vantage point the windows in my bedchamber." She smiled at him, knowing he was becoming more frustrated by the moment. "It's a narrow house, my lord, for all its grandeur."

"I already ruled that out, thank you."

"You did? Oh, so that's what you were muttering about. But you considered it, if only briefly. What turned you against the idea?"

"Why, Miss Foster, I have no idea. Unless I'm looking at her."

Dany was young, but women are born old as the world in some areas. "Your notoriety seems to have gone to your head, my lord, as you grossly overestimate your appeal."

"Wonderful. Now, mere aeons too late, you've decided to take umbrage. Did it not occur to you that you, Miss Foster, are grossly underestimating your charms?"

Now he'd done it, made her genuinely angry. And they'd been rather enjoying each other's banter, she was certain of it. Being friendly, even chummy, as Dexter would say. "That isn't funny. Nor is it flattering, if that's what you were aiming for with that ridiculous statement. I'd considered us partners in this adven—this arrangement. I can be of help. I want to help. Mari is my sister, remember. I release you of your obligation. You may leave. *Now.*"

"Do you feel better now that you've climbed up on your high horse?" he asked, shaking his head as if looking down at his favorite hound, just to see that it had piddled on his boots. "And I'm not going anywhere. No, that's not true. I am leaving now, but I'll return at half past four, to take you for that drive in the park. Or did you forget that?"

Rats. She had forgotten. He was going to lend his consequence to her entry into the Little Season, especially since Mari had taken to her bed, vowing not to leave it again for the Remainder of Her Life. *Who's the looby now, Daniella Foster?*

Sometimes it was wiser to bend, at least a little, in order to achieve one's ends.

"Very well, my lord, I accept your apology."

"I rather thought you would, even though I haven't offered one. We may or may not have much more to speak about during our drive."

"Really?"

He got to his feet. "Possibly. First, I'm going to consult the most unlikely physician anyone could imagine, and have him examine my brain. Until later, Miss Foster."

Then he bowed over her hand—she'd think about her reaction to that slight intimacy later—and left her where she sat, probably wise not to attempt standing anytime soon.

CHAPTER FIVE

DARBY TRAVERS FINISHED his examination of the two notes, an exercise that hadn't taken more than a minute at the outside, and placed them back on his friend's desk. "You aren't really applying to me for my one-eyed opinion, are you? My sole contribution, I imagine, is only to look aghast and exclaim, 'Good God, man, the handwriting is one and the same!'"

"As is the phrasing, yes, thank you," Coop said, still leaning against that same desk, a glass of wine dangling from his fingertips. "The bastard seems to have begun a cottage industry of blackmailing. I wonder how many others there are out there at the moment, suffering the same dilemma."

"If he's going after straying husbands and wives, my best guest would number in the hundreds. But then there's you, which makes a case for the man's diversity of ambition, and his, shall we say, *growth* in said ambition. Taking the time to both pen and publish two entire chapbooks for a mere ten thousand pounds? You may be his prize victim, the pinnacle of his nefarious career, if that flatters you at all, and I begin to think you're also a bird he will pluck more than once if you let him. I wonder how long he's been working at his trade."

"You're thinking of gifting him with a few pointers?" Coop picked up the note to the countess. "Five hundred pounds. I believe the countess has already considered selling some of her jewelry to pay him. The man isn't stupid, demanding more than she could possibly manage to produce."

"Not as much investment involved penning sappy, soppy letters to unhappy young matrons. I imagine he considers the amount a fair return on his efforts. No more than fifty pounds to blackmail our own Prinny, and even then he'd probably only receive our royal debtor's scribbled vowels in return."

"You're enjoying this, aren't you?"

"Not at all. I'm merely looking at the thing from our blackmailer's point of view, and must applaud his thinking. Five pounds from a shoemaker who passes off inferior leathers by means of clever dyes. Ten pounds six from the seamstress who delivers gowns and picks up various little rewards from milady's shelves and tucks them up in her sewing basket while inside the residence. That sort of thing could take considerable effort for small reward, but one has to begin somewhere, doesn't one? Gain polish, slowly grow your profits and then move on to larger targets?"

"You speak of this as if you're contemplating joining the man's ranks."

Darby grinned. "I *join* nobody, although I wonder why I never considered such a venture."

"I hesitate to guess, but perhaps because you're bloody rich as Croesus?"

"True enough. But the fact remains that there are few people who know more secrets than I do. Happily for the world, I am also a gentleman. Although I will say that if there's any truth to the fellow's veiled hint about your particular secret reaching all the way to the highest levels of the Crown, then either he's more daring than even I would be, or he has access to some prodigiously important people. We're looking to the ton for our blackmailer, Coop. You've figured that much on your own, I'm sure."

Coop downed the remaining contents of his glass. "I have. I flirted momentarily with the idea that a well-placed secretary or servant could be privy to many secrets, but it would take an entire small army of coconspirators to engineer something on this grand a scale. If there is a grand scale, and the more I think, the more I believe this is not one ambitious man, acting alone."

"There's an entire other world moving about in Mayfair, one many of us are sadly unaware of, I agree. So many consider them invisible, not to mention deaf and dumb. Ladies' maids, valets, tweenies quietly repairing the fire, footmen with large ears listening in foyers. But it would take someone to cultivate them, enlist them. The scope of such an enterprise, all the bits and pieces that make up the whole? I believe I'm feeling the headache coming on."

"Granted, it makes sense to believe there is an organized *gang* wreaking havoc all across Mayfair. Or we're wrong, and our blackmailer is just one person and his carefully selected targets."

"Oh, but what are the odds of that? Only one blackmailer and these few carefully selected targets of yours, and two of them they just happen to bump into each other on Bond Street—literally—and end up sharing their common predicaments?"

"I didn't share anything."

"No, but you'll have to at some point. For one, Miss Foster is far too clever to believe you'll be hunting down this scoundrel with all speed and fervor strictly because you're a hero. She took my measure within a heartbeat, much as it pains me to admit it, and found me both foolish and unnecessary."

"Don't go into a sulk. The countess doesn't want you involved. I doubt she wants me involved, for that matter. She's closeted herself in her chambers, refusing to come out again, even to shepherd her sister through the Little Season."

"The minx won't take that one lying down."

"I agree, but happily, that's not our problem."

"What's not your problem, darlings?" The questioning voice was loud, almost booming, thanks to the fact that the woman who owned it was slightly deaf and hiked her own volume as if everyone else would have trouble hearing her. On top of that often embarrassing trait—most discomfiting when she believed she was whispering—was the fact that she rarely *stopped* talking. "And for pity's sake, Cooper, don't slouch there against the desk like some lazy oaf. I raised you better than that. Stand up, stand up. There, that's better. Straighten your shoulders. Good posture is the sign of a gentleman, and a boon to regulation of the bowels. Look at Darby. See how straight he stands? *He* listened to his mother."

"Sadly, Mrs. Townsend, my mother flew off to her heavenly reward when I was not more than a mere infant in my cot. But I will say my nurse had a wicked hand with the birch rod if I ever slumped like a lazy oaf."

Cooper turned to look at his mother, tall of stature, strong of bosom and with a fierce, hawk-nosed face that would suit well as the figurehead nailed to a man-of-war. Add her natural curiosity and rather singular way of looking at most anything to the mix, and it was more than time they moved from the Pulteney, with its generous parlor but very little privacy.

"Perhaps I spared the rod to your detriment, Cooper. Curse my soft heart, but you were always *so* cute," she said as she grabbed Cooper's cheeks between her fingers and squeezed. "Look at that face, Darby. Just look, take it all in! How could anyone ever take umbrage with that face? So wonderfully kind. So infinitely understanding."

"Minerva, please," Cooper said, pulling away before she permanently dented his cheeks. He hadn't been allowed to call her Mother since his sixteenth birthday, which was the first time the woman realized she now had a son who apparently needed to shave. She didn't particularly want to be a mother, and felt they'd rub along much better as friends.

He looked past her now, to where her maid was standing just inside the entry hall, struggling to maintain her hold on a half dozen bandboxes. "And not infinitely, Minerva. May I be so ungentlemanly as to inquire as to how much your latest assault on Bond Street has set me back?"

Rose coughed. She and Cooper had established a series of signals to warn him that whatever his mother said next, he was certainly not going to be doing handsprings of joy once he heard it.

"I am aware of your miserly hold on the purse strings. But I have your reputation to uphold, even as you ignore the responsibilities incumbent on the proud matriarch of the new Townsend dynasty. You wouldn't dare send me out into Society in rags, now would you? *Rags*, Cooper."

Coop looked toward Rose, the maid-cum-companion, and a distant relation who had known him from his cradle. This time she rolled her eyes as she adjusted the bandbox straps on her forearms. Worse than a cough? My, this was turning into his lucky day, wasn't it? "Forgive me my unnatural tendency to avoid bankruptcy. I'm convinced you will do me proud each time you set sail into Society."

"My point entirely. Foresails flapping, flags waving, creating quite the wake as I pass by. It's only fitting, and Lord knows I'm built for it. I'm horribly shy, by nature, but I see this as a time when I must bite back on my natural reticence and hold up my end, as it were."

Rose's choked cough was ignored by the lady, other than for her to raise one strong brow and dare Cooper to add any comment to what she'd just said.

"All I do, I do for you. One cannot put anything so crass as a price on a son's love and a mother's obligations, dear. Even in my short time here in London, I've heard so many good things about a particular seamstress. Why, even Vivien gives her some bit of custom. Don't look confused, Cooper. Vivien Sinclair, Gabriel's aunt, and the Duchess of Cranbrook. I hadn't seen her in dogs' years, as she and her Basil were always flitting all over the world, but we ran into each other in the park yesterday, and it was as if we'd never parted. Good friends are like that, you know. All I had to say to her was 'Vauxhall Gardens,' and the pair of us went off into giggles like schoolgirls. There was this importune young scoundrel, you understand, and a proposed stroll along the Dark Gallery..."

"How pleased I am you and Gabe's aunt have rediscovered each other," Cooper said, simply to stop his mother before she launched into a litany of assuredly embarrassing reminiscences. "And the seamstress?"

"Such a sad, sorry generation you boys are, sticklers for propriety. I know Vauxhall has fallen out of favor for the ton, but in my time it was glorious. You should be delighted your mother had herself some fun, kicking up her heels and such during her grasstime. Don't growl, Cooper, it isn't polite. The seamstress, yes. I've just come from there, as a matter of fact. Mrs. Yothers—lovely woman. She gifted me with one of the gowns, and an enchanting purple turban. Itches some, but it'll do."

"Why would she do that? Not give you an itchy turban—give you anything?"

"Ah, Cooper, you still don't understand how the world revolves, do you, for all your fine education. The lady and I had a lovely coze—chatty woman, so I wouldn't dare pass on any secrets to her or they'd be all over Mayfair before the cat could lick its ear, but I was sure to keep *my* ears open!"

"You and I must have a lovely coze of our own someday, Mrs. Townsend," Darby interposed, his grin very much at his friend's expense.

"I highly doubt that, scamp. You know enough about Society for any three people as it is, and I am of course sworn to secrecy in any event. Now, back to Mrs. Yothers, if you will cease interrupting. Terrible habit. In exchange for the gowns and such, I've only to mention to two or three ladies—casually, simply in passing, and you know I am the epitome of discretion—that Mrs. Yothers is the only seamstress worth her salt in this entire city."

"A thousand pardons, Minerva," Cooper felt impelled to ask. "Did you actually say 'epitome of discretion'?"

"I can be, if I want. I simply don't always *want*. Now, to continue. We have, as you might say, struck a bargain, much the same as the arrangements I have with Mrs. Bell the milliner, the shoemaker Mr. Wood—pricey, that man! There are others. Oh, and I've established an account for you with Mr. Weston, who vows that you'd be poorly served by Stolz, who hires only ham-fisted tailors. I wasn't able to manage any sort of *arrangement* there, but he's still the best, or so I'm told. You have a fitting at eleven tomorrow. Now thank me."

Coop had long ago learned that, when it came to his mother, there existed no hole deep enough to throw himself into and pull the dirt back on top of him, so he simply said, "Thank you."

"Good, and as I've finished saying what I had to say, poor Rose can stop coughing like a consumptive, yes? Now, what's not your problem, darlings? From the tone of your voices as I entered, I believe you may be thinking something you're not saying. Come on, spit it out, and you know I can see through a lie, Cooper. You've much too much conscience to carry it off, which is why, Darby, *you* won't speak unless requested."

Darby raised his hand, waggling his fingers. "May I please be excused?" he asked cheekily.

"You most certainly may not," Mrs. Townsend told him sternly, and the viscount looked to Coop for help. Which he didn't get, damn it, for if Darby couldn't be considered reinforcements, at least Minerva Townsend might marginally mind her tongue while he was present. No, that wouldn't happen, but as long as Coop was stuck here, he didn't see any reason to allow his friend to escape unscathed.

"Really, Mrs. Townsend, it's nothing to concern you," Darby said, but there was little hope in his voice.

"It didn't sound like nothing. Whatever the problem, I have no doubt you're responsible for it. You, and those two other scamps, dragging my poor Cooper into your constant mischiefs. Now, I'm going to sit down— Rose, for pity's sake, are you still standing there? Go on, shoo, and put your feet up. You look totally fagged. And with me twenty years your senior and still not in the least deflated."

Make that thirty, and the number might be reasonably close. Oh, yes, Cooper McGinley Townsend knew an Original when he saw one. He'd grown up with one. Give Miss Foster another forty years of practice, and she'd be more than capable of taking up his mother's banner, to become the Terror of Society.

"Minerva, we were just speaking in general terms. Weren't we, Darby? Nothing to set your nose to twitching."

Mrs. Townsend adjusted her spectacles on her splendid, hawk-like beak. She didn't need them, or so she swore, and only employed them as a prop to give her gravitas. Coop had to admit that whenever she looked at him overtop the gold frames (not to mention the hawk-like proboscis), gravitas commenced to spew out all over the place as would hot lava on the unsuspecting villagers below in the valley.

She turned her stare on the viscount once more.

"I surrender," Darby said after a few seconds, smiling apologetically at his friend. "In my defense, she had a one-eye advantage on me. Tell her, Coop, or I'll be forced to squawk like one of Gabe's blasted parrots."

"Why not? Apparently I'm already standing in a hole of my own making that resembles nothing more than a grave."

"Cooper! You've never been so dramatic. A hole as deep as a grave? Where do you hear such nonsense? Are you reading poems again? I have warned you against them, again and again. They're all frippery and unrequited love and sad tales of woe no sane person would swallow whole. A thick volume on farming, that's what you need. You've got an estate to run now, you know. Learn to grow a proper turnip, that's what I say. Can't go wrong with turnips."

"Couldn't have said it better myself, Mrs. Townsend. Turnips, that's the ticket. Commit that to memory, my friend." Darby retreated to the drinks table, probably to pour a bracing glass of wine.

Coop was hard-pressed not to join him, but he'd ignore the glass and gulp straight from the decanter. His father had known how to handle Minerva. He'd learned to ignore her because, as impossible as it seemed, everyone save her husband and son found her vastly interesting and amusing.

Still, actually *handing* Minerva information she'd do God only knew what with? Coop didn't see how any good could come from that.

The blackmail threat, the chase through the alleyways, Miss Foster. Now this? He looked at the mantel clock and inwardly winced. It was only a few minutes past three? And he still had to run the figurative gauntlet of meeting with Miss Foster a third time. Was there anything else to go wrong for him today?

"And another thing," Minerva said, finally settling herself in a chair so that the gentlemen could sit, as well. "This Minerva business. That was all well and good before, but I realize the heavy mantle of responsibility now thrust upon me, thanks to your heroics, and believe it only commonsensible for me to once more take up the mantle of…" She sighed. "Mother. Or perhaps Mama?"

"You hate when I call you Mother. You have to be joking."

"I most certainly am not. Henceforth, at least in public—not that I consider this scamp's presence as anywhere near *public*—you will address me as Mother."

"The gifts heaped on your shoulders just keep mounting, Coop, you lucky dog. Either that, or this figurative hole you spoke of is growing deeper."

"Shut up, Darby. All right, *Mother*, since you insist. Now why don't you retire to your chamber, where I'm certain Rose has laid out some sort of refreshment."

"Perhaps even turnip pie," Darby said quietly. Too quietly for Minerva to hear, but close enough for Coop to not only hear but be forced to manfully repress a laugh.

Minerva looked from one to the other. "He said something, didn't he? Something amusing. What did he say?"

"Nothing Min—Mother. Darby's mouth moves, but he rarely says anything of importance."

Minerva smoothed the front of her gown, clearly settling herself in for the duration. "Well, at least we agree on something. Now, shall we travel back to the problem that isn't your problem, because it definitely seemed very much your problem when I arrived? Come on, lads, one of you open your mouth and say something important, because I'm not leaving here until you do."

"Race you to the door," Darby whispered, careful not to move his lips. "Unless you can come up with a convincing fib? Because you're wrong about the countess's retirement to her bedchamber, Coop—you need Miss Foster out and about in Society."

And that, Cooper was to tell himself later, was how Darby helped him dig that lifelong figurative hole even deeper, until he thought he could see a Chinaman's straw hat.

CHAPTER SIX

DRAT THE MAN, Dany thought, standing in front of the pier glass in the hallway just outside the drawing room, slapping her gloves against her thigh. And drat Mari, so firmly sunk beneath the covers that it would take an expedition to find her.

Does one have one's gloves on before her escort's arrival? Does one appeared gloved and *hatted* and panting like a puppy eager to be put to the leash? Does one race back upstairs, only to descend—gracefully, of course—when the gentleman is announced? Which would be past ridiculous, since that would mean his horses would be left standing while he waited for her to become gloved and hatted and fill the awkward silence with inane chatter such as, "Oh, dear, how the time has flown," or "Gracious, I had entirely forgotten I'd agreed to drive with you in the park."

Whopping great help Mari had been, only lamenting, "For the love of heaven, why won't she go away," when Dany had sat herself on the bed and asked these questions.

So here she stood, still not gloved, although she'd decided the military-type shako might take more than one attempt to settle it jauntily enough over her right eye and finally donned it. Amazingly, with her hands trembling ever so slightly, she managed the perfect level of jaunty in one try.

Did Emmaline ride with her? Did she, hopefully not, plunk herself down on the seat between the baron and her mistress? If he brought an open town carriage, there would be two seats, and she could have the maid facing her—and watching her—for the entire time. And wouldn't that be above all things wonderful, since Emmaline possessed an alarming tendency to giggle.

But no. Young gentlemen didn't favor such equipages. He was bound to show up with some outlandish curricle, or high perch phaeton (and wouldn't climbing up into that be interesting, while attempting to keep her ankles covered and her rump inconspicuous?). What about a tiger? Did the baron have one, some poor, terrified young lad in garish livery, balancing on a small step and hanging on to the back of the curricle for dear life? Did a tiger constitute a chaperone? Why would anyone need a chaperone in the middle of London, surrounded by everyone else in Society who had decided taking the air at Hyde Park was just the jolliest thing anyone could do at this hour?

Dany hadn't had time to ask those questions of Mari, although she had tried, even as her sister's maid was none too gently pushing her toward the door.

She'd ask Timmerly, but he'd only smirk at her in that obnoxious way he had, and make her feel twice the fool. Wasn't it bad enough that he'd positioned his smug self at the head of the stairs, pretending not to notice her for the past ten minutes? Honestly, some kind soul should bundle up all the rules of Society in one…

"Blast! Why didn't I think of that sooner?" she asked herself as she turned to the stairs, having remembered the thick tome her sister had handed her, commanding she commit every word to memory. The title, as she recalled, was nearly a small book in itself, and contained such words as *Circumspection*, *Comportment*, *Proper*. Dany had waited until Mari departed the room before kicking the offensive thing beneath the bed-skirts. Her big toe had hurt for three days.

She'd just put her hand on the railing when a footman called up, "Mr. Timmerly, sir, the hero baron has pulled to the curb. Miss shouldn't keep such a fine pair of bays standing."

"Miss Foster," the curmudgeonly old family retainer intoned gravely, "if you'll excuse my boldness, the foyer lies the other way."

"You enjoy this, don't you?" she accused as she headed for the curving staircase leading down to the foyer.

"You might wish to be more gentle with the countess, miss, now that she's in a delicate condition."

Dany halted with one foot already hovering over the first step, her right hand thankfully clutching the iron railing or she would have pitched face forward to the marble floor below. "My sister is *not*— Dear God, perhaps she is. It would be just like Mari not to know." She looked at Timmerly. "What do you know?"

"It isn't proper to discuss such things with young ladies."

Dany's mostly unpleasant day was growing worse by the moment. "It isn't proper for young ladies to plant butlers a facer, either, but if you were to apply to any of my family they would inform you I've never put much stock in *proper*."

The butler cleared his throat, clearly fighting a blush.

"It is sufficient to say that Mrs. Timmerly is certain we'll be welcoming the Cockermouth heir before the king's birthday."

Dany counted along her top teeth with her tongue until she got to nine (she might be young, but she wasn't entirely stupid). "Oh, that isn't good. That isn't good at all."

Timmerly straightened his shoulders and puffed out his chest. "I beg your pardon!"

"Oh. Sorry. It's the greatest of good news, isn't it? The earl will be over the moon when he returns." *Unless he believes his wife had taken a lover.* "I'll be going now, not that you care a button what I do. Mustn't keep the horses standing."

The footman was just opening the door for the baron when Dany went flouncing past him. "You're late," she told him before he could say the same to her, which the briefest glance at his expression warned her he was about to do. "We've a new problem to discuss."

"O happy day," Cooper said, following after her, and then standing back to allow his tiger—really, the livery wasn't so bad—to assist her up onto the seat of an admittedly fine yet sober curricle. No yellow wheels for the baron Townsend, clearly. And the bays were near to extraordinary.

"You've a lovely pair," she admitted once he'd gone around the equipage and boosted himself onto the seat.

His look was nearly comical. "I beg your pardon?"

"The bays are lovely, perfectly matched," she expounded further, wondering if the baron had possibly drunk away his afternoon. It wouldn't do well for either of them if she had to explain everything twice. "You haven't been drinking, have you?"

"If I have, clearly not enough. Shall we be off?"

"I suppose so. The sooner we're off, the sooner we're back, which should please you enormously."

"How well you know me, on such a short acquaintance," Coop said as he set the curricle in motion, his tiger still standing on the flagway.

"I think you forgot someone," Dany said, watching as the boy, no more than twelve, headed for the alleyway beside the mansion.

"Harry will go to the servants' entrance and someone will feed him a cake or something. It's all arranged. We've no need of a prepubescent chaperone, Miss Foster. We'll be far from alone in the park."

"Yes, I'd wondered about that. We'd look rather silly having to speak across my maid, plopped between us, her hands clapped to her ears. I really must read that book."

"Whatever book it is, yes, please do tend to the task posthaste. I know you're fresh from the country, but hasn't your sister explained anything to you?"

"She's been rather fully employed weeping into her pillow," Dany said, at the moment not caring what the baron thought of her, or her sister. It was enough that he was here, apparently still willing to play the hero for them. Why, she'd nearly forgotten all about his green eyes. Nearly. "Which brings us to our new problem. The butler's wife believes the countess may be increasing."

He made an expert but not showy turn into Hyde Park, having executed the tricky maneuver of inserting the curricle into the line of various equipages without muss, fuss or banging wheels with anyone. The man was not flamboyant, not in his speech, his dress, his deportment. He was the unlikeliest hero she'd ever imagined in her daydreams. He was simply a man who stood up when necessary, and did heroic things. Perhaps it was not only his eyes…and blond locks, and strong chin line, and…and all the rest that drew her to him. She'd like to think so, or else that would make her no more than one of the giggling, sighing throng of females who probably chased him everywhere. How he must hate that!

"Really. Increasing what— Oh. Miss Foster, I don't think this is anything you and I should be addressing. I'll correct myself. I *know* it isn't anything we should discuss. But since I have no doubt you'll address it, anyway, is there a problem of…timing?"

"Oh, good. I was wondering how I might gracefully get around that part. Yes, I think so. Probably only Mrs. Timmerly knows for sure, since I believe Mari only just figured everything out today. So you see, my lord, it is now doubly important we seek out this blackmailer and recover her letters. Oliver must never know, can never so much as think he may have been, um…"

"Usurped? I can think of other words, although I'd rather not."

She refused to blush. "I suppose that's as clear as we need make that, thank you. I felt you should know, since we are working together."

"We are? I don't believe I've agreed to a partnership of any kind."

Apparently men could be maddeningly thick. "Do you really have a choice?"

"I don't? Please, enlighten me."

"Yes, I should. In the interests of fairness, I feel it only fair to add that I don't like you. I may admire you, and even find you somewhat attractive, but I don't like you. You clearly resent that I've come to you for assistance, and you enjoy making me feel uncomfortable."

"Tit for tat, Miss Foster. I haven't had a comfortable moment since you threw yourself at me in Bond Street."

"I did not—oh, now you're smiling. I probably should look at you more often."

"And be in my company far less," he shot back. "What are you looking at, anyway? Clearly you aren't paying attention to our fellow travelers on this road to nowhere, or you would have commented on something by now. There are many finely feathered birds taking the air today."

"There are? Oh, goodness—is that man on the large gray actually sporting a parrot on his shoulder? How bizarre."

"You have no idea, Miss Foster. One day I might tell you a rather amusing tale about the tethered and caged birds still being seen around Mayfair by those not clever enough to have realized the joke. Our feathered friends are no longer in fashion."

"Yes, you do that." Dany really didn't much care either way about fashionable or unfashionable birds. "But no, I suppose I'm not really paying attention, am I? I suppose I thought the experience would have more to it than following everyone as they follow everyone else. What is the point, do you know?"

"The point, my fine country miss, is to see. And to be seen. You, for instance, are being seen in the company of the hero of Quatre Bras and a dozen wholly fictitious escapades of derring-do here in London. Even now, people are whispering to their companions. Who is she? Did he rescue her? Is she an heiress? Should we stop and ask, or would the hero take offense at our blatant curiosity? What to do, what to do."

"That's ridiculous."

"Most things are, Miss Foster. But remember, this was your idea."

Dany thought about that for a few moments. "You're right. It was my idea. I thought it would be interesting. I thought I would get to show off my new bonnet, which I couldn't do because I cut my hair and now even this shako had to be stuffed with paper so it didn't fall down over my ears. I used to have tons of it, you know."

"Paper? Or hair?"

"Hair, of course. I grew it for years, on my mother's orders. Do you have any idea how much trouble hair can be?"

"Not exactly, no. Is it as much trouble as having to stuff your bonnets with paper?"

Dany looked at him and grinned. "The bonnets are temporary. The hair was permanent. Or at least it was. By and large, I think what's left is rather fetching. Certainly different."

"Ah, yes, different. I believe that relieves me from having to ask why in blue blazes you hacked it all off. The color wasn't enough?"

"You don't care for the color?"

"Over the centuries, man has learned there is no safe answer to that sort of question, so I'll pretend you didn't ask it. Look here, Miss Foster, this is getting us nowhere, and we've much to discuss. For my sins."

His voice had rather trailed off on his last few words, but Dany heard them. "And what sins did you commit? I know I didn't commit any. Well, at least not connected to the pot my sister is boiling in at the moment. I'm not declaring myself free of failings."

Cooper exited the park as neatly as he'd entered it, putting the curricle back out on the street. "I hope you won't mind if I don't chivalrously exclaim that you could never be anything less than perfect."

"And now I'll ignore that. You know, my lord, I believe we're beginning to understand each other."

He kept his attention on his horses, but she did notice that his right eyebrow elevated in possible surprise. Certainly not in humor. "Does that prospect frighten you as much as it does me?" he asked as he took the bays into a turn down a rather narrow street.

"I don't know. At least neither of us has to waste our time or words in attempting to be polite. Which, you must admit, can only be considered a good thing, because we really don't have time to waste on conventions and silly rules of Society. Oliver will be home in less than a fortnight."

"I agree on the need for speed. The blackmailer's next communication could arrive at any moment."

"Yes, which means you need to reconsider the vantage point of my bedchamber. Where are we going? I've no fear you plan to compromise me, but if you have a destination in mind I suggest it not be Portman Square, as we still have much to discuss."

"More than you could imagine, Miss Foster," he said, pulling to the curb in front of a rather ancient-looking church stuck between a haberdashery and a tobacco shop. He set the brake and looped the reins around it. "Stay where you are until I come 'round and help you down. I only say that because you haven't read the book yet, whatever book that might be, and shouldn't attempt a descent on your own."

"It's not as if I couldn't do it, you know."

"I don't doubt that for a moment. Just...*don't.*"

She twisted about on the seat to watch as he walked behind the curricle, already tossing a coin to a young lad who had appeared out of nowhere to offer to "mind the ponies" for him.

"Perhaps you should have rethought the tiger," she said as she allowed him to assist her to the uneven flagway. It wasn't quite the same as being swooped up into his arms, but the touch of his hands at her waist while she rested hers on his shoulders for that brief moment wasn't exactly a distant second in how it affected her heartbeat.

If only Mari would climb out of her latest pit of despair; Dany really did have a few important questions for her.

"Tigers are for show, unless one employs an aging pugilist, and they don't look all that well in livery. Harry and his livery wouldn't last a moment in this neighborhood. You failed to tell me, Miss Foster. Do you possess any other talents save pickpocketing?"

She brought herself back from her new, unexpected curiosity concerning All Things Cooper. "That's not fair. The chapbook was mine. I was only retrieving it. What sort of talents?"

"Playacting. I've every hope you'll have no problem with a bit of fibbing."

Dany tipped up her chin. "I may have found the need in the past, yes. A fib is often more kind than the truth. Especially when one's mother asks unfortunate questions."

"Very good. Steadfast and upright honesty would do us no good at the moment." He offered her his arm. "Shall we remove ourselves from the sight of pass-ersby?"

Oh, we most certainly shall, Dany thought, quickly understanding that she should not be where she was, certainly not with him. They were in the process of being clandestine. What a lovely word—*clandestine*. How could she have, even for a moment, thought the baron was a sobersides? *What fun!*

"This chapel is no longer in use except for occasional weddings, but the frescoes are said to be in remarkably good repair. Aunt Mildred said we should not fail to see them before leaving London."

Aunt Mildred? Ah, so the fibbing had begun.

"Then how bad of you, for not telling me to bring my sketching pad. You always were a bit of a loose screw, Cousin Mortimer. Just for that, I believe I'll insist in inspecting every single fresco in some detail, and you'll be stuck chaperoning me for at least another hour before you can cry off and go chasing down your highly unsuitable friends."

Bless the baron's heroic heart. He winked at her! She'd get him to understand she would be more of a help than a hindrance.

They mounted the six steps to a pair of heavily carved wooden doors, pausing only as Cooper handed over a penny to the old man sitting on a wooden stool, curiously not showing any hint of curiosity upon seeing customers so late in the day.

"You always were a bit of a pill, Cousin Gertrude," he responded in just the correct tone of cousinly disgust as the old man creaked to his feet to push open one of the doors. "Next you'll say you want me to bring you back again tomorrow, and I won't. Not if you beg."

The old man cleared his throat. "There be sheets of paper and charcoal sticks inside, miss, for those who wish to take rubbings from some of the tombstones out back. Some lovely old stones we've got, we do. Only a penny for five."

Dany turned her most winning smile on the caretaker. "Why, thank you, good sir. Cousin, don't just stand there like the fool you are. Give the man a penny."

"Going to use them to stuff more bonnets?" Cooper asked, reaching into his small purse. "Here you go, sir, a six-pence. We'd rather not be disturbed."

"None of them never does," the old man grumbled, shaking his head as he returned to his stool as Cooper grabbed her hand and pulled her inside before she could ask the old man what he meant.

The door had barely closed before Dany turned on him, laughing. "Did you hear that? This place is used for assignations, isn't it? The man as nearly said that. Do you take advantage of this chapel often?"

Still clasping her hand, for there were only a few candles burning and the stained-glass windows didn't let in much light, he led her to a bench placed against one wall. "I thought I was being original, as a matter of fact. Here, sit down. You lie too easily for my comfort, Gertrude."

"Gertie. I much prefer Gertie. So you don't think the caretaker believed either of us?"

"Do you?"

Dany thought about that for a moment. "I'm not certain. I wouldn't want to be thought of as a loose woman. Or as someone as silly as my sister, who probably would have thought trysting with her unknown admirer in an ancient chapel the epitome of romantic expression. Of course, in either case, you're the rotter of the piece. Shame on you."

The baron sat down beside her. "You don't have a single nerve in your body, do you?"

"I don't think so, no," she said as every last nerve in said body commenced to tingle at his closeness. Not that he'd ever know that. "Papa vows I was a cuckoo hatchling. You do know about cuckoo birds, don't you? They lay their eggs in other bird's nests? If my great-aunt Isobel on my father's side hadn't had my same outrageous hair color, I believe Mama would have had considerable explaining to do. And don't look at me like that. Yes, that's how I know so much about...usurping. My brother explained it all to me. So, now can we get down to business? What time do you want me to meet you at the tradesman's entrance? Timmerly locks all the doors at midnight, but I managed to find an extra key for the side door that leads to the kitchens. It will be a simple matter of Emmaline letting you in, and sneaking you up the servant stairs."

"I will not sneak into your bedchamber."

"Oh, but I've already explained this to you. And we've already agreed that time is of the essence. Nobody will be any the wiser, and Emmaline can be discreet. There's no other way."

"Unfortunately, there is. Now listen carefully, Miss Foster, as we are limited for time."

"So formal? We're conspirators now. Please, address me as Dany. It's so much easier."

"And yet the clock continues ticking, Miss Foster," the baron said tightly, the look in his green eyes one of frustration bordering on contemplated mayhem, if Dany was any judge, and she was, having been the recipient of that particular look from members of her family time and again in her growing-up years (and at least twice today).

"Ticktock, ticktock. Yes, I understand, even as I wonder if you do. Go on."

"I'll ignore that. Here are the rules. One—there can be no clandestine surveillance nests set up in your bed-chamber. Not by me, not by you, not by any combination that includes you, me or any number of other persons, none of which would be considered a chaperone by any stretch of the imagination."

"Not even the Archbishop of Canterbury?" Dany couldn't resist. He was so handsome in his frustration. If he were her brother, he could box her ears or some such thing. But he wasn't, and he was forced by Society to treat her as a young lady of quality. Pity she didn't know how to behave like a young lady of quality.

Or perhaps she did; she'd certainly had years of les-sons behind her. She simply didn't see the point, when misbehaving was so much more fun.

"We'll leave that question for the moment," he said tersely. "Two. I did not ask for this assignment, I did not seek it out, I don't want it—but you and your crack-brained scheming has put me in this position. That said, and in words with the least syllables, *I* am in sole charge of what we do to aid the countess."

All right. Now he was ruffling *her* feathers. She clasped her hands and pressed them to her bosom, and then fluttered her eyelashes for good measure as she goaded: "My hero. I do fear I might swoon."

At last, he smiled. If he was a sobersides, at least

she seemed to have found a way through to his appreciation of the ridiculous. "Please don't let me stop you. I'm certain there's some water in that vase of wilting posies over there. Dumping its contents on your paper-stuffed head would count as my only pleasure since I woke up this morning."

Hmm. Perhaps he wasn't as amused as she'd thought, but was only delighting in contemplating a bit of revenge on her for all she'd put him through. Which was probably a lot, all things considered.

"Clearly entirely on the wrong side of the bed." Dany knew to retreat when she'd gone too far—she'd certainly traveled to that point often enough. "Very well, I'm sorry. No more interrupting. You're doing Mari and me a huge favor and I've given you nothing but grief in return. But," she added, because with Dany there was always a *but* somewhere, "you really needn't be so mean. I'm only trying to help."

The baron stood up, walked a few paces away from the bench and then turned to look at her. "I know, and that's what makes what I have to say even more difficult. You think you're helpful. Let me correct myself. You're *positive* you'd be helpful. Tell me, how much the worse would it be for me if I didn't include you in my plans?"

She got to her feet, applauding softly. "I knew you'd be brilliant, my lord. Never before has anyone asked that question."

"Although they certainly did get an answer?" he asked her, another smile actually beginning to evidence itself at the corners of his mouth.

That was a rough patch gotten over neatly.

"Indeed, yes, they did. I'm afraid I'm not a thing like Mari, or my mother, or most women for that matter. I cannot fathom dutifully tending to my embroidery when something important is afoot. It's against my nature. Sitting and waiting, perhaps sending up prayers in some chapel such as this one, with nothing to say about the outcome, would drive me mad."

"I'm after a petty blackmailer, Miss Foster, not marching off to the Crusades with your colors tied to my sleeve."

Oh, but if it were and if you did, I'd follow you without an instant's hesitation. With that thought came a blush that was the bane of her red-haired existence. Perhaps she was more like Mari than she'd considered. "Don't be facetious, my lord. But now that we've gotten that settled, what are *we* going to do next? And please don't say we'll be adding the viscount to our hunting party. I don't believe he would approach the problem with as much gravitas as I would like."

"He said you'd say that. But I'm afraid we may not have much choice. You might want to sit down again, Miss Foster."

"I'll stand, thank you."

"Very well, I suppose I can allow you to be stubborn when it makes no difference to me. We still do this with the understanding that I am in charge of anything over and above whether you choose to sit down or stand up. Agreed?"

"If I have no choice. Go on."

"That said, being in charge, it naturally follows that you'll be taking orders from me. You are not to circumvent those orders, you are not to improvise, you are most definitely not to question those orders. You are not to think up anything you believe to be a better solution than mine and go off on your own, leaving me to chase after you and pick up the pieces."

Yes, he already knew her very well. How had that happened? Did she have a warning sign pasted to her forehead, that only he could see?

"I hesitate to point this out, but you're sounding more like a tyrant than a hero. *That said*, I suppose I still agree, since it's clear you're leaving me no other choice if you're ever going to get on with this. That ticking clock, remember?"

"How you inspire my confidence, Miss Foster. Unfortunately, it has been pointed out to me, rather strongly, that I also have no choice where you're concerned. You see, Miss Foster, your sister is not the only person being blackmailed. I, too, am a victim of your sister's secret admirer."

Dany sat down. She sat down so quickly she nearly missed the bench entirely, but grabbed on to the front of it with both hands. "I... I beg your— *What did you say?*"

The baron raised his eyes toward the chipped, painted ceiling of the chapel, as if running his own words through his head for a second time. "Our mutual blackmailer is extorting money from the countess for her innocent indiscretion, and from me via threats that need not concern you. That's clear enough."

"No," she said, shaking her head. "I don't think it is. Are you less than a hero?"

"I'm not a hero at all, having only done what seemed sensible at the time. If not for those damnable chapbooks, I would be on my new estate now, learning how to grow turnips, Quatre Bras far behind me and forgotten." He ran his fingers through his hair, probably in disgust, but Dany thought the gesture charming. "I'm sorry. There's no need for you to know why I'm being blackmailed, other than to say I'm certain the same person is harassing your sister, and probably many more than the two of us."

"Why would you think that?"

The baron sat down beside her once more and explained his theory, and that of the viscount, putting forward the idea that the blackmailer had cultivated an entire list of victims, and not without some help from those he may have recruited to ferret out secrets.

"Servants, barmaids, shopkeepers. His most probable allies would be establishments in Bond Street, businesses frequented by the ton."

"Shopkeepers? In Bond Street?" Dany whispered, and shivered. "No, she was entirely helpful. Or was that *too* helpful? But she did hang about on the other side of the curtain, and send Mari's maid away. And to be so handy with an answer? Oh, how could I have been so stupid!"

"Are you enjoying this conversation you're having with yourself? Apparently not, would be my guess. I gather you're considering a shopkeeper in particular?"

Now it was Dany's turn to get up and pace. "I am, yes. The woman owns a small but thriving seamstress shop, and just as you said, in Bond Street. She had her ear to the curtain the whole time Mari and I were speaking in private this morning, but I didn't think much of it at the time. She gave me the chapbook, hinting broadly that what my sister needed was a hero. You, in particular. She…she also told us Mari's increasing."

"Dare I even ask how the woman would know that?" the baron asked, also getting to his feet. He was all attention now, and clearly anxious to hear more.

"She didn't. I mean, she told us she thought Mari was—although we didn't say she was—but now we know she was right. So what if she's in the employ of that horrible blackmailer and now he knows even *more* to dangle over Mari's head. She certainly can't be expected to suffer any more than she is now and still be healthy for the— We have to *do* something." She grabbed his hand. "The shops are still open, aren't they? Come on, we need to hurry."

Cooper looked down at their clasped hands. "Well, that lasted longer than I thought. Possibly even a full minute."

"What do you—oh." Dany released her grip even as she gave him a sheepish smile. "I forgot?"

"I understand completely, Miss Foster. It's not difficult to forget what you'd already chosen not to remember."

"That's not amusing. I was… I was overcome with worry, that's all. What if I've inadvertently made things even worse for Mari?"

"She picked up the spade and began digging long before you were involved," Cooper pointed out, which served to mollify Dany, if only a little.

"I suppose you're right. I only arrived in town a few days ago."

"Which explains your ignorance about Gabe's birds. I'm rather glad you missed that."

"There you go about the birds again. If they're not germane to the current topic, and I'm certain they're not, may we please return to the point? Mari is being blackmailed. And then there's you, and even more if you're correct. How many holes do you think have been dug across Mayfair?"

"Dozens would be my guess. Perhaps several dozens. Not that we can approach anyone and ask."

"That would be rather difficult, I agree. 'Good evening, my lord. Are you by chance looking so down at the mouth because you're being blackmailed to keep your wife from learning you've replaced her diamonds with paste?'"

Cooper smiled. "I can't think of a swifter way to get my nose relocated to the back of my head."

"And Mrs. Yothers, the dress shop owner? We can't approach her, either?"

For a heartbeat, no more, it would have seemed the baron had been turned into a statue. "Did you say Mrs. Yothers?"

"I did," Dany returned, tipping her head as she looked up at him. "Why? Do you know the name?"

"I've heard it mentioned, yes. Quite recently, as a matter of fact. I suppose that settles the thing—there's no getting out of it now. I was going to suggest we leave, but I think you'd better sit down again."

"Really? No getting out of what now? And we've already been here a good quarter hour. Even a sad country looby like me knows we've overreached at least a few bounds of propriety even by being here in the first place. Do you think it prudent to stay longer?"

"Under the circumstances, I'm no longer concerned, no."

"What circumstances?"

"Damn it, Dany—sit down."

"Well," she said, positively grinning at him, "since you asked so kindly, I suppose I probably will."

Oh, how wonderfully and darkly green his eyes went when he wanted to throttle her. He was so sweet...

CHAPTER SEVEN

COOP WAITED UNTIL she had seated herself, neatly arranging her skirts around her and then folding her hands in her lap, as if he might be about to tug on some imaginary bellpull and the old man would immediately appear, bearing a tea service and cakes.

Some, he imagined, might see this as acquiescence. Even this early in their relationship, Coop was certain acquiescence was not in Daniella Foster's vocabulary.

Her action was not an eagerness to please, but what she probably believed the shortest route between what she wanted to know and what he would say, a curiosity that would soon turn to—what? Shock? Outrage? Lord help him—amusement? Certainly not meek acceptance, of that much he was certain. He'd known her for less than a day, less than a few hours actually, but he'd already realized that another thing he could count on with Miss Daniella Foster was her unpredictability.

He wandered across the small chapel, either to put a safe distance between them or in search of some sort of inspiration in the faded fresco he stopped in front of, he wasn't sure.

He wasn't accustomed to feeling so helpless, so under the control of circumstances.

He didn't like the feeling.

If it weren't for the woman, for the Prince Regent,

Coop would have ignored the blackmailer's threat to call him out as a despoiler of innocent women and much worse, and damn the consequences. But he'd passed beyond that option the moment he'd accepted Prinny's offer in exchange for his silence.

Even if refusing that offer, he'd realized at the time, meant he would have most likely suffered an unfortunate fatal accident within hours of leaving Carleton House. He wouldn't have been invited to the Prince Regent's residence at all, but simply and quietly dispatched, had not the man wanted the reflected light of the hero of Quatre Bras shined upon him, to bolster his own reputation among an increasingly hostile populace.

Coop's mind went back to the conversation he'd had earlier with his mother and Darby. Neither knew now more than they'd previously known about the happenings at Quatre Bras, except that the Prince Regent himself would not be best pleased if the blackmailer penned another chapbook that would reveal "Shame That Rises to the Highest Reaches of the Crown Itself."

But Minerva did now know about the Countess of Cockermouth's predicament, about Daniella Foster… and her bedchamber…and after that, well, everything his mother and Darby hatched between them had become a bit of a blur in Coop's mind.

He just knew he'd agreed to do what they said. *For his sins…*

They'd convinced him to agree to this current mad course of action, or at least he'd allowed them to think they'd convinced him. He'd kept the hope alive that there could be another way, even as he'd drawn the bays to a halt in front of the chapel.

Inspiration had not struck.

But the hour soon would.

And then there were Darby's cheerful parting words to him as he'd mounted his curricle outside the Pulteney, still ringing in his ears: "Buck up, man, put a smile on that hero face. Our Miss Foster is the key to your salvation, remember. It's either you convince the girl, or you can help me pen your eulogy."

There was such solace to be found in the heartfelt concern of one's friends...

Coop took recourse to his pocket watch. Ten minutes. He had ten short minutes to come up with a better idea. Any idea at all. Ten minutes. An eternity. A single heartbeat in time.

He'd thought their fairly inane conversation since entering the chapel had eaten up a good ten minutes all by itself, but it had in reality only taken less than five. And then he'd run out of anything to say, any reason to keep her here, until Dany's mention of Mrs. Yothers had most probably taken away his last option, that of grabbing her hand and getting the two of them the hell away from the chapel.

So was this it? In less than a space of a day, was he about to irrevocably alter the perceived course of his life? He, Cooper McGinley Townsend. The steady one. The commonsensible one. The one who thought before he acted. Except for that moment at Quatre Bras when he saw children in danger...and again on the flagstones of Bond Street, thanks to a pair of mischievous indigo-blue eyes.

It was time to face facts. There'd been no escape, no real way back, ever since he'd ushered Dany inside the chapel. Probably not since he'd first looked into those same indigo-blue eyes, if he was honest with himself.

From that moment, he'd known that somehow she was going to be a part of his life, and him a part of hers.

He had at least partially accepted that. He'd heard of similar blows to the heart from other men, most particularly his friends Gabe and Rigby. He'd come to London to look for a wife in any case. In any other circumstances, having Dany stumble into his arms that morning could have been seen as a sort of less than gentle tap on the shoulder from some helpful gods.

In any other circumstances.

"You know something, don't you?" Dany asked from behind him. "Oh, did I startle you? I'm certain you don't mind, as I'd decided I'd sat long enough. You know something, something bad, and you don't know how to tell me. That's why you brought me here, and that's why you've been dancing about this whole time, attempting to find a way to say what you don't wish to say. It's about Oliver, isn't it? You've heard he's returning home sooner than expected."

"Oliver?" It took a moment for Coop to absorb that one, even as he continued his feigned interest in the fresco. "No, this isn't about Lord Cockermouth. Not directly, although it does remind us that our time to locate the blackmailer is limited."

"For you, as well," she pointed out. "You haven't really told me much about the nature of your problem with the blackmailer."

"We're after the same man. That's as much as you need to know."

"Probably. But not as much as I want to know. I'm sure the details are much more interesting than Mari's."

"Hardly. Contrary to my anonymous biographer's skewed version of my life, romance is not involved."

"Then it has nothing to do with the woman? How lowering to my expectations. I doubt you're protecting yourself, no matter what you might say to the contrary. And not the nonexistent owner of the signet ring, surely, as that's too much of a tarradiddle for anyone to swallow, that the woman would have turned over any such thing by way of a thank-you to a servant. The Prince Regent, then? I know you're a hero, but a title, an estate? That's quite the reward. Or is *reward* the proper word?"

He turned to face her, nearly bumping into her, for the love of heaven. One of the problems he'd have with Dany was that she was too intelligent. He opened his mouth, and the most ridiculous question came out: "How old are you?"

She didn't so much as blink. "Seventeen. I'm a bit late in making my come-out next spring, by which time I'll be the ripe old age of eighteen, but it was thought I'd needed some *seasoning* before my Season."

The answer had come quickly, without protest. Without guile. With a smile on her face.

Coop was amazed at how much he'd learned about her in one short day.

"I don't believe you."

She rather melodramatically slapped her hands to her cheeks. "Why? Do I appear as if I'm at my last prayers? Hagged? Fagged? Perhaps there's a wrinkle somewhere I haven't noticed?"

Coop felt his own cheeks coloring. "No, not that. My apologies. You just don't—it's difficult to believe you're so young. When you speak, that is. Again, my apologies. In my defense, it has been a rather trying day."

"Don't apologize." Dany shrugged. "I told them nobody with more than half a brain would swallow any such a crammer, but they would insist. Is the truth important?"

"Not to the world, no."

"But to you?"

"Probably not, except for my own satisfaction. Unless you're actually sixteen." *God, wouldn't that just put the capper on it?*

"Really. How interesting. A year makes that much difference?"

"I'm told even an inch is a lot, in a man's nose," Coop shot back, still trying to regain his usually unshakable composure.

Her eyes rather crossed as she attempted a peek at her own nose (lovely nose, quite perfect). "Eating soup and sipping wine could become quite the logistical dilemmas, couldn't they? I see your point. So it isn't the age, not in general. It's where that age is *applied*." Then she frowned. "No. I really still don't understand. But if it helps, my papa gambled a bit too deep and in the time it took for him to recover enough to launch me in anything more than Mari's cast-off gowns, I'd had the temerity to become two years older."

Coop began to relax. "So you're nearer twenty?"

"One and twenty in January actually, as I also lost a year to a broken leg. Mama's, not mine, and Mari was so newly married Mama felt she couldn't foist me on her, unattended. Now, frankly, I believe she's gone past caring. Do you really believe age means anything? My parents, and Mari as well, have sworn me to secrecy, saying it would put paid to my matrimonial chances should anyone know. Which also explains why Dexter—my large-mouthed brother—has been sent to tour the Continent with some of his ramshackle friends."

Cooper smiled. "You can't keep him overseas forever."

"Exactly! And may I say, another argument totally lost on my parents. Am I really wise beyond my years?"

"Wise? I don't recall saying that," he said facetiously. "I'd say you're much more of a trial than I'd expected from a debutante."

"Oh? And what attributes do you believe commendable in a debutante?"

"The usual, I'd imagine. Sweet. And biddable. Shy, not at all forward."

"Simpering? With a tendency to giggle? Smelling of nothing more than bread and butter, as Byron wrote? Proficient in discussing the state of the weather, as in it is fair, or coming on to rain, or beastly hot? No, not beastly. Horridly hot."

Even with the fraying cord holding a figurative sword of Damocles dangling over his head, Coop realized he could speak nonsense with Daniella Foster for hours, heartily enjoying himself. "Warm. Ladies of quality don't know the meaning of hot."

"Yes, I remember now. And moist. Ladies, even if lost in a desert, would get no more than moist. However, under the circumstances, I think you're much better off with me."

"Yes, in the end, that was the deciding factor," Coop murmured just as the heavy chapel door swung open, followed closely (too closely, really) by a woman's voice. "Aha! Basil, get yourself in here! Look what I've found. Oh, the shame, the shame."

Dany whirled about to see the intruder, or she would have if Cooper hadn't grabbed her by the shoulders and pulled her against him for a kiss. The kiss he was to have stolen just as the timepiece in his pocket chimed out the hour, which it had not yet done.

A kiss, he would later tell Darby when he recounted the scene, as being as inspiring as pressing one's lips against a block of wood.

"Basil, do you see them? Minerva's Cooper and some hapless gel, as I live and breathe. The hero of Quatre Bras—I recognized him immediately from the chapbook. Locked in a clandestine embrace."

"Yes, dear, I see them," the Duke of Cranbrook said, puffing only a little from his small climb up the stairs, as neither duke nor duchess would see sixty again. "Nothing we haven't done a time or three, eh, Viv?"

"Not now, Basil, not when we're being decorous," the duchess scolded, abandoning her husband to all but float across the stone floor in a compilation of skirts and scarves that, were it any darker in the chapel, would have put most in the mind of a ghost. If ghosts wore ruffled, tule-wrapped bonnets.

By now Dany was standing stock-still, her eyes all but popping out of her head, and Cooper had dropped to one knee, her hands held tightly in his.

So she couldn't run away. Or pummel him heavily about the head and shoulders, which he wouldn't dismiss as impossible. Not from the look on her face.

"Miss Foster," he said hurriedly, squeezing her fingers to get her attention. "Under the circumstances, it would indeed be my honor and privilege to ask for your hand in marriage, in front of these witnesses."

"You hear that, Viv? We're witnesses," the duke said, catching up to his wife and slipping his arm about her waist. "I've always wanted to be a witness."

"Basil, hush. Pretty little thing, isn't she? Minerva

was worried about that. Oh, dear, she hasn't answered yet. Go on, dearie, it's your turn now. Say yes," the duchess prodded, leaning in as if to not miss a word.

Cooper watched Dany as she looked to the pair of seeming cherubs beaming at them, actually dropping into a brief curtsy before redirecting her attention, and indigo eyes gone close to black, to him.

Suddenly, he felt himself transported to Bond Street.

Those eyes, like a mirror into her soul, told him her every thought, each rapidly transitioning emotion. Wide-eyed shock. Embarrassed innocence. Questioning. Recognition. Amusement, almost as if she was laughing at their situation, perhaps even at him.

"Just say yes, all right?" he whispered. "I'll explain later."

"Oh, my, yes, you will be doing that, won't you?" she answered just as quietly.

"Viv, I can hear them talking, but I can't quite make out what they're saying," the Duke of Cranbrook complained.

"She said yes, Your Grace," Coop told him, rising to his feet before raising Dany's hands for what he hoped resembled chastely devout kisses.

"Well, good, then," the duke chirped. "Good on you, young lady, and good on my nephew's chum. Oh, and good on me, because now I won't be late to dinner." He tucked his wife's arm within his. "Come on, sweetums, let's leave these two lovebirds alone, to continue their billing and cooing—and whatever else they might put their minds to, eh?"

The duchess tapped on her husband's arm. "You're *so* bad. Come along now."

As they turned to make their exit, the duke leaned

down and whispered something in his wife's ear that had her giggling like the worst of debutantes all the way to the door. "Oh, Basil, of course there will be time before dinner, you randy old goat."

"The Duke and Duchess of Cranbrook, aunt and uncle to their heir and my good friend Gabriel Sinclair," Coop said once the door was closed behind the pair. "Under the circumstances, I thought I'd leave introductions to some other time."

He let go of her hands.

"Miss Foster? You're not saying anything."

"I wouldn't know where to begin," she told him, and left him where he stood, returning to the bench to retrieve her gloves as he followed her. "Oh, wait, I suppose I do."

And with that, she went up on her tippy-toes and employed those gloves to slap his face.

"That's for bringing me here under false pretenses."

Coop kept his hands at his sides, fairly certain she was only getting started.

He was right.

Slap.

"That's for being so harebrained that you'd let the viscount talk you into this."

"In all fairness to Darby, my mother was in on it, as well. I was outnumbered at least ten to one."

"You said the viscount and your mother."

Slap.

"You're right. Make that outnumbered twenty to one. You'll understand when you meet Min—my mother. I had no plan—she and Darby did. We were running out of time, and it was and is plain as day that you'd involve yourself, anyway, and that was the end of that."

"We are *leagues* from the end of that, Cooper Townsend."

Slap.

"Ow. There are buttons on those gloves, you know."

"I don't care. I was to *obey* you. You were *in charge*. 'How old are you, Miss Foster?' Old enough to be compromised, or must I find another way? You couldn't simply *ask*? Does it feel more comforting to you to have been *forced* into marriage with me? I couldn't be trusted to have a brain in my own head?"

Slap.

It wasn't the force of the slaps, but the buttons, and the repetition, that were beginning to grate on Coop's nerves. That and the fact that she was right, all the way down the line. "We need to be able to be in each other's company at all times, and there's no time to devote to putting on a show of courting you, not while the blackmailer could be closing in on us, and probably many more like us. There are surveillance limitations to my current residence at the Pulteney. I need access to Portman Square. I need to be left alone by ambitious mamas and silly young ladies throwing themselves in my path, getting in my way. And once more, because it's important, you'd be in the way no matter what, so at least this way I could have some small chance of controlling— of watching over you. Our betrothal is a convenience. Don't worry. Once this is over I'll say you came to your senses and cried off. It's not going to come to marriage."

Damned if she didn't drop the gloves, and punch him square in the jaw.

"Why did you do that?"

"You can't mean you don't know."

The force may have been what finally drove some

sense into Coop's head. For a man of five and twenty, he'd had little interest in the ladies, and probably less experience. He'd been too busy being a soldier. From the moment the blackmailer had delivered his threat, he'd been almost exclusively occupied in finding the man before he could publish and Prinny had decided to bring back neck-chopping as a form of royal sport. He hadn't considered all of the consequences when he'd finally bowed to Darby and Minerva's plan, as long as it might work.

He hadn't put all that much thought into Dany's reaction. He was doing so now. In spades.

"You want to marry me? Why on earth would you want to do that?"

She bowed her head, avoiding his gaze, and his question. "I didn't say that."

He rubbed at his jaw. "Then I apologize, but I really don't understand. Although I'm certain I deserved it."

Now she looked up at him again. Those eyes. Damn those soul-bearing eyes. "I don't know why I did it, not precisely. I suppose I felt insulted."

Coop put a crooked finger beneath her chin and leaned in, gently kissing her on the lips before retrieving her gloves and handing them to her. Her lips were soft this time, not at all wooden, and he rather enjoyed the brief experience. He may have to try it again. Soon.

"Why did you do that?" she asked in that slightly husky voice that had intrigued him nearly as much as those eyes.

"I don't know, precisely. I suppose I felt an unexplainable urge. I think I've already established that I haven't been thinking all that clearly today. Are you going to slap me again?"

"No. I think I'd like you to take me back to Portman Square so that I can inform my sister of my new status as the betrothed of the hero of Quatre Bras. That ought to serve to catapult her out from beneath the covers. And you, sir, need to pen a note to my father, begging his forgiveness for presuming to take my hand before asking his permission to do so. I suggest a crate of fine claret accompany the note. Papa would forgive most anything for enough good claret."

Coop was astounded at her level of calm. He felt as tightly wound as a watch spring. Kissing her had only increased the tension. Maybe he should try punching something.

He helped her up onto the curricle seat, tossed another coin to the boy he'd charged with minding the horses and they set off for Portman Square.

Dany was once more sitting with her hands meekly folded her in lap. That couldn't be good.

"You're thinking, aren't you? I suppose you'll want me to post our betrothal in the newspapers?"

She answered without looking at him. "If that's what one does, then one who compromises ladies of quality probably does it, yes. I doubt the protocol for compromise is listed in the book Mari gave me. Is there a corresponding tome for gentlemen?"

"Probably. But I'm fairly certain I know what to do."

Coop knew he could have mentioned *Lord Chesterfield's Letters to His Son on the Art of Becoming a Man of the World and a Gentleman*. Minerva had given him the compilation of the letters on his fifteenth birthday, saying that since his father wasn't alive to instruct him, somebody else's father might serve as well, and probably do the job better.

She'd consigned the book to the fire a year later, after reading his lordship's observations on women being no more than children of a larger growth, devoid of real intelligence or good sense and prone to indulging themselves in silly little passions.

"Good. Then you know, as I know, that the side door will be left unlocked at a quarter to twelve tonight, and my maid will be waiting there to bring you to my bedchamber. Not that my romantical sister would blink an eye, anyway, now that you've compromised me. In fact, she'll probably be over the moon to assist us in any assignation. You've certainly gone to a whole lot of trouble to do what I'd already suggested you do."

There was probably something Coop could say to all of this, but he'd be damned if he could think of a thing. By the time they'd returned to Portman Square he'd half convinced himself that, no matter how the world may see him—soldier, patriot, hero, baron—when it came to managing the women in his life, he was a sad case indeed.

CHAPTER EIGHT

THE WORLD WAS a strange place, and London might perhaps be its very center of strangeness, or at least that's what Dany had concluded over the course of the past few hours.

Her sister, somewhere between her come-out and her nearly fourth year of marriage, had turned into a twit. Not that she hadn't always been a bit silly and romantical, but exposure to London air or a matrimonial bed or the silliness of Society had picked her up and launched her straight into the land of the cuckoos.

Mari had gone from Utter Despair to Near Euphoria once she'd heard her sister's news. She'd asked no questions, as if young ladies met a gentleman on Bond Street every morning and were betrothed to him by the time the sun set that night, without something fairly havey-cavey transpiring somewhere in between.

To Mari, apparently, nothing else mattered except how her sister's sudden engagement affected *her*. The hero had arrived. *Huzzah, huzzah*. He'd been immediately infatuated with Dany, and sworn on his sword to Save Them All from Shame and Ruin. One more *Huzzah!* All would be solved, Oliver would be over the moon to hear he was about to have an heir, there definitely would be more jewelry in Mari's future and her world would run knee-deep in milk and honey. "Oh, and here, darling sister, take these pearls as my gift to you. You can't be expected to go about town in grandmother's horridly cheap garnets now. Ollie will buy me more."

"Twit," Dany said out loud as she sat cross-legged in front of the fire and scrubbed at her still-damp hair, her fingers serving as the only comb she'd need. "Twit, twit, double twit." What did her sister think? That Cooper Townsend had just to wiggle his heroic ears, and the blackmailer would tumble into his lap, Mari's letters all tied up in a blue ribbon?

Then there was Timmerly. The condescending sneer the butler had conjured up each time Dany came into view had been magically replaced with an annoying series of bows and "Yes, miss. Anything you want, miss. Can I be so honored as to order anything for you, miss? Mrs. Timmerly is already planning a magnificent trifle for your first dinner here with the baron, miss."

Dany half expected the man to bodily throw himself in her path should an unexpected puddle appear in front of her on her way from the staircase to the drawing room. Why, at dinner, he'd actually offered to cut her meat.

And all solely because she was betrothed to the baron, the hero of Quatre Bras and those silly chapbooks. If everyone were to be as annoying as Mari and Timmerly, her pity for the baron would soon know no bounds. How did he *stand* all this fawning attention?

And all this business about him working under direction of "someone close to the Crown," going about the countryside, defending innocent young women from fates worse than death. What nonsense!

She'd read the second chapbook now, as a giggling

Mrs. Timmerly had offered her own copy, and she didn't believe the half of it. The quarter of it. Why, there weren't enough hours in the day to accomplish all the rescues written about in Volume Two.

And what was a fate worse than death, anyway? There certainly wasn't anything more *final* than death. Both volumes had been rather vague on that point. Just as they were vague on what the baron *did* with his rescued damsels. Especially at the end of Volume Two.

Dany picked up the book and read the section again.

Overcome by her Emotions, she cried out in Near Ecstasy as she grasped his strong shoulders, claiming the world could safely rest on their Broad Expanse, just as her fate had so lately done, and Never Fear for her honor, that which she then so Earnestly Offered Him.

"I may not be so sure on the worse-than-death business, but it would take a real looby to not understand what *that* means."

"You said something, Miss Dany?"

She smiled at the maid. "Nothing worth a second airing, no. Life is strange, isn't it, Emmaline? One moment you think you know everything, and the next you're certain you'll never really know anything. And yes, before you say it, in between those two opposing conclusions is the part where I do things like cut off all my hair."

"It will grow back, miss. It's doing it already. I would even go so far as to say it looks rather fetching, all clinging to your neck and your cheeks and such. Not that I'd say the same if your poor mama was to be sitting here with us."

"Value your position that much, do you?" Dany grinned at the maid as she got to her feet, already untying the dressing gown she'd donned after her bath. "Time for me to get dressed, Emmaline. Tell me, what does one wear to welcome one's betrothed into one's bedchamber just before midnight?"

The maid blushed to the roots of her thinning gray hair. Emmaline had been with the Foster family for decades, a sweet, homely woman who'd never so much as walked out with a young man during her youth. Dany had long ago given up asking her to answer the questions her mother avoided. "About what you've got on, Miss Dany, or so I've heard."

"Emmaline, for shame!" Dany giggled then, but she could hear her sudden nerves in that giggle, and quickly stopped. "I think the blue dimity, please."

The maid frowned. "The one with all the buttons, miss?"

"Precisely. What *do* you think is going to happen tonight, Emmaline?"

"I couldn't say as I'd know, Miss Dany. Begging your pardon, I haven't known what was going on with you since you could stand up and walk on your own."

"I'm a sad trial, I know," Dany said, giving the woman a quick hug. "If Evie hadn't married last year and gone to live with her innkeeper husband, you'd still be second maid to Mama, and not forced to deal with her unmanageable daughter. Shall we blame Evie?"

"No, Miss Dany, for if she hadn't married she'd be here with you, and I'm that happy to be in London, able to visit with my brother Sam in the stables on my afternoon off. Sam always said he wasn't built for sitting around in the country."

Sam was built for sitting, however—at the dinner table.

"That's right, I'd forgotten Sam is part of the earl's London staff. That might be something I should keep in mind," she ended half to herself, knowing no one could have enough allies. Sam, so rotund that at least two people could hide behind him, could also be set to watch the tree from the stables. It probably wouldn't take more than some leftover pudding to gain his allegiance. She needed to remember to tell Coop about Sam.

Coop. He'd be here soon, tapping his foot as he waited outside for Emmaline to let him in. How had the evening dragged on for days, and now in these past few minutes she had nearly run out of time.

Emmaline approached with the blue dimity, but it was too late for that. All those buttons.

"Here," she said, grabbing the gown and tossing it on the bed. Good Lord, Emmaline had turned down the covers! Well, that *invitation* had to be remedied, at once. "We'll forget this. Just bring me my green riding habit and take yourself off to the side door to let the baron in, all right? We don't want to keep him waiting."

"Your riding habit, Miss Dany? You're going riding this late? Ah, Sam won't like that, thinking he has the cattle all bedded down for the night."

"Tucks them in, does he?" Dany put her hands on the maid's shoulders, steering her toward the door. "No, I'm not going riding. It's one outfit I can manage by myself, that's all. Now go."

She didn't mention that it was also one outfit she could run in, thanks to its divided skirt, just in case the need arose. Certainly the baron didn't think she would meekly watch from the window if the blackmailer showed up and not follow after him when he set off to bring the rotter down. What was the sense of joining an adventure if she couldn't go *adventuring*?

After securing the skirt at her waist, she slipped her bare feet into a pair of half boots, donned and buttoned her jacket and was just about to wonder if Cooper had changed his mind when the door opened and he walked into the room.

Oh, my.

He was dressed in evening clothes, all severe black and pristine-white stock, all loosely tumbled blond curls and bright green eyes.

And big. She hadn't realized he was quite that big. The generously sized bedchamber suddenly seemed uncomfortably small, now that he was in it.

And with the bedcovers still turned down...

He greeted her with no more than a nod, and then turned to Emmaline. Dany imagined the look on his face as he did so, since the maid bobbed two quick curtsies and left, closing the door behind her without so much as a glance toward her mistress.

"That was ridiculously easy," he said, tossing his hat onto the bed, of all places. "Although I probably could have done without the butler and his wife, lined up with all the other staff in the hallway, welcoming me. Next time, if there is a next time, I might just as well use the front door knocker, and perhaps bring along a marching band."

"I had no idea…" Dany stopped, shook her head. "No, that's really not true. I should have known. Does this happen all the time? People turning near-imbecilic at the mere prospect of seeing you?"

"Since the chapbooks, you mean? More than enough

of them, yes. And if our blackmailer has one of his informers on the earl's staff, by tomorrow he'll know he can't risk returning here to carry on his knothole correspondence with the countess, so let's make the most of this single night we do have."

"You really think someone on the staff is in the blackmailer's employ? Really? And what are you doing?"

Coop was moving about the bedchamber, using a brass snuffer to extinguish the candles. "To answer your first question, nothing is impossible. As to the second, we need this room in darkness before we push back the drapes."

Dany pulled a face. "Oh, I did that wrong, didn't I? If he did think to deliver another threat, he clearly would have seen me outlined against the glass, wouldn't he?"

"In your defense, you're rather new at this," he said, snuffing the last candles, pitching the room into darkness save for the light from the fire. "Will you be staying here with me, or are you planning a midnight ride?"

She glanced down at her outfit, belatedly realizing she had foregone a blouse in favor of haste, and she looked decidedly *bare* above the last button of her jacket. She imagined it would be impossible to blow out the fire, to turn the room completely dark. Besides, it was fairly obvious he'd already noticed her missing bit of wardrobe. And he couldn't resist jabbing her about it, could he?

Really, once people got to know the baron, perhaps they wouldn't all be so loopy and silly when he was around. He was just a man, and a maddening one at that. Especially when his smile carried all the way to his eyes, as it was doing now.

"Let's be on with this, shall we? Or do you want to stand here being obnoxious until the blackmailer has been and gone?" she snapped, resisting clapping her hands to her chest only with the greatest of effort. She bared more to the world in her evening dresses, but there was something very different about showing that same skin above a severely cut riding habit.

Or maybe just in exposing that skin to one Baron Townsend...

"If he's going to appear at all."

"I know. He hasn't yet, and it has been five days—nights—since his threat. He's bound to show up soon."

She watched as he positioned the fire screen so that it blocked some of the light from the fire, redirecting it toward the bed, before he walked to one of the long pair of windows and pushed back the drapery as he sat down on the window seat.

"Tonight's our last chance, if I'm correct about someone in this house being in his employ. Did you have your sister pen the note and put it in the knothole?"

"I did, yes. She actually wrote *Dear Blackmailer* by way of salutation. She promised the five hundred pounds would be put into the knothole as soon as her letters were placed there for her retrieval. We also wrapped up our grandmother's garnets and put them with the note."

Coop turned to look at her. "Why would she have done that?"

"Because they're ugly, I never liked them and I'm fairly certain they're paste, thanks to our father's forays into the gaming hells a few years ago." She thought about what she'd said, because he was looking at her as if he'd never been anywhere near the inside of a woman's head before and that his first foray there was proving more than a tad unsettling. "To show her good faith, that is."

Coop shifted his gaze to the mews and the line of trees. "So you decided to show your sister's good faith by gifting the man with a down payment of paste garnets? Because you never liked them, anyway. You're a rather frightening young woman, but I imagine you already know that."

"I probably am, I think I do and he might not notice. They're very good paste," Dany said, defending her brilliant idea. Poor hero. If she'd found it sometimes difficult to be Dany, she could only imagine how other people could be uncomfortable in her presence. She was beginning to actually pity him.

"Well, then, that makes it all right, doesn't it? I suppose I should thank you for obeying at least half of my instructions."

"Probably. I can be a sad failure at matters requiring cooperation. I say it's because I have a mind of my own, although Mama insists I'm only good for driving others out of their minds," she admitted truthfully. "Can you see well enough to know if someone approaches the tree? I couldn't see much of anything the first two nights I tried to watch, but the moon is growing fuller now."

"Probably what the blackmailer has been waiting for. Enough light to see, but not a full moon, or he would chance being seen, as well. By the way, I've got Viscount Nailbourne stationed at one end of the alleyway and my friend Jeremiah Rigby at the other, prepared to act on my signal."

"What sort of signal?"

"Nothing too elaborate. If we espy anything unusual,

it would be a simple matter of cranking open one of these windows and giving a whistle," he told her. "How else could I do it?"

Pity him? Was she mad? It wasn't her fault he'd chosen to compromise her with those two adorable cherubs, just so he could run tame in Oliver's household.

"Indeed, yes, how else? How silly of me to badger the hero with obvious questions. What a brilliant plan. I stand in awe, my lord, truly. Such a shame that those old windows have been painted shut for what's probably decades."

"Damn." The baron tried the handle, and it turned easily, the casement opening just as easily. He swiftly closed it again. Without looking at her, he said, "You're worse than a menace. Go sit down."

Satisfied she'd gotten just a little of her own back, she walked over to the window seat and sat down beside him, twisting enough to be able to see through the narrow opening in the draperies.

They were shoulder to shoulder, their cheeks nearly touching. She could feel Coop's eyes on her.

"Dany," he said after a moment.

"What?"

"Over. There. At the other window. I said *go* sit down, not *come* sit down. And while you're at it, you misbuttoned your jacket. Fix it, before somebody comes in and thinks I'm responsible for your dishevelment and you'll have lost any hope of breaking our engagement without forcing me into a duel with either your father or your brother."

She practically flew from the window seat to take up her position at the other window, and immediately began to fiddle with her buttons in the dark. She hadn't misbuttoned at all.

One thing she could say for him—he gave as good as he got. Why, she could almost think, in other circumstances, they could have been the best of chums.

"You could have simply asked me to move. And to think at least half the people in this house, my sister most especially, believes we're in here being indecent. I was even beginning to pity you."

"Don't bother. The more I'm around you, the more I'm pitying myself. Damn, somebody's stepping out from the earl's stables. He'd better not stay long, or the blackmailer will never show himself."

Dany pushed the drapery aside and squinted down into the mews. It might be dark, but there was no missing her maid's rotund brother, even if he was mostly in shadow. "That's only Sam," she said. "He sleeps in the stables. Why is he looking around like that? Do you think he heard something and has stepped out to investigate? Let's hope he didn't scare off the— Oh, my heavens!"

She let the drapery drop just as Sam began lowering his trousers even as he turned to face the stone stable wall.

Coop's laughter, strong and clear, was so engaging that she couldn't help but join him in his mirth. It would be stupid beyond measure to pretend she didn't know what Sam was about.

"That's what peeking out of windows will get you, I suppose," she said when she could control herself again. "Is he gone yet?"

"He's gone. If the earl ever wonders why no ivy grows on that side of the stable doors, you'll have an answer for him, although you might be wise not to volunteer the reason."

Dany's only response was to carefully pull back the drapery again, and continue her surveillance, suggesting the baron do the same.

Which they did, for nearly two hours, during which neither spoke and many carriages made their way down the alleyway to return to stables that lined the mews.

Harnesses jingled, grooms and stable boys shouted to one another, stable doors banged and slammed. London certainly wasn't known for its quiet, no matter the hour.

Other than that business with Sam, Dany believed she had never been so bored in her life. She'd totally forgotten that she and her supposed fiancé were alone in her bedchamber. There was nothing romantical about their current situation, and if she yawned one more time she would have no recourse but to go over to her pitcher and basin and splash cold water on her face to stay awake.

"He's not coming," she said at last, breaking the silence. "This has been an entire waste of a compromise, you know, now that you've as good as said tonight was our only chance to capture the man. I can only hope you're not an efficient hero, and have already sent off a letter to my father. Or worse, a notice to the newspapers."

"It's too late to worry about that, I'm afraid. Since both my mother and her boon chum the Duchess of Cranbrook, who you met earlier today, were guests at the same dinner party this evening, I imagine the news of our coming nuptials will be served up at breakfast all over Mayfair tomorrow. Today," he corrected.

Dany left her seat and joined him as he kept his

watch over the mews. "Upcoming nuptials? Why would you phrase it that way? You said you were going to allow me to cry off."

"I remember. You punched me for it. The offer does remain open, but I've realized that hearing Darby and Minerva point out all the reasonableness and benefits of the thing and actually dragging you into this mess are two very different things. Therefore," he continued, still doggedly looking out the window, "I've decided to leave matters entirely in your hands. I came to London to search for a wife, my idea being that a wife by my side would put an end to all the nonsense. I'll admit to that, as well. Perhaps that's why I didn't throw away their idea, and allowed myself to be carried along, shall we say, by the tide of events."

He finally looked at her. "And you didn't say no."

"Oh, so now I'm part of the reason, am I? I am to shoulder my share of blame for the predicament *you* tossed us into today? And who is Minerva?"

"My mother. You'll meet her tomorrow. I've found myself rather looking forward to seeing the two of you together. Darby mentioned the possibility of selling tickets of admittance actually."

"I'm certain I won't like her. She sounds utterly overbearing, and obviously still has you tied to her apron strings. The more I know of you, Cooper Townsend, the less I understand how you ever became a hero."

"At least we finally agree on something. In my defense, I do have a very good reason for not wanting the blackmailer to publish his threatened third volume, and since you and your sister are my only current avenues to finding the bastard, I plead guilty to using you. The both of you."

Ah, *now* they were getting somewhere. Finally. "The chapbooks don't just embarrass you, do they? You're in a prodigious amount of trouble, aren't you? I felt it from the beginning, or at least I'd like to tell myself I did. Does the viscount know? Your mother? Are you going to tell me? I think you owe it to me. To tell me, that is."

He squeezed her hand for a moment. "I'm sorry. I can't. Nobody knows. Darby has made a few guesses, as have you, but mine isn't the only reputation at stake here. I was asked to swear to secrecy and rewarded for my agreement. That, too, doesn't make me a hero, in case you were about to point that out. But at least I'm still breathing."

Now it was her turn to place her hand on his. "For how long?"

"Pardon me?" He was leaning closer to the glass. "How long for what?"

"How long will you still be breathing?"

"I've entertained that question myself, and the only answer that seems plausible is as long as God gives me, if I find the blackmailer before he can publish whatever he believes to be the damning truth."

"Is there a damning truth?"

He turned and smiled at her, and her traitorous heart melted. "Isn't there always?"

"Yes, I suppose so. I'm sorry. I'm even more sorry that the blackmailer didn't show himself tonight."

"Because you were hoping for a good chase down the alleyway, or because you're still stuck with your grandmother's paste garnets?"

Dany smiled. "I know you're joking to be kind, but you really are a very nice man. I promise to be less of a problem to you, I really do. When I can," she added, because a caveat would at least keep her from feeling too guilty if she couldn't manage to keep herself from acting on her own if the opportunity arose.

He looked at her in the faint moonlight. "Thank you. I'm still not going to tell you why I'm being black-mailed, you know."

Dany shrugged, far from defeated. "You will. Eventually. You won't be able to help yourself. Just ask anyone. I'm very persuasive."

"You mean you wear people down to the point where it's simply easier to let you get your way."

She turned toward the gap in the draperies. "I take it back. You're not *that* nice. I thought women were supposed to be this huge mystery to men."

"Is that so? Then I suppose you'll have to leave off being so utterly transparent. Come on, I think we're done here for tonight. He's not going to show."

"Just five more minutes. There hasn't been a carriage coming back to the stables for a good quarter hour. He might feel safe now to approach. Oh, fiddle, I was wrong. Here comes another one."

Coop all but put his cheek next to hers as he took a look for himself. "That's not a carriage, it's a hackney."

"A what?"

"A hired cab. There's no reason for a hired cab to be in this alleyway. Move."

Dany moved. She had no choice but to move, because Coop had pushed her back enough so that he could reach the casement handle and begin turning it.

Dany ran to the other window to watch, her head pounding with excitement. Sure enough, the hackney stopped directly in front of the Cockermouth stables, and a dark-clad figure hopped down.

Carrying a stool?

"He's carrying a stool? Why on earth would he be carrying—oh, that's not fair. It's a child, isn't it? Look, he's put the stool down and stepping up on it to—yes, there goes Mari's letter. And my garnets. And now he's putting something into the..."

Coop's ear-piercing whistles, two in quick succession, cut off what she would have said next, although why she was telling him what he could readily see for himself she had no idea.

After all, she was already halfway to the door.

CHAPTER NINE

COOP CAUGHT UP to Dany just as she was about to throw open the side door. He grabbed her at the waist and hauled her off her feet, pulling her against him.

"There's no hurry. He's long gone," he said, doing his best to catch his breath. How did servants loaded down with trays and whatever navigate such steep, narrow stairs? He'd damn near tumbled a few times, which would have thrown him into Dany, so that they would have ended in an inglorious heap on the next landing.

"How do you know? And put me down, for pity's sake."

"Only if you promise not to bolt."

"I'm not a horse. And you're crushing my ribs."

Coop compromised. He turned about so that his back was against the door, and only then let her go.

She turned and looked at him, looked at the hat on his head. "You...you took time to retrieve your *hat*?"

"As I'll be leaving now, yes. Are you ready to check out the knothole?"

"But...but why aren't we chasing the hackney? I know we couldn't catch it, so don't look at me as if I've got two heads. But we may have been able to at least see the driver. Then we could go searching for him tomorrow."

"Yes, out of the several hundred hackneys in London, that should be an easy enough job." He held up the lit lantern he'd earlier requested Timmerly leave in the narrow hallway, opened the door and motioned for her to precede him. "I whistled twice, if you'll recall. That was to warn Rigby our target was heading his way. We might have had some slim chance if the hackney had come in the opposite end of the alleyway and was headed toward Darby, but Rigby has had too many good meals to hold his own in a footrace. Catching up with a hackney is definitely outside the realm of his capabilities. We can only hope he was able to catch a look at its occupant. Yes, and its driver."

"You don't have to sound so smug."

"Reasonable, not smug," he said as they approached the large tree.

"You let me think we'd be able to chase him."

"Hence the riding habit. Now I understand. Do you mind if I rethink your possible contribution to our small adventure?"

The lantern cast enough light for him to see the look of disgust on her face.

"The riding habit was easier for me to—oh, all right, yes. I chose it on purpose, but only as my second choice. Not to chase him if he showed up. I mean, not *precisely.* I made the first choice for its buttons. And we would have chased only if the opportunity should present itself. Mostly, I wanted to make certain I was dressed to accompany you when we retrieved any note he may put in the tree—and yes, I promise to stop babbling now, because I know I'm babbling. Go on, reach up and get it."

"Yes, my queen," he said, and then stopped, arm

half raised to do as she'd commanded. "No. You get it. You put your sister's note into the knothole, correct?"

"If you insist. But move aside. Mari's tall enough to reach it, but I have to step on that old broken mounting step behind you, and then hold on to the branch and— Oh. *Oh.*"

Coop retrieved the folded scrap of paper. "Yes, *oh.* Do we have a hired lad in the hackney? A less than tall blackmailer? Or do we have a…"

"Woman! The blackmailer could be a woman? Mari may have been pouring her heart out to another female? No wonder how she could have found all the right, soppy things to say to make Mari think she had finally found someone who *understood* her anguish."

"Some women have sympathetic, understanding sisters to confide in," Coop couldn't help but say as he tucked the note into his waistcoat pocket and moved Dany along, back toward the side door.

"I'd be insulted if Mari hadn't begun her illicit correspondence before I arrived in town, and if I were silly enough to applaud her for doing anything so harebrained. She doesn't need sympathy. She needs her letters retrieved before Oliver gets home. I'm being leagues more helpful to her than some sweet ninny who does nothing but pat her shoulder and say, 'There, there.' Of course, that also means we've ended up with *you*. So far, sad to say, that hasn't seemed to have helped much."

"Unfortunately, I have to agree with you, although at least you're rid of the garnets. Let's step inside and see what our mutual tormentor has to say for himself, or herself."

"But what about the viscount and your other friend? Don't you want to hear what they have to say?"

"They'll be waiting for me at the Pulteney, hopefully with a glass and a bottle, and my mother safely snoring in her bed. Do you want me to read this or not?"

She jammed her fists against her hips. It was possible she was running out of patience with him. Strangely, he found that very attractive in her. She was the only female he'd met since Quatre Bras who didn't all but drool over him.

"No, I want you to fold it into a paper bird, and then launch it out toward the mews."

"Yes, that's what I thought," he told her, putting the lantern on the table beside the door. "But I'll read it, anyway." He unfolded the note, biting back a sudden curse. "Since it appears to be directed to me."

"It is? Not Mari? Oh, God. That's not good, is it?" Dany grabbed at his wrist, pulling down his arm so that she could see the note, read it along with him.

Naughty, naughty, my lord Townsend, meddling in business that does not concern you, although I will say taking yourself off the marriage market was inspired, if your choice a decidedly odd duckling. Thanks to me, beating the drum of your undeserved popularity, you could have held out for an heiress. In any case, my congratulations; your mama appears well pleased, and it will leave you more time to contemplate the consequences of your rash actions. Because, you see, a price must be paid. Please inform the countess that my kind offer is rescinded. The earl will receive the letters upon his return. Oh, and your price just went up by a thousand pounds. After all, I must recoup my losses caused by your interference. Ten days until a copy of Volume Three is delivered to the Prince Regent. Less, if you get in my way again. You can begin counting now… I'll be in touch.

"He's not going to let her pay to get them back? I can't tell her that. What are we going to do?"

Coop looked at his brand-new fiancée. Her indigo-blue eyes were awash in tears.

He took her hands, her suddenly ice-cold and faintly trembling hands. "We'll find him, that's what we'll do," he said with as much conviction as he could muster. "Or her. Are you up to a trip to Bond Street at eleven tomorrow morning? I fancy buying you a betrothal present."

"You want to go *shopping*? What good is that going to— Oh, wait. I forgot. Mrs. Yo—"

He clapped a hand over her mouth and leaned down to whisper in her ear. "Nothing. Not another word. Not to your sister, not to your maid, not to anyone. And for God's sake, if you keep a diary, don't write in it about any of this."

She pushed his hand away. "How did you know I keep a diary?"

At last, he smiled. "A fortuitous guess? Now wait until I'm outside, throw the latch and get yourself upstairs. I've got to go meet my friends, hoping at least one of them saw something that might help us."

"I wish I could go with you."

It would take a stronger man than he to look into those eyes, see the pain and worry and not respond.

"I know. But everything will work out. I promise."

She nodded. "I think I'll hold you to that. My hero."

And then she went up on tiptoe and kissed his cheek,

the same one she had repeatedly slapped with her gloves that afternoon.

"I thought you said I didn't seem very much like a hero."

"I know. But now you rather have to be, don't you?" she said before pushing him through the doorway.

He stood outside, waiting until the sound of her footsteps on the servant stairs faded away, his hand to his cheek as he wondered what the devil that was all about, and why he was smiling, of all things.

Then he remembered the mess he was in, all of them were now in, and took off at a trot, hailed a hackney at the end of the square and directed that he be taken to the Pulteney.

As arranged, Darby and Rigby were waiting for him in his rooms, joined there by Sergeant Major Ames, the trio looking relaxed and comfortable, rather sprawled across the couches and chairs, drinks in their hands.

"Sir!" Sergeant Major Ames said, leaping to his feet to salute his employer. "We were just reminiscing about Champaubert. Fine mess that was. Called for a toast to the viscount's dimmed eye, you understand. I'll go now."

"Yes, thank you, Ames," Coop said, looking to Darby. How did the man do it, turn his injury into countless jokes at his own expense, even make it easy for the sergeant major to comment on it? The thing was, it was one thing to sacrifice an eye in battle, but quite another to lose it in a totally unnecessary defeat brought on them by that damn Russian general, Olssufiev.

"Are you all right?" he asked his friend after Ames had quit the room, no one commenting as he picked up one of the bottles and took it with him. It would be an hour or two of singular reminiscing for the sergeant major before he'd find sleep, Coop knew. Their losses at Champaubert, followed by their months of captivity until the deposed emperor was caught and put in a cage, had changed all their lives.

Their friend Gabriel Sinclair, his skull nearly bashed in by a French soldier's rifle butt, had gone into a funk, blaming himself for events he couldn't have changed, even though he'd felt certain an attack was coming. Coop himself had taken a ball in his side, and been little use to anyone when his wound had become infected. If it weren't for Ames's rough nursing and Rigby's suddenly discovered talent for finding food where none seemed to exist, things could have ended much differently for him. And Darby had lost the vision in his left eye.

Four schoolboy friends, now bound together more tightly than many brothers. They'd managed to return to their former lives, pick up the pieces and move on. But never alone. When Gabe had asked for their help, they'd come to him at once, fully prepared to make utter cakes of themselves with those damn birds. Now they were here for him, no questions asked, willing to do anything he needed of them.

"Did anyone hear from Gabe?" he asked now as he picked up one of the bottles and drank from it, not bothering to use the glass that had been placed next to it.

"I had a note from him this morning," Rigby said. "He hopes to return to town soon, sooner than that if you need him, if possible. He's still sweeping up after that little adventure last week, I'm afraid, dealing with what his Thea believes are her new responsibilities."

"In other words, hiding themselves away until the

scandal is replaced by something more interesting," Darby added. "Unless we get luckier than we were tonight, you might be able to help Gabe out in that quarter."

"So neither of you saw anything?" Coop had harbored a faint hope all the way back to the Pulteney, but it had been just that, faint.

"Au contraire, mon ami," Darby said, saluting him with his wineglass. "Being of a vastly superior intellect, I immediately realized a hackney had no business heading down the stable row behind the mansions. Therefore, still judiciously concealing myself, at great personal danger, may I add, within a mass of prickly shrubberies, I watched its approach and then, quick as a startled hare, jumped out into the alleyway just as some numskull—no names, please—whistled loud enough to bring down a mountain and the occupant of said hackney cowered into the darkest reaches of the vehicle."

"Wonderful. Even when my luck is in, it's out," Coop said in disgust.

"Not entirely. If I might return to my storytelling? The nag in the traces took umbrage at the whistle, reared up—chasing me back into the briars, may I add, so that I wouldn't end my evening with a stomping—but I managed to reemerge in time to use my knife to inflict a fairly long slice in the rear canopy of the hackey."

"Hopefully rendering it recognizable in the daylight," Rigby supplied in some awe. "That's more than I could do, I'm afraid. The hackney was on me before I could do more than realize I'd never be able to catch it, and then it was gone. Except—and you'll pardon me for this, Darby—that wasn't a hackney."

"I beg your pardon?"

Rigby took a sip of wine, clearly to delay his explanation until he was certain he had all attention on him.
"It was meant to look like a hackney, but the horseflesh
was straight out of Tatt's or I'm a monkey."

"You're a monkey," Darby said flatly. "But you know,
thinking back on it, and considering I was more intent
on keeping my one eye on the occupant, you could be
right. The animal was nervy, wasn't it? Hackney nags
don't move beyond a lazy walk if a cannon goes off next
to them." He looked at Coop, who was gnawing on his
bottom lip, deep in thought. "What do you think? Nothing blends in more on the streets than a hackney. Is our
blackmailer, far from being pinched for pennies, only
masquerading as someone less than affluent?"

"Or well placed," Coop said, mentally combining
this news with the proper spelling and phrasing in the
notes, the chapbooks. "Who better to move among the
ton than a member of the ton. Oh, and from deductions
I made tonight, this person might also be female. Or a
short male. Or," he added, sighing, "a lad hired from
the streets."

"Multiple-choice deductions now, Coop?" Darby
teased. "Tell me again about this blackmailer of
yours. Precisely what is he—she, or possibly them—
threatening to reveal to the world?"

"I won't tell you again because I didn't tell you in
the first place, although I commend you for trying now,
when I'm clearly in a weakened state. Which you would
be, as well, I should point out, if you'd just spent the
past several hours in Miss Foster's company. So you
can sit back again, Rigby. I'm not about to bare my soul
to either of you."

"Well, that's too bad," Rigby said. "I rather promised Clarice I'd have news for her tomorrow when I pay my daily morning visit to Grosvenor Square. She's particularly interested in those several hours you just mentioned."

"Ah, the beauteous and finely dimpled Miss Clarice Goodfellow, soon to be Lady Clarice Rigby, your blushing bride. It occurs to me that I'm the only one of us left."

"Left for what, Darby?"

"Left unattached, Rigby. How badly has infatuation fuddled your brain?"

It took a moment for Coop to digest Darby's initial remark, as he was still attempting to conjure up a mental picture of the person he'd seen in the alleyway. "What? How would you be the only one left?"

"You're engaged to Miss Foster, Coop," Darby pointed out, shaking his head. "How soon they forget."

Rigby's shout of laughter did nothing to make Coop feel any better. "It's so immensely gratifying to see you're both amused. I've left her with the option of tossing me out on my ear once all this is over."

"Dare I say she's being a really good sport about 'all this'?"

"Yes, Darby, you could. Although there'll be no decision to make if I can't stop the blackmailer before he publishes. She'd have every reason to cry off, and everyone's sympathy, to boot."

"Now, Rigby, why do you suppose I'm suddenly wondering if our friend here is more upset about the prospect of Miss Foster crying off than he is being of exposed as a— Damn, Coop, couldn't you tell us something? Just one small *something*?"

"May I remind you that I'm sworn to secrecy?"

"From *us*? We who are selflessly flinging our lives on the line for you? Oh, shame, Cooper, shame," Rigby said, and then winked.

"Tell you what," Coop said, considering the thing. "Ask me questions. I'll answer yes or no. Three questions, and that's all. Agreed?"

"That seems fair, doesn't it, Darby? All right, here we go. I'll go first. Coop, what's the gel's name?"

"Oh, for the love of—Rigby, pour yourself another drink, and allow me to handle this. Here we go, question one. Is the woman important?"

"And that's better than I could do? Haven't you read the chapbooks? Of course the woman is important. She's the whole reason we're here. Don't let him answer—ask another question. A better question."

"I'll stick with this one if you don't mind. Coop? Is the woman important?"

Leave it to Darby to see past the obvious. "Not in herself, no."

"No?"

"No, Rigby," Coop repeated.

"Hmm, I had wondered, but I will admit your answer comes as a small shock. All right, let's try this one. Is there a signet ring?"

"No. And you'll have to do better than that if you're attempting to appear brilliant. Miss Foster already deduced as much."

"Are you at all romantically interested in Miss Foster?"

"Rigby, for God's sake, you're asking that as our third question?"

"I rather had to," Rigby said sheepishly. "Clarice made it quite clear that I was to report back to both her and the duchess. In some detail. Oh, by the by, the duchess believes Miss Foster is full to the brim with spunk. Her Grace admires spunk. The duke was just pleased that he spied a fellow hawking meat pies on the corner when they left the chapel."

With Gabe and his Thea out of town, Rigby's betrothed—formerly maid to Thea but now Miss Clarice Goodfellow of the Virginia Goodfellows—was camping with the Duke and Duchess of Cranbrook, and would until her wedding. Which was rather the same as saying Rigby had all but taken up residence in Grosvenor Square, as he couldn't seem to exist for more than a few hours without breathing the same air as his beloved.

"Go again, Darby. I won't count that question against you."

"I suppose that's sporting of you," Rigby admitted. "Although it does me no good. I suppose I'll just have to make something up on my own. Even if I can't see why you won't answer."

"Not won't, can't. I don't know the young lady even twenty-four hours. Nobody knows such things in less than a day." *And now he was lying to his friends.*

"Yes, they do. I took one look at Miss Frobisher and knew I couldn't care for her romantically if someone held a pistol to my head. You remember her, don't you, Darby? The one my aunt was pushing on me a few Seasons back? Stands to reason that if you can tell who you don't want in an instant, it's just as simple to know who you do want. Look at Clarice. I took one look. Saw one smile. And here I am, soon to be a happily married man. Now will you answer, Cooper?"

"Once again, Rigby, *no.*"

But the man wasn't about to give up. This, Coop

quickly decided, was another strike against marriage; it made fools out of formerly intelligent males. "No, you won't answer? Or no, you're not interested? Clarice will ask, you know, and the duchess, as well. You could have a little pity for a man having to face those two in the morning."

"Consider yourself pitied. You have one more question. You might want to make it a good one. Darby?"

"Give me a moment, friend, if you please. The woman isn't important. The signet ring is not only unimportant but imaginary, as well. Yet the threat, the danger to our good friend here, obviously remains real. So where does that leave us? Ah—and forgive me this lengthy question, but the answer will still ultimately be yes or no."

"Go on," Coop said, wishing he hadn't offered to answer any questions.

"I fully intend to, yes. The woman unimportant, the signet ring no clue at all—which probably leaves out the small estate, the female guest, the servant—and we'll consign all the derring-do since Quatre Bras to the dustbin of fantasy, as well. And yet—and yet—the blackmailer has threatened exposing something so dangerous that you've called on us to help you, even gone so far as to betroth yourself to a woman you just admitted you don't known from Adam."

"Is this going to take much longer? I've had a long day."

"I'm getting there, friend. So what are we left with? We're left with this business of the *highest reaches of the Crown*, that's what. We're left with Prinny showering our hero with land, a title and even money—the latter something Prinny has precious little of, I should add. Are you paying attention, Rigby?"

"He could have just said he finds Miss Foster attractive. That might have appeased Clarice somewhat," Rigby mumbled into the neck of his wine bottle.

"We'll continue without you, then," Darby said. "Unless my question—yes, I've finally arrived at the sticking point—brings you back to attention. Cooper, requiring an honest answer of either yes or no—if we cannot find and stop the blackmailer, for the sake of all the others in similar predicaments but most especially in aid of you, dear friend, and if the blackmailer goes through with his threat to publish some *truth* in Volume Three—is it more than just conjecture that your life very likely will be forfeit?"

Finally. "Yes."

Darby retook his seat. "I see. Well, then, what do we do next?"

"Next being tomorrow morning, I'm forgoing my appointment with my supposed new tailor and taking Miss Foster to Bond Street to buy her a betrothal gift. You, Rigby—yes, the answer was yes, so are you going to close your mouth anytime soon?—will please me by escorting your beloved to Mrs. Yothers's dressmaking shop, armed with a bit of gossip."

"Gossip? Clarice lives for gossip. Oh, thank you, Coop. You may have just saved me. What is she supposed to say?"

"That, my friends, might take another bottle. Because I don't know which of you two will first *selflessly fling* yourself forward as volunteer."

"I'm game," Darby said without hesitation. "I take

it you have reason to believe this Mrs. Yothers is in the employ of our blackmailer?"

"I can't be sure, no, but Dany—Miss Foster—seems to think it's possible. If she's correct, and if our blackmailer isn't just tidying up all his victims before setting sail for parts unknown, another note demanding payment for silence could arrive on your doorstep within a few days."

The viscount nodded his understanding. "You have considered the possibility that Mrs. Yothers is simply a gossip, and could tell several of her customers, any of whom could be in the man's employ?"

"I did. But we have to start somewhere, damn it all."

"I agree. Just be sure to make this gossip something suitably salacious. I do have my reputation to uphold, you understand."

CHAPTER TEN

DANY WATCHED IN amusement and some admiration as her sister, so lately seen hanging her head over the chamber pot, entered the drawing room with the graceful glide and the upturned chin that were the result of long years of practicing to be perfect. Or snooty, Dany often thought.

Mari, with her uncanny way of spotting imperfection, took herself immediately to the large vase of flowers Dany had *rearranged* the previous afternoon, clearly in an imperfect way. Mari frowned in distaste, measured the bouquet with both eyes and hands and then removed four blooms. Four, exactly the number Dany had grabbed in her attempt to impress Lord Townsend. One, two, three—four, and the bouquet was perfect once more.

"A lesser person could hate you," she told her sister as Mari then sat herself down on one of the couches, arranging her yellow morning gown into precise folds. She entwined her fingers in her lap.

"A clever person might attempt to emulate me," Mari responded in her sweet voice. "As Mama has encouraged you to do. After all, look at me. Just another country miss from a respected yet fairly ordinary family, and now a countess. I worked hard to accomplish that, you know. Years of practicing with books balanced on my head as I walked, long days of being strapped to the backboard. Lessons in deportment, in music, voice, watercolors, embroidery. *Years*, Dany."

Her smile faded. "And all you do is carelessly break a heel, and less than twelve hours later you're the affianced bride of the hero of Quatre Bras, the most eligible, sought-after bachelor in all of England. If anyone should be considering hating someone, Daniella, I think that anyone should be me."

Dany's smile hurt, totally forced. "And he's going to retrieve your letters and Oliver will never be any the wiser. You believe that, don't you?"

"I *have* to believe that, yes. If not, my life is completely and utterly over."

Thank you, Mari. That added another row to the pile of bricks on my shoulders.

"Have you heard from the earl?"

Mari shook her head. "No, nothing since his last missive, telling me that he'd be home within a fortnight. And that was three days ago. That's enough time, isn't it? You must tell me that's enough time."

Dany crossed her fingers in her lap. "I told you. The blackmailer's note was quite specific. He will contact you another way rather than the knothole. He will arrange to return your letters on trust, and then your chosen emissary will hand over his letters at a designated place and time because he fully understands you have no more funds available, as you explained so eloquently in your note, and has accepted the garnets as payment in full."

So I can be assured the letters will be tossed in the fire, and not saved as some sort of romantical keepsake, only to be found someday and stir up a mess all over again. Because yes, sister mine, much as I love you, there are times you can be thick as a plank.

"He's being very nice, isn't he, in the circumstances?"

Like now.

Dany's eyes crossed, but she quickly agreed. "Your blackmailer is best of good fellows, definitely. Very nearly a gentleman."

Mari's chin went up. "Now you're being facetious. I know he's an odiously bad man, but he could have been worse, couldn't he?"

"Oh, yes, he could have written a chapbook about you."

Mari shivered. "A chapbook? Now why would you say anything so silly as that?"

Because I also can be a fool, with a very large mouth. "Oh, no reason. I think I heard one of the footmen open the door. Yes, I'm certain I did." She gathered up her reticule and gloves and headed for the landing leading down to the foyer. "Ta-ta, Mari. I'm off to Bond Street, to bankrupt the baron."

Coop had just stepped into the foyer when she came charging toward him. "I talk too much," she said, brushing past him. "Let's go."

He replaced the curly brimmed beaver he'd barely had time to tip in her direction, and followed her. "Am I allowed to agree, or would I be safer with a simple 'Good morning, my dear'?"

She stopped on the flagway, looking at the town coach. "What on earth? It's not raining. It's sunny and pleasant, even a bit warm. Why are we riding in that contraption? Are you ashamed to be seen with me?"

Coop put his hand beneath her elbow, and she studiously ignored the rather pleasant frisson that impersonal touch caused. "Sharp as a tack this morning, aren't you? Yes, that's it entirely."

"Oh, it is not. There's someone else inside the coach, isn't there? Don't tell me it's the viscount. I may not know him above a day, but I am fairly certain he hasn't yet left his bed."

"Or not yet reached it. I chose the privacy of the closed coach because we may be traveling together but we won't be arriving in Bond Street at the same time. We'll meet by accident."

"Then you do have a plan. Thank goodness one of us does."

"It's not brilliant, but it is a plan, yes. Now come along, I want to introduce you to my friends and allies."

"Does that make them my allies, as well?"

"I wasn't aware you needed allies."

"I'm with you, aren't I? I should think it wouldn't come amiss if I had an entire army behind me."

"I can see this is going to be a pleasant morning."

"Perhaps if I had been able to sleep after realizing Mari's now in twice the trouble she was before I was so fortunate as to find her a hero, I might be more *pleasant.*"

Why couldn't she stop talking? Really, the baron would be doing her a courtesy if he stuck a handkerchief in her mouth.

"I warned you I was no hero. Just get inside while I explain to myself why I persist in enjoying your company as much as I apparently do," Coop said as the groom let down the steps.

"You enjoy my company? Really?"

Yes, there it was, her heart once again going pitter-pat.

"Why look so shocked, Miss Foster? Or does that bother you as much as it does me? Now, please, we shouldn't keep the others waiting."

Since she was left with no other sensible choice— and told herself that was the only reason she was obeying him—Dany stepped up and pulled herself inside the coach, aiming for the empty forward-facing seat as Coop joined her and the coach moved off into the square.

Sitting on the facing seat was a pair of exquisitely dressed creatures, both of them grinning at her as if either she or they were the resident village idiots.

"Oh, Coop, she's beautiful!" exclaimed the dimpled young blonde in the bordering-on-outrageous bright pink redingote and high-crowned straw bonnet adorned with red cherries and a sprinkling of what most resembled sugared gumdrops, and tied with a wide green grosgrain ribbon that nearly obliterated her neck. Her voice was slightly high, but adorable in its honeydripping drawl that clearly stamped her as not being English born. "You didn't tell me she was beautiful, Jerry." She gave her companion's forearm a quick, light slap. "Details, my love. It's as the duchess says, if you're going to be of any use to us, you must remember the details."

"Yes, Clarice," the sweet-looking cherub of a man apologized. This must be Jeremiah Rigby, Baronet, the friend Coop had mentioned yesterday. Now here was a redhead who'd wandered too close to the carrot patch. Its color clashed badly with his heated blush. "But I did tell you about the hair, right?"

The woman he'd addressed as Clarice leaned over and planted a kiss on the cherub's cheek. "You did, indeed, precious peach." She turned her attention to Dany, who had just then been looking at Coop, hoping for some sort of explanation that clearly wasn't coming. "Hello, Miss Foster. I'm Clarice Goodfellow, late of the Fairfax County Virginia Goodfellows and soon to be Lady Clarice Goodfellow Rigby. That's my Jerry here," she said, hooking a thumb toward her betrothed. "Isn't he just the most handsome thing you've ever seen? Well, yes, of course he is. Say hello, Jerry."

"Miss Foster," Rigby somehow managed to choke out, tipping his hat. "Pardon me for not rising. It is my honor to meet you." He then looked at Cooper in some desperation.

"Sir Jerr—Sir Jeremiah," Dany answered, momentarily wondering if she should put out her hand for him to bow over, but then quickly deciding the man had enough on his plate without attempting such a maneuver in a moving coach. "Miss Goodfellow. It's a pleasure to meet you both."

Clarice put up her gloved hands, as if framing the last moments for posterity. "There, you see? That wasn't so terrible, was it? Introductions are so full of stuffy rules in England. Rough ground, I say, with all the folderol of who comes first and who comes last. Rough ground gotten over quickly is my answer to it all. And now, to settle it, I shall be Clarice, and Jerry here will be Rigby, because everyone save me calls him that, and then there's Coop and you. You're Dany, correct? Ah, I love when things are settled, and now we've all cried friends. Oh, and fellow conspirators, which is more lovely than anything, I'm thinking. I've always wanted to conspir-e-ate."

Dany saw a mental image of her sister's face if she could hear Clarice Goodfellow's opinion of the strict rules of protocol she and her sister had had drummed into their heads for years: her eyes bugging out, jaw dropped to half-mast, her maid fumbling in her mistress's reticule for some feathers to burn under her nose.

"What a wonderful suggestion, Clarice," Dany said, wishing she had been able to find a way beyond the *Miss Foster* and the *my lord* considering they were betrothed, for pity's sake. But now Clarice had done it for her. Americans were so refreshing. "Isn't it—Coop?"

She shot another glance toward Coop, who was still avoiding making eye contact with her or anyone else in the coach. Was he outraged? Dumbfounded? Embarrassed? No, wait, he was experiencing some difficulty with his breathing, wasn't he, and the eye she could see had begun to water slightly. He was near to killing himself, trying not to laugh.

Ahhh...wasn't that sweet.

She couldn't let him suffer like that, poor thing. He might burst something important.

"I couldn't agree with you more completely, Clarice. Formalities are so—oh, what could be the proper word? My lord Townsend—dearest Coop, I should say—as you have yet to contribute to this delightful conversation, could you be so kind as to assist me?"

His lips pressed tightly together, Coop's only answer was a quick shake of his head. Clearly he dared not open his mouth.

"No? Oh, that's too bad. Oh, wait, I've got it now.

Everyone, tell me if I've got it right, please. Formalities are so…formal."

Clarice pointed her finger at Dany. *"Exactly!"*

It was entirely possible Lord Cooper Townsend hadn't laughed, really laughed, in quite some time. If so, he was definitely correcting that lapse now, only able to catch his breath for a moment, at which time he managed to whisper to Dany, "I'm going to kill you," before going off again.

"It's the worry, poor man," Clarice said, nodding knowingly. "Jerry here told me he's in some sort of terrible trouble, although friend that he is, he won't say just what. But I'll get it out of him eventually. Oh, dear, now he has the hiccups, doesn't he? Jerry, check to see if there's a flask in the coach pocket. Nothing like holding your nose while downing some strong spirits to beat away the hiccups. Or, as my uncle Soggy, the privy master, often said, 'Make you not care that you've still got them.' Oh, Jerry, that's right, you don't have to nudge me. I shouldn't have said that, although for the life of me I don't know why, seeing as how all of you bow and scrape to your privy councillor. A privy is a privy, Jerry, and that will never change."

"Clarice," Rigby said in a strangled voice, "I've told you. There's a whacking great difference between your uncle Soggy, who digs privies, and the privy councillors who got their name because it once was the custom for kings to discuss secrets in the privy because that's the only place His Royal Highness didn't have to worry about being overheard."

"It seems to me you can hear lots of things in a privy," Clarice pointed out with a pout.

For a moment, Dany feared the baron might roll right

off the padded squabs, doubled up in hilarity. But he stopped himself, manfully, she decided, and somehow gathered up the pieces of his humor and tucked them back inside his gentlemanly self. "Forgive me," he said, pausing for one final hiccup. "Clarice, you are a treasure beyond price."

"Thank you, Coop, but that isn't true. Today, for scolding me when I said nothing so terribly wrong, I think that price will be a new bonnet. Won't it, Jerry, love?"

"Two, if you fancy more than one," her beloved promised as the coach drew to the curb. "And here we are, a mere block from Bond Street. How long, Coop?"

Coop pulled out his pocket watch and Rigby did the same. "Half past noon should do it. Remember, we'll stroll in after you by some minutes. We can't take the chance of raising Mrs. Yothers's suspicions. Do you know what you're going to say, Clarice?"

The blonde was busy gathering her things. Gloves, reticule and the lace-edged parasol she then handed to Rigby. "Don't you worry about me, silly. The duchess says I lie better than her best Aubusson carpet. That's a compliment, sweetie," she told Rigby as he managed to back out of the carriage with his walking stick and the parasol in one hand, Clarice clutching the other and warning him to mind her skirts.

The door closed and the coach moved on.

"Dany? You did nothing but sit there while I made an utter fool of myself. You weren't amused?"

He'd called her Dany. Well, about time, considering they were supposedly going to marry. Really, she was liking him more and more. Which was probably also a good thing, unless it became a bad thing, which could also happen.

The insides of her cheeks had nearly come to grief, holding back her own amusement, but somehow she'd remained silent, one might even say composed. "I was amused. A person would have to be my sister to not be amused."

"Then I congratulate you on your composure. In my defense, I was not making fun of Clarice."

"No, of course not. She does that very well on her own, and seems to enjoy doing so. You were probably chortling too hard to notice that she winked at me. Who is she, really? I mean, other than Miss Goodfellow of the Fairfax County Virginia Goodfellows."

"She was raised with Thea, Gabe's soon-to-be bride, and traveled here as her ladies' maid. But nobody can know that. Rigby took one look at her and tumbled into love, so now the duchess is turning her into a lady. She's doing very well actually. It's only been a few weeks, if that. She still has the occasional slip of the tongue."

"Deliberate slips," Dany told him. "I think I'm going to like her very much. But now, if you don't mind, perhaps you'll tell me what's going on, please. I thought we were going to Mrs. Yothers's establishment to…to reconnoiter."

"We were, but after I left you last night, Darby and Rigby and I came up with a different idea. We don't want to appear too suspicious or heavy-handed, you understand. Unless you planned to march inside, grab a hat pin and threaten her with it if she didn't talk."

"No, I dismissed that idea in the first five minutes. I spent the remainder of the night waiting for inspiration that never arrived, which is very lowering, because I'm usually quite good at what my mother would term *conniving*. In *my* defense, I believe worry for Mari froze my brain. I loathe saying this, but I fear this expedition is all in your hands."

"You wouldn't mind writing that down, would you?"

"And my sister accuses me of being facetious. Oh, speaking of Mari. I told her what you said I should tell her and she's completely happy and relaxed, certain her worries are over. For once in my life, I took no pleasure in lying to her."

"You couldn't tell her the truth," Coop said as the coach stopped again. "Are you ready?"

Dany peeked out the side window. "This isn't Mrs. Yothers's establishment. Where are we?"

He waited for the footman to lower the steps, and then helped Dany to the flagway before he answered. "Promise me you won't cause a scene."

"Why would I—where are we going?"

"Minerva—that is, my mother tells me this is the second best jeweler shop in town," he said as the footman ran ahead to open the door to a small shop. "Ah-ah, don't dig in your heels, Miss Foster. You are about to choose what will become the Townsend betrothal ring. Generations to follow depend on your good judgment."

"Generations to follow depend on your ability to find a willing bride, or they won't follow at all," she told him, her heart pounding.

"You and I know that, but if we're to convince the world differently, you need a ring, especially since my mother and the duchess spent last evening telling all and sundry that the hero of Quatre Bras is about to become leg-shackled. I've already had three impassioned, tearstained missives from young ladies begging me to change my mind, and my man had to turn away one persistent mama who declared it wasn't *fair* of me to choose a bride before her daughter recovered from her measles and could race hotfoot to town, at which point I would have no choice but to toss this opportunistic nobody country miss into the dustbin and declare for the beauty."

"'Opportunistic nobody'? Somebody actually said that? I'm sister to the Countess of Cockermouth. I'm daughter to Henry Erasmus Foster, Esquire. I'm grand-niece to Lady— No, never mind that. She ran off to Italy last year with her head groom. But that doesn't matter. I'm Daniella Foster, and I'm not nobody. I'm *me*."

To her surprise, Coop took hold of both her hands and raised them to his lips, depositing kisses on the back of each kid glove, his green gaze steady on her face.

She pulled her hands free, aware that her insides had begun to tremble in the most alarming way. "Why did you do that?"

Coop shook his head slightly. "I imagine because to kiss you on the mouth would seal your fate entirely, considering we're still standing on the flagway and several parties are feigning disinterest while watching every move we make. I just realized that, between your kindness to Clarice, your deliberate teasing me into a better mood with your silliness and your impassioned defense of your unique and increasingly appealing self, I was left with no other choice."

"Oh. Well. Um, all right." Dany's toes curled inside her shoes. "But you're only saying all of that so I'll politely accompany you inside."

"I don't think so, no," he told her in a voice that, if

not sincere, was residing next door to sincere. "But will you?"

Dany opened her mouth and idiocy came out before she could stop herself. "I'm sorry, will I what, my lord? Behave, or marry you?"

"For the sake of generations of Townsends to come, for the moment I'll be delighted if you don't bankrupt me in there."

"Yes, that probably is the best answer. But no garnets."

"On my word as a recently declared gentleman." He extended his bent arm, she slipped hers through it and for the first time in her life Dany was off to pick out a bit of jewelry that, at least temporarily, would be her own.

The first thing she noticed upon entering the long, narrow shop was that there was not a piece of jewelry to be seen anywhere. No necklaces, no eardrops, no rings. Not even a single stickpin for his lordship's cravat. The side walls were lined with wooden drawers, each with its own brass handle, keyhole and a white card listing its contents. Each side had its own wooden ladder that could be pushed along the drawers, making it possible to reach them all, and they stacked a good fifteen feet high.

A library of jewelry.

In front of each wall were long narrow cabinets and high stools with purple velvet cushions. The carpet on the floor was swirled through with gold, and so soft Dany's heels sank into it.

There were a half dozen male clerks wearing black leather visors, their shirtsleeves wrapped to their wrists in white paper, banded by black ribbons that kept the material tight to their arms. There would be no rings or other bits of glitter disappearing up a sleeve in this establishment, that was for certain.

Especially since each clerk was no more than three feet from what appeared to be the remains of a regiment of burly soldiers, each more fierce-looking than the next.

There were two customers in the shop—one a man currently examining a tray of diamond brooches, and the other deep in conversation with the clerk who apparently had been deemed trustworthy enough to wear his jacket.

"My goodness. I don't know if we've stepped into a church or a prison."

"Intimidating, isn't it? I think I'd rather face several dozen of Bonaparte's finest," Coop agreed. "Just remember, you're the customer. This is not the only jeweler in Mayfair."

"In that case, I shall be Mari. I warn you, she can be embarrassing. Oh, listen. That man is arguing with the clerk allowed to wear his jacket."

"The proprietor," Coop corrected. "But you're right. Since we're being ignored by everyone in favor of said argument, what do you say we eavesdrop?"

"My thought exactly. We do rub along together fairly well, don't we? I may only partway bankrupt your future generations."

Apparently Coop wasn't listening. "Hush."

"Yes, course. But first we'll strike my last statements. *Ooof!*"

Coop had rather roughly shoved her behind him, and just in time apparently, as the angry customer stormed past them in the narrow aisle and slammed his way out of the shop.

"Goodness," Dany said as she extricated herself from her position between Coop and one of the long cabinets. "What do you suppose just happened?"

Coop took her hand. "Let's find out, shall we?"

The proprietor was fanning himself with his handkerchief when he spied his new customers. He was a small man, almost painfully thin, his bulbous nose quite out of proportion with the rest of him, his pate as bare of hair as a polished egg even as his coal-black eyebrows were small bushes unto themselves. It was difficult to believe he was real, as he looked more like a pen and ink caricature than a man.

"My most sincere apologies, sir, that you should witness such outrageous behavior in my establishment," he said in a voice half an octave higher than Dany's. "Some people take umbrage at hearing the truth, sadly."

"He didn't care for the price you quoted?"

"More the fool I'd be if I were to turn over what he thought these were worth."

At that, the man pointed to a garnet necklace, bracelet and eardrops lying on the countertop in an inglorious heap.

"Oh, my," Dany said, eyes gone wide.

"But I suppose they're mine now, considering that he all but threw the necklace at me."

"Really?" Coop picked up the necklace and examined it. "Do you fancy it, my dear?"

She knew what he was asking, and gave him her best answer. "They put me in mind of the set I was given by my grandmother."

"You don't want these, sir. Pretty enough, but the stones are glass. Not even very good glass, as I pointed out to my unhappy patron. I am Mr. Jonathan Birdwell, proprietor," he then continued, collecting his dignity. "How may I be of service to the gentleman?"

Dany looked down at herself, just to be sure she hadn't suddenly gone invisible.

Coop allowed the necklace to fall back to the black velvet square they'd been resting on, the same black velvet square Dany had used to wrap the set before depositing it in the knothole. He looked to the door, but didn't make any attempt to follow the unhappy customer who was probably long gone at any rate.

"Actually, Birdwell, idle curiosity forces me to ask the name of our disappointed gentleman."

The proprietor wrapped up the jewelry and tossed the velvet square to one of the guards. "At least the gold is real—we'll melt it down," he said to the fellow before returning his attention to Coop. "I'm afraid I can't divulge that information, as the gentlemen deserves his privacy."

Dany saw that Coop was in the process of reaching into his pocket for his purse.

Oh, no, there was no reason for that. Not while Mari was around!

"You refuse? The insult! The sheer audacity! Little man, do you know to whom you are speaking?"

"For the love of…"

"…all that's reasonable and decent, yes, I agree. Come, Lord Townsend, we shall take our custom elsewhere," she continued over his rasped protest. "I may not yet be your wife, but I am your affianced bride, well aware of the respect due you."

And me. Just in case, Jonathan, old sport, you thought I was something other than a young, innocent miss, which I'm certain you did!

"Wait!" Birdwell all but shouted. "That is," he continued, grasping the shreds of his self-imposed dignity and wrapping them around him, "my deepest apologies, my lord. How could I not recognize your lordship, the hero of Quatre Bras…"

"And points west, yes," Coop interrupted dully, pulling back one of the stools for Dany, who grinned into his glare as she pushed herself up onto the purple seat. "I remember."

A little Mari, a sprinkling of Clarice…and a whopping big dollop of Dany. Why women did not rule the world was beyond imagination…

"You really wish to stay, my lord?" she asked, already depositing her reticule on the countertop. "Well, I suppose if this clerk here will deign to be more forthcoming…"

"I don't know the man by name, my lord, that being one of the questions you don't ask a moneylender."

Moneylender? Oh, this was getting interesting!

"I understand," Coop said. "He was here to sell the garnets?"

"That he was. We, um, we accommodate him from time to time. *His*, um, customer used it to pay a debt, or at least that is my understanding. I believe you know the rest."

Dany signed theatrically. "How very boring. And here I thought there would be a good bit of gossip to be had, but apparently not."

"Never say gossip, miss," the proprietor begged as his eyebrows nearly crawled onto his forehead. "Buying as well as selling is my business, but I would never buy anything I recog—that is, I only buy very sparingly."

"How reassuring," Coop said, taking a seat beside

Dany. "My fiancée, Miss Foster, and I are here to select a betrothal ring. One with a *new* stone, one that has never seen another setting."

"Yes, my lord, your mother's note this morning was quite specific. Um," he added quickly when both Coop and Dany frowned, "lovely woman, your mother. Quite…quite a presence about her. She established an account for you just yesterday. But wouldn't you care to step back into one of our private viewing rooms?"

"I like it here," Dany said, only because she was still feeling contrary, if no longer invisible.

"We'll remain here, Birdwell," Coop said. "Miss Foster becomes light-headed in small rooms."

Dany gave him a sideways kick, which was the least he deserved.

"Very well, my lord. I will get you a selection of my finest rings."

"Don't ask," Coop said as the proprietor walked away, shooing one of the guards ahead of him.

"I'm sorry, but I fear I must. Your *mother*?"

"Embarrassing, I know. I'll explain another time."

"Yes, you most certainly will. You did promise to introduce me to her."

"I know. I also promised myself I'd read the book on beekeeping she presented me with, but sadly, I don't keep all of my promises."

"Really? I'll have to remember that. So, our blackmailer is in debt to a moneylender? That is worrying, as it must make him even more desperate."

"Our *little man* didn't say that, not precisely," Coop corrected. "He assumed your grandmother's garnets were used to pay a debt. It's just as possible the blackmailer made an outright sale to the moneylender—

Wait. How do we know, how does the proprietor know, that the man we just saw is a moneylender at all? No names were exchanged. Damn. We may have just seen the blackmailer. If he's paid in jewels, he then sells them."

"I suppose that's possible. I didn't see his face thanks to you pushing me behind your back. Did you get a good look at him?"

"No. He was angrily jamming his hat on his head as he passed by, his arm fairly well covering his face. Upon reflection, that may have been deliberate, if he'd recognized me. Tall, but not as tall as I, well dressed, but not remarkably so. And we didn't hear him speak. In other words, he could have been anyone."

"Yes, but you said tall. That would mean tall enough to reach the knothole. Doesn't that prove that we're dealing with more than one person?" Dany felt excitement, but only for a moment. "That doesn't really help us, does it?"

"Probably not, no. Oh, and by the way, my compliments on your clever handling of Birdwell."

"He deserved it, assuming I was your light-o'-love, or some such thing."

Coop shook his head. "Damn, I was hoping you hadn't noticed. I told you I'm new to all of this, so I apologize for bringing you in here. Clearly, choosing betrothal rings are the duty of the groom."

"I don't see why. The groom doesn't wear the thing."

"True, but we won't point that out."

"Or ask costs."

"With my betrothed present? No, I—*we*—definitely will not ask costs."

Dany couldn't help herself. She laid her hand on his

forearm and batted her eyelashes at him, just as Mari did from time to time with Oliver. "As true love has no price. Aren't you a dear."

Coop shifted rather uncomfortably on the stool. "Are you done?"

"I don't think so, no. Do you think it's the red hair? Dexter's said more than once that redheads are often mistaken for females of negotiable affections. Birdwell may only have been making a natural assumption."

"Can we possibly have this conversation another time? Or are you getting some of your own back for something I did?"

"I'm not quite sure. I'll have to think about that. It may just be that otherwise I'd feel rather overwhelmed in such stuffy surroundings. Either that, or I'd enjoy seeing Birdwell's eyebrows climb his forehead like bushy black bugs a few more times. I do know I'm enjoying myself. Are you enjoying yourself?"

"More than I'd believe, yes. I'm nearly on the edge of my seat, wondering what you'll do next."

"Well, I could be good. But what fun would that be?"

"No fun at all, I agree. Ah, and here comes our smugly smiling proprietor, followed closely by a parade of clerks toting drawers undoubtedly filled with gems and rings. I can't believe I'm saying this, but let the bug crawl begin."

She watched as the drawers—she counted seven in all—were reverently placed on the countertop at exactly the same time, the purple velvet cloth covering each just as reverently removed, one after the other. The pompous precision of the thing nearly caused her to giggle.

The clerks stepped back, actually clicked their heels and then turned as one, retreating, leaving behind only a man nearly as large as a mountain. He took up a position behind the diminutive Birdwell that seemed innocuous enough, but warned that there would be no pilfering going on as long as he was around or else there would be a cracked head in someone's near future.

"My lord, for your kind consideration," the proprietor intoned importantly, sweeping a hand over the assembled glitter and glory. "My very best, at your disposal. Diamonds, rubies, sapphires, emeralds, pearls, aquamarine, topaz."

Dany wanted to scream, laugh, jump down from the padded tool and dance about in a circle. She'd never seen so much *marvelous* all in one place. She was having trouble controlling her breathing; swallowing was definitely beyond her, blinking out of the question.

Yet once again the proprietor was ignoring her, selecting rings and presenting them to Coop, just as if she wasn't there.

"No," she heard herself say as the jeweler held out a heavily engraved gold band encrusted with diamonds, the center stone so immense as to seem unreal.

Both Coop and the jeweler turned to look at her, which was when Dany realized she'd spoken.

"You don't care for it, Miss Foster?" Coop asked, clearly inviting her to do mischief.

Wasn't he a sweetheart!

"Assist me," she said to Coop rather imperiously, extending her hand so that she could slide off the stool rather than jump from it. Ladies clearly weren't often accommodated in jewelry shops, or else at least some of the stools would be shorter. "Yes, thank you. Now step back if you please."

He squeezed her hand encouragingly. "You don't care for diamonds?"

"I don't care to have the Townsends' soon-to-be ancestral betrothal ring chosen by you two gentlemen. If that were to be the case, you shouldn't have brought me here."

He leaned closer, to whisper his next words in her ear. "And what fun would that have been?"

She bit her lip so that she wouldn't smile. He was going to give her her head, let her do what she wanted, even if it meant she was about to embarrass him all hollow.

But she had an idea, and he'd given it to her.

She walked along the counter in grand imitation of her sister at her most imperious, pointing a finger at first one velvet-lined drawer, and then the next. "No, not this one, take that one away, no, no, definitely not the diamonds. That one," she declared, stopping in front of the drawer of emerald rings.

Emerald. Like his eyes.

This drawer had been her destination from the moment the assortment had been placed on the cabinet, a decision solidified when he'd looked into her eyes and he'd seen a twinkle of her own mischief there.

Birdwell motioned for the other drawers to be removed and the clerks hustled forward to do his bidding. That left the single drawer in front of Dany, and she hopped up onto the stool once more and began examining its contents, row by row.

The settings and stones all looked so impressive, and so very heavy. Why, Mari very nearly had to have a maid walk beside her, holding up her hand, when she wore the Cockermouth ancestral ring. Dany had supposed the first Cockermouth bride had been nearly Amazonian, and the countesses that followed had all been saddled with the thing, like it or not. Mari swore she adored it, but Mari wouldn't tell the truth about something like that if someone held a knife to her.

The Townsend brides would not be burdened with anything so monstrously large, or so garish. She slipped off her gloves, more than ready to try on dozens of rings, just because she could.

But that turned out not to be necessary.

"That one," she declared, pointing to a large but otherwise unadorned rectangular-shaped stone held in place by thin prongs, the gold band itself fairly wide, flat and completely plain. Simple. Elegant. And not likely to bankrupt his lordship.

"Yours is a lady of taste, my lord. This stone has just recently arrived from Columbia, home of the most exquisite emeralds in the world." If Birdwell had wings, he probably would have lifted completely off the floor. As it was, he seemed to grow about two inches as he reached for the ring.

But Dany was faster. She snatched it up and slid it onto her finger, where it fit as if fashioned for her. And yes, the stone was a perfect match for Coop's eyes, at least when her behavior elicited any sort of emotion from him, be it amusement, frustration or downright anger.

"My lord," Birdwell all but bleated, keeping one eye on Dany's hand, as if she was about to make the ring disappear. "You understand that the emerald was only inserted into that setting to, well, to display the stone. That's not a complete ring. You'll wish now to choose a setting worthy of the stone. May I suggest diamonds?

A veritable *cushion* of them, wrought into rosebuds on either side of the stone, raising it a full half inch above a heavily engraved band. I have just such a setting."

"Absolutely not. That will just muck it up," Dany said, closing her fist. The ring was going nowhere!

Coop took her hand, and she unclenched her fist. "Are you sure, Miss Foster? It's beautiful, no doubt, but it is rather plain."

"I'm being considerate. It's probably the least expensive stone in the drawer," she whispered as Birdwell flew off, probably to bring them the setting he favored. "Besides, you said I could choose, and I do like it." She looked up into his eyes, but couldn't read them. "Please?"

He bent and kissed her knuckle, just below the ring. "And there it stays until the day you take it off, mostly probably to fling it in my face."

With that, he turned to the approaching Birdwell and said, "Miss Foster and I have decided. The ring goes with us today."

It was only then, watching the proprietor's face as various emotions flitted across it, that Dany realized that the man was caught between elation and his reputation, should anyone know the unadorned, rather *outré* ring had come from his shop.

Apparently elation won the battle, and he ordered the man mountain to take the drawer away as if its inferior contents offended him.

She looked down at the stone once more. It was large. It was deeply green, and very likely without flaw. Birdwell had said he'd only put the gem into the plain setting in order to display it. So it wasn't the ring that could cost the earth, but this single, solitary stone itself.

Oh, dear.

"Um," Dany whispered, tugging on Coop's sleeve. "You might want to ask him the cost. I may have... misjudged."

"Just now figured that out, did you?" Coop whispered back. "But don't worry. My crafty mother already arranged for a discount, so you've probably only halfway bankrupted me." He grinned at her. "And as that same mother used to warn me, you may want to close your mouth now before a fly wanders into it."

CHAPTER ELEVEN

DANY WAS STILL sunk in a sulk as she and Coop walked along the Bond Street flagway. What a mess she'd made, believing herself to be so brilliant.

But she did love the ring.

Not that it was hers, not *really*.

Although it could be.

But only because Cooper Townsend was a gentleman, and a man of his word. A hero, who insisted he was not a hero.

Not that she'd hold him to their supposed compromise and proposal. They would find the blackmailer. Coop would give him a good thrashing and suggest an ocean voyage, perhaps to India. She'd worry that another man might eliminate the blackmailer in a more *permanent* way, but not Coop. Still, the man would get the message! They would retrieve and then promptly burn Mari's letters; the damning chapbook would never be published; and Coop's secrets would remain safe and his head continue to ride secure on his neck, the Prince Regent or whomever never the wiser that some deep dark secret was nearly spilled all over London.

And then it would be over. Coop would go his way, and she would go hers.

Maybe they could remain friends…

Suddenly she wasn't walking anymore, because

Coop had halted, nearly pulling her to a stop when she continued on, not noticing.

"Whoa," he teased. "Are you ready?"

She looked up at Coop, realizing she'd been concentrating her gaze on the flagway and the tips of her shoes each time she took a step, just as if fascinated by the sheer action of locomotion. How far had they walked? A block? Six? Were they even still on Bond Street?

"Uh, um, where are we?"

"I'm standing a short distance from Mrs. Yothers's dress shop. I don't know where you are, although I will say you've been the object of some curiosity from passersby, as you so neatly cut everyone dead while I was apologetically tipping to my hat to all and sundry."

Dany looked to her left and right, feeling her cheeks flushing. "I was...woolgathering?"

"Circling the moon might be more to the point. Not that I'm complaining. I find I like a peaceful woman."

"Then you'll have to look elsewhere, my lord," she shot back, still angry with herself, "for I'm feeling far from peaceful. It's my own fault, I know that. Only Mari should be Mari. I should be myself. As myself, perhaps I would have realized the stone was too extraordinarily beautiful to be less than— Stop smiling. I'm serious about this. I've bankrupted you."

"You're forgetting Minerva's discount."

"Yes, your mother. But I'm afraid I don't understand a Minerva discount."

"Birdwell, and several others, realized that being able to say they've won the custom of the hero of Quatre Bras could do wonders for their business. If they didn't realize it, Minerva pointed the fact out to them. And before you say anything else, yes, I was appalled when I learned what she'd done." He smiled at her. "Admittedly no longer quite as appalled as I was before you set eyes on that emerald, as she wrangled a fifty percent discount from the man. Now, are you ready to step inside and be delighted to see your new friend Clarice? We're already late, which means it might be Rigby who's in danger of being bankrupted."

"You still haven't told me what this is all about, and why I'm meeting her."

"I know. I want you to be surprised, and react genuinely. Don't worry, Clarice knows what to do."

"But it's better that I don't?"

"See that? I was certain you'd understand. Good girl. Shall we?"

Dany was close to grinding her teeth. "Do I have a choice?"

"You'll always have a choice, Dany," he said, suddenly and unexpectedly serious. "That's a promise."

"Oh. Oh, my," she said, attempting to catch her breath. "I wasn't expecting that." Then she wrinkled up her nose, realizing what she'd said. "That is, I mean…" she rushed to say. "I mean, we're talking about…about the— *What* are we talking about, Coop?"

"I'm not sure," he said, tipping up her chin. "I just suddenly felt a need to say the words. And perhaps to bring my mind back to the matter at hand, as you've managed to distract me from our mutually pressing problems. How do you do that?"

Dany wet her lips with the tip of her tongue. "I don't know. I don't set out to do it. Is there anything special that, um, that distracts you?"

"You," Coop said, a rather rueful half smile causing her to catch her breath. "I could enumerate at some other time, with much less of an audience, but for now? For now, Miss Daniella Foster, *you*. Just you, being you."

"Oh." Her voice was nearly inaudible. Her world seemed to be tipping on its axis, and she felt her body begin to move toward his, drawn to him by the intensity in his eyes. Nor did he seem unaffected, or even aware of where they were.

Wasn't that…interesting.

"There you are! You're late."

Dany shook her head as both she and Coop turned to see Rigby coming toward them from the direction of the dress shop, his cheeks flushed, very nearly splotched.

"My pardon, friend," Coop said. "How late are we?"

"Two bonnets and a reticule late, I'd say," he told them, retrieving a handkerchief from his pocket and dabbing at his brow. "Miss Foster," he said, belatedly acknowledging her with a slight bow. "That is, Dany. If you would be so kind as to join Clarice in the shop? And possibly talk her out of the reticule? It's fairly drowning in *pearls*, you understand."

"Surely not real pearls."

"I don't know," the baronet told her. "She wants to bite one, to see for certain, but I've so far talked her into waiting for you, as I've told her you're an expert on pearls. *Please*."

It was good to laugh, and Dany wanted to give Rigby a kiss on the cheek for taking her mind away from all the many dangerous areas it had traveled to in the moments since Coop had turned so suddenly serious.

"I don't want to be seen just yet. Therefore, having happily encountered Rigby here, you sent your maid to the coach to unburden herself of the bandboxes containing your purchases, while he offered to escort you to meet with your friend Clarice," Coop told her, nodding his head in the direction of Mrs. Yothers's establishment. "Are you ready? Time to go."

"You've thought of everything, haven't you?" she asked, not all that happily. Why on earth did she say he could take the reins into his hands? She'd have to correct that at some point, she supposed, although it probably didn't matter, since they would soon part ways from their sham engagement. Did he already know how he was going to do that? "I could have made up my own fib, you know."

"Next time," Coop said. "Perhaps we can take turns."

"Now you're being facetious again. Not that I won't hold you to that suggestion. After all, we may *get along*, but that doesn't mean we, well, we *get along*, if you know what I mean."

"Unfortunately, Dany, I believe I do. We're playing at a sort of game, aren't we? And it's not always mutually enjoyable. But all games have an end." He tipped his hat at her, turned and walked off down the flagway, away from the shop.

And now he's frowning, and probably second- or even third-guessing this ridiculous arrangement, from the ring to the kiss...and beyond. Are you happy now, Dany? she asked herself, and decided that she wasn't. She could only get back to the *game.*

She spied Clarice within moments of entering the shop with Rigby, and called out a cheery, "Yoo-hoo," as she raised one hand and waved wildly, in the manner of her mother when seeing someone she knew (and embarrassing both her daughters in the process).

Clarice waved back and hastened to join them, before commanding Rigby to vacate the premises, as his presence wasn't necessary.

Rigby made his escape without complaint, most probably to rejoin Coop and the two of them off on the hunt for cigars or some such thing.

Clarice grabbed Dany's arm and pulled her toward a corner of the shop, even as Mrs. Yothers approached from behind the curtain covering the dressing room Mari and Dani had occupied only a day earlier.

A day? Why did it feel like whole weeks had passed?

"Come on, come on, I've a secret to share. That's why I sent poor Jerry away," Clarice declared in a less than secretive voice. "I've been all but dancing out of my britches, waiting for someone to tell. It's just the best secret *ever*."

Dany smiled. So this was it? She was to allow Clarice to tell her—and Mrs. Yothers—a secret? And then she was to appear summarily impressed by said secret, obviously, which was why Coop hadn't told her the particulars, so that neither their meeting nor the secret-telling would seem contrived. Very well, she'd act surprised. But first she'd give Mrs. Yothers time to make her way to within earshot. At the moment, she was fussing with some scarves on one of the nearby tables, her back to them, just as if she didn't know she had customers.

"A secret, Clarice? You mean gossip, don't you?" Dany shook her head, and tsk-tsked into the bargain. "I'd rather not listen if you don't mind. I'm afraid I'm not a believer in gossip."

Clarice's blue eyes went wide. "But…but *everybody* loves gossip. You *have* to love gossip. Oh, wait. You're only saying that because you're a lady, and think you should. I understand. But you still want to hear it, don't you?"

The shopkeeper was closer now.

Dany laughed. "Found me out, did you? Are you suitably impressed with my *ladyness*?"

Clarice shrugged. "I suppose so. I'm just happy you aren't all prunes and prisms, whatever that means, or else I'd have to be on my best behavior, whatever *that* is, because just when I think I am, the duchess informs me I'm not. She's a dear, the duchess, but I do miss my mis—my good friend Thea," she said, and then shook her head. "I meant to say, my good friend Miss Dorothea Neville. She's to marry Mr. Gabriel Sinclair, heir to the dukedom, you understand. But you and Thea both are more friendly than starchy, so you won't mind if I make the odd misstep or two, will you? It's so important that I don't disgrace my sweet Jerry, you understand."

"I doubt he's worried about that," Dany told her, reaching for the small reticule Clarice held tightly in both hands. "My, isn't that pretty. May I see?"

The reticule was handed over and Dany-the-pearl-expert carefully turned it about in her hands, sniffed dismissingly and placed it on the nearest tabletop. "Yes, pretty enough, but the construction is pitifully shabby. Why, one wrong move and its owner would be scattering paste pearls behind her as she strode into the ballroom. Now, what were you saying?"

Clarice was still looking at the reticule. "I don't remember. Shabby?"

Knowing Mrs. Yothers most definitely was in earshot by this time, Dany replied, "Oh, yes. These shops mix the bad in with the good, hoping no one will notice. My mother explained that all to me before I came to London." She leaned forward to whisper none too quietly in Clarice's ear. "I'd wager you a new lace handkerchief that the sheen would slide right off those pearls if so much as a drop of rain fell on them."

There, that will fix you for the moment, Mrs. Yothers. Because you're guilty as sin of something, I just know it!

"Really?" Clarice's whisper was about as effective as Dany's. "So if I were to sort of, well, spit on my fingers, and then just happen to rub one of those pearls…?"

"Good afternoon, ladies!" Mrs. Yothers exclaimed brightly, all but tripping over herself as she made her way past another table and approached them. "I beg your forgiveness for not realizing Hilda wasn't assisting you. Stupid girl, always wandering off. Oh, my, Miss Foster, isn't it? Yes, of course. And if you'll pardon me for being so bold as to inquire, how is your sister the countess?"

"Quite well, thank you," Dany said, trying not to laugh as the clever shopkeeper surreptitiously covered the pearl-laced reticule with a patterned scarf she'd brought with her from the other display table, "and still so delighted with the gowns she chose."

"How…delightful," Mrs. Yothers responded, her brow furrowed as if she might be pondering the wisdom of her next statement. "Have you yet found the time to enjoy the book I gave you, miss?"

"Alas, not yet. I've been otherwise occupied."

As you'll know soon enough, or perhaps already do know, even if you're not letting on that you do. None too tall, are you, Mrs. Yothers? The sort who might need to step on a stool in order to reach high places? Please be guilty. It would make things so much easier if you were guilty.

"Well, now, isn't this too lovely and chummy," Clarice said, her words pleasant, her tone far from it. "I'm certain Miss Foster was raised to be polite, and is willing to stand here while you make nonsense conversation all the afternoon, but I am not. Kindly take yourself off, and take that sorry excuse for a reticule with you. Don't think I didn't see you attempt to hide it. Imagine what would happen if I were to tell the duchess! We'll summon you if we need you."

For a moment Mrs. Yothers appeared ready to remind her customer that she was not about to be dismissed from her own shop, but then apparently thought better of it.

She curtsied, first to Clarice, then to Dany, mumbled something about finishing up Hilda's neglected chore of refolding the scarves and took herself off.

Dany took hold of Clarice's arm and walked the two of them a few steps closer to the corner. "You're probably going to rule Society, you do know that, don't you?" she told her new friend. "I don't believe there's a soul alive, chimney sweep to king, who doesn't tread warily around those who might open their mouths at any moment to say just what they think."

"Jerry doesn't believe that. He'd rather I just smiled and curtsied for some space of time yet, perhaps until the spring Season. As it is, he can't wait to get me out of London, the dear thing. As if I'd go. Oh! I remember now why I was so happy to see you. Jerry told me something yesterday, something truly extraordinary and impossible and, even worse, true. But I'm not supposed to repeat what he told me. Naturally, I'm bursting at the seams to do so. Please let me tell you."

Sensing Mrs. Yothers hovering even though she'd

turned her back to the woman, Dany said, "If it's true, then I suppose it wouldn't be gossip, would it?"

"That's the spirit!" Clarice rubbed her palms together and bent her head close. "You've met Darby, haven't you? I'm sure Jerry told me you did. Darby Travers, Viscount Nailbourne? He has that patch over his eye and all? Handsome devil, if a bit too amused, if you take my meaning. Gabe—Thea's fiancé—is a happy soul, and up to most any mischief, and Coop is so upright and commonsensible, while my Jerry is very nearly their pet, bless him, and I'd never say such a thing to him. Such good friends, for such a long time. But this?" She shook her head. "Even Jerry is appalled. You're really going to let me tell you?"

Dany wondered which one of them, Mrs. Yothers or herself, would be the first to grab Clarice Goodfellow by the throat and choke this supposed secret out of her.

But she managed to retain an outward calm as she nodded. "If only to ease your mind, Clarice. Yes, I'll hear your secret."

"Damned well about time," the young woman whispered, this time so that Mrs. Yothers couldn't hear her. Dany barely heard her, but she was fairly certain she knew what Clarice was saying.

Now the girl took a deep breath, held it for some moments and finally said: "He owns a brothel. Him. The viscount of Nailbourne."

Dany gave a quick shake of her head, as if she hadn't quite understood what she'd just heard. In truth, she was having some difficulty believing this was the secret Mrs. Yothers was to hear. "Pardon me? You couldn't possibly have that right. Could you?"

Clarice gave a rather haughty push at her blond curls. "My Jerry doesn't lie."

"No, no, of course not. I wouldn't imply any such thing. But this is terrible, Clarice. Very nearly as scandalous as if he'd gone into trade. My parents have been most clear on that point. Rather a privateer than a coal merchant. But this is worse, isn't it?"

"Jerry thinks so. He said the brothel is right here in Mayfair, and that would mean that the viscount is rubbing shoulders with the men who pay to use his services. I mean, not *his* services. But the services he provides. Is that what I mean?"

"I'm sure I have no idea," Dany lied, wishing she hadn't listened so well to her brother when he was telling her things she shouldn't know. "Clarice, Rigby was wrong to tell you. I understand you must have been bursting to tell someone, but now you can't tell anyone else. Not a single soul. The viscount would be ruined. Disgraced. Forced to leave Society."

Was that enough, or should she add a few more hints?

Clarice was vigorously nodding her agreement, so Dany decided she had made herself clear.

"Good. Now we'll not speak of this again. Truly, it's something we shouldn't know, should we? Although I wonder if Coop knows. I may just tell him. But only him, and nobody else. This is our secret now, Clarice. And a terrible one it is. Why, it's put me quite out of countenance. I don't think I could look at a single thing in the shop today, even as I'd returned specifically to select materials for a few gowns my sister promised me. Shall we leave now, and hope you haven't chased Rigby too far?"

They hadn't. As soon as Dany stepped outside the shop she saw Rigby nervously pacing the flagway.

"There you are!" he exclaimed while Clarice held out her hands to him, as if they were meeting after an intolerably long separation. "Did you do it? Did she hear you? Where are your packages? Don't say you didn't buy anything. That would be too suspicious."

"I'm not such a sad looby," Clarice scolded as she slipped her arm through his and Dany joined them for what appeared to be a walk to the corner. "The bonnets will be sent to Grosvenor Square, but I allowed Dany to talk me out of the reticule, just as you wanted."

"Ah, caught out, am I?" Dany said, laughing. "What gave me away?"

"Nothing," Clarice told her as she winked. "I was merely guessing. Shame on you, Jerry. You just had to say no."

"I would never say no to you, Clary. I wouldn't know how."

You'll always have a choice, Dany. That's a promise.

Two men. Saying two very different things. Yet both employing that same suddenly serious tone.

What did it mean? Did it mean anything? Rigby was a man in love. Coop was...well, he wasn't, that's all. Why, they barely knew each other.

She spied him as the trio turned the corner. He was standing beside his coach, propping up a light post, his arms folded, his feet crossed at the ankle. He looked like a man bored to flinders, and she felt a sudden mad desire to fling herself into his arms.

Rigby and Clarice gifted him with cheery hellos before climbing into the coach, but Dany stopped right in front of him to say, "Brothel? That couldn't have been your idea."

"True enough. Darby picked it. He wanted something salacious. Do you know what comes next?"

"I do, or at least I think I do. We come back when the shop closes this evening, and then hopefully get the chance to follow Mrs. Yothers as she goes racing off to meet with her blackmailing employer."

Coop held out his hand to assist her into the coach. Once they were settled on the squabs and dutifully ignoring Clarice and Rigby, who were greeting each other as if parted for years (and why did she feel suddenly jealous?), he corrected her assumption.

"Darby has all of that in hand. *We* are attending the theater, to see and be seen, as last night's dinner table gossip will have spread to every corner of Mayfair by then, and it's important we make an appearance. We can't have the world thinking you've locked yourself in your bedchamber, hiding from the man who compromised you, now, can we?"

Dany pointed to the cooing lovebirds on the facing seat. "Do we have to do *that*?"

Surely he couldn't hear that smidgen of hope in my voice.

Coop smiled. "God, no. Nobody does that. Only the two of them. Unless, that is, you believe it necessary."

"I don't think so, no," Dany said with all the conviction she could muster, stealing another peek at her new friends, who apparently had remembered where they were and broken off their kiss. Either that, or they'd run out of air. "Do you really think it will work?"

"That?" Coop asked rather incredulously, also pointing at his friends.

"No, of course not. The viscount flushing out the blackmailer. That is what you want, isn't it? Mrs. Yothers taking him information he can use to further line their pockets?"

"You'll pardon me for not always running fast enough to catch up with your mind as it skips ahead like a flat stone skimmed across a pond. But that is the plan, yes."

"You should have spoken with me before you launched it, you know. Or did you consider the possibility that Mrs. Yothers is not involved with the blackmailer, and is only a silly gossip, so that our *engagement* may be completely overlooked as the world turns as one on the viscount?"

Coop muttered something under his breath.

"Pardon me? I don't believe I quite caught that," Dany said, feeling rather smug.

"I said, men shouldn't think when they drink. I believe we did consider that possibility, but not seriously. I suppose we'd better hope Mrs. Yothers is guilty, shouldn't we?"

"Yes, *we* most certainly should. You men should also confine yourselves to war, and leave intrigue to the ladies. We're much better at it. A brothel. I suppose that's better than saying he murdered his valet, or some such thing."

"That also was considered, but Darby pointed out that then he'd be forced to polish his own boots, which he deemed totally unacceptable for a man of his stature."

Dany looked at Coop in astonishment but quickly noticed the twinkle in his eyes—those marvelous green eyes, more priceless than any emerald—and the two of them fell against each other in shared laughter.

It was as if they'd known each other forever. And wasn't that wonderful? They had bumped up against the edge of ridiculous and, oh, what a marvelous collision it was.

Dany could believe they were simply two people who had met and liked each other, and could possibly be passing beyond mere liking and on to something else, something perhaps even rare and magical. For this moment, these few fleeting moments, it could be believed that their lives were perfect.

Save for the blackmailer, the chapbooks, Mari's letters and her soon-to-return husband, a totally ridiculous engagement and the constantly ticking clock hanging over all their heads…

CHAPTER TWELVE

Coop believed he had never so enjoyed an evening at the theater, and he had yet to more than occasionally glance toward the stage. There could be dancing elephants in pink tulle skirts twirling on the boards for all he knew, or cared.

Watching Dany's reactions to all that was transpiring around them was so much more entertaining. She was by turn amused, dismayed, curious, as excited as any child, and just the once, had waggled her fingers (the hand with the emerald riding atop the glove) at a rude dowager across the way who had aimed her lorgnette at their box, until the woman looked away in shame.

Not that most every eye hadn't been directed at them at one time or another once they'd entered the box and taken up the chairs in the front row. There was nothing like the ton to speed news across all of Mayfair with the velocity of a volley of loosed arrows.

At the moment, Dany was leaning slightly forward, her toes tapping, as the corps de ballet—Coop believed they were meant to be angels—performed on the stage. After all, there were wings involved, although most Covent Garden dancers were, as a group, farther from innocent angels than most any group Coop could think of. Darby, it was rumored, had bedded all of them.

Darby had probably launched that rumor.

In any event, this evening Dany and he were the guests of the Duke and Duchess of Cranbrook, who insisted on the more informal Uncle Basil and Aunt Vivien, which was what Coop, Darby, Rigby and of course Gabe had called them in their youth, when they were frequent guests at Cranbrook Chase and Basil was still thrice removed from the dukedom, intent only on staying as distant from responsibility as a generous allowance permitted.

But one by one, Basil's older brothers, each just on the eve of their sixtieth birthdays, had, or so it was told to Coop by Gabe, unexpectedly opened their eyes wide, said something on the order of "Erp?" and mere seconds thereafter shuffled off this mortal coil for "a better place."

Eventually, the trio of *erps* left Basil the dukedom and, as he was approaching his sixtieth birthday in November, the notion that he was next. He had fallen into a sad decline, refusing to leave his rooms at the ducal estate. Boosting the man from his doldrums had fallen to Gabe, which meant Coop, Darby and Rigby were immediately called upon for their assistance.

Them, and the parrots.

Basil had gone from a man hiding from his own fate to a happy fellow who, if he was going to have to die, would make the most of his remaining time. He now spent that time doing what he pleased, when it pleased him, and chasing a giggling Vivien around the bedroom. He did a lot of the latter, and not always in the bedroom.

Not that there was anyone, Gabe included, who was about to point out that, since Clarice was living under their roof; they just might be setting a bad example for

Miss Goodfellow and her ardent Rigby when it came to public displays of affection.

As if Clary and her Jerry gave a fig for conventions. Clarice was Rigby's first love, and love had fairly slammed him in the face like the broad end of a shovel, convention be damned. Their wedding, slated for Christmas at Cranbrook, couldn't come too soon.

Just as Gabe's marriage to his Thea, especially as he was heir to the dukedom, had only been put off until after the duke's birthday celebration—or funeral, whichever way a gambling man might wager in the clubs.

Lovebirds. Coop knew he was surrounded by lovebirds. Thank God for Darby, the happily dedicated bachelor who had— Wait a moment. Hadn't Darby been in on the plan to have his good friend compromise Dany into a betrothal?

Why would he have done that? Why had there been such a twinkle in his eye as he'd convinced Coop it was a necessary strategy if they were to catch out the blackmailer?

And then he remembered. They'd been at Oliver's residence that first day—and how long ago it seemed now. Darby had said that he was an observer, and Dany had asked him what he was observing at the moment. That's when he'd looked at Coop for a long moment in that *way* he had and said, "No, not today. I think I'll wait. It might be safer." And then he'd made an excuse to leave Coop and Dany alone.

No, that's impossible. The viscount Nailbourne in the role of matchmaker? He couldn't have seen something neither of us saw. Still don't see.

Do we?

Do I?

Coop looked over at Dany, who was still tapping her foot, even sighing in pleasure, as the angels continued their hopping, skipping dance about the stage. There was so much joy encased in that small body, so much energy and love of life. Clearly, she wanted to stand up and dance.

Suddenly he wanted to dance with her, right here, at this very moment, and the world be damned. He, Cooper Townsend, good friend, granted, but occasionally accused of being a bit of a sobersides, voluntarily making a cake of himself?

Had Dany caused this change in him?

Was there another answer?

No, none that he could think of at any rate.

It was as if she'd been fashioned especially for him, to shake him awake, make him realize all he'd been missing by being so rigid and commonsensible. Why should the duke be the only one to see life as something to be enjoyed to the hilt?

But now what? This was a temporary betrothal; he'd promised Dany as much. Damn Darby for a troublemaking soothsayer; now what should he do?

"Look at the third one from the left, dearies. Her plump bakery shop bouncing and jiggling like blancmange. She could do with a wide strip of linen tied around her bosoms, to my way of thinking. Many more years of flapping those things about and they'll be at her knees."

Thunk. Welcome back to reality, old sport. Unexpectedly tumbling into love isn't your only problem.

How had he forgotten that his mother was seated in the row directly behind them, and what were the chances he'd be killed instantly and painlessly if he stood up and threw himself out of the box and down into the pit below?

"Minerva, please, you can't say things like that around…" he said, but then closed his mouth as he realized Dany was laughing. Her slim shoulders shaking, her gloved hands concealing a wide grin. Why, there were tears gathering in her eyes from attempting to hold back her amusement.

"Ah, sterling. Just testing," Minerva said in some satisfaction, sitting back on her chair once more, tossing one end of her just-short-of-garish purple pashmina stole around her neck as if pleased with a mission successfully accomplished. "She'll do nicely, Cooper, just as Darby said. You may keep her. Although you may want to tell Ames to remove some of the starch from *your* collars."

His mother would never change, and he loved her. Dany was not his mother, but she clearly delighted in nonsense. Maybe that combination wasn't as bad as it might have seemed a day earlier. Actually, the two of them, together, could be fun, if fun was the correct word. Still, he had to say something, admonish his mother in some way. "Mother—"

Applause rose around them at that moment, and for an instant Coop wildly thought both Minerva and Dany would stand up and curtsy to the audience. But it was only Intermission, and an unforeseen rescue as he grabbed Dany's hand and all but mowed down Rigby and Clarice as he dragged her past a canoodling duke and duchess in the shadows, and out of the box.

"Where are we going?" she asked him as he raced her along ahead of any other patrons also intent on escaping their boxes for a bit of air and refreshment. "And can we get there before anyone can follow us?"

Coop turned to grin at her, because once again she had peeked into his mind and seen his intentions. "Had enough of our jolly friends for a while, have you? The royal box is empty and curtained, and only five boxes down this way. It's our best option."

Carefully looking in all directions to be certain they weren't observed, he then pushed back the velvet curtains and entered the royal box. Because the front of the box was also draped shut, the move cast the two of them into near-total darkness.

"Won't we be arrested and clapped in chains if anyone discovers us in…"

He didn't allow her to finish. He was too intent on turning her about, pulling her into his arms and taking possession of her incredibly enticing full mouth.

To silence her, of course.

Bloody hell that was the reason!

Perhaps she'd sneaked a few lessons from Rigby and Clarice's performance earlier in the coach, because this time there was nothing wooden or missish about her response to his kiss. Instead, she rather melted against him, even as her arms slid up his chest and she wrapped her hands around his neck.

His reaction to this unexpected capitulation was anything but that of a seasoned seducer.

His throat seemed to swell, his heart rate doubled and damn if there wasn't a small show of fireworks going on behind his eyelids.

Other parts of his body reacted in a purely masculine way.

She seemed to notice that, as well. And not shy away.

Coop deepened the kiss, sliding the tip of his tongue inside her mouth, tasting her sweetness, marveling when she returned ardor for ardor. His thigh somehow found its way between hers and he moved his hand down to cup her firm round bottom, move himself against her.

He broke the kiss but not their embrace, moving his mouth along the side of her throat, pressing kisses against the exposed skin above the neckline of her modest gown, lightly squeezing her breast as she threw back her head in the age-old signal of acceptance.

Coop, with the last shreds of sanity he retained, knew he had to stop. This was not the time, and most definitely not the place.

And who knew she'd be so willing? God, she was willing.

It was that thought that truly stopped him.

He had to know. Curse him for a fool, he had to know.

He put his hands on her shoulders and put a careful six inches between them, attempting to make out her expression in the darkness.

"Are you in any way serious, or is this just another adventure?"

The sound of her palm hitting his cheek could not be considered one heard 'round the world, or even outside the royal box, but it was one totally deserved, and Coop knew it.

"Oh, God, Dany, I'm…"

"Not another word, my friend. You've more than dug this particular hole deep enough. Although I was going to stop you, anyway, for the sake of my own delicate sensibilities."

Coop and Dany turned as one, to see the dark outline of one Darby Travers standing just to the left of the railing overlooking the theater.

"How did you…?"

"Where else were you going to go?" Darby interrupted, stepping toward them to bow over Dany's hand. "I knew you couldn't remain in the duke's box throughout the entire evening, not without running stark, staring mad into the streets, and this was so wonderfully convenient. Or am I wrong, and Minerva is behaving herself?"

"She was behaving exactly like Minerva," Coop said, putting a protective arm around Dany's shoulders—why, he didn't know, since he could be considered the enemy at the moment. "But Dany has passed muster by allowing herself to be amused."

Dany shook off his light embrace and wrapped her silk shawl more closely around her. "If I may be allowed to speak?"

"I don't know," Darby said. "Coop, do we dare?"

"I'd ask you to go away," Dany said in some heat, "but that would only amuse *you*, my lord. Why are you here? Aren't you supposed to be following Mrs. Yothers?"

"Ah, dear lady, but I am. Or at least I was. I followed her directly here from her shop. She purchased a ticket, stepped inside, ignored the staircase to the highest balconies and made her way to a box situated directly across from this one, as coincidence would have it. Conveniently, at least for us, she extracted a folded paper from her reticule before stepping inside the box. She tarried inside but a moment, and is now on her way back to same said shop, I'd imagine, having delivered her missive to her—I suppose I should say *employer*?"

"Tipping him to the carefully fed gossip about you."
Coop took a step toward his friend. All right, they were
making progress. "Good, at least something is going as
planned. Who occupies the box?"

"Yes, that's where it gets a bit sticky. I suppose now
I have to reveal that I was using the royal box as a vantage point, to see who occupies that box, and that you
shocked me all hollow when the two of you stepped in
here and began— Well, that's enough of that."

"I knew you weren't that perceptive," Dany said with
readily apparent satisfaction. "But you are lucky, I will
admit to that."

Darby touched his fingertips to his patch. "That's
me, Miss Foster. I've been basking in good fortune all
my life."

"Oh. I'm so sorry…"

"Don't fall for that one, Dany," Coop warned her. "If
the ball had been an inch lower we'd be putting posies
in front of his headstone once a year."

"But that's not lucky, it's only *less* unlucky," Dany
pointed out in what Coop had come to understand to
be typical Daniella Foster logic. "Again, I'm sorry, my
lord. But if I may admit to a concern I've had ever since
my trip to Mrs. Yothers's shop this morning? What if
Clarice and I weren't as convincing as we supposed,
and all Mrs. Yothers wrote in her note this evening is
that we're onto her?"

"Does it matter, Miss Foster?"

"No, I suppose not, unless you've set your heart on
being blackmailed, but it would be disheartening to believe we were that unconvincing. Now, tell us who is
sitting in the box."

"Doesn't cling to things until they become maudlin,

does she?" Darby joked, and then suggested they vacate the royal box before someone else got the bright idea for a quick assignation at the king's expense.

They exited carefully, Coop and Dany both, and were followed a few moments later by the viscount, who promptly propped himself against the wall, so that Dany and Coop had no option but to become his audience.

"Prepare to be amazed, my friend, although I suggest you don't so forget yourself as to exclaim, 'Aha! Now it all makes sense!' Which, by the way, it does, even as, considering the objects of his blackmail, I suppose my secret is safe with him. In case you still were worried, Miss Foster."

"Could you just please get on with it," Coop said, shaking his head. "I've realized you're only amusing when you're teasing someone other than me."

"I never tease. I build anticipation. But very well. The box itself, to the best of my recollection, belongs to the ancient and revered Lanisford family, with Ferdinand Lanisford serving as the current marquis. You remember Ferdie, don't you, and a certain event?"

It didn't take long for Coop to jog his memory. Ferdie had been at school with them for three terms, and a more repulsive specimen would be difficult to imagine. He whined, he bullied, he snitched on his mates. He screwed his badly dyed hair into a near corkscrew at the top of his head; he dressed rather like a circus clown, brayed like a donkey when he laughed and often smelled like one, as well.

"Oliver was with me that night, and a few others," Coop said, nodding. "Yes, Darby. *Aha.*"

Dany looked from one to the other, clearly frustrated.

"Is anyone going to explain any of this to me? Why are we suddenly talking about Mari's husband?"

"Later, Dany, please. For now, who else was in the box?"

"Ferdie, of course, his lovely fiancée, Sally Bruxton—you once thought her a pretty little thing, I believe. That was before the frown lines, I'm sure. Knowing her father's gambling debts, I imagine this is not a love match."

"Just the names, Darby," Coop said as Dany looked ready to open her mouth yet again.

"Now you're forcing me to admit I don't know the name of the other person present. However, after observing the box through a slight gap in the draperies, I believe the gentleman seated behind the happy pair could be Miss Bruxton's brother. I seem to remember him only as being vastly unmemorable. The sole other occupant is a maid, sitting in the shadows at the rear of the box. And now, just to prove that our dear Miss Foster is not the only one who can flit from subject to subject—do you happen to remember who else was with you and Oliver that night? We may want to have small chats with them tomorrow."

"I don't have the faintest idea what he's talking about," Dany said, tugging on Coop's jacket sleeve, "but I want to chat, as well. *Now.* My lord, you are excused."

"I beg your…"

"I don't think begging would work," Coop said, laughing. "But don't depart in complete haste, if you please—at least not before stopping by the duke's box and informing Minerva that Miss Foster has developed the headache and I'm escorting her home."

"I don't have my reticule. Besides, she won't believe that obviously trumped-up story," Dany pointed out.

"No, but she won't kick up a fuss, either," the viscount countered. "None of them will, or haven't you already noticed that adhering to convention isn't of paramount importance to any of them."

"Well, I like them, my lord," Dany replied staunchly. "I like them all."

"As do we all, Miss Foster," Darby said, bowing in her direction. "Sometimes, however, not all in one bunch, at least when not armed with a large bucket of cold water. And yet, friend to the end, I'll now take myself off to do as I'm bid. Coop? Until later?"

Coop felt Dany's gaze on him and turned to smile at her. "What can I say? He's my friend."

"And a good friend," Dany answered, slipping her arm through his as they made their way through the throng of theatergoers on their way back to their boxes as Intermission was signaled to a close. "But he does see a lot for a man with only one eye, doesn't he? At the very least, he could have said hello, or at least cleared his throat or something when we entered the royal box."

"Until I spoke, I imagine he didn't know the identity of his fellow occupants," Coop pointed out as they made their way down the first long flight of stairs to the street. "It was nearly dark as pitch in there."

"He heard what you said. He heard the sound of my slap."

"What I said was inexcusable. Your response was quite in keeping with the gravity of my indiscretion."

"Oh, piffle. I only slapped you because otherwise I would have had to answer you, and I didn't have an answer. Not that you should have asked. You might want to stop doing that, asking decidedly personal questions

I can't answer, at least until I can think up another way to divert you."

"I can think of several, just off the top of my head."

How strange. His friends hadn't been able to corrupt him, as it were, in all their years together, yet Dany had managed to strip away whatever *starch* Minerva had always complained about in less time that it took for a cat to lick its ear.

She looked up at him, clearly measuring, digesting his words. He prepared himself for another well-deserved slap.

"I think that was naughty. It was naughty, wasn't it? Is that your coach?"

Coop looked to his left, where she had pointed. The coaches had begun circling the theater, as many patrons departed at Intermission, to move off to another engagement scheduled for the evening. "It is. Like Darby, it would appear our luck is in. And as my coachie has recognized us, he's already stopping."

The steps were let down by the tiger-cum-groom, and Coop handed Dany inside.

"Portman Square, my lord?"

"Not yet, Harry. Please tell Simmons to drive through the park until I signal for a return to Miss Foster's residence."

"Yes, sir! And he's to go right slow, too, sir." And then the lad winked.

Coop looked at the boy curiously. "Aren't you too young to— Never mind. I forgot you've been escorting my mother about town, as well. Carry on."

He settled himself beside Dany, waiting until the coach had moved away from the front of the theater before leaning forward to lift the shades three-quarters of the way and secure them, preserving their anonymity but giving them enough light to at least see past their noses.

She didn't say a word. Which, of course, spoke volumes.

"You'll want me to start at the beginning, I suppose."

"If that means you'll start with Oliver, yes, I think so. You've figured out something, haven't you?"

"Darby did first, I'd have to say, but yes, I believe we now have some answers."

"I had only one question. Who is the blackmailer? Is it this Ferdie person?"

He took her hand and raised it to his lips, and then kept hold of it as he lowered their hands between them. "I want you to think about something, Dany. Have you wondered why the blackmailer singled out your sister for his attentions? After all, there was considerable effort involved on his part. Searching out the premises, finding that knothole. All those letters to write as he cultivated her to the point where she wrote something… well, shall we just say embarrassing about her husband the earl."

"He was *using* her? To get to Oliver? Is that what you're saying? But…but what about the five hundred pounds?"

Coop shook his head, knowing he'd been guilty of the same incorrect assumption. "Ferdie's family is what many would term odiously wealthy. Money never had anything to do with it. Or with me, for that matter. This is a matter of revenge. Inflicting suffering, offering false hope, turning the screw again and again and then applying the coup de grâce, destroying the person. Persons. There was never a way out, not from the beginning."

"Revenge? On you? On Oliver? Why?"

But Coop was still thinking, considering. "It had seemed such a coincidence that two victims of the same blackmailer would learn about each other. And it was, really, except that without mention of Oliver's name, I may have walked away. No, that's not true. Walking away was never an option. A broken heel, a pair of indigo eyes. Fate, intervening. He couldn't have foreseen that, simply proving that no crime can ever be perfect."

Dany squeezed his hand, and not gently. "Could you possibly stop talking to yourself and tell me what you mean? Especially that business about indigo eyes."

He smiled at her in the darkness. "Don't tell me you weren't using them to their best effect when we stumbled on to each other."

"I would *never*— You're grinning at me, aren't you? Never mind. Go on. You have a mutual enemy, you and Oliver. And perhaps there are others, since the viscount asked if you remembered the *names*. Am I guessing correctly so far?"

"Because you're brilliant, yes. Again, I'll begin at the beginning."

"With Ferdie the marquis. Because he's the enemy."

He ran a fingertip down the side of her cheek, and then gave her chin a gentle flick. "Are you telling this story or am I?"

"Sorry. Carry on," she said. She divested herself of her shawl and then snuggled against his side just as if they'd been romantically involved for years and such an action was only natural.

It certainly felt natural, just as raising his arm so

that she could move in closer before he draped said arm around her shoulder felt natural.

Before I beat Ferdie into flinders, I really should thank him...

"Once upon a time," he began, earning himself a playful elbow jab in the ribs, "there was an exemplary student on the subject of military tactics as first presented by the legendary Sun Tzu in his writings, most commonly called *The Art of War.* At the request of several of his fellow students, he agreed to an evening of drinks and conversation."

"You were that student, of course," Dany interrupted, a hint of pride in her voice.

"Your high opinion of me is truly humbling, and I'd like to say I was, but that's not true. I was one of those hoping to learn something that might keep me alive if I ended up facing Bonaparte, which most of us were convinced we would. My friend Gabriel Sinclair was our informal instructor. In any event, we met in a local tavern, and then returned to our rooms as a group, except Gabe, who had caught the eye of one of the barmaids—but that isn't important save for the fact that he wasn't with us."

"But Oliver didn't catch the eye of one of the barmaids. Nor did you. Good."

"I'm relieved that I have your blessing on that, but we weren't feeling all that fortunate at the time," he told her, daring to drop a kiss on her hair.

He could say anything to her. They...they could be two halves of the same person. A person he barely knew, even as he was sure he knew her more than anyone else ever would, and she him.

"Who was with you? The viscount? Rigby?"

"Neither of them, no. I don't remember where they'd gone off to, but I'm certain it had nothing to do with ancient teachings. All right, I have it now. The others were Oliver, Johnnie Werkel, Thad Wallace, Geoff Quinton, Edward Givens and— No, that has to be wrong."

He turned on the seat and took Dany's hands in his own. "There was someone else. David Fallon. He was the youngest of all of us."

"Yes? But what has to be wrong? I can tell you're upset."

Davy's dead, that's what's wrong. He was found hanged in his mother's attic. Rigby was the only one who could travel to the services, but Davy's mother showed him the note he'd left behind: *I can't let it happen, this is the only way. Forgive me.*

"I'm sorry. Davy suffered a fatal accident, not quite six months ago. He'd made it through the war without so much as nicking himself shaving. You're right. It still upsets me."

She put up her hand to stroke his cheek. "I'm sorry, too. What about the others?"

Coop lightly rubbed at the skin she'd touched, mentally taking roll. "Johnnie died on the Peninsula. Thad emigrated, to Jamaica I think it was, to take charge of his uncle's holdings there. We weren't that close. I believe Geoff is in town, and I know where Ned is. The ton turned its back on him when he was exposed as a card cheat, his creditors immediately called in all his accounts and he now resides in the Fleet for debt."

He held up his hand. "Yes, and before you say anything, that suddenly sounds suspicious."

"We really must visit him. I've never been to a debtor's prison. I've read they lower baskets from between the window bars, begging for food and far-things."

"Your family must keep an interesting library. And no, you're not going to visit the Fleet. Besides, you haven't heard the rest of the story."

"Well, that's true enough. You may continue, I suppose."

"Thank you." Coop smiled. "I was heading back to my room, along with the aforementioned others, when we heard a slight whimpering, some low moaning, coming from Ferdie's quarters. Curious, I knocked, only to be told to take myself off if I knew what was good for me. That's nearly an exact quote."

"You didn't, of course. Know what was good for you, I mean. Did you knock again, or simply kick down the door?"

"A little of both," he admitted. "Remember, I'd just come from a tavern, so I wasn't entirely sober, and felt rather opposed to being told what to do, especially by a bas—a person I didn't care for in the first place. Once inside, we discovered someone sprawled on the floor, and not in a pretty state."

"A woman? You said *pretty*. You mean a woman, don't you? Perhaps a female of negotiable affections?"

"You're rather enamored of that phrase, I believe. Yes, a prostitute. Ferdie had taken his riding crop to her. So—" he was having some trouble being so frank, but Dany really did make it easier for him "—so I wrestled the crop from him and returned the favor. Someone, probably Geoff, shouted, 'All or none!' or something similarly ridiculous. In the end, everyone had taken turns with the crop before dumping a now-unconscious Ferdie in front of the dean's door, a note pinned to his shirt, confessing to his crime. I'm not proud of any of that, but we were young, we were all three-parts drunk…and it happened."

"You were young," Dany repeated, nodding her head. "Was he expelled?"

"The woman died the next day, and suddenly Ferdie was gone. The marquis made a sizable donation to the school's chapel, and Ferdie was banished to a distant cousin somewhere in the wilds of north Ireland, not to leave unless he wished to be disowned. I seem to remember that the cousin was some sort of fire and brimstone holy man who had eschewed money, wine, women and most probably indoor privies. And yes, before you ask, we all found great pleasure in hearing that via Ferdie's suddenly unemployed valet. When his father died last winter, Ferdie came into the title. I really don't know more than that."

"Yes, you do. Or you think you do. We're almost there, aren't we?"

He took both her hands in his, lightly rubbing his thumbs over her soft skin. "I'll reserve judgment until I've spoken to Ned and Geoff. But yes, I think we've found our man in Ferdie, although he wasn't the person who brushed past us in the jewelry shop. As to where *we* are, you and I, I have no answer for you."

Dany sighed. "I know. Neither do I. We don't even know each other, do we?"

He leaned in, to whisper his next words in her ear. "How long do you think it takes until two people can be said to know each other?"

Her sigh was rather shaky, and lit a small fire inside him. "Surely longer than two days, don't you think?"

"Perhaps—" he paused, pressed a light kiss against

her ear "—perhaps it takes a lifetime to really know someone else. Or you can know them in an instant, and spend the rest of your life delighting in the knowing."

She moved slightly away from him, although she didn't withdraw her hands. "That sounded lovely, if a bit romantical. My parents are…comfortable. Do you think all people who know each other for a lifetime are comfortable with each other?"

He pulled her closer, knowing he should consider her question carefully. "I'm comfortable with you now."

"Really? That's nice, I suppose."

Nice? Well, wasn't that encouraging?

"You'd rather I were uncomfortable?"

"I suppose I'm thinking about Mari and Oliver, and how she worries that he's…he's not as interested as he had been when they married. I don't think I wish ever to be thought of as a pair of comfortable old slippers."

He smiled. "I'd say you may rest assured that would never happen."

"You say that now. But perhaps we're simply friends. People can strike up friendships quite easily, especially in times of crisis. I already feel as if Clarice is a friend."

Was Dany sounding just a tad desperate? Attempting to find rhyme or reason in feelings she'd not expected and didn't know how to interpret?

Should I tell her I'm struggling with the same attempt?

He changed the subject, if only to give them both a chance to relax.

"This sham betrothal was a mistake, for too many reasons to mention, one of them being we seem to have solved the question of who is the blackmailer with almost stunning ease. In fact, all we've succeeded in doing is warning Ferdie that we know both your sister and I are being blackmailed. Worse, that Yothers woman showing up with gossip about Darby—my good friend Darby, no less—could very well have tipped him off that we'd planted that gossip, and that the woman had done just what we'd hoped, leading us straight to him. At this point, he may go underground."

"Retire from the game, you mean? I don't know the man, of course, but he seems to have gone to a prodigious amount of trouble to seek his revenge. I doubt he'll turn away at the first fence."

Bless her, she was always ready to jump from subject to subject, and put her very good mind to very good use. More discussion of their impromptu proposal would wait for another day.

Coop had a sudden memory of Ferdie's bloody face, where one of the blows from the crop had sliced him to the bone. No, with the scar that wound must have left behind, greeting him in the shaving mirror every morning, it was doubtful he'd give up now.

"Damn."

"Excuse me?"

"Hear me out. Ferdie has had a long time to build on his hate, plot his revenge on us. We fairly well destroyed his life for the past half dozen years or more, maybe forever, in his mind. That's not something easily forgotten. But first he had to figure out how to target his victims, or his oppressors, as that's probably how he sees the thing. Two of them were out of reach—Johnny and Thad—but he's already gotten to two others."

"Two? You said Ned Givens was exposed as a card cheat. Who's the other?"

"Davy. It had to be. I said he'd suffered an accident, but that's not true. He killed himself."

Dany's body went taut with excitement; clearly she loved a mystery, but not as much as solving that mystery. "Because Ferdie was going to expose him? Is that what you're saying? What did he do wrong?"

"Nothing that I know of, but there had to be something."

He loved a man, that's what he did wrong, at least according to the world. What else could he have meant with that note? Somehow, Ferdie had found out, and threatened him with exposure. Lord knew he had enough money in his pockets to buy most any information he wanted.

Including information on me? Yes, of course.

"I'm sorry," she said, putting her hand on his forearm. "This is difficult for you, isn't it?"

"If by difficult you mean it's taking everything in me not to rush you back to Portman Square before hunting the man down to wring his neck, then yes, it's difficult. I have to get to Ned tomorrow. I'm already certain he's in the Fleet because of Ferdie, but I want to hear it from him."

"He did cheat at cards, didn't he?"

"He did in school, but after we skinned him to his unmentionables and ran him up the flagpole by his ankles, he promised never to do it again. Which he didn't, as far as I know, even if it was because no one would sit down with him again. He was really quite good at fuzzing the cards, I'll hand him that, so he may have tried it again, just to keep in practice. What we need to know is if Ferdie had a hand in exposing him."

Dany nodded. "Once we know for certain what we're

already convinced we know, what do we do? Mari needs those letters, Coop, and you need to stop this horrible Ferdie person from publishing another chapbook. Only then can you wring his neck, which I wouldn't suggest doing because people get hanged for that sort of thing and I'd rather miss you."

"How gratifying. No, I learned my lesson that night at school. Giving in to violence is no answer to anything."

"Wait a moment. Is that why you're a sobersides— although I certainly don't think you are, not at all."

"No, that would be my friends, and my own mother," Coop said, hoping she could hear the smile in his voice.

She squeezed his hands. "The others weren't with you, or perhaps they'd feel the same. Your life changed that night, didn't it?"

Her conclusion was something he'd considered. He'd learned that with enough money and position, a person could be bought out of being charged for murder, and that some lives apparently meant less than others. All he could say for certain was that, although they were all of the same age, he'd felt older than his friends after Ferdie than he had before Ferdie.

"At least I didn't swear off strong spirits, or my own mother wouldn't speak to me," he quipped, drawing a smile from her before they could both sink into solemn silence.

"You can't turn him over to the courts," she pointed out, her mind leaping ahead. "Not without exposing Mari, or yourself. So how will you stop him? Really, it's a shame he has no secrets you can reveal, turnabout being fair play and all of that."

"What did you say? No, wait, I heard you. Turnabout is fair play. Dany, you're a genius!"

"I am? Oh, good, at last someone has recognized what I've always believed." She leaned toward him. "How am I a genius?"

"I'm not quite sure yet, but we'll think of something."

"Before I'm too delighted, I'd like you to clarify something for me. When you say *we*, do you mean you and the viscount and Rigby? Or do you mean we, as in the way I'd prefer you say it? As in you and the viscount and Rigby and the genius?"

"I wouldn't take a step without you. I don't think I'd dare."

"Wonderful, because I'd hate having to run to catch up. Still, and even as friends, I think perhaps we should shake on it. You know, to seal the bond, as you men do?"

He saw an opening and, crass as he could consider himself, he took it.

"I'd rather seal the bond the way men and women do."

Or perhaps it was the opening she had sought. With Dany, he knew he would never be sure which one of them, as it were, was driving the coach.

"Well, for goodness' sake, Coop, it's about time. I was about to begin wondering if I'd become repulsive to you now that we're supposedly betrothed."

He relaxed…but he certainly wasn't comfortable. "Or that I'd become too comfortable?"

"Yes, that, as well, I suppose. I fear I may share some of my sister's romantical failings, and would really like it very much if you were to kiss me."

Apparently both of them had a hand on the reins, and seemed to be heading in the same direction.

He closed the gap between them to little more than scant inches. "If you haven't noticed, I've been of the same mind all evening."

She closed her eyes. "Yes, I think I did notice."

"But it's wrong. I mean, for both of us. As a gentleman, shaky as that term is at the moment when applied to me, I still feel I need to point that out."

"I believe most of the world would say so."

He released her hands, to rest his on her shoulders. "Which begs the question—do we care what the world says?"

Now she looked at him, her indigo eyes looking black as the deepest part of the sea. "I should say we do, that *I* do. Would you mind if I didn't?"

"No," he breathed, just before finally closing the gap between them. "I don't mind at all."

CHAPTER THIRTEEN

HIS LIPS WERE cool against hers—for what else could cause a shiver to run down her spine at his merest touch?—and Dany instinctively pressed her body closer to his, to take in his warmth.

The heat was sudden and intense.

Gone was the teasing, the pleasant camaraderie. Friendship had nothing to do with what she was feeling now. It couldn't.

This was something new, different.

This was desire.

And she liked it.

Maybe it is the red hair, she thought before she decided not to think anymore. She much preferred to feel.

Coop's kisses were short, teasing, testing and tasting, as if gauging her response, her willingness.

She wanted to grab on to his ears and pull him firmly against her, because if he were testing her, he'd soon learn that he was politely driving her mad.

So Dany wrapped her arms about his neck, lifted her feet off the floor, swinging them onto his lap, and deliberately propelled herself backward.

Down they went, onto the tufted velvet squabs, their mouths still locked together. Coop somehow sorted out arms and legs until he was lying half-beside her, their lower limbs comfortably entangled, holding her securely so that she didn't topple to the floor, which would be embarrassing as well as probably putting an end to this exciting interlude.

He was kissing her face now, more of those quick, tantalizing kisses.

And talking.

Good Lord, why is he talking?

"You're so beautiful."

Aren't you sweet? Now hold still and kiss me again. Kiss me a thousand times. Yes, like this. Just like this. Kiss me all night long...

Her mouth opened half in shock, half on a sigh, when she felt his hand on her breast. Cupping her. Rubbing his thumb over her until her nipple responded by going taut, sending unsettling sensations throughout her body, but mostly spreading low, to her belly, and beyond.

He was kissing her. He was touching her. His breath had become fairly ragged, just like hers. She'd dug her fingertips into the cloth of his jacket, able to feel his shoulder muscles, and now wished the jacket gone, even his shirt gone, so she could press her hands directly against his strength.

It had to be the red hair. Or Coop.

They were two people in the most awkward of physical positions, in the most complicated of contrived engagements, behaving like any other two people who couldn't be close enough, couldn't hold back, were no longer in control of the situation they had created.

Something else had taken over, and was apparently very much in charge.

And I've known this would happen from the first moment I fell into his arms. Two days, two weeks, two years. What did time matter? Because I knew. I think he did, as well...

Dany couldn't hold back a soft, anguished moan when Coop broke their kiss, moved his hand from her breast.

But then he was kissing her again, trailing those kisses along the side of her throat, down onto her chest, at the same time managing to slide her gown from her shoulder.

When he took her into his mouth, Dany knew that whatever she had felt before this moment in her life had been nothing. Not happiness, not sorrow, not pain nor pleasure. Nothing compared with the waterfall of feelings pouring through her now. Hunger. Joy. Fulfillment. Conquest. Surrender. Chinese rockets exploded behind her eyes, filling her world with color.

She pressed her lower body against his, raising herself up because it felt natural to do so, and encountered his strength, his ardor.

He wanted her.

She wasn't the baby sister anymore, the too-inquisitive one, the impetuous one, the dare-anything, risk-everything, trust-too-easily bane of her mother's existence.

Or maybe she was in the process of proving that she was all of those things.

Coop lifted his head, slid her gown back in place. He looked down at her in the near darkness.

"You're right," he said, as if he'd read her mind. "We're not ready for this."

"We aren't?" She hoped he didn't hear the mix of relief and disappointment in her voice.

He kissed her, a long, drugging kiss, the sort that had

started all this in the first place. She'd remind him of that, except then maybe he wouldn't do it again.

"We won't give this up," he said as he broke the kiss, long enough for them both to breathe, and then took her mouth once more, even as he righted them on the squabs.

"Stay right there," he said, dropping a kiss on her nose before shifting to the facing seat, in order to open the small door and tell the coachman to proceed to Portman Square.

And then he was back.

And she was waiting.

Each kiss was better than the last, his strong arms around her, her hands on his shoulders, holding him close.

Each time they broke a kiss, she felt a stab of loss go through her, until he healed her with another kiss.

All night. Kiss me all night.

But when the coach came to a halt and the flambeaux outside the earl's mansion turned the interior of the coach brighter, it was time to say good-night.

Dany's bottom lip trembled, and she felt tears stinging behind her eyes.

"Until tomorrow," Coop promised in a tone so sincere her toes curled in her evening slippers.

He kissed the palms of her hands; he pulled her close to take her mouth one last time.

"I don't want to leave you here."

He may as well have told her he loved her. Dany nearly burst into tears, something she never did.

"I don't want you to go," she whispered, astonished at her feeling of loss, even as she could still look into his eyes. "One more?"

She could see his smile as he tilted his head and took her in his arms again.

The door opened, and the tiger reached in to let down the steps.

"You have to go."

"I know."

"Give me your hand so I can help you down."

Dany nodded. Her throat was too full to speak.

Together, the backs of their hands brushing against each other, they ascended the steps to the door of the mansion, where the light was brighter and Society's conventions most definitely ruled.

He kissed her hand as a footman opened the door and Timmerly stepped into the light cast by the candles in the foyer.

"Miss Foster, it has been my pleasure," Coop said, bowing over her hand again. "Good night."

"Good night, my lord," she answered, knowing her eyes were begging him not to leave.

She watched him descend the half dozen steps before he turned, to look at her. "Good night," he said again.

"Yes. Good night."

"There's a chill, Miss Foster," the butler pointed out. "Come inside now and allow Martin to shut the door."

"In a moment."

Coop reached the open coach door and turned once more.

"If it's all right with the countess, I'll call on you to-morrow at noon. We'll go for a drive, perhaps a picnic in Richmond Park if the weather cooperates."

"Noon would be fine. As would earlier," she added, and quickly wiped at a tear that had escaped down her cheek.

Anyone would think he was going off to war, and she might never see him again. Yet that's how she felt. Lost. Bereft.

Coop nodded, and stepped into the coach.

"Now, Miss Foster. The countess would not approve."

"Dany—wait."

She turned to see Coop all but bounding toward her, her scarf in his hand.

"You forgot this," he said, draping it around her shoulders.

Suddenly everything was awkward.

"Th-thank you."

"My pleasure, Miss Foster." He leaned toward her and whispered, "What's his name?"

"His— Oh. Timmerly. Why?"

"Timmerly? A word."

"Yes, my lord? You wanted something?"

"Indeed I do. Bloody shut your eyes," Coop said as he pulled Dany to him for one last, lingering kiss.

This time, when they broke their embrace they were smiling. Smiles that turned to laughter, at the butler's expense, surely, but also laughing at the world, life in general, and with a happiness neither seemed ashamed to show to that world.

"Tomorrow," Coop said, and bounded down the steps once more.

"Harry. To the Pulteney. Quickly, before I change my mind."

The tiger closed the coach door and climbed back up onto the seat next to the coachman. "Queer as folk, all of them, that's what I say," he commented loudly enough for Dany to hear him as the coachman flicked the reins over the horses.

"*Now*, Miss Foster?"

"Yes, thank you," she said as she stepped inside the mansion, still struggling not to laugh. "I'm a sad trial, Timmerly, do you know that?"

"There have been rumors to that effect, yes, miss."

"So you're going to tell the countess?"

"No, miss. His lordship is the hero of Quatre Bras and you are betrothed. Besides, Mrs. Timmerly and I were once young."

"But you're comfortable now."

He cocked his head to one side, as if considering her need for an answer. "There's love, Miss Foster, and then there's love. The first, when it strikes, is all we believe we can wish for."

"And the second?"

He looked at her for another long moment, and something about him seemed to soften. "And the second, the love that remains, sustains, is all we never realized we needed. Good night, Miss Foster."

Dany felt tears stinging at her eyes again, and went up on her tiptoes to kiss the butler's cheek. "Thank you. You're really a very nice man."

Timmerly cleared his throat with an imperious *harrumph*. "I'm nothing of the sort. Upstairs, young lady. Martin, close your mouth."

"Yes, Martin, before a fly wanders into it." Laughing, Dany lifted the front of her skirts and took off up the stairs, feeling light as a feather, almost as if *she* could fly.

"Decorum, Miss Foster," Timmerly called after her. "*Decorum* at all times."

Dany turned at the head of the stairs, ready to ascend

the next flight, but then hesitated. Mari really should know there are two kinds of love.

Besides, she knew if she didn't talk to *somebody* she probably was going to burst!

She crept down the hall on tiptoe, not wanting to alert Timmerly as to what she was doing, knocked lightly on the door of the master's bedchamber and slipped inside. There was still light from the dying fire, and for some unknown reason, a candelabra still burned on a table beside the bed. Was her sister still afraid of the dark? After all these years? She tiptoed across the floor, heading for the partially curtained four-poster.

"Mari? Mari. *Pssst. Mari.*" She pushed the curtains farther apart. "Oh, for goodness' sake, Mari, *wake up!*"

The Countess of Cockermouth, serenely beautiful by day, sat up all at once, and Dany jumped back a step, clapping her hands over her mouth so as to not cry out.

"What do you have on your face?" she asked as her sister pulled off a quilted satin sleeping mask, to blink furiously in the light. "My God, Mari, you're *green*! And why were you wearing that mask? And...and where's your hair?"

"I am not green."

"You are so," Dany said, hopping up onto the bed. She reached out to remove a bit of something that was hanging from Mari's cheek. "And you're *molting.* Ugh!"

Mari put her hands to her face and likewise came away with a little bit of peeling *greenery.* "Now you've gone and ruined it, Dany. The instructions were to wear it for a full twelve hours in order to wake with a dewy, flawless complexion."

"Whose instructions?"

"Mrs. Angelique Sweet, of course. She comes straight from Paris. And before you say it, no, she's not a witch, like that old crone Mama used to visit in the village to buy her elixir, until Papa drank some and took it for himself. But her results are magical. She's a highly respected...purveyor of beauty. All the best ladies of the ton seek her custom."

Angelique Sweet. I'd wager my best new gloves the woman's real name is Agnes Clump and she hails from Cheapside.

"And if all the best ladies of the ton stuck their fingers in their ears and quacked like ducks, I suppose you'd join them in that, too. I can see you all now, marching through the park on your way to wade in the Serpentine."

"You always think you're smarter than me, but you aren't. I have every confidence in Mrs. Sweet."

Dany sniffed the bit of dried potion, which smelled rather like apples, and then sniffed the air...which didn't. "You have something on your hair underneath that toweling, don't you? Or are you hiding a chicken leg you stole from the kitchens?"

Her sister patted the wrapped toweling. "If you must know, Mrs. Sweet's recipe for maintaining a lush, full head of hair does contain some...some chicken fat in it, I believe." She rushed to add, "But she warned me that many women lose handfuls of hair when they're increasing, and this is the one sure way to prevent that. Nourishing the...the follicles, whatever they are."

"Feeding the follicles. With chicken fat," Dany said flatly. "I begin to understand the multitude of bottles and pots on your dressing table." She reached out to put a hand on her sister's. "Don't you know you're already beautiful?"

"Yes, I suppose I do. Mama always says I am her beautiful daughter."

Dany rolled her eyes. Just when she wanted to hug her sister, she said something like that. Lord bless her, she never meant anything mean by what she said. Or perhaps that was the pity of the thing.

Mari plucked at another thin apple scraping. "But being beautiful can be a curse as well as a blessing."

Dany pulled her legs up under her, cross-legged, and rested her elbows on her knees, pretending her sister had her fullest attention. "Not that I'd have reason to either understand or worry about that. But, please, do go on."

"I'd be happy to explain."

Sarcasm was something else that eluded Mari's comprehension. It must be nice to be so completely and dedicatedly involved only with oneself.

Mari unwrapped one side of the toweling and used it to wipe away the drying, flaking green potion. "It's simple, really. Oliver saw me and was immediately smitten. He told me that, told me how beautiful I am. But I was four entire years younger then, Dany. If I'm to keep him, to hold him, I have to *remain* beautiful. And—" she sighed soulfully "—clearly I'm failing. Soon I'll be a hag."

Dany was all attention now. She shifted uncomfortably on the bed. What had Coop said to her when she was wishing he'd shut up and kiss her? Oh, yes, she remembered. *You're so beautiful.*

"I think you're wrong," she said, partially to reassure herself. "Men always say things like that. Especially when they're...when they're being romantical."

"And how would you know that?"

Dany blew out her cheeks, and then smiled. "I've read a few of Mama's books."

Mari motioned for her to move so that she could put down her legs and get out of bed. "Oh, that's too bad, Dany. I thought perhaps your *betrothed* kissed you."

"And what do you mean by that?" Dany asked, following her sister to the dressing table and the basin and pitcher of water that sat there. "Not the kissing. The way you said *betrothed*. As if you—how did you— *Emmaline?*"

"It wasn't her fault, so don't fly up into the treetops, for goodness' sake. After my initial jubilation, I got to thinking, that's all. What would the hero of Quatre Bras see in my fresh-from-the-country sister? You only did it so that he could be closer at all times, to help me retrieve my letters. Really, Dany, I'm extremely grateful to both of you. What I don't understand is how you'll manage to cry off without looking the greatest fool in nature. Turning away the hero, that is."

"The debutante who turned off the hero. I imagine it will do wonders to enhance my reputation when I make my formal debut in the spring."

It seemed a reasonable answer. For three full seconds.

Mari was bent over the washbasin but, unfortunately, every word she said was clear as the pealing of a bell— perhaps a death knell. "But, Dany, haven't you realized yet? With me increasing, and probably *huge* by the spring, I can't possibly chaperone you, and Mama swore she would rather have splinters stuck beneath her fingernails than try to ride herd on you in Mayfair.

Your debut is going to have to be delayed again. How old will you be then? I mean, in *real* years?"

"You missed a spot on your forehead," Dany said dully once her sister was done scrubbing at her face and turned around. "I'm going to bed."

"Yes, all right. No, wait. Why did you come bursting in here in the first place?"

"Oh. That. I was… I was just going to say that Coop believes we've identified the blackmailer, and you'll have your letters well before Oliver comes home."

Mari gave a ladylike screech and held out her arms as she raced to gather her sister close. "Oh, you're the best of sisters, Dany. Thank you."

"I'm your only sister," she returned, attempting to avoid being coated with chicken fat and whatever else was clinging to Mari's hair.

"Yes, but you know what I meant. You didn't say. Do you have a name for this horrid blackmailer? Is he anyone I know?"

"No, Coop plays his cards quite close to his chest, as the saying goes," Dany lied. "I'm just the make-believe fiancée, as you so kindly pointed out. I don't know anything more on the subject. You'll be fine. No matter what, Mari, Oliver loves you. Please remember that."

Her sister gave her another hug. "Thank you. I love him *so much*. And now we're going to have a baby, and we'll live happily ever after!"

Dany struggled for humor. "Only if you don't wear Mrs. Sweet's concoctions to bed once he's home. You've given me a lot to think about. Good night."

CHAPTER FOURTEEN

COOP ARRIVED AT the Fleet before ten, having partaken of an early breakfast with Darby, who was now on his way to see Geoffrey Quinton.

Divide and conquer wasn't quite their strategy, but time was of the essence, so they'd split their chores between them.

Besides, Darby had never really cared for Geoff, a man too slow with his brain and too quick with his fists, and had admitted to looking forward to watching the man squirm. "I'm a true believer in taking my pleasure where I can," had been his exact words.

After bribing a burly fellow at the gate, Coop was escorted up several flights of stairs covered in residue of dubious origins, and stood back as the fellow rapped his hairy knuckles on the door to what he presumed to be Ned's cell.

The man *knocked*? As if requiring permission to enter?

Hmm.

"Master Givens," the man called out, his mouth inches from the door. "It's Clem, sir. Oi gots a gentry mort out here wot wants ta see ya. Crossed me palm with a copper and said please, too, jist loik you tol' me real gentry morts do."

The jolly, disembodied voice of Ned Givens came

from the other side of the door. "The gentleman *rewarded* you, Clem? Good on you! By all means, send him in."

Clem reached for the latch, but before he could grasp it, the door opened and nearly took off his nose. A tall, spindly shanked man pushed past them, but not before Coop saw that he had a copper shaving basin, some brushes and other clear advertisements of his trade hanging from a leather strap around his shoulders.

Checking again, to make sure he was correct, and there was no lock on the door, Coop stepped inside what was not a cell at all, but a generously large and tastefully appointed apartment containing other doors leading God only knew where.

There were tall windows. There were draperies. There were couches, chairs, a writing desk, a large fireplace, even bookcases containing a small library. A chandelier hung from the high ceiling.

It all seemed impossible, but then again, Ned had always found a way to land on his feet.

The man himself was standing before a tall dresser equipped with a mirror, and was in the act of tying a pristine white linen neck cloth, as if he planned on taking the air sometime that day.

"Cooper Townsend, is that you I see reflected in this mirror?"

Ned turned around, presenting a face and build that had barely changed since their years at school. The same dark copper hair, the same overabundance of large white teeth and the same slim-shouldered body with its unfortunate tendency to spread in the middle.

"Ned," Coop acknowledged. "You're looking well."

"Expected to see me huddled in a corner, covered in rags and sores, weeping, mumbling incoherently?"

Coop took up a seat on one of the striped blue satin covered chairs. "Very nearly, yes." He spread his arms as if to encompass his surroundings. "How did you manage all this?"

Ned sprawled his frame nearly sideways onto the closest couch, somehow making Coop feel like a starchy-backed headmaster.

"You know why I'm here, don't you?" Ned asked, not waiting for an answer. "That business about fuzzing the cards. Happily, I was forewarned, you understand."

Coop leaned forward. He had to mean Ferdie. "Not really, no. Tell me how you were forewarned."

"I suppose you have a reason for asking. Otherwise, why lower the hero of Quatre Bras to bringing his esteemed self to the Fleet, hmm? Very well. But it will cost you. Five quid."

"You'll have it. And more, if I like your answers."

"I suppose I'll trust you. Never gave me a reason not to, did you? I always admired you for your loyalty, your clear head, your sense of right and wrong. I couldn't even dislike you when you had me run up the flagpole, because you explained why you did it. To point out that actions come with consequences, wasn't that it? Shame I didn't listen better, I suppose."

"Ned?"

"Yes, yes, I'm getting to it. Clearly you're not here to reminisce about our salad days. It was nearly six months ago, as I recall. I received a note, one warning me to pay over a certain sum or else be prepared to be exposed as a card cheat."

"Were you cheating? Not to condemn you, but purely out of curiosity."

"You know I'm not going to answer that. Although I'm a proponent of people doing what they're good at, you understand."

Coop smiled. "That's answer enough. Did you pay this person?"

"Now, Coop, why would I do that? He'd only come back for more, having had success the first run out of the gate. No, I did what was prudent. I *collected* as much money as possible—became quite the social butterfly, although usually only confined to my hostess's card room. I sold all but the furnishings you see around us, and in my bedchamber, all of which I put in the hands of a good friend who delivered them here. I sent a good portion of my wardrobe, my horses and equipages, the family silver and anything else portable to a cousin in Wiltshire, and prepared to meet my fate."

"Your fate being the start of the rumors and the eventual arrival of the duns."

"A rabid group," Ned said, shuddering. "They found me sitting in the only chair remaining in my rented flat, and damn me for a tinker if they didn't fall to fighting over it."

Coop couldn't help but laugh. "And now you're living here."

"Residing here temporarily. And with no dint of fellow residents unwilling to sit down at cards with me, which keeps my pockets full so that I have yet to dip into my, shall we say, *capital*. Clem is a good man. I keep him supplied with coppers, and he allows me to join him nights in his favorite pub. There's one barmaid in particular I favor. The duns have fairly well forgotten me, if the ton will never forget. It's not a splendid life, Coop, but it's a good one, and I intend to quietly leave the city soon, winter with my cousin and then set off for adventure. I'm considering Spain, as well as Austria. What do you think?"

"I think you'd want to know who attempted to blackmail you."

Ned shrugged. "Does it matter?"

"It might, if I were to tell you it was Ferdinand Lanisford."

Ned fairly leaped to his feet, his fair cheeks gone scarlet. *"Ferdie?"* From there he progressed to mouthing a string of profanities so inventive, so exquisite in its detail, that at any other time Coop might have applauded.

"Do you want to know why?"

Ned sat down again. "I don't think I have to ask. I also know now why you're here. Ferdie's out to bring us all down, all these years later. 'A man that studieth revenge keeps his own wounds green.' Francis Bacon said that. I've spent much of these past months catching up on my reading."

"He's come after all of us who were close enough to strike at, yes. Oliver for one, me for another. Johnnie died at Waterloo. Thad's in Jamaica, I believe. I'll soon know if he's come after Geoff. Now I've added you to the list."

"You forgot one. What about Davy?"

There was no other way but to say it. "Hanged himself around the same time you ended up here. Leaving behind a note about how it was the only way to keep anyone else from *knowing*."

The two exchanged looks, and then Ned nodded his

understanding. "Poor bastard. He didn't even want to be there that night. What's he holding over your head?"

"That's the devil of it for me. I can't really be sure. It could all be a bluff on Ferdie's part. I just know, as you did, that it isn't money he wants. It's revenge. I only wish I'd realized that sooner."

"You can't be blamed for not thinking like me, Coop," Ned said as he walked Coop to the door, an arm around his shoulders. "I'm a gambler, I think in odds. To me, odds were that whoever it was would come back a second time, and then a third. So I...prepared. You need to prepare, old friend, you and Oliver and Geoff."

The two shook hands, a purse ending up in Ned's.

"Excuse me," a man said, brushing between them and into the room. "Eleven o'clock, Givens. You promised me a rematch."

Coop looked at the well-dressed but faintly shabby about the hems man just then unfolding a card table that had been propped against one wall. "Isn't—isn't that...?"

"It certainly is. All sorts end up in the Fleet from time to time, him only until his next quarterly allowance, or so he says. There are several apartments here for those who can afford them, you understand, although I shamefully would declare mine to be one of the best. I've no end of whist partners eager to part with their money. I may leave here a very rich man."

"You'll be all right, won't you, Ned," Coop declared, stepping through the doorway.

"I always am. Now go take the bastard down. For Davy. For all of us. I can't think of a better man for the job."

Coop left the Fleet with a smile on his face, which

he believed fairly ridiculous of him considering the circumstances, and stepped onto the street to see Darby standing there, lounging against a lamppost.

"I saw your curricle and sent mine on its way," his friend told him as the two fell into step along the flagway, heading toward young Harry, who was waiting at the corner, growling at any passersby who might be looking too hard at the horses and equipage. "Well? What did you learn?"

"Ned's not subsisting on stagnant water and stale crusts of bread, if that's what you want to know. But you probably want to hear me tell you yes, he was being blackmailed. He was."

"Not unsurprising. Especially since your friend Geoff…"

"Aquaintance. Not friend. They all were. Although I'm beginning to wish I'd gotten to know Ned better. I think he could have taught me a few things."

"About hoarding aces?"

"About life actually. How has Ferdie come after Geoff?"

CHAPTER FIFTEEN

COOP AND DANY drove away from Portman Square beneath a reasonably warm London sun, Harry and a wicker picnic basket behind the curricle seat.

Dany considered the picnic basket a good omen. She wished Harry to John O'Groats or some other place equally distant.

She was fast becoming A Very Bad Person.

Her fingertips itched to stroke Coop's cheek, to run through his hair.

She probably shouldn't imagine any plans beyond that. For now, she could barely look at him without her stomach twisting into knots.

He seemed perfectly in control, however. Almost as if last night hadn't happened. She could only hope he was also hiding his true feelings.

"Excuse me?"

Coop had said something, and she hadn't heard him.

Had the events of last night turned her suddenly stupid? Yes, that was entirely possible. Look at Mari, for goodness' sake.

"I said, I was surprised to have you meet me in the foyer, ready to leave. I was convinced your sister would have had a few questions for me."

Dany brought up a mental picture of Mari as she'd last seen her, weeping over her hot chocolate while holding up a mirror to her red, splotchy face, her usually beautiful dark hair hanging in greasy strands, wet from two washings yet still clearly clinging to the chicken fat.

She couldn't resist.

"I believe she plans to confine herself to her chambers for the next several days. A slight mishap with foodstuffs."

She felt him looking at her and hoped she appeared suitably solemn.

"Foodstuffs? I don't want to know anything more about this, do I?" he asked.

"I don't think so, no. Suffice it to say, although I'm confident she'll be fine, she told me she doesn't care where I go, what I do, nor whom I do it with, as long as I don't say, 'I told you so,' one more time. You and I, Cooper Townsend, are free as birds."

Coop reached over and squeezed her hand. "I don't know that I'll ever be free again. And before you fly up into the boughs, little bird, I'm deliriously happy about that."

"Oh." Dany took in a breath, not deep, because even shallow breaths seemed suddenly difficult with her chest feeling as tight as it did. "We rather made fools of ourselves last night, didn't we?"

She waited for an answer.

"Well? Aren't you going to say something?" she asked at last.

"Oh, you wanted some sort of validation?"

She rolled her eyes. He loved to tease her, obviously. And she apparently loved to be teased. "You could tell me I'm wrong. That might help, yes."

He turned to her, his smile knees-melting. "Forgive me. I was fully occupied in contemplating how we might be *foolish* again today."

Dany bit her bottom lip to keep from laughing. "I like a gentleman with a fine mind."

"And I like an honest woman. But first, we do have to talk. Darby and I learned a few things earlier today."

"You visited the Fleet?" Dany allowed herself to be diverted. After all, one couldn't think about being *foolish* all of the time. Although she'd have to delve more deeply into reasons why they shouldn't. "Was it a dreadful place?"

"Most of it, I'm sure. Ned Givens, on the other hand, apparently lives better than half of London. He explained that he was *prepared* to be clapped in the Fleet, and made appropriate arrangements. And before you ask, yes, Ferdie demanded money or else he'd expose him as a cheat."

Dany tipped her head to one side, considering this, what *prepared* meant.

"How did he know this Ferdie person would expose him in any case?"

"He didn't know it was Ferdie. He just knew that if he met with success, the hopeful blackmailer would be back for more money until Ned's well ran dry, and probably then expose him, anyway. Ned didn't like the odds."

"Never play at cards with the man," Dany warned, but then she smiled. "I wish you'd taken me with you. I think I would have enjoyed your Mr. Givens."

"I thought of that, yes. Now do you want to hear what Darby learned about Geoff Quinton?"

"I suppose. If he's also being blackmailed by Ferdie— such a silly name, Ferdie. I can't seem to stop saying it."

"I'm happy it amuses you. I'm not feeling inclined to find anything silly about the man right now."

"Your friend Davy." Dany nodded. "I'm so sorry."

"Yes, so am I. Sorry for Oliver, for Ned, and I reserve some pity for myself, if truth be known. But not for Geoff Quinton. Unless we should feel sorry for him now that he seems to have suffered a broken arm."

"He's—he's had an accident?" she asked, although she was fairly certain she knew the true answer. "Darby visited him this morning. Was the man injured before the viscount arrived?"

"No, he wasn't. I understand he was in his dining room, shoving dripping eggs and kippers down his gullet. And before I say more, let me tell you again how wonderful it is that I can speak freely to you, without fear you won't understand, or that you'll swoon or some such thing."

"Thank you?"

"You're welcome. And stop looking at me that way or Harry is going to receive an education he's too young for at this moment. And here we are," he said, pulling the curricle onto a narrow lane. "I'll answer your questions soon enough."

They rode in silence for at least a half mile before he brought the horses to a halt once they'd arrived at a wonderfully thatched and cross-barred cottage, the sun shining off dozens of mullioned windows. It was at least five times the size of any cottage she'd ever seen.

"I admit I haven't been paying attention ever since we left London behind," Dany said as he helped her to the ground, looking about the grassy, parklike setting. "Where are we?"

"Just outside Wimbledon. This is Darby's estate, or

should I say one of them. It's currently in dust covers, and with only a skeleton staff, as he didn't see the point of residing here just for the short Little Season, and prefers his mansion in town."

"Yes, of course, I certainly can see his point," Dany said, tongue in cheek. "Is he here?"

"Mercifully, no. But he did suggest we picnic here. Do you mind?"

Dany nearly snorted at the absurdity of that question. "No, I suppose not. We do need to…talk."

Coop took her hand. "There's a gazebo, discreetly located behind the house, beside the stream. Harry? The basket, if you please. Tend to the horses, and then you're expected in the kitchens, where you will remain until I call for you."

"Yes, my lord, I'll take m'self off," the boy said, already grabbing at one of the bay's bridles and heading along the gravel path that led to the stables.

"That probably couldn't have been more obvious, could it?" Coop said, leading Dany in the complete opposite direction, toward the stream. "We've dropped many a line into this water over the years, to little success. But the conversation, and the wine, have always been good."

"It's a lovely stream. The gazebo is lovely. I'm certain the food in that basket will be lovely. And wasn't someone very kind to have spread out that blanket for us. Can we say hello to each other now?"

He put down the basket, and took both her hands into his, stepping closer.

She'd been good. She'd been good for an entire hour. Now anticipation curled her toes in her slippers.

"Hello," he breathed quietly, bringing his head down

to hers, his mouth to within an inch of hers. His green eyes were so darkly intense. He smelled so good. He untied her bonnet and flung it somewhere; she didn't care if it was now bobbing along downstream, as long as the dratted thing was out of their way.

And then, finally, he kissed her, and her heart leaped in her chest.

Last night wasn't a fluke. It wasn't the moment. It hadn't been curiosity. It was the man. It would always be the man. This man.

She felt him scoop her up into his arms, then carefully deposit her on the blanket, coming down with her, his lips never leaving hers. They couldn't, really, for she had her arms wound tightly around his neck.

She was home again.

He drew slightly away, then kissed her again, his lips slanting against hers, smiling against hers.

He was happy. She could feel his happiness. Touch it, taste it. As he most surely could touch and taste hers.

"I'm afraid that will have to suffice for now," he said, levering them both up and away from the blanket, so that they were sitting, facing each other. He ran his fingertips down her cheek, and then, unexpectedly, ruffled her hair.

Just as she'd longed to do to him.

"What does it look like, long?"

"Prettier, I suppose. But also heavier."

"I like it this way. Rigby commented that you could be a pixie. Do you have magical powers? I've considered that."

"Have I cast a spell over you, do you mean? That would be nice, but I don't think so. Are you hungry? Because I'm starving."

She reached for the basket, hiding her blush at his compliment. At least she'd take it as a compliment.

He helped her, extracting a dark bottle of wine and uncorking it as she laid out plates and utensils, along with a container of cold chicken and a crusty loaf, a pot of butter and some thinly sliced cucumbers. She loathed cucumbers. Ah, but the grapes, fat and purple, looked perfectly scrumptious.

She broke off one and motioned for Coop to open his mouth so she could have a clear target.

"Very good," she said when he caught it between his teeth before it disappeared into his mouth. "Now, while I deal with this chicken, tell me about the unfortunate Geoffrey Quinton and his broken arm."

"Yes, my queen." He retrieved a pair of wineglasses and poured a quantity into each one. Her portion was rather miserly, but that probably was sensible.

He began by explaining that Quinton was not anyone's bosom chum. He was an earl's son, yes, but a sadly disappointed second son—his older brother having already produced four male progeny with his fertile wife. He possessed no title, no prospects, little allowance and a predilection to breaking noses as often as most people broke bread. He'd avoided fighting in the late war, something that Coop apparently saw as a large black mark against the man, and was whispered to have rented out his fists. He clung to the fringes of Society, but only because of his father's title.

"But, at the heart of it, Geoff is a coward," he told Dany as she settled in with a chicken leg, ignoring the utensils in order to grasp it in both hands. "I've never known him to confront anyone remotely larger or stronger than himself. Which brings us to the man's predicament. Steady yourself, Dany, because you won't like this."

"He beat someone to death? He's attempted to slaughter his brother and nephews? What? Tell me."

"He was instructed to kill me."

Dany paused with the chicken leg halfway to her mouth. "Kill you? How?"

"Messily, as a matter of fact. With his fists. He has fists like small hams, by the way," Coop told her, looking at her overtop the brim of his wineglass. "The demand for blackmail would go away once I was dead, while punishment for not complying would mean his own death. He was given three days to complete his 'mission.' According to Darby, the man was in a high state of agitation, and seemed nearly overjoyed to be able to share his dilemma with him."

Dany's mind was whirling. "So Darby broke the man's arm, to put him...what? Out of the game?"

"He told Geoff to consider it a favor, yes. And said he'd return to break the other one if we so much as sniffed one of his cohorts following me. Geoff was ordering his man to pack him up for a visit to his father the earl even as Darby was leaving. Yes, Darby had also suggested that he do so."

"I knew the viscount could be dangerous. He's too silly not to be." Dany put down the chicken leg, her appetite gone and her hands noticeably shaking. Sucking lightly at each faintly greasy fingertip, she spoke as she thought. "He...but would he have done it? Killed you, I mean. In the next *three days*? Oh, God, Coop. If we hadn't...if you and I had never met, if we hadn't found out about Mrs. Yothers...if we—what do you mean, three days? And who are these cohorts?"

Coop drained his glass. "I was waiting for you to pick up on that, although I admit to being distracted, watching you at the moment."

Dany spoke around her middle finger, which she was just then lightly sucking on, using the tip of her tongue to, she hoped, discreetly coax a bit of chicken out from under her fingernail. "Why are you looking at me like that? I don't understand."

"Good. Now, to get back to what we know. Geoff had been approached over a month ago, for blackmail, to avoid having the world know he supplements his allowance robbing coaches with his small gang of undoubtedly dangerous hired cohorts. Ferdie found out about that—how I don't know, save to say he's been planning his revenge on us for a long time. The demand to rid the world of me arrived by note just this morning, in fact, only an hour ahead of Darby. Apparently Geoff's problem didn't seem to affect his appetite."

"This morning. Because he—Ferdie—knows we're onto him. We truly have backed him into a corner, haven't we? And ourselves, I suppose."

"We have. Third chapbook or not, Ferdie must believe it won't be published in time to save him from me."

"Because you would go straight at him, chapbook be damned," Dany said, not without pride.

"Miss Foster, such language!" He poured them each more wine. "Luckily, our friend Ferdie isn't aware that we've yet to come up with a plan to best him, to get your sister's letters back, to stop the publication of the chapbook."

"We were working on it," she told him, patting his hand. "We would have come up with something soon. We will, won't we?"

"There's no more time for finesse, I'm afraid. I'll have to directly confront him, find out what he really knows about…about Quatre Bras."

Dany withdrew her hand. She couldn't let him know how that prospect terrified her. Besides, she had something else on her mind. "Probably more than I know, which is nothing. Do *you* know something, my lord Townsend? I believe I'm rather more angry with you than I'm frightened for what Ferdie is planning. What do you intend to do about that?"

"At the moment? Nothing."

"Nothing? How—how can you say that?"

"Dany, it's not my secret to tell, only mine to keep. Besides, Ferdie may be bluffing. He certainly didn't have the thing correct in the chapbooks, thank God."

"The signet ring." She nodded her understanding. "And not the woman? I know what you said, but I feel compelled to ask again."

"I had rather thought you would. I've been putting some thought to that. He seems bent on condemning me as a rotter with women, which is a far cry from the truth of the matter. The more I consider the thing, the more I really think he's been bluffing about knowing something havey-cavey about Quatre Bras, and just made a lucky guess on that end, probably so that I'm disgraced in the eyes of the Crown that, remember, showered me with a title and estate. Not that I wouldn't be destroyed, in either case, not to mention imagining my head on the block if he did somehow know the entire truth." He stood up, and held out his hands to assist her to her feet. "Come on, we'll take a walk. This might be easier if you're not looking directly at me."

Dany quickly complied. She was getting what she

wanted. Now to see if she might have been better off not knowing. "Do you want me to put my bonnet on again, to act as blinders?"

He slipped an arm around her waist, and she returned the favor. "No, you're short enough. As long as you don't raise your head and skewer me with those resolve-melting eyes of yours," he joked, planting a kiss on her hair.

She couldn't be bothered with feeling happy about his clear admiration of her eyes. "Just tell me one thing before you begin. Have you told Darby and Rigby the truth? Anyone?"

"I've been lying, hopefully convincingly, to anyone who asks, mixing fact with a bit of fiction. I don't think I've given the same answer twice, so that I'm even confused from time to time as to which lie I told last. To know the whole truth would put them in danger. I also feel the truth doesn't show me in the best of lights, I'm afraid. Are you sure you still want to know?"

"I'm not going to have anyone drive me around Mayfair, shouting out the truth to anyone, so yes, I think I'll be safe enough, thank you. Besides, men usually don't tell women anything important, do they?"

Coop laughed. "Would you like an abbreviated listing of the empires that have fallen, just on that mistaken assumption? Oh, and notice that I'm telling you something important, and have been, since the day we met."

Dany sighed. "Yes, but I'm very persuasive." Then she lowered her head to cover her blush, as the true import of what she'd just said struck home.

They walked along the bank of the stream, Dany ignoring the beauty of their surroundings, barely able to contain herself as Coop apparently searched for a way to tell her about that day at Quatre Bras.

"You know that we were in Brussels, awaiting Bonaparte, hoping he'd lag behind Blücher's arrival, as we were very possibly outnumbered. Plus, it was Bonaparte, the acknowledged master of military strategy. Wellington had his victories, but he'd never before faced the emperor."

"May I nod, indicating I do know that?"

"Yes, you may nod," he agreed, dropping another kiss on the top of her head.

"Good. You may also take that nod as meaning please get to the point."

"I'm more used to giving orders, you know. But I will attempt to be brief. Bonaparte was on the loose, and gathering support at an alarming rate. This less than a year after the Peace Celebrations and Prinny acting cock of the walk as the man who'd bested the upstart Napoleon. Our Prince Regent apparently was curled up under the covers in his bed, fearing the English populace might rise in support of the common man. Remember, our returning soldiers had not come home to a land suddenly running with milk and honey, but to half pay and soaring prices, and were quickly forgotten. The French had to be soundly defeated in Belgium, once and for all, and Bonaparte put in a cage he could not possibly escape. Wellington and our allies were a strong force to be reckoned with but, rather like Ned Givens, Prinny didn't quite like the odds. He, or probably his advisers, decided to even those odds."

"That was fairly concise, thank you. Go on."

"I suppose I should release you from your vow of silence, since you seem beyond adhering to it, anyway.

Very well. Bonaparte had one weakness. Two actually. His wife, the Empress Marie Louise, and his son, Napoleon the Second, born the King of Rome, among other titles. Both had fled France and were safely ensconced in Austria, where the empress supposedly formally renounced her husband as a criminal, opening the door for all of Europe to capture and cage him."

Dany nodded again, and then again. She was aware of the story, and had wondered how much influence the empress's family had exerted on her to brand the father of her child a criminal.

"Bonaparte was desperate to be reunited with his wife and child. Prinny and his advisers…well, it appears they decided to give him that opportunity. If not them precisely, somehow or other Prinny had to be in on the plot up to his third chin, or else I never would have been declared the hero of anything, let alone named a baron."

"The woman in the field. That was the *empress*?" Dany quickly lowered her head, and apologized. "Forgive me. Go on. But please hurry."

"I don't know who the woman was—we didn't exchange introductions—but she could curse like a fishmonger, in both French and German, and gifted me with a few nasty scratches on my cheek. Once I got her safely into the trees and stood her up, and her cloak fell away, I was immediately struck by her resemblance to the empress. I'd seen portraits, you understand, not that I wasn't helped by the fact that she was wearing what appeared to be diamonds, and had Bonaparte's seal embroidered on the bodice of her gown.

"The children, as I found out once the woman promised the truth in return for her release, were local orphans, most all of them the same age as the Prince of Rome. They—the *they* to always remain a mystery to me—had been deciding which orphan best resembled the boy, and had all of them stashed in a cottage, presumably safe while they went off to negotiate with one of Bonaparte's marshals. She heard the sounds of approaching soldiers, the servants ran off, leaving them behind, and she decided it would be safer to follow the servants' lead than find herself trapped behind the stone wall. At any rate, the Grande Armée surrenders, all the marshals are given pardons and Bonaparte is generously allowed to meet with his wife and heir one last time. Oh, and with the son officially named heir to the throne of France. He would never get close enough to realize he wasn't seeing his true wife and son, of course. They'd simply be *displayed*, from a distance."

"Would his marshals have agreed, would Bonaparte? Again, I apologize. But it sounds so far-fetched."

He stopped, turned her about and they began retracing their steps to the gazebo.

"Again, we'll never know. Bonaparte's love for his son, and his own legacy, could have been the deciding factors. He had to know, in his heart, that his cause was lost. But regardless of the possible outcome, the world could not know that England had even attempted such a dishonorable scheme, especially if it failed. I let the woman go—or should I say she ran off the moment I released her arm—and took the orphans back to camp with me.

"I believe she must have met up with her employers and told them what happened, and they would have immediately realized I'd seen the woman, spoken with the woman, seen the crest embroidered on her gown. Directly after Bonaparte fled the field that last day, since I hadn't conveniently died in battle, I was scooped up and whisked back to England, to meet with the Prince Regent and his cronies. You know the rest."

"The title, the estate. The threat that accompanied them. Yet what else could you have done?"

"I could have died in battle, and His Royal Highness could have merely commissioned a statue in some far corner of Green Park or somewhere, and spent far less money. Still, I like to tell myself I made the only sensible choice in the circumstances. I wasn't about to open my country to ridicule and censure. I wasn't quite ready to spend my days waiting for some sort of fatal accident. I reluctantly allowed myself to become the famed and feted hero of Quatre Bras, and Prinny basked in that reflected glory. I think it was another good fortnight before any oranges were flung at his carriage when he went out and about."

Now Dany did raise her head, to smile at Coop, to see her smile returned.

"And that's the whole of it?"

"That's the whole of it, yes. Strangely, I feel better, having told you."

"I'm glad. Will you tell the others?"

"Never, no. You'll have to keep the secret with me."

"I will, I will," she vowed fervently. "Not because you weren't brave and honorable, but because you *were* brave and honorable. You do know that, don't you? At the end of the day, you saved those children, that woman, at great danger to yourself, and with no expectation of reward. You're a hero, Cooper Townsend. Don't ever forget that, please."

They were back at the gazebo now, and Coop held

her elbow as he assisted her up the three steps to the interior, hung with gauzy white draperies and sporting padded benches along its eight-sided perimeter, with a large white linen chaise at its center, a soft yellow blanket draped over the back.

Dany imagined Darby had personally designed the interior, and the placement of the gazebo itself, to his own specifications.

And here comes another blush to give away my thoughts. Shame on me for even thinking about such things in the first place.

Still, she tugged the coverlet half onto her lap as she semireclined on one side of the chaise. She bounced twice, testing its softness. It was very comfortable.

And secluded.

And...convenient.

"Dany?"

She looked up at Coop, blinking.

"Yes," she said. She didn't ask, inquire, question. She said *yes*.

Hopefully he would understand...

CHAPTER SIXTEEN

HER INDIGO EYES were wide with wonder, anticipation, a hint of humor only slightly shadowed by apprehension.

He wondered what she saw in *his* eyes.

He wondered if she was having as much trouble breathing as he was, as if his body had turned that responsibility solely over to him, and if he didn't concentrate he would not breathe at all.

She didn't know. She'd never questioned.

Or she'd never doubted.

Did it matter?

She was his, convenient betrothal be damned, the ring be damned, the world be damned.

She was his. From the moment she'd first looked into his eyes. Then. Now. Forever.

Her mouth was warm beneath his, her skin soft and silky as he kissed away her clothing, his senses fired by her tentative touch as she returned the favor.

Stroke. Touch. Learn.

With all the time in the world, with all the care he could hope to convey through each new gentle advance.

Always ready to stop. A constant prayer in his head that she wouldn't ask that of him.

That he wouldn't ask it of himself.

She moaned softly as he took her nipple into his

mouth, raising herself so that he could cup her, hold her, introduce her to the world of sensual pleasure.

He moved to kiss her again, keep her at a level of pleasure unmixed with pain as he managed to somehow unbutton his breeches.

Advance. Retreat. Kiss, and kiss again. Taste and touch and swirling passion mixed with a tenderness that threatened to bring him to tears.

God. Thank You, God. What did I do to deserve such a precious gift?

Coop lifted his head, to look down into Dany's face as he slowly slid his hand down her perfect body. He pressed his palm against her lower belly, and watched as her pupils went wide and dark.

She licked her lips with the tip of her tongue. He watched as her throat worked when she swallowed, blinked up at him.

His heart pounded. With the rapid beat of life, of the exquisite pain of love he hadn't known existed.

He moved his hand, slipping it between her thighs even as he claimed her mouth once more with lips and tongue.

She opened for him. Flowered for him.

He mimicked his motions, tongue and exploring fingers. Cajoled. Comforted. Knew the moment when apprehension was replaced by pleasure. Pleasure he was giving her, longed to give her.

She moaned quietly, moving her hips as if she thought he'd leave her.

He dared to become more intimate, but she immediately stiffened, her thighs tensing.

"It's all right, it's all right," he soothed against her mouth. "I'll stop."

She shook her head. Rather violently actually.

He couldn't help but smile.

What had he been thinking? Dany would never call a halt at the first fence. It wasn't in her nature.

Slowly, as he levered a leg between hers, he began whispering in her ear. "I don't want to hurt you. I never want to hurt you. But just this once, I will, I must."

She wrapped her arms around his back and lifted her lower body against him. No words. No fear. Just a silent yet definite *yes*.

"But quickly," she told him, her fingertips digging into his back.

"No going back," he warned.

"No going back," she agreed on a sigh.

That was all the encouragement he needed. He felt her tense; he knew the moment he'd broken beyond the thin barrier. He held her close as he gave her everything, as she took him in.

He wanted to be gentle. He had every intention of being gentle, slowly introducing her to what he hoped would be a building pleasure, at least enough to give her the promise that next time, and all the times after this, there would be nothing but pleasure.

But he hadn't counted on Dany.

Somehow, amid the tangle of clothing and the soft, sun-warmed cashmere throw, she managed to free her legs, bringing them up and around his back, keeping him close as he began to move inside her.

Her courage lent him courage. Dany was a woman now, of her own free will, her own free choice.

She could walk away once this business of blackmail was settled, and Mari was settled. He could walk away, both of them having agreed this was only a sham betrothal.

Yet she'd given herself to him. Without a backward glance, without demanding anything of him. And damn the consequences.

Or did she trust him that much? Was there even more there than trust? He dared to hope.

"Dany…" he breathed, claiming her mouth again. He could never, would never, get enough of her kisses. He could survive for days with no other sustenance but the sweet taste of her.

Coop was in awe, reverent even as his passion built, but he would continue to hold back, be gentle, slowly, carefully, bring her at least some measure of pleasure… even if it killed him.

But Dany wasn't so reticent.

Her fingertips dug into his back would leave marks. She raised herself to meet him each time he dared to go deeper, matching him move for move. He could hear her quick, shallow breaths. He could feel her heart beating against his chest.

He raised his head, looking down into her eyes. Those deeply blue, all-expressive eyes. The expression of wonder was still there, now accompanied by revelation, and perhaps even a bit of impatience.

Bless her. Dany, the fearless.

"Are you certain? I'm not hurting you? Because…"

She scissored her legs higher on his back.

He had his answer.

Nature has a way of protecting the innocent, and that's what they were at this moment, two innocents, navigating their way through unfamiliar territory, guided only by instinct.

Sex. Any two people could fumble their way through that age-old act.

But to care, really *care*? Adding that unexpected dimension to what came naturally?

Being with Dany this way, Coop felt himself as much the virgin as she had been until a few short minutes ago. As his passion grew, another emotion grew with it, blossomed, burst into full flower the moment he felt her body convulse around him. Her pleasure ignited him, took him beyond anything he'd known, and when he spilled inside her he felt tears stinging at the backs of his eyes.

He lay on top of her for long moments, both of them recovering their breath, waiting for their hearts to ease back from the mad gallops they had been that had helped them race to the brink, and beyond.

He looked down on her face, again attempting to gauge her reaction, only to see tears running out of the corners of her eyes, sliding into her ears. Yet she smiled, raised a hand to cup his cheek.

He turned his mouth into her palm, pressed a kiss against her warm flesh.

"That…that was interesting."

Only Dany could say something like that and make him laugh.

"I agree," he told her, carefully levering himself away from her, just enough to remove some of his weight. Still watching her, he fumbled for the cashmere throw, drawing it up and over her.

Dropping a kiss on the tip of her nose, he sat up, his back to her, located his jacket and retrieved the linen square handkerchief.

"Stay," he told her as he got to his feet, one hand

holding up his pantaloons. He felt he presented a less than romantic figure, but there was nothing else for it.

"Stay? Am I graduated now to your trusty hound?"

"Absolutely," he told her with a smile, and then took himself off to the stream, dipping the handkerchief in it, catching his breath in his throat as he saw the merest streaking of red that clung to him.

Once buttoned and tucked and reasonably decent, he rinsed the handkerchief and carried it back to the gazebo, only to see that Dany apparently had fallen asleep.

So much for any niggling worries he might have harbored about tears, uncomfortable questions or recriminations.

He lifted the throw and bent over her, kissing her awake, whispering into her ear, even as he slipped the wet handkerchief into her hand and then took himself off again, only returning when she asked his assistance in rebuttoning her gown, standing behind her to secure the buttons, kissing her shoulder, smiling as she tipped back her head against his chest.

"We have to go," he told her as she busied herself folding the throw and replacing it on the back of the chaise.

"I know. We have to go back to the world, and all our problems. Including the fact that I doubt I will be able to look Darby, or Harry, for that matter, in the face ever again."

"Harry was trained to be discreet, having been in my mother's employ since he was out of leading strings, and Darby has what he terms a selective memory. At least he won't tease. Well, he won't tease you. I don't think I'll be so fortunate."

Together, stealing kisses across the expanse of the

blanket, they gathered up the remnants of their uneaten meal before Coop took her hand and led her back toward the cottage.

Harry was already waiting with the curricle, holding one of the bay's heads, a bit of residue from what had probably been a cherry tart clinging to his chin and a wide smile on his face.

Once they were away from the estate and heading back to Portman Square, Coop felt the world slipping back into his consciousness, doing its best to crowd out more recent, definitely more pleasant memories.

Dany appeared to be suffering from the same depressing letdown.

"Have you decided *how* you're going to approach this Ferdie person? You more than hinted that finding something with which to turn the tables on him is no longer possible now that he knows he's been found out. But then what do you do? What can any of us do? To stop the publication of another chapbook destroying you, of retrieving Mari's foolish letters?"

"Some plans are in motion, but they won't suffice on their own. Ferdie attempted to coerce Geoff into killing me. I doubt that having Geoff conveniently sidelined by injury will stop Ferdie for long, once he discovers that Geoff did a flit."

He turned to look at her, sure he was about to set off their very first verbal fight, and not a half hour after they'd made love. "In any event, until he's taken care of, you are confined to Portman Square."

"I will not!"

He needed to be direct, and firm. "Dany, don't I have enough on my mind?"

She faced front, her arms crossed, and pouted.

"Dany?"

"Yes, yes, I was going to answer you. Reluctantly. You're right," she said at last, sighing rather theatrically. "But I expect Rigby and Darby to have your back. They will, won't they?"

"Yes." But Coop was far from relaxing. Dany obeyed when she wanted to obey. He'd learned that well enough in only these few days. "I'd move you to the duchess's mansion, but you need to remain with your sister. What if Oliver were to return before we have the letters? She'd need you."

"Again, I have to agree. Will you at least tell me what these other plans are that you have set in motion?"

He attempted to hold back a smile, but failed. "Minerva and the duchess are involved, along with an eager-to-help Clarice Goodfellow. And believe it or not, the whole thing was Rigby's idea. I only had to agree to not interfere and 'Get on with it,' as Minerva told Darby and me to…"

The shot came from the trees to their left, and Harry cried out in pain.

Coop reacted with a soldier's quickness, never slowing the curricle.

"Harry!"

"Here, sir. It's m'leg, sir."

"Hold on! Dany, can you take the reins?"

She already had her hands out to accept them. "We all need to learn sometime. Grab him, Coop, before he tumbles off."

Coop didn't have time to worry about her inexperience. The roadway was far from crowded, and straight as far ahead as he could see. He turned on the bench seat, snagged Harry by the front of his shirt, lifted him clear of the seat and pulled him forward so that he landed facedown between them, then managed to right him on the seat before taking back the reins.

The time—from the sound of the shot, to Harry's yelp of pain, to taking back the reins while Dany cradled the tiger tightly against her—had been no more than a few seconds.

Seconds that had seemed like a lifetime.

"Holding on?"

"Holding on," Dany replied. "Ferdie heard the news about that Geoff person sooner than you thought?"

"And made other plans, also sooner than I thought. Are you certain you're all right?"

"I am, at least as all right as anyone would be in similar circumstances, I suppose. But Harry's bleeding."

"Jist a nick, ma'am," the boy said cheekily, his head against Dany's breast as he smiled up at her in some adoration. "Jist a wee dizzy, that's all." He then wound both arms around Dany's waist.

"I'll pull to the side of the road, once I'm certain nobody's in pursuit."

"That sounds reasonable," Dany told him. "From the look of his trousers, he was only grazed by the ball. Mostly, it ripped them. Um, could you spring the horses a little more? This may sound silly, but I think my back itches."

He grinned at her. "Mine, too. We're already seeing more traffic on the road. I'll soon have to slow down in any case."

"Then do that, and I'll tend to poor Harry here as we keep moving."

"Poor Harry, m'mum's only baby," the boy said on a sigh, snuggling even closer, until Coop was tempted to give the boy a clap on the ear. Except that the lad had taken a shot clearly intended for him, a shot that could just as easily have found Dany.

They'd put a good mile between themselves and the failed assassin, and now there were two coaches riding behind them, and an empty farm wagon in front of them. They were slowed to a near walk.

"You can let go now, Harry, unless you think you might faint?"

"Yes, m'lord."

"Close your eyes, Harry," Dany told him as she bent forward, lifted her skirt and proceeded to tear a strip off her petticoat. "There. Now let's just wrap this around your leg, all right?"

"Yes, ma'am. Should I...should I be droppin' m'drawers?"

"No!"

"Honestly, Coop, there's no need to shout," Dany told him, laughing. "Thank you, Harry, but that won't be necessary. I only want to put pressure against your wound. That's what my papa did for my brother the day he thought it would be fun to see if he could toss his new knife in the air and catch it."

"Don't have no brother," Harry said. "No papa, neither. Jist me and m'ma, and she's still on the baron's estate, all alone an' lonely like."

Dany finished wrapping the leg and tying the ends. "You'll see her soon enough. Won't he, my lord? And with a nice new set of livery. He's been so brave, hasn't he?"

They were entering the outskirts of London. "Anything else, Miss Foster? Perhaps his very own pony?"

"M'very own *pony*!" Harry grabbed Dany in a fine

rendition of a bear hug. "Oh, thank'ee, Miss Foster, ma'am, *thank-ee!*"

Dany patted his head and made a silly face at Coop. "You're very welcome," she said, obviously content to take all the credit.

Coop shook his head and made the turn that would lead back to Portman Square. She made Minerva look like nothing more than a rank amateur...and somehow, he couldn't be happier.

CHAPTER SEVENTEEN

"ARE YOU ALL RIGHT?" Dany asked her sister as she peered through the semidarkness in the bedchamber, as all the draperies had been pulled tightly shut.

She probably should have asked that of the pair of maids collapsed on chairs, mounds of toweling at their feet, one still holding a horsehair brush in one hand. Both scrambled to their feet when Dany spoke, gathering up the toweling and hastening from the room, probably to beg the housekeeper for restorative cups of tea and buttered biscuits.

"*No*, I'm not *all right*," the countess answered sourly from the bed. "Only you could ask such a ridiculous question, Daniella. My head aches from all the repeated washings, my face is still covered in splotches and I have all but *begged* someone to bring me some cucumber pickles in cream and no one has paid me the least amount of attention. *Where* have you been?"

"You said you didn't care where I went," Dany reminded her as she hopped up onto the bed. "Your hair looks much better, Mari. And it definitely smells better in here."

"I will not consume chicken again, not for the remainder of my life!"

"Yes, *fowl* creatures," Dany agreed, although she knew she was the only one who would appreciate her small joke. "But you're all right? I mean, in general? With the baby and all?"

Mari pulled a pink lace bed jacket more closely around her. "You certainly are persistent today. Yes, I'm fine. Has the baron recovered my letters as yet? Is that where you were? With the baron? Where did you go?"

There wasn't much that could be *circumspect* in Dany's answer, not if she answered truthfully. So she summoned a lie.

"We took a stroll along Bond Street and then another in Green Park, where his lordship took my hand and we disappeared into the trees so that he could kiss me. Twice, if you can imagine."

"Oh, you did not. The baron would never so compromise you, not when he has no real plans of wedding you. Nor you him? Dany, you aren't getting any foolish ideas, are you? I appreciate what you're doing, but I don't want you hurt. You *are* my sister."

"No, no, of course I won't be hurt. Yes, I was fibbing, silly. As if he'd kiss *me*. I wanted to be certain you were paying attention. You often don't, you know. I don't know why Mama thought you'd be a good chaperone."

Mari burst into tears, which was the very last thing Dany wanted.

"I'm so, *so* sorry," the countess said, taking Dany's hands in hers. "I'm a wretched sister. I've set a poor example, I make silly mistakes and now I've confined myself to my room until these nasty, horrid splotches go away, and the Little Season will be over before we know it. What can I do to make it up to you?"

"Well, um, I'm sure I can't know. I mean, really, Mari, you're the best of sisters, and I'm so delighted that I am to have a niece or nephew in a few months, and I truly love being here in London in any case, even if I don't attend another ball or musical party. Although…"

Mari squeezed her hands. "Yes, yes? What is it? Honestly, Dany, unless you want to do something totally outrageous, I'm sure I can approve. Will I approve?"

"Oliver is still traveling?" Dany asked, getting down from the bed. "He won't come strolling in the door in the next four and twenty hours?"

"No, no. I counted out on my fingers, from the day he first said he'd return. It will be at least another three days. I simply *have* to be healed by then. Mrs. Timmerly said I will be, using the cream she said her mother swore by, and her mother before that. Why? Isn't that enough time for the baron to retrieve the letters? Tell me the truth, Dany. I must know the truth. You said he knew the identity of the blackmailer."

"True enough, but he wouldn't tell me. Aren't you simply *itching* to know?"

Mari shrugged. "I suppose so. I may have to meet him in Society at some point." Now she shivered. "Can't the baron just shoot him or some such thing? After he retrieves my letters, I mean."

So much for diverting her, Dany thought, smiling inwardly. *Now we're back, as always, to Mari's favorite subject. Herself.*

"You'd ask a near-stranger to sacrifice his freedom in order to retrieve your silly letters?"

The countess sank back against the pillows. "Not for me, Dany. For the *child*."

"Oh, yes, of course. The child. How could I have been so silly. Babies need fathers, don't they? Fathers and being named the heir without any niggling little questions as to just who that father might be."

"You know very well I would never— Oh, Dany, this *has* to work. It just has to!"

Ah, and now, finally, they were where Dany wanted to be.

"I couldn't agree more. That's why I wanted to be certain you were all right. Because the duchess has asked me to dinner, and possibly to spend the night, as she believes her guest, Miss Clarice Goodfellow of the Virginia Goodfellows, you understand, is pining for home and could use some female company more her own age. Are you certain you'd be all right here, on your own?"

"I'm surrounded by people, Dany," her sister said, actually sounding reasonable. "Besides, how does one, especially one with no prospects or dowry of any import, turn down an invitation from a duchess? No, no, that's not possible."

Dany was already heading for the door. "Are you certain?"

Mrs. Timmerly herself entered the chamber, carrying a silver tray holding a china bowl filled to the brim with pickled cucumbers in cream sauce.

Mari sat up, all excitement, and fairly shook in anticipation of her treat.

"What? Oh, yes, yes. I'm sure. Just go. *Ahhh*," she said, all attention turned to the tray placed in front of her, employing her fingers to lift one round slice and hold it in front of her eyes. "Heaven."

Dany didn't wait to see the dripping thing disappear into her sister's mouth. As far as she could remember, Mari didn't even *like* pickled cucumbers.

Within an hour, fresh from her bath, her short hair hopefully attractively mussed and blessedly dry, a

stuffed bandbox already handed over to a footman—
and assuring herself that Harry was resting in the servants' quarters—she was standing in the foyer, awaiting
the arrival of the earl's town coach.

"Miss Foster?"

She turned about, to see Timmerly descending the
staircase, a worried look on his face and a folded letter in his hand.

"Yes? Does my sister want to see me?"

The butler shook his head. "No, Mrs. Timmerly is
with her. I don't know if you are aware, Miss Foster,
but longtime retainers, such as myself, are privy to information one might think withheld from them. Such…
such is the case with her ladyship's current dilemma.
Not that I would say that I…*snoop*, but there are moments when it may be necessary to…"

Dany had been watching Timmerly's hand, and the
broken seal on the letter he held in that hand. "Give it
to me."

"Oh, thank you, miss. It arrived this morning, but
Mrs. Timmerly said her ladyship is already too overset to…"

"'My dearest wife,'" Dany read out loud, holding
out her hand for silence. "'I've left my luggage and the
others to follow, frustrated by their slow pace when all
I wish is to be home, to see your beautiful face again.
Expect me within a day of receiving this. With loving
affection…' *Oh, my God!*"

"Yes, miss. Mrs. Timmerly is doing her all to soothe
my lady's, um, complexion. But it won't do to overset
her ladyship in her current condition."

"Her *splotches*? Ah, Timmerly, if only that were her
sole problem. Is the coach outside? I must get to the

duchess to, um, assist her and her other guests with a small project."

And to hopefully find out Coop's plans for the evening, as they were sure to involve confronting Ferdie.

Ten minutes later, she was being ushered into the private sitting room of the Duchess of Cranbrook.

The duchess was already there, she and all her flounces and filmy draperies. As was Coop's mother, the infamous Minerva, dressed much more severely and in her clearly favored purple. Clarice Goodfellow, blond curls hanging, was sitting at a writing desk, quill in hand, as the older ladies stood on either side, bent over her.

None of them appeared to have heard Dany being announced, and all the butler did was look at her, shrug and retire from the room, closing the double doors behind him.

"No, that's not it, Minerva. *Clandestine* is spelled with two *d*'s, I'm certain. Clan…*des…dine.*"

"Did you hear that, Clarice? You shouldn't. You should be clapping your hands over your ears, rather than to be exposed to such nonsense. The woman doesn't even know how to pronounce it. Clan…des…*tine*. Go on, strike it out, write it correctly."

"Yes, Minerva," Clarice said, dipping the quill pen and attacking the page once more. "But what does it mean? What is a clandestine assig—assig—nation?"

The two older women exchanged glances, and the duchess put out her hand, indicating that her friend should answer.

"It means, my dear, meeting—lovers most usually—in secret, for reasons of amorous…exploration."

"Oh, like when you sneak out of the house after midnight to meet up with the cook's son and do the naughty behind the barn. Why can't you just say so?"

"You warned *me* I should be careful of my language around her," Minerva said accusingly.

The duchess fussed with one of her ruffles. "It wasn't the girl I was thinking might be embarrassed if you were to in any way encourage frankness, Minerva. And you're blushing, aren't you? Clarice is wise beyond her years. We just don't like to think about that."

Dany's unleashed laughter had all three females turning to look at her, and she hastened to approach, curtsy first to the duchess, then to Coop's mother, and then to simply grin at Clarice.

"Your pardon, ladies. Please believe I wasn't purposely— Oh, yes, of course I was. Purposely eavesdropping, that is."

Minerva Townsend looked at Dany from overtop an impressive pair of spectacles. "Does my son know you're here?"

"Oh, yes. He sent to me to help, as a matter of fact."

"He did not," Minerva told the countess. "She lies well, doesn't she?" She turned back to Dany. "But only when left with no alternative, I'll wager, while I look at lying as a pleasurable hobby. Do you know where he is?"

"You don't?" Dany seated herself in the nearest chair, feeling as if all the air had suddenly been knocked from her. "I had so hoped you would. I came to see you, Clarice. Rigby couldn't keep a secret from you if he tried. Do *you* know? Somebody has to know. After what happened."

Minerva came around the desk, the other two close behind her. "What happened? I haven't seen my son since he left the Pulteney, having turned down Ames's offer of breakfast. Come on, gel, *speak*."

Dany spoke. Stronger people than herself would have broken beneath Minerva Townsend's stare.

She told them about Ned Givens. She told them about Darby's visit to Geoff Quinton. She told them about the assassination attempt on the roadway.

She did not tell them Coop's secret that he was only keeping for someone else, nor did she mention her own sister's dilemma.

She most certainly did not tell them about…well, *about*.

"Someone shot at my son? My *son*?" She dropped into a chair with a thud. "Viv, I need a restorative. Quickly!"

Clarice moved first. "I'll ring for some vinaigrette. Or we could burn some feathers."

"Unnecessary," the duchess said, walking over to a gilt-and-mirrored cabinet and opening the doors, extracting a decanter and two glasses. "Gin, Minerva? I believe it was once your favorite."

Minerva nodded, keeping her head down even as she shot out her arm, her fingers opening and closing until the glass was in her hand. She downed its contents in one loud gulp, and then held out the glass again. "The first for its effect, the second to help me think."

Suitably fortified, Minerva leaned forward on her chair, elbows on her knees, and Dany sat back as far as she could on her own.

"From the back, I'll presume," the woman said, rubbing the empty glass between her palms. "That's how cowards operate, from cover, and from the back. Who is he?"

"You...you don't know that, either?" This surprised Dany. It would seem she was Coop's only true confidante.

How very lovely.

"I'm sure I couldn't say, ma'am."

"Minerva. I'm Minerva to you unless I tell you otherwise. Can't say, or won't say?"

Clarice put her hands on the back of Dany's chair. "Be careful. I've never known a woman who could ask the same question so many different ways, until you simply give up and tell her what she wants to know."

"I don't know, so it doesn't matter how many ways she asks me," Dany said, putting all her conviction into her words. "Wherever Cooper is, I do know this—he is in control of the situation. He's the hero of Quatre Bras, if you'll all recall, and knows no fear."

Surprisingly, this caused Mrs. Townsend to pull a large white linen square from her pocket and dab at the corners of her eyes. "That's just what I'm afraid of, my dear. I know my son, and if he ever did experience fear, it would be because you were with him when the shot came. That poor Harry was hit, that either one of you could have been killed in his place? No, I'm convinced Cooper is not feeling fear. He's angry. He's incensed. I've never known him incensed. It's never prudent to anger a normally calm man. Someone has poked a stick at a sleeping bear. God only knows what will happen now."

"My Jerry's with him, Minerva," Clarice soothed quickly. "And where they are, Darby's sure as check to be, as well. Our job is to be strong, and to finish what we were commissioned to do. Aren't I right, Your Grace?"

"Yes, my dear, you're correct. Sadly. Come, Minerva, we must get back to work. We're nearly done, but then the whole must be gotten to Paternoster Row by this evening if it is to see publication tomorrow."

Dany looked to Clarice, who was already seating herself behind the writing desk once more. "You…you're writing a chapbook?"

"Indeed, yes. Took a devilish long time to come up with a new title. Viv, read the girl the title."

"Certainly." The duchess extracted a pair of diamond-studded spectacles from the bodice of her gown, and carefully wrapped the ends around her ears before sorting through the small pile of papers until she found the correct one. "Here it is." She cleared her throat, and read, "'The Chronicles of a Hero: Wherein the Hero of Quatre Bras Is Tried and Tempted to the Limits of His Endurance, and Boldly Decides on His Future and His Rightful Place in Society: Third and Final Volume.'" She looked to Dany, who did her best to summon a compliment, and decided to simply lightly applaud instead.

The duchess removed the spectacles, tucking them back into her gown. "Yes, it might still need some work, I agree. But we had to move on."

"My Jerry thought of it," Clarice said proudly, picking up the quill once more. "He and I spent all day yesterday visiting the print shops up and down the road, offering a tidy sum to the owners if he could purchase a print of the handsome hero of Quatre Bras as it appeared on the cover of Volume Two. For me, you understand, who would die, simply *die*, if I didn't have one for my very own."

Dany was amazed. "And that worked? You found the print shop that has been producing the chapbooks?"

"We did. On only our very second try. I cry most convincingly, you understand." She grinned, and then patted at her ample and well-displayed bosom.

"Nothing like a perky young pair to convince a man to do what he wouldn't believe he would. Cooper should have thought of that on his own," Minerva said, obviously recovered. "Not the method, of course. That wouldn't have worked for him. But he should have thought to trace down the printer. Still, hard to believe he was outthought by Rigby, of all people. The printer admitted rather proudly that he had been commissioned for the other two, and had actually been in the process of readying his presses to print Volume Three."

Dany clapped a hand to her mouth. "Were you able to stop him?"

"We were. I told you Rigby had brought along a purse. It was a comfortably heavy purse. The man was also promised something else to print, another Volume Three to replace the handwritten one he was setting in type. Would you like to see it? We're keeping most of it the same, but making drastic changes to the ending, because that certainly did not flatter the baron."

"Coop was right. Volume Three's planned ending was to brand my son as a despoiler of women, including allusions to doing so at the direction of the Crown for some ungodly reason. I only skimmed, since it was all nonsense. Quatre Bras wasn't even mentioned save for a demand Coop be stripped of his land and title and cast out of Society."

The duchess was pouring herself another measure of gin. Her cheeks had already gone rosy, and she was smiling, pretty much to herself. "The populace is expecting an end to the hero's story, and we are going to give it to them. Otherwise, there would always be speculation, and poor Coop has suffered enough. Minerva, I've just had the most delicious idea. Instead of sneaking out into the gardens for a clandes*tine* assignation—so very *done*, my dears, by others—we could write about the time Basil and I tiptoed past the guards and up into the bell tower of Saint Paul's. We had to hurry with what we were about, of course, because of the bells, you understand. Our heads would have *rung* right off our necks. So what we did was—girls, leave us. Minerva and I will finish up here."

"But…but won't we just be able to read the chapbook when it's published?"

"Yes, Clarice," the duchess said. "What I'm going to say to Minerva is *not* going to be published anywhere. Titillating as it might be otherwise, in *our* Volume Three the assignation leads to yet another silly young twit being rescued from her own idiocy by the hero, who then returns to his estate, to live out his days—what was that he's going to live out his days doing, Minerva?"

"Cultivating a new variety of turnips in order to feed more of the masses," Mrs. Townsend answered dully. "We'll have to work on that, as well, won't we? Ah, well, we'll think of something. So long as London knows that Volume Three is the very *last* volume."

The duchess clapped her pudgy hands (with much more enthusiasm than Dany had been able to muster). "Yes, that's it. The turnips stay. We'll first titillate, and then *bore* them to flinders, that's what we'll do. They'll have some other nonsense to engage them soon enough, and your son can get on with his life. Ah, we're brilliant. Go on, girls. Minerva and I needs must *create*."

Dany was more than agreeable to leaving the room, taking Clarice's hand and all but dragging her back to the hallway.

"Where can we be private?" she asked her.

"We could walk in the square."

Dany shook her head. "No, that's not good. Coop wouldn't approve."

"Would he approve of you being here?" Clarice asked, winking at her.

"Probably, if he thought about it long enough. He would not approve of me being foolish, putting myself in possible danger."

"And walking in the square would put you in possible danger?"

"We were *shot* at earlier today, Clarice, remember?"

"Crikey, you're right. No sense in the chicken stretching out her own neck on the block all helpful like, while the farmer sharpens the ax, hmm?"

Dany put a hand to her throat. "Yes, that seems to about sum up the matter. Now tell me where they are. I have something I must tell him. Where did they go?"

"I don't know."

"You don't know, or you're not supposed to say?"

"I don't know, Dany. I'm so sorry. I just don't know." Then she put out her arms and Dany walked into them, at last giving in to the fear that had settled in her heart earlier, and let herself cry.

CHAPTER EIGHTEEN

THEY WERE SITTING at the table in the drawing room of Coop's Pulteney hotel suite, listening to the small fire as it crackled in the hearth. The only other sound came from the ticking of the mantel clock and the creaking of Rigby's chair as he occasionally rocked it back and forth, then stopped each time Darby threw him a cutting look.

They'd been sitting there for over an hour now, the clock having struck the hour of seven not long since.

"Do you ever remember Coop being so quiet, Darby? I don't remember him ever being so quiet. Not that he's the sort that talks your ear off, never was, but he's just sitting there, Darby, just sitting there, staring at the drink he isn't drinking. Making me nervous, that's what he's doing. What do you think, Darby?"

"I'm thinking how you'd look with your neck cloth stuffed down your gullet," the viscount said in his affable tone. "Let him alone. He was shot at, remember?"

"That's not it," Coop said, dragging himself out of his thoughts. "I've been shot at more than once. By people with better aim. Dany was with me. Do you understand what that means?"

"I don't think so, no," Darby said, looking at Rigby, who only shrugged his shoulders. "Why don't you explain it for us."

"She could have been hit, you idiots. She could have been killed, just because she was with me. Because I was stupid enough, selfish enough, to want to be with her today, and damn the consequences. Because I underestimated Ferdie's ability to improvise once he'd heard about Geoff's broken arm."

"We've all underestimated Ferdie. You weren't the only one."

Coop shook his head. "That's still not it, not all of it." He looked to his friends, and then lifted his drink, let the wine run down his gullet before flinging the glass into the fireplace.

"Sad waste, that," Rigby said. "They'll put it on your bill, you know."

"The ever practical Jeremiah Rigby," Darby said, chuckling.

They subsided once more into silence.

Rigby laid his head in his arms on the tabletop, and actually began to snore not two minutes later.

Darby had pulled a slim book of poems from his waistcoat pocket, and was slowly turning the pages.

The clock struck eight.

"I'll tell you what it is," Coop said into the silence.

Darby closed the slim book and replaced it in his waistcoat pocket.

Then he nudged Rigby with the tip of his Hessian under the table, waking him. "It's time."

"What? What? What did I miss?"

"Nothing. The oracle is about to speak."

"I don't know how either of you put up with me," Coop said.

"We like you, that's why. Gabe says you keep us anchored, isn't that right, Darby? Lord only knows where we'd all be if it weren't for you being so commonsen-sible. Not that we're half so wild now. Gabe's all mel-low with his Thea, me soon to be with Clary. Settles a man, having a woman in his life."

"And me, Rigby?" Darby asked.

"Don't even attempt to answer that," Coop warned, still trying to shake off his doldrums.

"I agree. I might be put to the blush. All right, Coop, you said you're going to tell us something. We're more than ready to listen."

"I learned something about myself today. I'd already figured out some of it, or else I'd have to condemn my-self as a bastard, but it truly wasn't until I heard the crack of that shot that it hit me squarely between the eyes, nearly jolting me from my seat."

"But the ball missed. Didn't come anywhere near your eyes."

"Rigby, let the man speak."

"Sorry. Go on."

"No, that's all right. I'm the one being melodramatic here. It…it's just all so new to me." He looked at his friends once more. "I realized, in just that split sec-ond, that if I died today, my only regret would be leav-ing Dany. And…and if she had died today, I'd have no reason to go on."

Rigby put a hand on Coop's forearm. "I understand."

"Unfortunately," Darby said, "so do I. And it's my fault. It was my plan to have you two engage in that sham betrothal. How will you ever convince your Miss Foster that you truly love her? That's what this is all about tonight. You're intent on stopping Ferdie, yes. We all are. But for you, there's a separate problem. Because, although it's most certainly obvious to us that you love the woman—yes, even to me—it may not be quite so visible to her. I'm sorry."

"Now I don't understand," Rigby said. "The truth should serve well enough. Just tell her, Coop. *Tell* her. Do you want me to…?"

"No!" The answer came from both Coop and Darby.

"There's more," Coop said, lacing his fingers together, squeezing until his knuckles turned white. "All I wanted to do was deliver Dany and Harry to her sister and then drive straight off to run Ferdie to ground, and wring his neck. I was seeing the world through a red haze of anger, and it took everything within me to return here, wait for the two of you to talk me out of throwing away every happiness I might hope for, just for the satisfaction of seeing that bastard dead."

"See? He's still the sensible one," Rigby said, sounding satisfied. "You did just right, Coop. You always do. Now, what do *we* do?"

Coop reached across the table and picked up the wine bottle. As he raised it to his lips, he smiled. "Now, you see, Rigby, I was hoping you might have the answer to that question. You've been bloody brilliant so far."

His friend blushed to the roots of his hair. "Yes, I have been, haven't I? Although it was Clary who first complained that things certainly would be easier all 'round if *we* could pen the third volume. I pointed out that we'd need a printer for that, and she, dearest, dearest Clary, gave me a slap on the arm and said, 'Well, then, Jerry, let's go find ourselves one.'"

"You're marrying above yourself, friend," Darby commented drily. "Did she happen to mention how we're to rid Coop of his nemesis?"

"No." Rigby's chin sank into his neck cloth. "I asked,

mind you, but she said she'd been brilliant enough for one day and her shoes pinched so I should take her back to the duchess. Perhaps tomorrow I could apply to her again?"

"I don't think there's anything more we can do tonight, in any case," Coop told them quickly, before Darby could comment on their friend's last statement. "Unless you two are of a mind to climb Ferdie's gutter pipe and take a turn at housebreaking. There's still the matter of the countess's letters to retrieve, remember? I doubt Ferdie will hand them over willingly."

Darby gestured down at his well-cut evening clothes. "I fear I'm not dressed for the occasion. I hesitated to mention it earlier, but it appears you've both forgotten Lady Huddleston's ball this evening. As his lordship is known to keep a high-stakes card room to amuse the gentlemen, most everyone will be there, either to gamble or to watch."

"Including Ferdie," Coop said, his mind already whirling. He was beginning to feel better, even if not fully in charge of himself quite yet. It was good to have his anger behind him, his fear for Dany behind him. And Darby and Rigby had patiently waited for him to come back to his senses. He couldn't have better friends. "And if he's there, then housebreaking doesn't sound all that impossible. Rigby, are you up for a small adventure?"

"Not yet nine. I'd told our friends here we'd give you until ten to come up with a plan. Congratulations. Rigby, I believe I owe you ten quid." Darby was already getting to his feet. "Now, since I'm the only one dressed for it, I'll adjourn to Lady Huddleston's, and keep an eye on Ferdie. What do you say? Two hours for you to locate and recover the countess's correspondence? But not a minute more. If he surprises me and leaves the ball before that, you'll have forced me to trip him on the stairs or some such thing. Not that I'd be crushed to have to appear so clumsy."

"Agreed." Coop put out his hand above the table and the other two clapped their hands atop it.

And then, suddenly, there was a fourth hand capping the others.

"'Once more unto the breach, dear friends, once more,'" Gabe Sinclair said, as was the friends' custom before battles during the late war.

"Gabe! How the devil did you…?"

"Get in here? Quite easily, old friend. Or did you forget you stationed Sergeant Major Ames outside your door while you all sat in here like brood hens, hatching plans. You have hatched a plan, I take it?"

"Yes, but first tell us how you knew we'd be here."

"Uncle Basil summoned me, saying I was missing all the fun. Thea's with the ladies, and Minerva directed me here as a hopefully good starting point. I met your Miss Foster, Coop, and was given strict instructions to guard your back, and that the letters—whatever they are—must be recovered by tomorrow morning. She said you'd understand."

Oliver must be closer than we'd hoped. As for her finding her way to the duchess? He had to resign himself—Dany did what she did for reasons privy only to her.

"Yes, I understand. Thank you. At least I know where she is."

"Don't thank me. She wouldn't let me leave until I'd promised to tell you. Not precisely shy and retiring, is she? Very unlike anyone I would have supposed you'd choose, when you finally got around to it. I like her. Oh, and Rigby, Clarice informed me that you're to *hightail* it back to the ladies, with the mission of delivering an opus to Paternoster Row. I didn't ask questions, not once Minerva told me our friend here was shot at today. Now that I've fulfilled my role as messenger, what are we going to do about that pernicious gray worm?"

Coop glanced at the mantel clock. "I'll explain on the way. Gentlemen?"

It was good to be moving again; he'd sat and stewed and wrestled with the unfamiliar feeling of helplessness long enough.

Within moments, Rigby was on his way to the ladies, Darby was off to the ball and he and Gabe were in the back of a hackney cab and en route to Ferdie's residence.

They left the hackney a block from the Lanisford mansion and proceeded on foot, turning down an alleyway so that they could approach from the mews.

But then Coop stopped, putting out an arm to halt Gabe's progress, as well. "No. We go to the front door. I'll be damned if the man will turn me into a housebreaker, let alone the future Duke of Cranbrook."

"Hopefully, unless the Cranbrook curse my uncle is so worried about is true, I have a long time before I'm duke of anything," Gabe pointed out. "Are you certain? I was beginning to feel some excitement about the whole business of the clandestine approach."

"Yes, but that's why you've all always let me be in charge of strategy. Just follow my lead, all right?"

"This should prove interesting," Gabe said, lifting his hat to slide his fingers through his blond hair. "Am

I presentable enough to pass muster for a marquis's majordomo? I've been on the road all day."

Coop smiled, as he was sure he was supposed to do. "Just stay clear of the light, and we probably won't be sent around to the tradesman's entrance. All right, here we go."

Coop climbed the marble steps to the impressive front door and lifted the heavy brass knocker. Banged it three times in quick succession, with enough force to have those inside believe they were about to usher the Prince Regent into their humble abode.

And so far, so good. A liveried footman pulled open the door, to reveal an imposing figure who had to be Gabe's imagined majordomo.

"Step aside, king's business," Coop commanded, already advancing into the black-and-white tiled foyer.

The majordomo moved to physically block him, but Gabe could always be counted upon to step into any breech. "Here, here, man, what do you think you're about? Don't you know who this is? My lord Cooper Townsend, the hero of Quatre Bras. Oh, and I'm Gabriel Sinclair, heir to the Duke of Cranbrook, not that I believe that's of any real import at the moment. I am here only at the request of Lord Townsend. Now—*step aside.*"

"Your pardon, my lord, sir," the man implored, clearly impressed.

Coop took a moment to feel comforted that he was finally getting some sort of benefit out of being the hero of Quatre Bras.

"Very well, but step lively, my man. As I said, I am here on the king's business. Show me to your employer's private study. Come on, man, don't dawdle."

"But…but to his lordship's private study? If I may be so bold as to ask why, my lord?"

"You most certainly can do that. Gabe, summon the guards from outside if you please, and have them escort this inquisitive fellow to— Well, no names need be mentioned."

"Certainly," Gabe said, already turning for the door.

"No! Wait! I've read the chapbooks," the majordomo rushed on, nearly breathless. "I know you serve the Crown, my lord. I… I… Forgive me. If George here can be allowed to relieve you gentlemen of your hats and gloves?"

"Certainly."

Lying becomes easier the more one engages in the practice, Coop realized as he stripped off his gloves and handed them to the young footman. *I imagine Dany could have told me that. I'll have to warn her that I'm fast becoming more proficient in the practice.*

The majordomo preceded them down the wide hallway to the rear of the mansion, the typical location of private studies.

Although Ferdie's study's decorations were not as ordinary. The leather couches were there, the bookcases, the large, intricately carved desk, a well-stocked drinks table. But rather than globes and busts of ancient Greeks, the marquis had chosen to display an array of brass and stone carved nudes, a few of them faintly artistic in nature, but for the most part rather grotesquely enlarged in certain areas, very nearly cartoonish.

"Suits the man," Gabe said quietly. "All that's missing is an assortment of riding crops hanging in pride of place on the wall."

The majordomo had remained in the open doorway. "If I might be of any further assistance…?"

"You can't," Coop told him, closing the door on the man's face, and then leaning up against it, to grin like a schoolboy who'd just made off with his father's pipe and tobacco.

Gabe had already begun searching the bookshelves, to be sure none of the decorative boxes held the letters. "Did you imagine it would be this easy?"

"No. But I had hope. Minerva sails through life like a man-of-war, and for the most part everyone she encounters is quick to hasten out of her way. I merely tore a page from her lesson book. I'll take the desk."

He pulled out the chair and sat down, opening one drawer after the other until he realized one of them bore a keyhole. Locked, of course. "Gabe, do you have a knife?"

"You mistake me for Darby. Here, try this letter opener."

"There's no need for that, gentlemen."

Coop froze where he was, as did Gabe, and they watched as a not too tall, not homely nor handsome—indeed, a totally unmemorable—young man entered the study via the French doors that led out to a balcony.

"You," Coop said, careful to keep his hands still until he saw that the man's hands were empty. "You're the one from the jewelry shop."

The man bowed. "One and the same, yes, for my sins. Allow me to introduce myself. I am William Bruxton, brother to Miss Sally Bruxton, who is soon to be wed to the marquis. If I don't kill him first. Now, who are you?"

"We're here on the king's business," Gabe said, surreptitiously sliding his fingers around a slim bronze statuette and slipping it behind his back.

Bruxton smiled. "No, you're not. You're here to find Ferdie's latest incriminating manuscript. You're too late. He had me deliver it to the printer this morning."

"Just as he had you take the garnets to the jewelry shop."

"As you say, yes. I recognized you that day, which is why I hid my face as I rushed past. Not that anyone ever remembers my face. It's both my curse and my blessing."

Coop stood up. He felt more comfortable, standing. "So you're in league with your soon-to-be brother-in-law."

"Hardly. Like my sister, and courtesy of our gambling-mad father, I am firmly held beneath the thumb of my soon-to-be brother-in-law. There is a discernible difference, if one cares to look."

"I do. The jewelry you attempted to sell. That wasn't your first visit to the shop to do such business."

"No. The other visits were to deliver minor pieces of the Lanisford family's enormous collection, to have the larger of the genuine stones popped out and replaced with glass."

"Why would he do that?" Gabe asked, relaxing enough to put down the statuette and take up his position, seating himself on one edge of the desk. "Ferdie's rich as Croesus, last I heard."

"The late marquis's will left several of the minor, unentailed pieces to his late wife's sisters and nieces. Ferdie figured out that his father's will did not demand they be given in their original condition."

Coop actually saw the humor in that. "Sounds just

like the man. What is that Irish saying? Oh, yes—'If he had only an egg, he'd give you the shell.' Now tell me why you continue to cooperate with him—and if you were the man who shot at me today from the trees."

"You might still be able to stop publication if I tell you the address of the printer," Bruxton said, which fairly well answered Coop's question.

"That information won't save you. The chapbook is already in our possession. You shot my tiger. You could have killed my fiancée."

"I could have hit you squarely in the back of your head," the man said, actually boasted. "Instead, at the last minute, I came to my senses, and shot low, knowing I had to hit something, or else you might not even realize your life was in danger. My apologies to your tiger. It was only a graze."

"That graze cost me a pony, the four-legged kind. So now you've come to your senses. Why?"

Bruxton pointed to the drinks table. "May I?" He walked over and poured himself a glass of gin, downed it and then poured another. "Do you know what it's like to be poor, my lord? Poor, after years of *not* being poor? I think that's even worse, because you've known better, and don't precisely know *how* to be poor. At any rate, when Lanisford decided he fancied Sally, asking no dowry, and paying Papa's gambling debts, his mortgages into the bargain, it became easy, at least for a while, to turn my head away from what was really going on with my sister."

"You once pursued Sally, didn't you, Coop? Pretty girl, as I recall, and always with a smile. What happened there?"

"She had to leave town in the middle of the season. Her mother fell ill, I believe it was."

"Our mother was fine. It was our finances that suffered a near-fatal affliction. And if you haven't seen Sally since her engagement, she doesn't smile much anymore. I think I miss her smiles most of all. I told her tonight. The marriage, the title, the prospect of never being poor again? They're simply not worth another day of Ferdie and his curious predilections. That's why I'm here tonight while he's on the town, to collect my severance upon departing his employ. You're standing on it, my lord, by the way—my severance. Sally and I take ship on the morning tide, for Boston, and the home of our mother's sister. There, that's honest for you, gentlemen. Since you say you already have the chapbook, why are *you* here?"

Coop looked down at his feet, then pushed the chair away and lifted the small rug. There was a thick iron ring cut into the floor, and the wood was carefully cut on four sides. "A trapdoor? Where does it lead?"

"Nowhere. It's more of a secret compartment. Open it. Oh, and if you'd be so kind as to turn the black metal box over to me, I'll be on my way. Time and tide wait for no man, you know."

"Chaucer," Gabe said. "You are an educated man. You and your sister should land on your feet."

Coop had checked the contents of the box, and then handed it to Bruxton. "I believe they'll be reasonably well cushioned until our new friend here finds employment. My quick guess is ten thousand pounds."

"More than twelve actually. I counted it last time I was fortunate enough to be left alone in here. My aunt has already secured a position for me in a school named

Harvard. You may have heard of it? I'll be instructing students in classical literature. And now I'm off. I hope you find what you're looking for."

"I think we just have, yes, thank you. And thank your sister, for it's only because of her that you aren't leaving this room with two blackened eyes. Gabe?" Coop held up a nearly inch-thick stack of letters tied with a black bow. "A lesser man might even cry out, *Eureka!*"

"Archimedes," Bruxton called over his shoulder, and then he was gone.

Gabe joined Coop behind the desk. "Is there anything else in there?"

"There is more, yes. But we've got what we came for, as did Bruxton. I don't know that I feel justified delving any deeper."

"Really? Well, let me tell you, friend-straight-and-narrow, *that's* why you need the rest of us. Move aside, and let me do the delving."

"All right, but be quick about it. I don't trust that dragon at the door to not have sent off a note to his employer, alerting him to our presence."

"True. Ah, here we go. I believe I'll just take these interesting bits, and we can look at them more carefully later. Are you ready?"

Coop rolled his eyes as Gabe stuck several sheaves of paper into his waistcoat. "Not quite, no. I thought we'd have someone come stoke the fire and share some of Ferdie's brandy while we have a pleasant coze—of course I'm ready. And for the love of all that's holy, wipe that grin from your face. We're here in service of the king, remember?"

"The king who's locked up in the castle, convinced he can fly? Yes, yes. We needs must show all gravitas."

"Rigby said you'd settled yourself, perhaps even become domesticated."

"So much for Rigby's powers of observation. Thea would never let me *settle*."

Taking one last look about the room, Coop picked up one of the less revolting statuettes and opened the door to the hallway.

The majordomo rushed to meet them, wringing his hands.

"Sirs! That's one of his lordship's most favored pieces."

"I'm certain it is, my good man," Coop told him as he brushed past. "Unfortunately for your employer, it is also the property of the Crown, having quite recently resided in its own secure case in the Tower. Please inform his lordship that he is to make himself available tomorrow at ten of the clock, when another colleague of mine will arrive to discuss the matter further. Good evening to you. George—our hats and gloves, if you please."

The young footman hastened to assist the gentlemen, and in another minute they were on the flagway, clear of the mansion, and increasing their pace until they exited the square and were safely ensconced in the back of yet another hackney.

"What the devil am I supposed to do with this monstrosity?" Coop asked his friend, who was sitting at his ease on the cracked leather seat, chuckling in amusement.

Gabe took the figure and leaned forward, to wave it in the driver's face. "Hey—you up there. How would you like this for your mantel?"

"Don't got me no mantel, but it'd fetch me a right snootful in m'tavern, Oi wager."

Gabe handed it over and sat back once more. "There, another problem solved. Whatever would you do without us? Although I must say, your actions tonight bordered on genius. Where to now?"

"Back to the Pulteney, to retrieve your coach, and then I'll follow you to the duchess, where I'll gather up Dany and take her back to her sister."

"Do you think that's wise?"

"I don't see why not."

Coop believed he could actually feel Gabe's smile in the dark inside the hackney. "No, of course you wouldn't. But you've forgotten something, Romeo. We're meeting Rigby and Darby back at the hotel."

"Damn." Coop felt ten times the fool. How could he have forgotten that? But he had news for Dany, and she'd be overjoyed to see her sister's letters. *Really* overjoyed. Even grateful. "Gabe, I'm turning into a very bad man."

"Yes, that happens when a man tumbles into love," his friend said matter-of-factly. "We also at times act like fools, and make rare cakes of ourselves. I'm saying this, you understand, as a man who rode to London in the back of a wagon filled with birdcages, just so I could be near Thea."

"Why was your fiancée riding with what I will assume were your uncle's parrots?"

"I didn't say we men are the only ones who make cakes of ourselves when we tumble into love, did I? But that's another reason why it might be best if you allowed Miss Foster to remain where she is, surrounded by women who will be more than happy to— You know, Coop, you may be right. Perhaps you should escort her back to the countess."

"My mother was still there when you left?"

"She was. Also prepared to stay the night. And my aunt Vivien, of course."

"And Rigby's Clarice?"

"And my Thea," Gabe added, chuckling. "They were all in the drawing room, having a lovely chat, when I left. Although perhaps *escaped* might be a better choice of word."

Coop thought about the situation, thought about his mother, the duchess, Clarice. "I have to get her out of there."

"A true den of female iniquity, I agree. Complete with whispers and feminine giggles and, for the matrons, a decanter of gin employed to stiffen their cups of Bohea. But first, the Pulteney. If what I saw when I quickly looked at the papers I pilfered from Ferdie's hidey-hole contain what I believe they do, I think the last of your problems may just have been solved and you can return to your new estate, to grow turnips."

Coop's head turned so quickly he should have been in danger of snapping his neck. "Did you say turnips?"

"Yes. Turnips. I was given a quick summary of the grand climax to *The Chronicles of a Hero.* You rescue the fair damsel—I think that would make five now, yes?—and the Crown declares you a hero once more and releases you from further obligations so that you can return to your first love as a botanist, eager to serve the Crown in another way, by inventing new varieties of winter-hardy turnips meant to ease hunger in the masses."

"Gad! Minerva. I suppose I won't have to worry about being mobbed on the streets anymore, there is that. But...*turnips?*"

"Turnips," Gabe repeated, and then went off into howls of laughter until, against all reason and even sanity, Coop joined in.

CHAPTER NINETEEN

DANY HAD RELUCTANTLY gone up to her borrowed bed just after midnight, still hoping Coop would come knocking on the door with good news.

Now she not only had to worry about Mari, but she was forced to worry about Coop, who could have failed, could be bleeding in a ditch or could have just not considered it necessary to seek her out because he didn't care if she was going quietly out of her mind with worry.

And what did that say about the man?

What did it say about her?

"That I'm a fool," she told herself as she punched once more at her pillows, unable to sleep. And what did Clarice say, hmm? Men don't buy the cow when they can get all the milk they want for free. Yes, that was it. And everyone else had laughed, except for Thea. Dany hadn't understood at first, and when she did, her cheeks had gone hot with embarrassment.

"But they do come back," Clarice had gone on to say. "My goodness, sometimes there's no getting shed of them. Isn't that right, Minerva?"

"I like this gel," Coop's mother had said, saluting Clarice with her well-laced cup of tea. "Knows the way of the world, she does. And when they come back for more? Ah, that's when a wise woman plays the maiden all over again, until the poor sot can't stand anymore and begs—pleads!—for her hand in marriage. Then, of course, you're really stuck with him. Look at you, Viv, for pity's sake. You've been stuck with Basil for nearly forty years. Stuck *to* him, in your case. Randy old goat."

"Yes, but that's all right, if there's love," Clarice had argued. "I love my Jerry straight down to my toes. What do you have to say for yourself, Thea? And remember, I was there when you and Gabe were courting, so don't try to play the innocent with us, for it won't fudge."

Thea had just smiled and lifted the tray of lemon squares. "Anyone care for another?"

Dany had grabbed one, and shoved the entire thing into her mouth, so that she didn't have to say anything at all.

Now here she was, where she didn't want to be, knowing nothing she needed to know, and caught between worry for Coop and a strong desire to box his ears for not dutifully reporting back to her on what had transpired since she'd last seen him.

And when she'd last seen him, he had been all tight-lipped and clamped jaw and looking very, very dangerous.

She threw back the badly mussed covers and stood up, fully prepared to pace away the remainder of the night, but when she heard the faint click of the latch she quickly dived back beneath the covers, to lay on her side, her back to the door, and feign sleep.

The last, simply the last, thing she needed at the moment was one of the ladies—dear women, all of them—stopping by to share something else she really didn't want to hear.

She felt the faint pressure of someone joining her on the mattress, and prayed the next voice she heard wouldn't be that of Minerva Townsend, who had already heard the story of the assault on the roadway twice—and why had the two of them driven so far from London in the first place?—and still believed there must be more details being kept from her.

"Dany? Dany, are you asleep?"

Coop? Here, in the duke's residence? In her bedchamber? With the mansion chock-full of people—his mother!—any of them fully capable of discovering him here?

Was he insane?

She didn't move. It would be better for both of them if she feigned sleep and he went away.

Was she *insane?*

"Coop!" she exclaimed, throwing off the covers so she could sit up, launch herself into his arms, pressing kisses all over his face.

"Happy to see me?" he joked after he'd finally captured her mouth in a long, satisfying kiss that ended with the two of them reclined against the pillows.

"You could have come sooner," she said, remembering that cow and milk business Clarice and everyone had thought so amusing. "Are you all right? Where have you been? What were you doing? Did Thea's husband find you? You didn't shoot anyone, did you? Who let you into the house? Who told you where I— You didn't just prowl up and down the halls, looking in every room until you found me? *Say something.*"

"I was waiting for you to run out of breath. Although I must say your concern—for most everything—has been amusing to hear. I have something to show you."

"The letters?" Dany felt as if she couldn't breathe. "You have Mari's letters?"

She watched as he shrugged out of his jacket and reached inside his waistcoat, pulling out what had to be her sister's letters. "We're not going to read them."

She grabbed the packet, could feel its thickness. Mari had always been long-winded. "No. No, of course not." Her fingers strayed to the tied length of black grosgrain ribbon. "Not even one?"

"Not even one," Coop told her, taking them from her and tossing them behind his back, where they landed with a soft thud on the carpet. "I think we have much better things to do right now, don't you?"

"Here? Now? But what if…?"

"Dany, are you seriously telling me to leave?"

The milk. The cow.

"I *should* tell you to leave. I mean, you've done what I'd asked you to do, so there's no real reason for you to remain now that we have the letters back, and you apparently have bested terrible Ferdie without permanently dispatching him so that you have to flee the country, and I know we said we'd be betrothed, but there's no longer any reason, is there, for us to— Are you going to stop me anytime soon, Lord Townsend? Because I think this has been the longest, best and worst day of my life, and…"

His kiss stopped her just as she felt herself ready to burst into tears, and she held on for all she was worth as they rolled together on the bed, limbs tangling, hands searching, seeking, finding.

She knew now. Knew what lay at the end of the long, sweet and winding path he was leading her down, and she was determined, this time, to be a more active participant in that journey.

What had been new, even strange, that morning now

seemed as natural as breathing. They were two, and the goal was to become one.

Her rising passion didn't frighten her now; she welcomed it.

She unbuttoned his waistcoat and shirt with sure, confident fingers, and gloried in the warm, hard strength she encountered beneath. She traced his rib cage, marveled at the scarred flesh that must have come from an old wound, longed to kiss it, remove any memories of the pain he must have suffered.

When he lifted her night rail, her breath caught in her throat and she bent her knees, opening to him, longing for his touch, the hot moist center of her his for the taking.

Please. Please.

She sensed his urgency, and it mirrored her own.

"Yes," she breathed against his mouth, just as she had earlier. *Yes, Coop, yes.*

When he sank into her there was no real pain, but only a moment of soreness, easy to ignore, for now she knew what possession felt like, and welcomed the feeling of being filled, consumed while consuming.

"God, Dany," he whispered, raising himself up on his hands, to look down into her eyes. "You don't know... you can't know how I've worried that you might have changed your..."

She slid her hands behind his back and held him, attempted to comfort him, until slowly, he began to move inside her.

"Please," she said, "no more talk. I know there's more for you. I don't need you to be gentle tonight. I just need *you*."

He leaned down to kiss her, even as he moved his

lower body against her, beginning slowly, building a rhythm she had no trouble matching, because they were one, they moved as one, reacted as one.

She'd let him go. If she had to, she'd let him go. She wasn't here, holding him, flying, soaring, floating with him, with any thoughts of forever.

She wanted him, now. He wanted her, now.

They'd been through so much in only a few short days. They needed each other; they'd given in to temptation.

And she'd never regret a moment.

Colors swirled inside Dany's tightly shut eyes; her heart raced, pounded, her whole body tensed in anticipation as Coop took her beyond anything she could have dreamed existed, into a world that held only the two of them…and then beyond the realm of what seemed possible.

His back was slick with sweat as he collapsed onto her, and she nuzzled into his neck, licking at his salty skin, holding him while he shuddered, then seemed to melt against her.

After a few moments she would have given half her life to cling to forever, he rolled onto his back, taking her with him, so that she could snuggle against his shoulder while he dropped light kisses on her hair and they both recovered their breath.

She didn't know what to say. It seemed entirely the wrong time to tell him that he was free now, that she regretted nothing.

It didn't seem fair to question him, either, not when he was clearly as caught in the moment as she was, and have him say something he might spend the rest of his life regretting.

There simply wasn't anything either of them could say. Or so she thought.

"Turnips?"

Dany looked up at him, saw the smile on his face.

"Pardon me?"

"That's all they could come up with? Turnips?"

Dany smiled. It was all right. He was still Coop, and she was still Dany. And they both, thank God, could still see absurdity for what it was, even in the midst of all that had been so very complicated and frightening.

"The Townsend turnip. The Hero Turnip."

"Never," he said, pulling her close once more. "If I'm to discover some fine, hardy new turnip, it will be the Minerva."

"That seems only fair," Dany told him. "Followed by the Vivien and the Clarice. You're not leaving, are you?"

"Not for a while, no. I don't think I can move."

"Good. Well, then…good night," she said, and then snuggled closer, suddenly able to find sleep. Tomorrow would just have to take care of itself.

CHAPTER TWENTY

Coop was gone by the time one of the duchess's maids crept into Dany's chamber the following morning. She shifted and slithered her way to the opposite side of the bed, looked down at the carpet.

Drat. The packet of Mari's letters had departed with him.

He didn't trust me not to peek. How wise!

And Ferdie was no longer a problem. Wait. Had he said that, or had she? It was difficult to remember, but she suddenly had the niggling feeling that she might have assumed Coop was no longer in danger from the man, and he'd let her think that because, well, they did have other things pressing on their minds, hadn't they... like making love.

She quickly rolled over onto her back, rubbing at her sleep-sandy eyes before squinting across the room to look at the mantel clock.

"Ten thirty! Who let me sleep until ten thirty!" She hopped out of the bed so quickly she nearly knocked the silver tray bearing scones and a pot of hot chocolate from the maid's hands. "Oh, I'm so sorry. Quickly, I need a basin of warm water and the clothing I brought with me yesterday. I have to return to Portman Square at once."

"Yes, miss. Lord Townsend said you are to be ready,

waiting and, um, tapping your foot in impatience for him to arrive at eleven o'clock. But his mother said you probably needed your sleep because—I don't rightly know why, miss, but she winked at me. Scary, that wink, and if you don't mind me saying so, her smile beats the wink all to flinders."

"Oh, Lord…"

Dany was downstairs and, yes, tapping her foot, when the hall clock struck the hour of eleven.

Thank her lucky stars for her short hair, which needed no more than a quick brushing, and for Maisie, the maid assigned to her, who probably couldn't wait until all these extra, giggling and apparently hard-drinking ladies were gone from the mansion.

She'd have been waiting outside, on the wide portico, if the steely-eyed butler hadn't informed her that was *not done*.

Really, Timmerly would have said the same thing, but at least he would have shown her some sympathy.

But when she heard the slowing hoofbeats and the jingle of harness through the heavy door, the major-domo didn't stand a chance in Hades of holding her back any longer.

Coop and his wide smile met her halfway up the marble steps.

"You're late," he teased as he helped her up onto the seat of his curricle. "You know Oliver is arriving home today? I told Mr. Sinclair to tell you."

"His name is Gabe, and yes, I know. But we're fine. The farm wagons coming into town for the markets would have slowed his pace, unless he's on horseback."

"He *is* arriving on horseback! Didn't Mr. Sin—Gabe tell you that part? We have to hurry."

"Do you suggest I command my horses to produce wings, and fly us over all these other carriages and equipages?"

"Oh, stifle yourself."

Coop laughed. "I see the romance of the night quickly fades in the morning."

Dany put her head down, still tapping her toes on the footboard. "I'm sorry. It's just that Mari needs me. I never should have left her alone, but I was so desperate to find you, warn you that the letters *must* be retrieved at once."

Then she'd ask him more about Ferdie. One crisis at a time, and right now, surprising even herself, Dany realized that her main concern was for her sister. After all, Coop was sitting beside her, and apparently feeling odiously cheerful.

They turned into the square, and Dany sighed in relief, a relief that lasted only until she saw the familiar round shape of Emmaline's brother Sam leading a horse down the alleyway beside the mansion, on his way to the stables.

She bounced on the seat, wishing she could fly. "He's here. He's home. He's already inside. Oh, if Mari refuses to see him? Worse, if she feels some overpowering urge to *bare all* to him?"

"By 'bare all,' you mean tell him about the letters, correct?" Coop asked as he eased the curricle to the curb and Dany hopped down to the flagway before he could set the brake.

"What did you think I—oh, will you please hurry. A groom will be out in a moment, and you've set the brake. Do you have the letters?"

"Gabe's right," she heard him say as he joined her on the flagway. "Nothing's ever the same. Are you ready?"

"Am I—no, I'm not ready. If we're too late, I don't know how Mari is going to be able to go on."

A footman opened the door as they approached and Dany ran inside to see Oliver standing in the foyer, looking up the length of the staircase.

She turned to where he was looking, and there was Mari, her foot poised just over the first step, looking so beautiful, so frightened, so much the little girl she'd been when she and Dany had been children together—Dany younger but always in the lead, Mari reluctantly following.

"Mari," Oliver said, taking two steps forward. "My darling Mari."

A pause followed, a silence so profound Dany could hear her own heart beating.

"Oliver," her sister said at last, slowly descending the stairs. "You're home."

Dany heard a slight rustling behind her and could imagine Coop removing the bundle of letters from his waistcoat, waving it in the air behind an oblivious Oliver.

The sun came out. Right there, on the curved marble staircase in Cockermouth mansion, it shone as brightly as the most glorious of dawns, and suddenly Mari was running down those stairs and straight into her husband's outflung arms, her smile bringing tears to Dany's eyes.

"Oh, Oliver! You're *home*!"

The Earl of Cockermouth lifted his wife high in the air and spun her around before lowering her to the floor once more and kissing her, holding her. After a moment, he scooped her up against his chest and headed for the staircase.

Timmerly, who always seemed to be present when anything of import was going on, turned to Dany and winked before passing by them to personally open the door—a silent invitation for them to leave.

"Come along before those tears make a puddle on the floor," Coop whispered in Dany's ear even as he pushed a white linen square into her hand. "Apparently we're not necessary at the moment."

Once they were back on the flagway, to see the curricle and horses being held by a footman, Dany let herself be lifted onto the padded seat this time, and continued to dab at her tears while Coop walked around the rear of the curricle and retook his own seat, tossing a coin to the footman.

"Where...where are going? I'm starving, by the way. I didn't realize that until now."

"Yes, I figured as much. We're going back to Darby's estate, as a matter of fact. The others are probably already there, anxious for us to arrive. We're promised food, if that still concerns you. On the way, you might want to look at this."

So saying, he reached into his waistcoat again and pulled out what had to be Volume Three.

She grabbed at it, quickly reading the cover. "They didn't change a word, did they? It even *reads* boring. And it's already being hawked on the streets?"

"Being given away actually. We want to be sure everyone reads or has read to them the mundane conclusion of my exploits. I am about to embrace the obscurity I hadn't realized I would miss quite so much."

Dany's heart was beginning to sink. "So you're off to grow turnips?"

"Not quite yet, no. Are you by any chance wondering why I have no qualms about exposing us to another attempt by Ferdie to rid the world of what seems, to his mind, to be his greatest enemy?"

"I had thought about it, yes, and I might add that you're looking as smug as a cat with bird feathers clinging to its whiskers, so you'd best speak quickly. What happened last night when you confronted him, demanded Mari's letters? Is it over? Is it really over? How can you be certain? What did you say when you confronted him and demanded Mari's letters? Please say you didn't feel it necessary to kill him."

"Kill him? We never saw him."

She kept her gaze on the roadway ahead, delighting when she noticed that the traffic all seemed to be heading toward the city, not away from it, so that Coop could spring the horses a bit. "You're deliberately being obscure, aren't you? Forcing me to drag each bit of information from you."

"Actually, I'm trying not to crow too loudly at what Gabe found in Ferdie's study. Other than your sister's letters, Ferdie had hidden away some other papers that spell out, quite clearly, that he has been corresponding with a small, rather volatile group of Irish sympathizers bent on revolution. You'll remember that he spent several years in Ireland. It appears he used at least some of that time forging alliances."

"But...but that's treason."

Coop's smile was both wicked and amused. "I adore how quick your mind is to come to the correct conclusion, or at least the one that matters most to anyone who would rather not spend another moment wondering what the bastard might think up next to revenge himself on me. We doubt there's any true conviction or loyalty involved in Ferdie's schemes, but there was mention made of a very large estate just outside Dublin being transferred to him."

"Do you think he knows you know?"

"Actually, two gentlemen representing themselves as agents of the Crown demanded entry to his domicile last evening, something Ferdie would have learned when he returned home. It's highly possible he then checked on the contents of his clever hidey-hole and discovered a few pertinent items missing."

"You and Gabe bullied your way past the servants and ransacked Ferdie's study to find Mari's letters and fell straight into a honeypot of evidence against the marquis. Wouldn't that be the way it happened?"

"Again, my compliments." Then he grinned. "Ah, Dany, it was fun. I shouldn't say that, admit to it, but Gabe and I enjoyed every moment last night. Finding the evidence against Ferdie? That made it all even better. I expect he'll be arrested later today, if not already facing some very probing questions. Gabe went directly to one of his friends at the Royal War Office first thing this morning, you understand. And now we're here, with some unfinished business of our own."

He pulled the curricle straight around to the stables and handed Dany down to the ground, taking her hand as he led her across the lush grass, the gazebo soon visible, and everyone either standing about or sitting at one of the tables set beside it.

Minerva. The duke and duchess. Clarice and Rigby, Thea and Gabe. Darby, standing off on his own, propping up one post of the gazebo. The only people missing were Mari and Oliver, but she knew where they were, and could only imagine they wouldn't mind not being included.

"We're having a celebration?"

"Hopefully," Coop said, squeezing her hand.

She looked up at him, even as she returned cheery waves from the group. Did he sound nervous? He did; he sounded nervous. What on earth?

"Your Graces, friends, thank you for being here, to lend your support at this time," he said as he stopped a good ten feet from them all and bowed as Dany, now equally as nervous, dropped into a curtsy.

"As you are all well aware, it has been quite the eventful week. Early on during that time, with judgment fairly clouded, and decisions made in haste, Miss Foster here suddenly found herself caught up in a sham betrothal to a man she supposed to be the hero of Quatre Bras."

"You *are* the hero of Quatre Bras," she objected, but then bit her lip, for she had begun to realize what was happening, and she didn't know whether to run or cry or simply stay where she was while her entire world fell apart.

"But the danger has passed, and it's time to make amends, not to go back and change events, because that is impossible, but to make clear to all that Miss Foster—Dany—is not to be held to her agreement any longer, and I hereby release her from any obligation she might feel."

Dany couldn't breathe. Her entire body had gone numb.

Everyone was looking at her.

Nobody said a word, not a single word.

"Dany," Coop whispered. "Give me the ring."

She looked at him, unable to believe what was happening. How could he do this?

"Dany. Please. Give me the ring."

Her gaze locked with his, she stripped off her glove and handed him the ring.

"Thank you."

"I should have thrown it in the stream," she told him, even as her bottom lip trembled, even as she longed to fling herself into his arms and remind him that he'd left it a little too late to play the honorable gentleman.

But she'd known they'd just been pretending. Even as she'd given herself to him, she'd told herself that she could be content with that, and nothing more.

"Will you take me home now? Please."

"If that's what you want," he said. "But first…"

Taking her hands in his, he dropped to one knee in the grass.

"Miss Daniella Foster," he said in a clear, carrying voice easily heard by all. "Although I have proven myself unworthy in so many ways, my deep love and affection for you will not allow me to sink into despair without first asking you if you will consider sharing the rest of our lives together. Dany, dearest, dearest Dany, will you do me the honor of becoming my wife?"

"You…" She looked at everyone watching them, Minerva softly weeping into a handkerchief, Clarice all but dancing as she hung on to her Rigby, everyone watching, waiting. "Them…? You all…you *planned* this? Do you know how you *frightened* me? All because you wanted to be *honorable*? All because you wanted me

EPILOGUE

DANY SNUGGLED AGAINST Coop as they reclined against a wide tree trunk, the two of them looking out over the stream. Remnants of their meal lay scattered on the blanket, and from time to time he lifted her hand to his mouth, kissing the ring he now saw as the true promise of their shared lives.

"Forgive me yet?" he asked her when she sighed, hopefully in contentment.

"I do. But you could have just told me, couldn't you? I would have understood."

"I wanted *everyone* to know, to see. Darby most particularly, since he was feeling guilty about having come up with the idea of a sham engagement in the first place. Now there's no question. I love you, Daniella Foster. In fact, I'm fairly dotty about you."

"But Darby isn't. You did notice that, didn't you? He smiled and kissed my hand, and said all the right things, but he seemed distracted, as if still bothered by something."

"That's because he is. He took me aside while you and the ladies were talking, and told me about a letter he found waiting for him when he arrived here this morning. It seems our friend has found himself in a bit of a pickle."

"Don't say pickle. I don't even want to *see* a pickle for another five years. What's wrong?"

"It's a long story, and Darby's to tell, but while we were stuck in a French prison—this was a year before Waterloo—he struck up a friendship with one of the physician captives who helped care for us. The man had a daughter, and when Darby asked how he could repay the man for saving his eye, if not his sight, his answer was that, if anything happened to him, Darby would take charge of that daughter."

"And Darby said yes? And the man died? But—but that was years ago. You already said that."

"No, the physician didn't die. He was wounded attempting to steal food from the French soldiers guarding us, but he didn't die. Then. Apparently he now has, and the daughter is keeping Darby to his word. In fact, according to the letter he showed me, she'll be arriving here at the cottage within a few days."

Dany pushed herself up to a sitting position, to look toward the others, sitting a good distance away from them. They were all laughing and talking and thoroughly enjoying themselves. But Darby was once more standing alone, his hands shoved into his pockets, a look on his face that didn't bode well for anyone who might decide to approach him.

"What is he going to do? I can't imagine him with a ward, let alone a female ward."

"I don't know. I do know he's asked his friends to help him, which of course we will. So, if you don't mind, before traveling to see your parents and ask for your hand yet again, do you mind staying in town a little longer?"

How old is this child? Is she still in leading strings?

Is she ready for a come-out? How many hoops will
Darby have to jump through before he's shed of her?

"Oh, no. Goodness, no," Dany said, settling against
Coop once more. "I don't mind. I don't mind at all…"

* * * * *

HOW TO WOO A SPINSTER

pinned to the twins' luggage, had stated so cruelly. But all under the guise of being caring and compassionate.

Lady Emmaline knew her late brother's widow could be a kind person, in her own way. She simply wasn't a kind person frequently.

In that way, Helen had fit very well with the Daughtry family, who seemed to belong to another age, the more rough and tumble—and most definitely profane—age of two decades past. Marital fidelity was a joke to them, kindness considered a weakness and selfishness a near art form. Or else today's Society had simply learned to hide their failings and vices better...

Her morals had, however, been the only way her sister-in-law resembled the Daughtrys. Helen always said she'd married the wrong brother when she'd wed the second son, but even that marriage had been quite above her social station. Yet, ever resourceful, she'd made do with a husband who had tired of her within a few months, and built her own life, her own circle of London friends.

When Emmaline's brother Geoffrey had died, Helen had tricked herself out in crushingly expensive widow's weeds, impatiently waited out a full month of mourning and then deposited her son, Rafael, and the twins on the doorstep of Ashurst Hall and returned to London and those friends. Over the years, the children had spent more time at Ashurst Hall than on their own estate, until Rafe had left to serve with Wellington.

Emmaline had been as thrilled by these additions to the family as her only surviving brother had been appalled—which may have been one of the reasons Emmaline had been so delighted. After all, it wasn't as if there was any love lost between Charlton and herself.

Charlton and Geoffrey were so very much older than Emmaline, and males to her female, so it was not surprising that the three had never been especially close. And Emmaline could have accepted that. But Emmaline's mother had departed this earth the same day her only daughter was born, and for that, Charlton and Geoffrey would never forgive her. Even their father, the Duke of Ashurst, had been no more than occasionally aware of his daughter's existence. Not that he'd much cared for his sons, either. Emmaline always thought his children would have garnered more affection from their sire if they could run on four legs, go up on point when they spotted the fox and then lay at his feet at the banquet whilst he celebrated his latest glorious kill.

And then Geoffrey had died, and their father had looked around and noticed that, by Jupiter, he was in danger of being outnumbered by petticoats. Charlton's wife was enough to have twittering about Ashurst Hall, complaining that he came to dinner in his hunting clothes, or tossing fierce looks at him when he belched or scratched satisfyingly whenever the spirit moved him. It was time to marry off the one he could get rid of, by Jupiter!

So Emmaline had been hauled off to London upon the occasion of her eighteenth birthday, where she was put under the supposedly watchful eye of Helen Daughtry. Which was the same as to say Emmaline was left to her own devices while Helen flirted outrageously with any man who happened to look at Emmaline in a matrimonial way.

Not that Emmaline hadn't had her chances during the Seasons she'd suffered through under Helen's haphazard chaperonage. There had been at least a few gentlemen who hadn't taken one look at Helen's décolletage and deserted Emmaline as if she'd just told them she had contracted the plague. There had been Sir William Masterson, a widower with six children under the age of ten. He'd made no bones that he was looking for a woman to ride herd on his...well, on his herd. Lord Phillipson had loved her.

Emmaline had been very aware of that fact from the way he had all but drooled on her shoe tops, but as his breath would fell an ox at ten paces, she'd felt she had to decline his proposal.

There had been no third Season, as her father had died, and Emmaline had insisted on a full year of mourning (Helen had actually laughed when she'd heard that, which was, in fact, as she headed out the door on her way to London less than two hours after the duke had been put to bed for his eternal rest in the family mausoleum).

Charlton, now the thirteenth duke, had given Emmaline one more chance the following Season, sending her off with a warning that an only passably pretty woman of three and twenty shouldn't be so damned choosy and she'd better find some fool who'd come up to scratch because he was done paying through the nose for gowns and gloves and other fripperies.

The Season hadn't gone well. Emmaline sometimes wondered if she had deliberately sabotaged herself and her matrimonial hopes simply to spite the new duke.

On the event of her twenty-fourth birthday, Charlton's gift to her had been a half dozen white, embroidered spinster caps and the information that, while he and his sons George and Harold (their mama having succumbed to a putrid cold three years previously) would be going to London for the Season, she was to remain at home.

Emmaline hadn't protested. Indeed, at the time, she had been rather relieved. After all, in her many Seasons in London she had met, danced and spoken with nearly every eligible bachelor not risking his life on the Peninsula, and none of them had excited her in the least. She could find little attraction in men who cared more for the cut of their evening jacket than they did the notion that Bonaparte might somehow best Wellington and they'd all be speaking French. How on earth was she supposed to take any of these men seriously when none of them had been any better than her brother and nephews, some of them actually worse?

But now the war was at last over and Bonaparte was on his way to a deserved exile, and the world could welcome home all its fine, brave soldiers…who to a man would surely be on the lookout for ladies much younger than Lady Emmaline.

No, she was destined to remain forever on this estate, sitting in this same garden, season after season, year after year, birthday after birthday, waiting for her perfect lover who would never arrive. How she had tired of watching Charlton eat with his fingers at the dinner table, hearing George and Harold brag about their latest bouts of drinking and gambling, wretches that they were, not to mention listening in some fear to her brother threaten to send her off to their great-aunt in Scotland because he was weary of looking at her.

Yes, having Rafael and Lydia and Nicole so often in residence these past years had been Emmaline's main comfort, and she missed them sorely.

She did not miss Charlton or his sons, who had left

her alone without a kind word about her birthday, most probably because they'd forgotten the date. No, they'd gone off five days ago to play with George's newest toy, a yacht he had won at the gaming tables. As if any of them knew the first thing about steering a boat, or whatever it was one did with a boat.

Would it be terrible of her to hope that all three of them spent most of their voyage hanging over the side, sick as dogs and casting up their suppers into the Channel?

Emmaline sighed, folding up the letter from her nieces as she tried to shake off her depressing thoughts. She wished her good friend Charlotte Seavers, who lived in Rose Cottage with her parents, right next door to Ashurst Hall, could share her birthday with her, but her mother was still not quite well. But, no, Emmaline wouldn't think about that particular sadness tonight, either.

Cook had promised her a special treat for supper, and she really should go change out of her simple sprigged muslin gown and into something more festive. She didn't wish to disappoint the servants, who she knew had been busily polishing silver especially for what would be a solitary meal in the cavernous dining room, followed by a quiet evening of reading and an early bedtime.

Perhaps she should reconsider those caps Charlton had given her along with the warning that she was only living under his roof because of his kind and generous nature. She considered this idea for a full three seconds before declaring to the flowers and the trees: "The devil I will. With or without my family, I'm going to celebrate my birthday. By Jupiter."

And then, after surprising herself with her outburst, Emmaline quickly bit her lips between her teeth as she heard the sound of firm, purposeful footsteps approaching along the brick path. How wonderful. Now she was talking to herself, a very spinster-like thing to do, and someone may have heard her.

She turned her head at the sound of her name. "Yes. Here I am," she said, knowing she did not recognize the male voice that had called to her.

The gentleman who appeared momentarily was a complete stranger to her, for she surely would have remembered such a tall, darkly handsome man as this if she had ever seen him.

"Lady Emmaline?"

"Yes…um, yes, I am she," Emmaline said, feeling rather shaken by the sight of the man's coal-black hair and blazingly blue eyes. As her own eyes were a very ordinary brown and her hair so typically English blond, she had always had an attraction to dark hair and blue eyes. Indeed, she had secretly envied young Nicole her ebony curls and nearly violet eyes, knowing that when she and the differently beautiful Lydia came of age and headed to Mayfair, their suitors would probably have to be beaten away with stout sticks.

"Please pardon the intrusion, ma'am. Your butler told me I would find you here."

Belatedly, Emmaline held out her hand to the man, her hopefully subtle inspection unnoticed by him. She recognized his uniform as belonging to the Royal Navy. *And on my birthday, too—what a lovely present.*

She mentally slapped herself for her frivolous thoughts, probably old-maid thoughts, or those more often entertained by someone like Helen. Then again,

Emmaline reminded herself, she was not exactly a deb-utante, was she? "Captain?"

"Alastair. Captain John Alastair, ma'am," he said after only a slight hesitation, taking her hand in his and bowing over it before releasing her and rising to his full height once more. "I've brought news. If we might step inside, ma'am? And do you have other family in resi-dence at the moment?"

Goodness, what a glorious uniform, right down to the bicorne hat he had tucked up under his arm. Now this was a man worth meeting. *Stop that!* she warned her inner self, who was certainly not behaving as a spin-ster should. But, my, he was so handsome...

"No, I'm quite alone," Emmaline answered after a moment, feeling slightly dazed. When he'd taken her hand she'd felt a tingle of awareness skip up her arm, and knew she was disappointed that he had not kissed her hand. Which was ridiculous. It wasn't as if someone had sent her the man as a birthday present, for good-ness' sake. Still, the image of him being presented to her, all tied up with a lovely satin bow, persisted in her traitorous brain. If this was what reaching the lofty age of eight and twenty got her, what would she be doing at thirty? Chasing men down the streets of the village? Shame on her!

His frown told her she had given him an answer he could not like. "Then perhaps your maid? A compan-ion?"

Reluctantly, Emmaline brought her mind back to attention. "Captain Alastair, I don't understand. I'm certainly past the age of needing a chaperone. Or have you come to the front door of Ashurst Hall and intro-duced yourself to my brother's butler all with the intention of either robbing us or killing us, or both? If so, you may want to reconsider housebreaking as a way to make your way in the world now that the hostilities are a thing of the past."

Had she really said all of that? Why, she was babbling, that's what she was doing. But he looked so serious. So handsome and so serious. It seemed necessary to keep speaking, even babbling, so that he didn't say what he had obviously come here to say. Something he would say that, it would seem, required that she have some other female conveniently on hand for the moment when she would either erupt in hysterics or faint dead away.

A sudden fear invaded her. "Has this to do with Rafe? My nephew, Captain Rafael Daughtry? He is with Wellington. But no, that can't be it. For one, the hostilities are over. And you are a navy captain, and Rafe is with the—I'm sorry. I should stop asking questions and ask you to accompany me inside, shouldn't I, as that is what it would seem you wish me to do?"

"That was another question," Captain Alastair pointed out, not unkindly. "If I may?" He held out his arm to her, and she took it, suddenly believing she might need some sort of support.

Neither spoke as they made their way along the brick path to one of the many sets of French doors leading into the large formal saloon. The captain held open the door for her, and Emmaline stepped inside to see that not only was the silver tea service already set up on the table between the two couches near the center of the room, but that both Grayson and the housekeeper, Mrs. Piggle, were standing just outside the room, pretending not to be watching for her.

She shot them a look they both seemed to understand, and the double doors were closed. Not that Emmaline didn't feel certain that both servants had stepped no more than an inch away from the doors. Knowing Mrs. Piggle, the woman was probably already down on her knees, one eye to the keyhole.

"This is about my brother, isn't it?" Emmaline asked as she sat down and waited for the captain to take up his seat on the facing couch. "What have he and his sons done? Did they somehow ram and sink one of His Majesty's boats? Has the navy put them under arrest?"

"No, ma'am," the captain said, reaching for the teapot. "May I?"

"Oh! I should have offered. I'm so sorry...yes, please do. Would you rather some wine?"

He looked across the table at her, those blue eyes unreadable. "I'm pouring the tea for you, ma'am. You might consider it a restorative, unless you'd rather a glass of wine. I'm afraid I'm the reluctant bearer of very sad news."

"Yes, I believe I've rather sensed that, Captain Alastair. Please forgive me for attempting to delay delivery of this very sad news. I'm trying to keep my wits about me. Unfortunately, I believe I'm sadly failing at the effort. I'm imagining all sorts of things, none of them very palatable."

"Then please allow me to say this as quickly as I can, and I apologize now for being so abbreviated. Lady Emmaline, it is my sad duty to inform you that your brother and his sons were lost at sea last evening off Shoreham-by-Sea. My own ship arrived on the scene just as the yacht was disappearing beneath the waves with all save one soul still on board. I'm… I'm profoundly sorry we could not save them."

Emmaline sat very still. She may have breathed, but she couldn't be sure. Her mind objected in the most ridiculous way: *But it's my birthday. Isn't it just like them to do this to me on my birthday?* She twisted her hands in her lap, and then pinched herself, just to be sure she was awake, and not in the middle of a nightmare that incongruously somehow included a man best described as the perfect lover of her more pleasant dreams.

"Lady Emmaline? May I please summon someone now?"

She shook her head, unable to speak. She waited for the tears, but they didn't come. In all, she felt rather numb. What had been the last words Charlton had said to her five days ago before climbing into his traveling coach behind George and Harold? Oh yes, she remembered. *Make me a happy man, sister mine. Run off with one of the grooms before we get back!*

Her nephews had laughed hard and long at their father's joke. She could still hear them laughing as the coach moved off down the drive.

Emmaline snapped herself back to the moment at hand.

"Was…um, was there a storm?" She didn't know why she asked this. But she felt it was something at least halfway sensible to say, something to break the oppressive silence.

"No, ma'am. Not anything I'd call a storm, at least. As I understand the thing from speaking with the survivor, a Mr. Hugh Hobart, the captain was intoxicated and belowdecks at the time, and one of your nephews was at the helm. Waves are powerful things, ma'am, even on a day that could only be called choppy from the wind along the Channel. Ride with the waves and you fly across the water. Hit one of them wrong, and even a sturdy ship can crack like an egg."

He looked at her, wincing. "I'm sorry. That was stupidly clumsy of me. I shouldn't say that the tragedy could be laid at your nephew's door."

"The yacht was a recent…acquisition. I can't imagine what either George or Harold could have been thinking, to attempt to take the wheel like that. But that's what this Mr. Hobart told you?"

The captain nodded. "The man was rather overset and unintelligible. But, yes, he said his friend Harold was at the helm. That is—was—one of your nephews, correct?"

Emmaline nodded, still waiting to cry. She should be crying, shouldn't she? Clearly Captain Alastair believed she should be weeping, in need of comfort. She was an unnatural sister, that's what she was, and an unnatural aunt.

Because all she could feel, of the little she seemed capable of feeling, was relief…

CHAPTER TWO

JOHN ALASTAIR WAS certain he'd felt more uncomfortable in his lifetime, but at the moment he could not recall anything that measured remotely close to the impotence he felt as he sat across from the bravely stoic Lady Emmaline Daughtry.

He wasn't certain what he'd been expecting from the woman once he'd delivered his terrible news. Tears, protestations that he was wrong, slightly buckling knees or even an outright swoon necessitating burnt feathers being passed beneath her nose to revive her.

He was in considerable awe of the woman, even as he was grateful that he wouldn't have to deal with a hysterical female, as he did not believe playing the role of sympathetic comforter was one of his stronger suits.

Although the thought of having Lady Emmaline in his arms as he comforted her probably appealed to him more than it should.

The late duke's valet, whom John had run to ground at a tavern in Shoreham-by-Sea, had rather grudgingly informed him that Lady Emmaline was the late duke's closest relative, and then gone back to drinking himself under the table, bemoaning the loss of his master. John had asked that the man accompany him to Ashurst Hall, but the valet had demurred, pointing out that there was nothing for him there anymore so he'd stay where he was for the nonce before returning to Ashurst Hall, thank you very much, and then maybe take himself to London to find a new position. When the valet began loudly complaining that he'd have to find that new employment without aid of a written recommendation, considering that the duke was currently fish food, John left the useless man where he was, and good riddance.

He left feeling certain that whatever belongings of the duke and his sons had remained in their rooms at the tavern would soon be sold in order to line the servant's pockets, but it wasn't as if he could command the fellow to show him the way to Ashurst Hall. Instead, he'd commandeered the duke's crested traveling coach and set out to be the Bearer of Sad News.

News Lady Emmaline Daughtry seemed to be taking exceedingly well. What sort of men were the late duke and his sons? The valet had cried...the sister had not?

John studied her as she spooned sugar into her tea and then added cream, her hands steady, her movements graceful. She was a mature woman, little of the girl about her. Her blond hair was styled very simply, swept up and back, away from her face, which showed her smooth chin line and remarkable cheekbones to his admiring eyes. Her brown eyes were rather long, their shape definitely bordering on the exotic, although she did not use them to their best advantage.

Not that he'd expected her to flirt with him. For the love of heaven, what was he thinking? This was probably what happened when a man hadn't stepped foot onshore, let alone been in the company of a beautiful woman, in more than half a year.

"Lady Emmaline?"

"Yes, Captain?" Still slightly bent toward the tea tray,

she looked up at him from beneath her curiously dark eyelashes. *Now* she was using her eyes as they were meant to be used. Except he doubted she realized that, even as he was certain she couldn't know how his traitorous body had reacted to the look of vulnerability he saw in those soft brown depths.

"I apologize again for being the one to bring you such disturbing news, and feel I have intruded on your sorrow long enough. I took advantage of having your coachman drive me here in the duke's coach, so I would be most appreciative of the loan of a horse so that I might be installed at an inn before nightfall. I'll see that the horse is returned tomorrow."

"You...you're leaving?"

It seemed a strange question. But he couldn't ignore the sudden apprehension in her voice. What was wrong with him? She'd told him she was alone here. Alone, and most probably completely at sea as to what she should next do.

As if to help decide the question of his departure, there was a loud boom of thunder just as the skies seemed to open in a downpour that would have had him soaked to the skin in moments were he to step outside.

Lady Emmaline turned to look out through the panes of the French doors, and then returned her gaze to him. "You were very kind to have come here today, Captain. Please, allow me to offer you the hospitality of Ashurst Hall for the night. Unless it is imperative that you return to your boat?"

"Ship," he corrected with a slight smile. "A frigate, to be exact. But not mine. I was merely traveling with the *Fervant*, as my duties have concluded. I was on my way home via the port of Hove, in fact, when we came upon…when we came upon the wreckage."

She ignored his mention of her brother's yacht. "Have you been away from your home and family for a long time, Captain?"

"My home, yes, my lady. Four years or a little more, when last I thought about it. As for my family, my three sisters are wed and gone. My parents are also gone— to their eternal rewards. Not to belabor the thing, but as I have spent a solitary bachelor existence at sea for so very long, I will be returning to a home as empty as this one must feel to you at the moment."

"Then I wouldn't be delaying you overmuch if I were to shamelessly beg you to remain here until I…until I can think what next to do. I should be doing something, shouldn't I? Should I be asking you to take me to Shoreham-by-Sea?"

John shook his head. "There's nothing for you to do there, no, my lady. The *Fervant* circled the area for hours, and only Mr. Hobart was located. He'd somehow been lucky enough to free the small boat the yacht had been dragging with it before it, too, was pulled beneath the surface."

"How fortunate for Mr. Hobart. Will there be an inquiry, do you suppose?"

John didn't have an answer to that question. "I suppose that will be up to the authorities in charge of such things. But Captain Clark has already written his recounting of what we found, what we did. I'm fairly certain the ruling will be death by accident, not misadventure."

"Yes, I would agree with that. Not misadventure, but adventure. Is that what men call heading out to sea with a drunken captain, and with less knowledge of how to pilot a boat—ship—than a strutting barnyard rooster?" She entwined her fingers together as she looked at John in some surprise. "Why, yes, that's it. That's what I'm feeling. I wasn't certain. But now I know. I'm angry, Captain Alastair. My brother and my nephews are dead, leaving me to do Lord only knows what, and I'm very, very angry with the three of them. Is that wickedly unnatural of me, Captain?"

John lifted his shoulders in a small shrug. "I suppose that, in some ways, you could believe that they've behaved rather inconsiderately toward you. Dying, that is."

They looked at each other for a long moment, and then John felt the corners of his mouth attempting to embarrass him with a smile.

But rather than be appalled by his inappropriate levity, Lady Emmaline's brown eyes began to twinkle, and a smile played about her lips as well, before she stood, so that he, too, hastened to his feet.

"I need to have Grayson summon all the servants and inform them of the duke's demise. Oh, dear. The duke's demise. That sounds rather like a farce at Covent Garden, doesn't it? Do you know something, Captain Alastair? I think I may be about to become slightly hysterical, after all."

"I sincerely hope not," John told her frankly. "I've no experience with hysterical women, and I was hoping to be of some use to you as long as it would appear I am to be your guest for the evening." He was liking this woman more with each passing moment. Her courage, her strength—her honesty. And those lovely soft brown eyes...

"Very well, then, I won't be hysterical. Not even

slightly, I promise. But you'll come with me, won't you? You'll speak to Grayson for me?"

"Would you rather I hunted him down and brought him in here?"

"I suppose. But you won't have to look far, I'm sure. Just open the door. Oh, and be careful Mrs. Piggle doesn't topple in on your feet."

Lady Emmaline's strange warning had John thinking that the woman still wasn't very far from a complete breakdown, but when he opened the doors that led into the foyer, it was to see a rather red-cheeked, pudgy woman of an indeterminate age attempting to regain her feet just on the other side of the door.

"You could at least have offered your arm in helping me up, Mr. Grayson," she complained to the butler, who was now eyeing John as if he was some bit of vermin he'd unintentionally let into the house.

"Let me assume that you've heard the news," John said before turning to close the doors behind him, blocking Lady Emmaline's view. She'd mentioned a farce, and he sought to spare her the one now taking place in this foyer.

"How can we know they're dead? We've only your word for it. And who are you?" Grayson asked, accused, the moment those doors were shut.

John nearly told him, but then mentally bit his tongue. A duke of the realm and his two heirs didn't all perish together without repercussions that would reverberate for weeks, if not months. There was enough turmoil at Ashurst Hall at the moment, without him making some grand announcement. Besides, Lady Emmaline might not be as ready to appeal to him for help if she knew who he really was. As things stood now, she could accept his assistance and retain the illusion that she was in charge. John believed she needed to feel in charge, competent.

"I am who I said I was when I arrived here, Grayson. Captain John Alastair, late of His Majesty's Royal Navy. I'm also the man who would consider your words an insult to his honor if not for the grief that has just settled over this household."

Grayson's chin lowered slightly, the older man seeming to understand that he had spoken out of turn to a gentleman who didn't take insolence lightly.

"I'll have one of the grooms ride to the village to summon the vicar. Lady Emmaline will wish for spiritual guidance."

"Hummph," Mrs. Piggle snorted, and then quickly covered her mouth as she turned her less than laudatory reaction into a cough. "Suppose someone'll want the chapel taken out of Holland covers. Ain't been a Daughtry in there since the last duke was carried in feetfirst. I'll set the maids to it first thing tomorrow."

"We all worship the Almighty in our own ways, Mrs. Piggle." Grayson quelled the woman's insolence with a stare that would have made any sergeant major proud. "Lady E. attends services in the village, you understand. His Grace and his sons…preferred to worship our Lord in their own way."

"You don't need to explain. I will tell you that I'll be staying here tonight at Lady Emmaline's request," John said, not wishing for any more confidences from the servants at the moment. "See to it that a chamber is made ready for me. My bags are still in the coach, I imagine. I'd like to bathe and change into a fresh uniform before the dinner bell is rung."

"Oh, laws, Lady E.'s birthday! Mr. Grayson, we forgot. Lady E.'s birthday celebration. And Cook has prepared all of her favorites, and now we're all at sixes and sevens, what with the duke and those horrid boys drowning and all. Ah, what a misery this day is. Poor little dab. What a misery…"

John cocked a look at the butler. "It's Lady Emmaline's birthday?"

"Just as Mrs. Piggle said, yes. She's had more than her share of birthdays under this roof, that's what His Grace would always say. He may have forgotten this one, I'm afraid."

"They'd all still be alive if he'd remembered this one. Excepting he probably would have gone sailing at any rate." Mrs. Piggle took a step away from the butler as Grayson frowned. "I'm only speaking the truth, you know. I can't remember the last birthday any of them paid a bit of mind to. Poor little dab."

John took a step toward the butler. He was beginning to feel rather proprietary toward Lady Emmaline Daughtry. "But we're not going to forget it, Grayson, are we? Whatever has been planned shall go forward. So, what is planned?"

Mrs. Piggle answered. "Just her favorite meal, sir, and a simple confection she also favors. And all to be served in the main dining saloon, with the table shining with all the silver and candles and such. The staff is quite fond of Lady E."

"Thank you, Mrs. Piggle. It all sounds lovely and thoughtful. I would ask that another place be laid, as I will be joining Lady Emmaline at table. There's time enough for the vicar tomorrow, Grayson. For tonight, we will discuss the duke's death only if her ladyship wishes it. Agreed?"

Grayson nodded. "Agreed, sir. And I will inform the staff. Her ladyship should not have to worry her head about a thing, not if we can be of assistance." He frowned, hesitated and then added, "The new duke will be here soon enough, if he's not dead, too."

"And who might this new, perhaps deceased duke be, Grayson?" John asked, anxious to get back to Lady Emmaline, who probably shouldn't be left alone with her grief for too long.

Grayson sighed. "The most unlikely person, that's who. The late duke's brother's son. One Rafael Daughtry, and a captain serving under Wellington. I cannot imagine anyone less suited for the title."

"And don't be forgetting the mother," Mrs. Piggle said, rolling her rather bulging eyes. "There's one would make a stone statue blush, what with her outlandish ways. We're to be taking orders from the likes of her?"

"Shush, Mrs. Piggle. That will be quite enough." Grayson turned to John once more. "Forgive us, sir, the both of us. We've had quite the shock. We've known the late duke ever so long, and the boys since they were born. And then, of course, Lady Emmaline holds all our hearts. It's…it's a trying time. But we will overcome it, sir."

"Then you're all finished with being shocked now, aren't you, and from this moment on you will all do whatever is in your power to assist Lady Emmaline during this trying time—without further comment. Am I correct? Very good." What a poorly run household this was, John thought. He'd never met the Duke of Ashurst or his sons, but he felt fairly certain he had nothing to regret in not making their acquaintances.

At last, the butler seemed to pull himself together. "Yes, Captain. I'll see to having your bags taken up to the west wing and a bath called for. I'll have one of the footmen escort you directly. Dinner is at six."

"Thank you, Grayson. But before you do that, please summon Lady Emmaline's maid to her and explain that I will rejoin her in an hour."

"Yes, of course. And again, Captain, our apologies. We will strive to draw ourselves together and carry on." The butler put his hand to the small of the housekeeper's broad back. "Come along, Mrs. Piggle. I know you can't wait to be the one who tells everyone the terrible news."

John looked at the closed doors to the main saloon, part of him wishing to rejoin his hostess, while another part of him longed to be out of his uniform and sunk in hot soapy water to his chin. Bathing aboard ship was always a spotty thing, and he was sorely in need of not only soap and water but clean linen and even a razor.

He should have stopped at an inn along the way from Shoreham-by-Sea and made himself more presentable, but he'd believed time was of the essence, that news of the duke's demise—as Lady Emmaline had termed it—must be brought to his estate as quickly as possible.

Still, it wouldn't hurt to just step back inside the room for a moment, to assure himself that the woman was still as bravely stoic as she'd been since first hearing of her now vastly altered family situation.

Giving in to his curiosity, if that was the proper term for it, he opened the door only slightly and peered toward the couches set in the middle of the large room.

Lady Emmaline was no longer seated on one of the couches.

John stepped fully inside, casting his gaze around the room, only to discover that it was empty of all but its furnishings.

Where could she have gone? A quick glance toward the French doors told him that the rain was still coming down hard, so she wouldn't have gone back outside into the gardens.

Then he noticed another door in the far right-hand corner of the room, and he approached it quietly, to see that it was slightly ajar.

"Lady Emmaline?"

"Yes. One moment."

He stepped back from the doorway and she joined him in a few moments, as promised, a new look of determination on her beautiful face.

"How do I best get a message to Paris?" she asked him without preamble. "Or at least to France. I think Rafe's in France."

"Rafe. Your nephew?"

Lady Emmaline nodded. "Yes, my nephew. He has to come home, doesn't he? Ashurst Hall cannot be without its master."

"You should not be alone here, no. I would suggest a personal courier, ma'am. Perhaps a former soldier? A Bow Street Runner? It's an orderly turmoil now that Bonaparte has retreated to Paris, but it is still turmoil, and will be until the man officially abdicates."

She looked up at him, her eyes fearful. "Is Rafe in any danger?"

"Hopefully not. But as I said, Bonaparte is still in

Paris, and one can never consider the man as being entirely toothless."

"Oh, dear," she said as she turned and stepped back into the room she'd just left. She crossed to a small table, the top of which was more than completely covered by what looked to be an open Bible. "I want Rafe to be safe. There's no question of that. But there is more than just Rafe's safety that is at stake now."

John walked over to the table and looked down at the writing on the inside of the back cover of the Bible. "The next in line after your nephew is a real rotter?" he asked, hoping to make her smile.

"Hardly. The next in line after Rafe is nobody. I was certain that is the case, but felt it necessary to check my conclusion by looking at our family tree in the Bible. And there is nobody. The titles, these lands, this estate and others, they would all revert to the Crown. That can't happen, it simply cannot. Someone must be sent to find him, immediately, and bring him back here." She laid both her hands on his forearm and looked up into his face. "Please, Captain Alastair. Help me."

"I will. I promise." He didn't know how he would help, but if she'd asked him to move a mountain he would have agreed to that chore, as well. How could he deny this woman anything when she looked at him with those soulful brown eyes?

CHAPTER THREE

EMMALINE SURREPTITIOUSLY TURNED her head toward her left shoulder and sniffed. Maryanne, her maid, had sworn to her that the black gown did not smell of camphor after being packed away in the attics these past half dozen years or more, since her father's death, but Emmaline was still not convinced.

What she was convinced of, however, was that the gown, never a favorite, was woefully out of fashion. According to her sister-in-law, Helen, it had been out of fashion the moment it had been stitched up by the seamstress in the village, as anyone with any sense knew there was no hope of cleverness to be found in Mrs. Watley's hamlike fingers. To Emmaline, that had meant that Mrs. Watley had flatly refused to lower Helen's bodice another two inches for fear that the deceased would take one look at those exposed bosoms and sit up straight in his coffin.

The last time Emmaline had worn this gown (the one with the depressingly *ordinary* neckline) had been during her year of mourning for her father. That grief, although not overwhelming by any means, had been genuine, as it was difficult to fault the twelfth duke for being the man he had been: rough, gruff and fairly oblivious. Summoning up authentic grief for her brother and his sons was still proving problematic, however, and she'd once again felt a fraud as she'd come down to dinner in this gown.

Emmaline paced the main saloon, unable to settle herself, wondering where she'd summoned the courage—no, the audacity!—to enlist a complete stranger's assistance in dealing with the repercussions of her brother's death. But there was something about Captain John Alastair that instilled confidence in him and his ability to, if not make things right for her, at least shepherd her through the next difficult days.

She closed her eyes and thought about him, and the way he'd looked as he'd approached her out in the gardens. His tall, handsome form so splendid in his impressive uniform, his bicorne hat neatly tucked beneath his arm, the slight shadow of an evening beard on his lean cheeks. He'd looked weary, and more than a little nervous, most probably because he was certain he would momentarily be presented with a wildly hysterical, weeping woman.

Emmaline walked along behind one of the couches, lightly running her fingertips over its curved back, and then stopped to look up at the portrait of her father that still hung in its place of honor above the fireplace. Yes, she'd wept when the twelfth duke had died. Why couldn't she seem to weep for the thirteenth duke and his two sons?

There had to be something unnatural about a woman who would see their deaths as a problem to be solved rather than the tragedy that it was. There had to be something perverse about a woman whose primary occupation since hearing of those three deaths had been to worry for her own future…when she wasn't peering into every mirror she could find to assure herself she and this horrid gown wouldn't frighten Captain Alastair when next he saw her.

"Emmaline?"

Emmaline turned in time to see Charlotte Seavers racing into the room, tossing her shawl in the general direction of Grayson, who was now wearing a black armband and a suitably stern expression.

"I just heard the news," Charlotte said, approaching Emmaline and taking her hands. "Is it true? Harold's dead?"

Charlotte, who lived on a small estate that bordered Ashurst Hall, was not only Emmaline's dearest friend. She had also recently been betrothed to her younger nephew, a fate Emmaline had considered worse than death for that beloved friend. Indeed, for the past month, since Charlotte had become betrothed to Harold and she had learned the circumstances behind that engagement, Emmaline had lost any remaining love she'd harbored for her brother and nephews.

"All three of them, yes. It's over, Charlotte. You're free."

"Oh, but I...that is, I shouldn't..." Charlotte shook her head and sighed. "Surely I'm going to hell, Emmaline. I want to dance a jig!"

"Oh, thank God," Emmaline said, pulling Charlotte down on the couch beside her. "You're the only one who understands how I feel, and I don't have to pretend with you. We can travel to hell together."

"Perhaps not. Lord knows George and Harold and your brother are already there. Perhaps we'll go somewhere else. Would you like to see Paris, Emmaline?"

"I know you're joking, but perhaps we could. It is imperative that Rafe be informed of his changed station as quickly as possible. Would you like to see Rafe, Charlotte?"

The younger woman colored, her eyelids fluttering shut for a moment. "No. I… I wouldn't know what to say to him. It has been six years. We're no longer children, are we?"

"He will be coming back here as the new duke," Emmaline reminded her friend. "You won't be able to avoid him. And if you were to tell him the truth, he'd certainly understand. Or I could explain everything to him for you."

Charlotte shook her head. "No, don't do that, please. He can't know. I couldn't possibly look him in the eye once he knew, not knowing what I'd see. Please, Emmaline, let's not speak of this anymore. Just take this," she said, pulling off the heavy betrothal ring and putting it in her friend's hand. "There, that's better. It was as if I had a small millstone circling my finger. From now on, we shall pretend it was never there, and Rafe never needs to know. Are we agreed?"

"Agreed, although I doubt such a secret will stand for long, not once Rafe has returned." Emmaline examined the fine Ashurst ruby set inside a cluster of diamonds. "This ring has been in our family for untold generations. How often do you think such a pretty thing was employed to hide an ugly truth?"

They sat silently for a few minutes, each lost in their own thoughts, before Charlotte asked what she might be able to do for Emmaline in the coming days.

"I really can't be sure. There are no…that is, there is nothing to be laid to rest in the family mausoleum. I suppose, for the sake of propriety, there must be a service of some kind at some point. The few relatives we have left need to be notified. Nicole and Lydia. Oh, dear. You know whom else that means, don't you?"

"Helen," they said at the same time, and then Emmaline smiled.

"I could say I sent a letter off to London and it became lost in the post?"

Charlotte nodded, not quite suppressing a smile of her own. "The post has been notoriously erratic recently, hasn't it? Why, by the time your letter arrived in Grosvenor Square, it could be whole days after the service, and with the Season already begun. No one could expect Helen to leave Mayfair in the midst of the Season."

"Least of all Helen," Emmaline pointed out, her smile widening, until the two of them dissolved into guilty laughter, which is how Captain Alastair discovered them a few moments later as he entered the main saloon.

"I'm sorry. Am I interrupting?"

Emmaline wiped at her moist eyes and looked up at the captain, who appeared bathed and shaved and positively resplendent in his brushed and pressed uniform. "Oh, no, no. Miss Seavers and I were…we were just reminiscing about a family memory. Captain, may I introduce you to my dear friend and neighbor, Miss Charlotte Seavers. Charlotte, Captain John Alastair, who was kind enough to personally inform me of…of the tragedy."

She quickly explained the man's continued presence to Charlotte, and his generous offer to help her wade through the necessities that must be dealt with in the coming days.

"Captain, I cannot thank you enough for your kindness to my friend," Charlotte said, holding out her hand. He bowed over it elegantly, Emmaline thought. And then Charlotte got to her feet after only one quick, interested look at Emmaline, saying she was needed at home and must leave. "My mother is not quite well," she explained to the man. "I only stole a moment to sneak here once the rain stopped, to see how you were, Emmy."

"You can't stay for supper?" Emmaline inwardly winced, wondering if her lack of disappointment was evident in her voice.

"No, I'm sorry, I can't. Oh, but I forgot!" Charlotte reached into her pocket and pulled out a small package wrapped in ivory paper and tied with a small red bow. "Happy birthday, Emmy. It's only a silly bookmark, and I'm afraid my embroidery isn't what it should be. But please know I give it with love," she said, and then kissed her friend's cheek. "Captain," she said, dropping into a quick curtsy, "it was a pleasure to meet you, and I thank you for being so considerate as to offer your support to Lady Emmaline during this trying time. I'm sure I'll see you again, at the memorial service?"

The captain looked to Emmaline, who realized she was suddenly holding her breath, and then back to Charlotte. "Why, yes, Miss Seavers, I shall look forward to that."

Emmaline watched the captain as he watched Charlotte depart the room, and then she quickly looked away as he turned back to her, so that he shouldn't know that she'd been staring. But who could resist staring, when the man's presence seemed to fill the room with light, charging the very air with an excitement she could not name, yet knew she had never before experienced.

"May I add my congratulations to Miss Seavers's

sentiments, ma'am, and wish you as pleasant a birthday as possible under the circumstances," he said, inclining his head toward her.

She didn't know where the words came from, what part of her normally reticent self had allowed such a thought to enter her head yet alone escape her lips, but suddenly Emmaline heard herself saying, "Captain, I would consider my natal day to be more of a blessing and less of a reminder of my continuing gallop into old age if you could please resist addressing me as ma'am again."

His low chuckle sent hot color flooding into her cheeks. "A thousand apologies, Lady Emmaline. Are you feeling quite decrepit? Surely you're not anything so ancient as ma'am would suggest. At six and thirty, I believe I have some years on you."

"Good Lord, yes," Emmaline shot back, suddenly willing to give as good as she got. "You're positively tottering on the brink of the grave." Then she realized what she'd just said. "Oh, dear. No matter what anyone says, we seem to keep circling back to Charlton and the boys, don't we? I still imagine they'll all come storming back in here at any moment to put the lie to what I know is true."

Did she sound as if that was a prospect much to be wished, or the thing she would dread most in the world? Really, she had to take control of her tongue, and quickly, or the captain would wonder if he'd blundered into a madhouse.

"May I?" Alastair asked, indicating with a small gesture that he'd like to join her on the couch.

"Oh, yes, please do," she said, tucking her horrid black skirts more closely around her just as if he'd planned to plop himself down right next to her when the couch could easily accommodate a half dozen people. "And would you care for some wine?"

"Thank you, no," he said as he sat, and then bent down to pick up something that had fallen to the floor. "Yours?" he asked, holding up the ruby ring.

Denying the dratted thing would open up questions about Charlotte, and as the story could only reflect badly on her brother and Harold, she quickly claimed the ruby as her own. "Thank you, Captain," she said, reaching for it. "It was my mother's, and always much too large for me."

And then the dratted ring made a liar out of her by stopping at her second knuckle as she attempted to slip it on her finger. She resisted the urge to fling it across the room.

"Ma'am—Lady Emmaline...?"

"Just Emmaline, please," she said, sighing. "And I shall call you John, since we're just the two of us here. And then, John, I should tell you that I just quite blatantly lied to you, shouldn't I?"

"About the ring. Yes. But you don't have to explain."

She relaxed. "Good, because I really don't want to." She slipped the ring into her pocket and picked up the small wrapped present. "Shall we open this instead? I love presents, and Charlotte is always so inventive with hers, even if she insists she has no talents. Just this past Christmas she gave me a small, smooth rock she'd painted to look like a toad."

Actually, Charlotte had given the toad a face that greatly resembled that of her nephew George, but the captain didn't have to know that.

The captain put his hand on her wrist. "Lady... Emmaline," he said, so that she forgot all about Charlotte's present. "I should leave."

"Leave?" Emmaline squeezed her eyes shut for a moment, hating that she had seemed to squeak out the word. "But…but why? I know the rain has stopped, but it's coming on to dark soon, and we'll be called in to dinner at any moment, and—"

"I didn't mean tonight," he said, cutting her off, thankfully, before she could say something so silly as to mention how much she really wanted him to stay. "I would go only as far as the nearest inn, if you still wish my assistance for a few days, until we can summon your brother's solicitor, set up a search for your nephew and anything else I might do for you."

"You're saying without saying it that we are unchaperoned here."

"No, I'm saying without saying it that you are unchaperoned here. I would suggest that Miss Seavers come bear you company, but as she is quite young, and there's the problem of her mother being unwell…"

"John, there are twenty-seven servants in this house, at least three of whom, I have every certainty, are spying on us even now. I hardly call that being unchaperoned."

"No. However, Society would. You've just been dealt a serious shock, Emmaline, but one of us must think clearly."

She nearly let her shoulders sag as she realized what he was saying. "You feel responsible for me. Because it was you who brought me the news about Charlton and the boys. And I did nothing to dissuade you of that impression, absolve you of your gentlemanly impulse to protect a clearly helpless woman."

His slow smile sent her stomach to doing a small flip inside her. "That sounds so very noble, doesn't it? Actually, I came here to deliver my news and then depart as quickly as possible. Until I saw you out there in the gardens and thought you the most exotically beautiful woman I'd ever seen. You've had the most immediate and remarkable impact on me, Emmaline. I am in no hurry to leave."

"Oh."

"Yes—oh. And, hopeful idiot that I surely am, I don't think you have taken me in disgust. Now do you understand? The proprieties must be adhered to, no matter the circumstances. I won't go far, unless you've now decided that I should, but I cannot remain here, the two of us beneath the same roof."

"There are sixteen bedchambers under this roof," Emmaline said, as if that meant anything to Society, that same Society that had condoned Charlton's behavior, George's and Harold's behavior, but would condemn her, a confirmed spinster, for the most minor infraction of their silly rules. "There's no need for you to be put to the expense of staying at the inn."

His smile in response to that statement had her looking at him strangely, and she quickly attempted to explain what she'd said.

"Not that I'm intimating at all that you might be... that you cannot afford, um, that is— Oh, stop that! I'm not saying anything in the least amusing."

He took her trembling hands in his and raised the right one to his lips, turned it over, and pressed a bone-melting kiss against her palm. Just for an instant, the tip of his tongue lightly stroked her sensitive skin. And then, holding her hands against his chest, he looked at her with those soul-destroying eyes. "Now, Emmaline? Now do you see why I need to take myself off to an inn tomorrow morning?"

"Yes… I rather suppose I do."

CHAPTER FOUR

JOHN DIDN'T KNOW if Grayson's entrance into the main saloon to announce that dinner was being served had been fortunate, or if it had been the worst timing in the history of Affectionate Old Family Retainers. Probably the former, as John hadn't known what in bloody blazes he was going to do next, once he was looking so deeply into Emmaline's glorious eyes.

He had wanted to kiss her. No, he had needed to kiss her. He *would* kiss her before this night was over. As a man who had spent many years at war, he knew that opportunities were just that, and often fleeting. For too many years of his life, he'd put his own wishes aside in the name of the Better Good. Now it was time for him to think about what John Alastair wanted.

And he wanted Lady Emmaline Daughtry.

Curiously, knowing this, he was finding it best suited to his purpose to keep his true identity hidden just a little while longer. He wanted Emmaline to see him as Captain John Alastair, accept him that way…perhaps discover feelings for him that way; the simple man, the man she could be concerned about if he had to pay for his lodgings at the local inn.

He also wanted to know more about the late duke and his two sons, but would she find it as easy to confide in him if she realized his true rank? Emmaline had been shocked by the news of their deaths—anyone would have been shocked at the suddenness of it—but John felt certain he'd also seen a measure of relief in her eyes.

Having experienced much the same feelings when he'd opened the letter from Warrington Hall, informing him of his father's departure from this earthly coil by way of collapsing after a hard ride on one of the local tavern wenches, John wondered what sort of man the late duke had been. What sort of brother he'd been to Emmaline. Obviously not a beloved one.

John sensed that applying to Grayson for enlightenment would get him nowhere, but he had higher hopes of Mrs. Piggle, and planned to speak to the woman in the morning. In the meantime, he would not press Emmaline for details, not knowing how painful it might be for her to share them with him.

This decision left him free to concentrate on Emmaline herself, which was what he'd much prefer to do in any case.

He entered the cavernous dining room with Emmaline on his arm, only to see that their places had been set at opposite ends of a table that could easily serve as a bowling green. Once he'd assisted her to his chair and Grayson had withdrawn his disapproving face, John picked up his gold charger plate, utensils, serviette and wineglass and carried them all down the length of the table, placing them to Emmaline's right.

"This way we won't have to shout at each other," he said as he sat down. "And I might add that I cannot think of more pleasant company than you in this, my first meal in months in which I won't have to worry about my wineglass sliding off the table as the ship cuts through the waves."

"Grayson will not be pleased," Emmaline told him as a young girl entered, two bowls of soup balanced on a tray. "He's quite the stickler for propriety."

"Among other things, yes, I can see that propriety would be one of his sticking points. Does that worry you?"

Emmaline cocked her head slightly to one side, as if considering the question. "No. No, I don't think it does. Thank you, Mary. It smells delicious."

"Yer fav'rit, milady. Cook remembered. All yer fav'rits tonight. All whats yer likes best, right here."

"Yes, I believe you're right," Emmaline said, sneaking a quick look at John from beneath her lashes, a delightful flush coloring her cheeks.

The soup was country thick and flavorful, or so John remembered it later, even though the rest of the courses were eaten without him tasting them. He was much too well-occupied answering Emmaline's intelligently probing questions about his service in the Royal Navy, much too enthralled by the way the candlelight danced in her golden hair, the grace with which she patted her lips with the snow-white serviette…the way she listened to him as if he was reciting words he'd brought down from some mountain on stone tablets.

He did remember the dessert course, because it seemed that Emmaline's favorite sweet consisted of a simple dish of strawberries and heavy cream. Whenever some of the cream clung to her upper lip, and she surreptitiously employed the tip of her tongue to swipe it away, John began to wonder if taking himself off to the inn the next morning could be seen as in the way of cruel and unusual punishment for a man who definitely had another destination in mind.

At last the meal was over, and John suggested they take a stroll in the gardens now that the rain had disappeared and a setting sun still lent enough light for a pleasant inspection of the grounds.

Good Lord, he sounded so stiff, didn't he?

"Emmaline—I want to be alone with you," he whispered in her ear as he pulled out her chair for her. "And to hell with the posies."

She looked up at him, her smile tremulous, and laid her hand on his as she got to her feet. "The herb garden is well away from the house at the bottom of the gardens. And fenced," she said quietly. "With rather tall shrubbery."

"I've always liked herbs," he said as, together, they departed the dining room through the French doors conveniently placed there so that gentlemen could end their meals by stepping outside to blow a cloud, spit or relieve themselves over the railing of the stone terrace. John's father used to hold contests as to who could aim best and shoot farthest, much to his son's embarrassment. He pushed the memory from his mind.

"Rosemary is one my favorites," Emmaline told him as they descended the flagstone steps into the gardens.

"Mine, as well. Along with parsley and sage and…"

"Thyme," she finished for him. "I've always thought 'Scarborough Fair' a most confusing poem. If you wish someone to be your true love, why would you then make impossible demands on that person in order to become that true love?"

John bent and broke off a perfect pink rose, stripped it of its thorns and then bowed as he handed it to her. "'Love imposes impossible tasks,'" he quoted from memory, "'though not more than any heart asks.'"

"Oh? And do you think that sounds as asinine as I do, John? Why should a heart that cares make demands?" Emmaline asked as she held the rose beneath her nose and sniffed. "Ah, nothing complicated about a rose, is there? It is pretty, it smells heavenly, and if you aren't careful in the way you handle it, it pricks your finger. Still, you can see the thorns, so it isn't as if you weren't warned, correct?"

They threaded their way along the curving brick path. "Am I being warned, Emmaline?"

She stopped, turned to look up into his face. "Someone probably is, but I'm not sure which one of us that person might be. John... I think you should know that I'm not a very...nice person."

"Is that so?" He cocked one eyebrow as he offered her his arm once more and they continued down the pathway. "Do you abuse kittens? Snore in church? No, wait, I have it—you pull faces behind Grayson's back."

"Well, sometimes—that last bit about Grayson. But I'm attempting to be serious here, John. I'm... I'm an unnatural sister, an unnatural aunt. I've been trying all day long to work up even a single tear over Charlton and the boys, and I simply can't manage it."

"You didn't love them?"

"No, no, of course I loved them. One doesn't have much choice in that, seeing as we're related. The question is, did I like them? And I didn't."

John kept moving toward the tall thick shrubbery that he was sure concealed the herb garden. "They weren't likable?"

"I suppose that would depend on whom you applied to for their opinion. Their friends seemed to like them well enough."

"And did you like their friends?"

They stopped at a slatted wooden gate and John opened it. "No, I didn't. Why would you ask that?"

He ceremoniously bowed her through the entrance to the herb garden, where they were immediately cast in the shade of the towering evergreens. "I don't know. It simply occurred to me that, if you didn't care for the people who cared for them, then perhaps the only reason you cared for your brother and nephews at all was because of an accident of birth. We can't choose our relatives, Emmaline. Only our friends."

"You're only trying to make me feel less guilty."

"I know," he said, leading her to a curved stone bench at the center of the small garden. "Am I succeeding?"

She sat down, gracefully arranging her skirts around her, and looked at him. "Why, yes, I believe you are. Charlton and his sons are dead, and I'm sorry they didn't lead better lives while they had the chance. I think I could weep for that."

He joined her on the bench. "Now?"

Emmaline was slowly twirling the rose stem between her fingers, and looked up at him in some confusion. "Pardon me? Now what?"

"I was asking if you were going to weep now," he explained, biting back a smile.

"Oh. Oh, no, I don't think so. But at the service it will be better if I don't disappoint Vicar Wooten. So then I shall think about what might have been." She sighed. "What might have been is always so sad, isn't it? What we could have done, what we should have done. What we missed because we didn't dare to—"

John brought his mouth down on hers, cutting off

any chance that either of them would ever look back at this moment and think, If only.

He pulled back slightly, smiling into her eyes. "I'm sorry, I couldn't seem to resist. In fact, I still can't…"

This time when he kissed her he also slid his arms around her, pulling her closer against his chest. She responded by sliding her arms around his back, signaling without words that she didn't dislike what he was doing to her.

What she was doing to him.

A kiss. A simple kiss. And yet his world was tilting on its axis. He prodded at her with his tongue, and she responded by opening her mouth to him, and the flame she had lit inside him the first time he'd seen her threatened to consume him.

He kissed her hair, her perfect shell-like ear, her throat. He heard her quick intake of breath as he moved his hands forward, to her rib cage…and then slowly slid them upward, to cup her firm breasts.

"John…" she breathed, but not in protest, as she still held him tightly, her head tipped back as he dared to press his lips against her bare flesh above the neckline of her gown.

Her mourning gown.

Christ!

He took her hands in his and raised her to her feet, not letting go of her as he looked deeply into her eyes. "I'm sorry. I had no right…"

"You were not lacking an invitation, Captain Alastair," Emmaline told him quietly, shifting her gaze to the ground at her feet. "Shall we just put this down to an aging spinster feeling reckless, even desperate, on the event of her twenty-eighth birthday?"

"I don't think so, no. Not unless we explain my behavior with the notion that I've been too long at sea, and haven't seen a woman in months and months, so that any woman will do. You're not that old, Emmaline, and I'm not that young."

She smiled weakly and pulled one hand free, turning so that they could retrace their steps to the house. "You've quite the way with words, or else I'm eager to be convinced."

She shivered then, only slightly, as the setting sun had slipped behind a blanket of thick clouds, and John slipped his arm around her shoulders, pulling her closer beside him as they walked along the path.

"I had an idea as I dressed for dinner," he told her as they approached the doors to the main saloon. "I've remembered the name of the brother of Josiah Coates, my steward aboard ship. Phineas. Yes, I'm positive that's it. Phineas Coates. He's with the Bow Street Runners, but Josiah told me the man is unhappy with his position, so that he's actively seeking employment as a valet. Josiah and his other brothers are all gentleman's gentlemen, in one form or another, you understand."

"Not really, not yet," Emmaline admitted as they stepped inside the main saloon, to see that Grayson had already ordered the evening tea tray, a not-quite subtle hint that he believed her ladyship should soon be saying her good-night to the captain. "But you'll explain?"

John availed himself of the well-stocked drinks table, pouring a glass of wine while Emmaline prepared a cup of tea for herself. He returned to the main seating area, but did not sit down.

"Josiah left for his home at the same time I was coming here, to Ashurst Hall. I know his direction, and I'm sure he'll be there by the time a letter from me reaches London." He didn't add that Josiah had only gone to the city to visit his widowed mother before heading to Warrington Hall, as that was information best kept to himself for the moment.

"Ah, you're thinking this Phineas Coates might be the man who can find Rafe for me."

"Yes, that's exactly what I'm thinking. You could go through the War Office, but the extremely busy people there might not consider the mission as important as you'd like."

"And, since Mr. Coates is a Bow Street Runner, he should have no problem in running down Rafe if we tell him what we know, that my nephew is in Paris. He could even, considering the man's desire to leave the Runners, offer his services as the new duke's valet, and stay with him, accompany Rafe home to Ashurst Hall. All very neat and tidy."

"Only if you're agreeable. I don't know Phineas, but I can vouch for Josiah."

"Very well, then, that's what we shall do. I'll write to Rafe tonight, and you can include the letter along with your instructions? And, yes, I'd feel much more comfortable if this Mr. Phineas Coates stayed at Rafe's side until he's home safe. I might even suggest they stop in London for a few days, to do something about Rafe's wardrobe. The boy has been in uniforms for half a dozen years. Now he has to dress himself as befits a duke. Oh, dear, I wonder if he's going to like that. He left here a boy, but he's a man now. I wonder if he's going to like any part of this, to be truthful. He had no ambitions in this direction, and no training, when it comes to that."

"Three hearts away from the title, two of them young and I'll assume vital, I can see why your nephew might not have considered that such a day might arrive. The title, this estate and, I'm sure, several others? He's inherited considerable responsibility. Is he up to it, do you think?"

Emmaline nodded. "Rafe is a good, sound person, boy or man, I'm sure. He may be somewhat discommoded to see how his sisters have blossomed in his absence, and I don't envy him having to ride herd on his mother once she decides she is now the dowager duchess—but, no, I have no serious qualms for the title now that it is in Rafe's hands."

She put down her cup. "John...about what happened in the gardens..."

He shook his head slowly. "No, let's not talk about that now. You've had a long and extremely trying day, one way or another, and I certainly wasn't any great help to you."

"I feel as if I've just been told to take myself off to bed," she said to him, smiling. "All right. And I'll have that letter for you in the morning. Oh, and I suppose there are others I'll need to write. To some distant aunts...perhaps the newspapers?"

"Tomorrow, Emmaline. There is nothing you can do anymore tonight that can't wait until tomorrow."

"Do I look that exhausted?"

"No, Emmaline. You look that vulnerable. And I'm not as strong as I thought myself. Not since I kissed you, at any rate."

He watched as hot color invaded her cheeks once again. "Oh. Well, then, all right. It has been a long day."

"Until tomorrow, which is already much too far

away," he told her, not daring to kiss her hand because he knew neither of them would be able to stop with such a simple, formal gesture.

He watched her walk, chin held high, toward the foyer, and then drank the rest of his wine, resisting the temptation to then fling the glass into the fireplace.

What in bloody hell had he done out there in the gardens? The woman had just had a terrible shock. Had he really believed that seducing her was the answer to all her problems?

And lying to her? How was that helping her?

His deception had begun easily enough, but there had been ample opportunity for him to correct her when she addressed him as captain.

She'd been impressed to hear he was a captain in the Royal Navy, that he had, like her nephew, gone to war to defend his country. And all of that was true enough.

She'd also felt comfortable with him, possibly because he was, to her mind, a relatively simple man. She'd felt free with him. Free to tell him the truth, bare her troubled soul to him. Free to lean on him in her time of need.

Free to let him kiss her.

She was Lady Emmaline Daughtry; daughter of a duke, sister of a duke, aunt to a duke. There would be no real social consequences for her if she kissed a captain in the Royal Navy. Kissed him…or more.

John poured himself a second glass of wine, preparing to settle himself in for at least another few hours of thinking, and most probably drinking. He had to tell her. He couldn't put off telling her.

How would he tell her?

"Your Grace?"

John's head turned toward the door before he could stop himself, and he watched as Grayson entered the main saloon, to bow in front of him.

"Excuse me, Grayson? That's Captain, not Your Grace."

"No, Your Grace, it's not. I took it upon myself to personally unpack your bag. There were letters inside. I left them tied as they were, but could not avoid reading what few lines I saw. You are His Grace, Captain Jonathan Alastair, Duke of Warrington. I've taken the liberty of removing your belongings to the large bedchamber just to the left at the top of the landing, Your Grace."

"Lady Emmaline?"

"Doesn't know, no, Your Grace. May I ask why?"

"I was just sitting here asking myself the same question, Grayson. She seemed…she seemed pleased that I served in the navy."

Grayson nodded, transformed from the stiff and stern butler to the sort of old family retainer who had come to look upon his employers as well-loved children. "Her ladyship is very admiring of those who chose to defend this country from that rascal Bonaparte, yes, Your Grace." The butler bowed, turned to leave, and then turned back to look at John, his expression stern once more. "She is also, begging Your Grace's pardon, quite fond of honesty and truthfulness."

"Yes, thank you, Grayson. Lady Emmaline is, indeed, a very truthful, forthright person. She deserves nothing less in return."

Grayson bowed again. "As you say, Your Grace."

CHAPTER FIVE

...SUCH SAD AND shocking news. I imagine you reading this wherever you are, and marveling at how quickly lives can change. In truth, I have been thinking much the same thing ever since Captain Alastair walked into the gardens of Ashurst Hall this afternoon.

Emmaline lifted her pen and stared at her words. Why had she written them? She should tear up this letter as well, and put it with the other discarded efforts she had begun and then abandoned. But it would make no difference if she began again; no matter how she tried to concentrate on the matter at hand, John Alastair kept creeping back into her thoughts, and onto the page of the letter to her nephew.

She dipped the pen once more and continued:

You are, of course, needed home as soon as you are able, but I understand the demands of your service, and wish to assure you that we are all quite safe here, and capable of holding things together until you find it possible to return. I ask only that you write to us as often as you can, and that you allow Mr. Coates to be of any and all assistance to you.

Rafe, you will make an exemplary Duke of

Ashurst. You hold my deepest confidence and
blessings.
 Yrs. In Greatest Affection,
 Emmaline

Before she could change her mind, Emmaline sanded
the page, folded it and then used the Ashurst seal to
press the warmed wax onto the folded page. There, it
was done. She'd arrange for funds to be given to Mr.
Coates, who would carry them with him to Paris, so
that Rafe would not feel penny-pinched as he made arrangements for his transport back to England.

She kept the letter separate from the small stack that
would go out with the morning post, informing a few
distant aunts of Charlton's death, and then reluctantly
added the letter to Helen, Rafe's mother, to them. She
could not in good conscience delay sending that particular letter, especially since the London newspapers
were bound to make a huge announcement in the next
few days.

After all, it wasn't every day that a duke and both
his heirs drowned in the Channel thanks to their own
utter stupidity.

"Stop it," Emmaline muttered under her breath as
she rose from the small writing desk in her bedchamber
and turned to contemplate the mantel clock. She was
surprised to see that it had only gone past midnight.
She'd hoped for more, perhaps that it was already after
three, or even four.

How long before she would see John again at the
breakfast table? Knowing she would not sleep, could
not sleep, she believed the hours between now and then
could be more easily measured in months.

In any event, it was no longer her birthday, although she could still consider it such until the sun rose in the morning. The next time she marked her birthday, it would also mark the day she'd learned that her brother and nephews had died. How odd. Which was worse, she wondered: To grow older every year, or to be reminded how many years it had been since those deaths?

"If they were going to die, anyway, they could have been just a *little* bit more considerate," Emmaline told her reflection in the dressing table mirror as she pinched at her cheeks to bring color into them and then checked the neckline of her ridiculously virginal white night rail and dressing gown.

And then, before her better self, her saner self, could talk her out of it, Emmaline headed for the door to the hallway, intent on spending her twenty-ninth birthday thinking back over a much nicer memory of her twenty-eighth.

She headed for the west wing, hoping her courage wouldn't desert her, but halted before she got to the center staircase, having seen light peeking out from beneath the double doors to the bedchamber reserved for their highest-ranking guests. The prince regent himself had stayed in the chamber twice, this last time breaking a fine antique chair just by sitting his bulk in it.

Why would Grayson put John in this chamber? It wasn't like the butler to stray from the strict rules of social protocol that made up such things. Captain Alastair should have been put in the west wing, and probably at the end of the corridor at that, right next to the servant stairs.

Perhaps Grayson had taken a liking to John. Although Grayson rarely took a liking to anyone.

And what did it matter where Grayson had put John, or why? She told herself that all she was doing now was standing in a drafty hallway, possibly to be seen by any servant who might be up and about for some reason. Either she was going to do something for herself or she was going to die old and dry and with a regret that had her sighing into her teacup while her relatives murmured behind her back: "Poor old Emmy, unlucky in love, you know."

She raised her hand, hesitated as she took one last, deep steadying breath, and then closed her fist and rapped her knuckles on one of the doors.

Emmaline winced as the sound of that knock seemed to fill the quiet night like cannon shot woke the world to mark a dawn battle.

"You wanted something, Emmaline?"

She nearly jumped out of her skin, whirling about to see John standing almost directly behind her.

"Why aren't you in bed?" she asked, saying the first thing that came into her head.

"I should perhaps ask you the same thing," he responded, his magnificent eyes slipping lazily up and down her dressing-gown-clad body.

Her toes curled in her slippers.

"I didn't hear you come down the hallway."

"Or up the stairs, either, I'd imagine," he said, smiling. "Perhaps, next time, I should have one of the footmen lead the way, blowing on a trumpet."

"Now you're making sport of me."

"No," he said, his tone serious as he stepped closer to her. "I'd never do that. For one thing, I'm too grateful to see you. It has been hours and hours."

"Yes, it has," Emmaline told him, daring to look

straight into his eyes. "And it's just as you said, John. Tomorrow is much too far away…"

He put his hands around her upper arms and then leaned in ever so slowly, touching his mouth to hers with a gentleness that brought her closer to tears than she had felt all day.

At first she thought she was floating, but quickly realized John had picked her up, lifting her high against his chest, even as he went on kissing her. She sensed his knees bending slightly as he tried to manage the brass latch. She was about to tell him that romance was lovely but perhaps they were both a few years too old for such gallantry when the door opened and he walked her inside, kicking it closed behind him.

By now she had her face buried against the side of his neck. "That was quite…impressive," she whispered, keeping her eyes shut as he carried her across the large chamber and toward the bed that had housed kings, queens and rotund princes.

"Thank you. I thought so, too," John told her as he laid her on the already turned-down bed. Bless Grayson, he was nothing if not efficient.

Standing next to the bed, John stripped off his uniform jacket before joining her on the lush satin sheets, pulling her once more into his arms. His mouth mere inches from hers, he said, "I've wanted this for so long."

Emmaline thought that a lovely thing to say. "We barely know each other."

"No. We've known each other forever, my dearest one, always known the other of us was out there somewhere in the world, waiting. We only just happened to meet today."

They made love slowly, because it was her first time,

because they had the rest of their lives, because to rush something this beautiful, this perfect, would be tantamount to a crime.

He kissed away her silent tears when the lovemaking threatened to undo her; the unexpected intensity of her arousal, the tenderness of his every intimate touch, swelling her heart and wordlessly telling her she was cherished, she was beautiful to him, she was desirable.

But there was more. She hadn't expected what she'd felt so far, what he'd caused her to feel, and her surprise manifested itself in a rather startled gasp as he found the very heart of her most intimate place and touched it, teased and stroked it, doing amazing things to her suddenly eager body.

She lifted her hips to him, wanting to know more, wanting to learn her feelings even as he was learning her body. A new tension invaded her every muscle, urging her forward, telling him without words that, yes, yes…there. And again, there. Do that…please do that. Don't stop doing that…right there…*please*…

And when he mounted her, when her body relieved her of the responsibility to think and just reacted to his, when he settled himself deep inside her, Emmaline knew that every word he'd said to her was true. She'd been waiting for him all of her life.

Their bodies had become one, their hearts and minds, as well. He whispered sweet words in her ear, urging her to move with him, feel with him, fly with him.

Emmaline had already waved goodbye to all of her misgivings and inhibitions of eight and twenty long years. She lifted her hips to him, met his every thrust as she held on tight, pulling him deeper, deeper inside her. She felt her most secret parts bud, unfurl, bursting into the full flower of her womanhood.

And then more. Just when she felt she had nothing more to give, to take, to feel, her body began to throb around him, sending stunning sensations through her, glories both wonderful and frightening.

"John!"

And he knew, somehow he knew. His hold tightened on her and he thrust one more time as he held her close, his mouth on hers, taking in her frantic breaths, her wondrous sighs.

She felt his body clench. Clench, and then release. Again and again and again, until he seemed to collapse bonelessly against her, his warm breath audible next to her ear.

"I will never...leave your side. Never. At last I'm alive..." he whispered, and her tears fell once more as he kissed her hair, her eyelids, even the tip of her nose, before settling once more against her mouth. "Neither of us will ever be alone again."

EMMALINE ALLOWED HERSELF to be convinced another black gown she'd always loathed would be extremely fine for the morning, especially since she would have to meet with the vicar at some point, and headed down the stairs to see if John was already at breakfast in the morning room.

He'd proposed to her an hour before dawn, promising her his love and all of his worldly goods. He'd gone down on his knees; he'd held both her hands in his as he looked so deeply into her eyes. Had she said yes before he'd kissed her, before they'd fallen onto the bed once more?

And did it matter? He had to know her answer was yes.

She would still have a personal maid when she was John's wife, as well as a cook and housekeeper, if not a butler. Her dowry was such as to make them both comfortable, and to support any children that might come of their union.

Children. Emmaline stopped on the bottom stair and smiled into the middle distance. She'd never thought she would have children, and now she wanted a houseful. And she and John would never neglect them, never treat them as if they were a nuisance.

No. They'd live in a lovely thatched cottage, possibly near the sea—John loved the sea—and they would spend their lives quietly, happily. Watching their children grow, together. The two of them growing old, together.

After all, being the daughter of a duke had gained her nothing. She had no qualms about exchanging that role for that of wife and mother.

There was a knock on the door and one of the footmen hastened to open it, stepping back quickly as Helen Daughtry swept (Helen swept better than most anyone else in the world) into the foyer.

"Emmaline!" she called out, already drawing off her black gloves and untying the smallest wisp of a black bonnet that must have cost the earth. And if the bonnet had cost the earth, the black cashmere shawl tipped with ermine and the black mourning gown covered in lace and edged with pearls had cost the remainder of the universe. "I came as soon as I heard. Oh, the horror!" And then her eyelids narrowed. "Has my son been notified? He's the duke now, you know."

"Yes, Helen, I know," Emmaline said, descending

the last few stairs and allowing herself to be lightly embraced by her sister-in-law's scent as the woman pursed her lips and kissed the air about an inch from Emmaline's ear. "And you are now the dowager duchess."

Helen Daughtry's eyes widened in horror. "Dowager? Oh, no. Oh, no, no. I think not! We'll have to do something about that. But for now," she said, taking Emmaline's hand and leading her down the hallway, "I'm famished. Ah, Grayson, there you are."

"Your Grace," the butler said, his bow stiff, as if it was restricted by a rusty hinge rather than a spine. "I'll have someone see to your luggage, and that your usual chamber is prepared."

"Oh, no, don't do that. I'm staying only a few miles away with Lord Edmunds—dearest Ferdie—marvelous house party. You weren't invited, Emmaline? Shame on them! Just because you said your last prayers years ago doesn't mean you couldn't be included, at least for the tamer entertainments. At any rate, I heard the news, and knew I must have someone drive me over here for a few hours," Helen said with a wave of her hand.

"How fortunate you managed to pack that gown," Emmaline said without inflection.

"Yes, isn't it, darling? I had to borrow the bonnet, but I wear black quite often in the evening, as it shows off my hair so well. Strange that we're both blonde, and yet black…well, perhaps a little visit to the paint pots, hmm? At any rate, I'm only here to make certain my son is being installed as he should be…and to lend you my support of course, my dearest Emmaline. So alone in the world now. How difficult it must be to be a spinster. Being a widow is much more fun! Why, only Rafe's charity will keep a roof over your head now, won't it? But not to worry—I'm sure he'll find some-place to put you."

Grayson and Emmaline exchanged looks as Helen wandered off ahead of them. "As my late brother said, Grayson, the woman has a tongue that runs on wheels, but only rarely engages with her brain box. She means well."

"As you say, my lady. His...that is, your guest awaits you in the morning room."

Emmaline hastened down the hallway, realizing that putting Helen within fifty yards of any young, hand-some man was akin to setting a plate of sugar cookies within easy reach of a precocious child.

She stopped to take a settling breath, and then turned the corner and entered the morning room, just in time to see John bowing over Helen's hand.

Her sister-in-law turned to her with a wink and a smile. "Well, now, aren't you the naughty one? While the cat's away the mice will dance, hmm? Or did Charl-ton know about this...houseguest of yours?"

"Captain Alastair was there on the scene, just after the yacht sank, Helen. It is he who brought me the sad news."

"And then decided to stay for the funerals? How ac-commodating of you, Captain. I may have to attend the services myself, after all," Helen said, once more turn-ing her back on Emmaline. "Alastair? John *Alastair.* Now why is that name so familiar to me, hmm?"

John shot a quick look past Helen, to where Emma-line stood. "John is a fairly common name, Your Grace."

"Common as dirt, yes. But Alastair? No, I think I... oh, wait! I think I remember now. Not John Alastair. *Jonathan* Alastair. You're William's son. The sailor.

How he loathed that you'd put the line in jeopardy, haring about on the high seas and all of that nonsense. Poor William, although Dame Rumor has it that he died quite happily." Helen sank into a graceful curtsy. "It is so delightful, again, to meet you, Your Grace."

Emmaline found that she couldn't breathe.

And Helen, who always noticed such things, noticed. "Emmaline, dearest? Are you quite all right? How could you have forgotten to tell me that the Duke of Warrington is your houseguest? Your Grace, you simply must return to River's Edge with me, as there is nothing quite so dull and dreary as a house of mourning. So sorry you won't be able to join us, Emmaline. What with your brother so newly dead and all."

"Emmaline, I—Emmaline, wait!"

But Emmaline was gone, turning about so quickly she nearly tripped over the hem of her gown before running out of the room.

He caught up with her in the large foyer, before she could mount the stairs and lock herself in her bedchamber, where she would remain for the next hundred years, if possible.

"Grayson," he said, his eyes on Emmaline, his hand holding tight to her arm, "if you'd be so kind as to keep Her Grace occupied elsewhere."

"But…but how should I do that, sir?"

"I don't care if you tie her to a chair. And it wouldn't depress me if you included a gag. The woman is a feather-witted menace. Go, and everyone else—leave."

"John, you cannot just go ordering the servants to—and let go of my arm."

"I was going to tell you, Emmaline, I swear I was. This morning. I don't know why I didn't tell you immediately…but it all just seemed…easier if you thought me a more…a more simple man."

"I thought we'd live in a cottage. And…and raise our children. I thought… I thought I would be your help-meet, your companion."

"And how does my being a duke change any of that? Granted, Warrington Hall is not a cottage, but as for the rest of it? Being duke and duchess does not preclude us from being loving parents. From loving each other, staying true to each other. We won't ever have to go to London at all, if you don't want to go. Is that it? Have you taken a firm dislike to London, to Society?"

She shook off his hand. "I'm not a recluse, John. Charlton refused to take me, that's all. I adore London, at least most of it."

"Oh, good," he said, relaxing slightly. "Because I really think we need to go there from time to time. That is, if you can love a duke even half as much as you could love a simple sea captain?"

Emmaline looked down at the floor. "I'm being silly, aren't I? I saw us as being so simple, our lives so uncomplicated. Being Charlton's sister was…very complicated." She turned her gaze on the man she loved. "How did you know I felt that way?"

"I don't know. I felt that if I told you who I am, about the damned title, then you'd not relax your guard around me, tell me the sorts of things you told me yesterday. About your family, about your life."

"Well, I wouldn't have, you're correct about that. I don't think I would have worried about how you'd pay for your room at the inn, either."

"Darling, do you remember when I said we can't choose who we love, but we can choose who we like?"

"Yes," she said, allowing him to take her hands in his.

"I knew I loved you the moment I first saw you. That was the easy part. But then I knew I liked you when you showed such concern for my welfare, when you were more worried for me than concerned with the suddenly altered circumstances of your life. Now, am I forgiven?"

"I don't know," she said coyly—imagine, a twenty-eight-year-old almost-virgin, being coy! "I really believe I may have had my heart set on a thatched cottage near the sea."

He slipped his arms more fully around her and brought his mouth down to nearly meet hers. "We'll work on that…"

EPILOGUE

THERE WERE TWO musty old aunts in the second pew, a quiet and reserved-looking Charlotte Seavers and her father in the third, and only Emmaline and John sitting in the first pew as the vicar looked uncomfortable in the small chapel hung in black crepe but glaringly absent of coffins.

Helen Daughtry had not only sent her regrets, but had forbidden her twin daughters from attending the service. "Much too depressing for the young dears," she'd insisted, which was, Emmaline knew, another way of saying, "If they're there, then I have to be there, and I don't want to be there."

Last night, while the two of them were in bed together after the rest of the household was asleep, John had proposed a wine toast to Helen's absence. If it were possible to love him even more, she did, because he was so impervious to Helen's beauty and wiles.

The quickness of the memorial ceremony and the absence of the trio who would provide raucous entertainment for them had kept Charlton's friends firmly in London. As for George and Harold, they were the sort who had acquaintances, men to whom they either owed money or were owed money. Not friends.

It was a sad statement about three wasted lives, lives that could have been so rich as well as privileged.

Now Rafael Daughtry was the Duke of Ashurst, even if he was probably still unaware of his new title. His mother would drive Grayson and the other servants to distraction when she was in residence, and Nicole and Lydia would make them happy again, as all the staff adored the twins.

But Emmaline, who had thought she'd never leave Ashurst Hall, would be departing in the next few weeks to become the Duchess of Warrington. It was obscene, unheard of, for a woman in mourning to wed so hastily, but when she and John had realized that neither cared what Society thought, Emmaline had set her maid to bringing down trunks from the attic so that they could begin packing up her belongings.

"We mourn our brothers, Charlton, George, Harold," Vicar Wooten droned on—he'd been droning on for nearly an hour and even he seemed fatigued. "Dust to dust, ashes to ashes…um, well, not perhaps in this particular case, begging your pardon."

One of the aunts stifled a giggle and, for some reason she would never understand, that caused Emmaline to shed her very first tears for her brother and nephews.

Not in this case. No, nothing was quite like this case. The deaths had been senseless, unnecessary and much too soon.

She dabbed at her moist eyes with the corner of her handkerchief, knowing her tears now were for what might have been, for the past that could never be changed.

And then John slipped his hand into hers, squeezed

Into Historical Romance?
We have the perfect read for you!

Looking for more reads from Harlequin®?
Go back in time with Harlequin®
Historical and Love Inspired® Historical
for stories of life and love set across many
time periods.

H HARLEQUIN®

HISTORICAL

Where love is timeless

HISTORICAL

Historical romances of
adventure and faith

Be sure to check out our
full selection of books within
each series every month!

#1 *New York Times* bestselling author

STEPHANIE LAURENS

delivers the first passionate and exhilarating tale in *The Adventurers Quartet*.

Declan Frobisher, scion of a bold, seafaring dynasty, is accustomed to getting his way. He chose the beautiful Lady Edwina Delbraith to be the wife who graced his arm, warmed his bed and remained safely at home when he returned to sea. But Declan soon discovers Edwina is unconventional and strong-willed, and his marriage promises to be as tempestuous as the high seas.

With her aristocratic birthright supporting her and Declan's ring gracing her finger, Edwina expects to forge a marriage by his side. So when, bare weeks into their honeymoon, Declan is recruited to sail on a secret mission, Edwina declares she must accompany him.

Facing unforeseen perils and unexpected enemies while battling to expose a dastardly scheme, Declan and Edwina discover that their unusual marriage demands something they both possess—bold and adventurous hearts.

Available now, wherever books are sold!

Be sure to connect with us at:

Harlequin.com/Newsletters

Facebook.com/HarlequinBooks

Twitter.com/HarlequinBooks

MIRA®

www.MIRABooks.com

REQUEST YOUR
FREE BOOKS!

2 FREE NOVELS
FROM THE ROMANCE COLLECTION
PLUS 2 FREE GIFTS!